DEC 2 7 1996			
FEB 1 2 1997			
NOV 2 1 1997			
JUN 1 7 2000			

The
IRON
HAND
of MARS

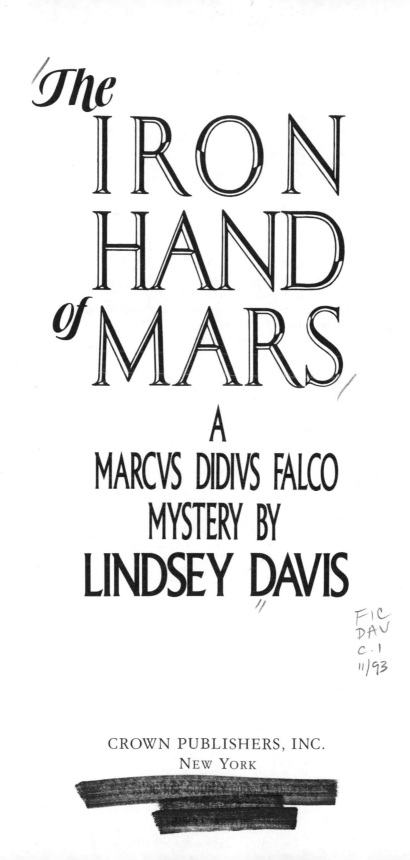

The IRON HAND of MARS

A MARCVS DIDIVS FALCO MYSTERY BY LINDSEY DAVIS

CROWN PUBLISHERS, INC.
NEW YORK

Published by Crown Publishers, Inc., 201 East 50th Street, New York, New York 10022. Member of the Crown Publishing Group. Random House, Inc. New York, Toronto, London, Sydney, Auckland

Originally published in Great Britain by the Random Century Group Ltd in 1992.

Crown is a trademark of Crown Publishers, Inc.

Manufactured in the United States of America

LIBRARY OF CONGRESS CATALOGING-IN-PUBLICATION DATA

Davis, Lindsey.
    The iron hand of Mars / Lindsey Davis — 1st ed.
        p.   cm.
    1. Falco, Marcus Didius (Fictitious character)—Fiction.   2. Rome—History—Vespasian, 69-79—Fiction.   3. Private investigators—Rome—Fiction.   1. Title.
PR6054.A8925175   1993
823'.914—dc20   93-19265
                                                                                                           CIP

ISBN 0-517-59240-1

10   9   8   7   6   5   4   3   2   1

First American Edition

To Rosalie,

in memory of two Roman legionaries

on the 29A

ROME; ROMAN GERMANY; GERMANIA LIBERA
September–November AD 71

'*The story upon which I embark is one full of incident, marked by bitter fighting, rent by treason, and even in peace sinister . . .*'

Tacitus, *The Histories*

PRINCIPAL CHARACTERS
(Not all of whom are free to appear)

The Emperor	
Vespasian	who needs an agent he can trust, eg:
M. Didius Falco	an informer in need of work, who wants:
Helena Justina	who wants the impossible, but not:
Titus Caesar	who wants Falco off the scene

Plus in Rome, or thereabouts:

A widow in Veii	a mere distraction (honestly!)
Canidius	an unwashed clerk of censored archives
Balbillus	a one-legged free-speaking ex-legionary
Xanthus	a sharp barber who wants to see the world
Silvia	wife to Petronius (who keeps out of the way)
Decimus	Helena's father, an apologetic man, also parent to:
Camillus Aelianus	(in Spain); a high-minded youth

And in History:

P. Quinctilius Varus	a disastrous general (long dead)
Petilius Cerialis	a renowned general (not as disastrous as Varus)
Claudia Sacrata	a woman of intrigue (preferably with generals)
Munius Lupercus	a missing officer (probably dead)
Julius Civilis	a rebel chief in need of a haircut
Veleda	a priestess who lives alone with her thoughts and:
Some relatives of hers	who live there too

In Gaul:

A Gallic potter	who will soon be a long way from Lugdunum
Two German potters	who may never go home

In Germany:

Dubnus	a pedlar who sells more than he should
Julius Mordanticus	a potter who knows a few things
Regina	barmaid at the Medusa; an angry girl
Augustinilla	Falco's niece, laid low by love and the toothache
Arminia	her little flaxen friend

Belonging to the famous Fourteenth Legion:

Florius Gracilis	their legate; another missing officer
Maenia Priscilla	his wife, who is not missing him
Julia Fortunata	his mistress, who says she is
Rusticus	his slave, who is just missing
The Primipilus	the Fourteenth's sneering chief centurion
The Cornicularius	their snooty commissariat clerk
A. Macrinus	their arrogant senior tribune
S. Juvenalis	their truculent camp prefect

In the much-less famous First Legion:

Q. Camillus Justinus	Helena's other brother; an *ingénu* tribune
Helveticus	a centurion with a problem, which includes:
Dama	his servant, who yearns for Moesia, and
Twenty rather dim recruits including:	
Lentullus	the one who can't do *anything*

Also featuring:

The aurochs	a legendary beast famous for ferociousness, and:
Tigris	a dog who finds an interesting bone

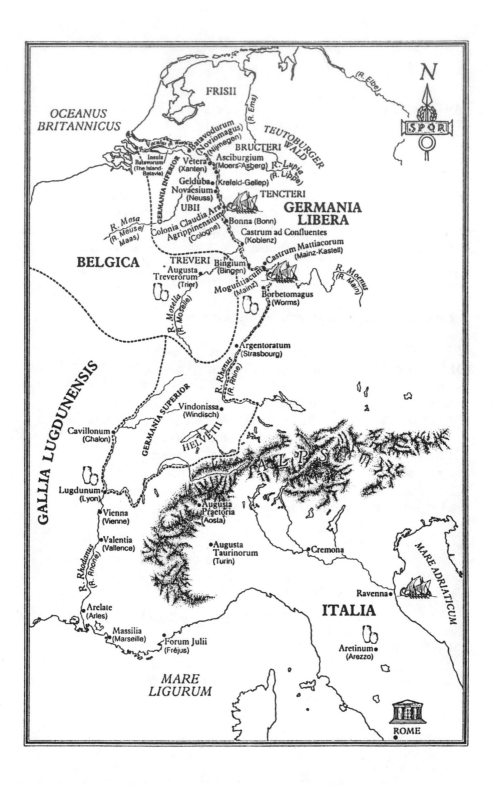

PART ONE: REFUSING TO GO

ROME
September, AD 71

'My official career owed its beginning to Vespasian, its progress to Titus . . . I have no wish to deny this.'

Tacitus, *Histories*

I

'One thing is definite,' I told Helena Justina; 'I am *not* going to Germany!'

Immediately I could see her planning what to pack for the trip.

We were in bed at my apartment, high up on the Aventine. A real sixth-floor bughole – only most bugs grew tired of walking upstairs before they ever got this far. I passed them sometimes, flaked out on halfway landings, with droopy antennae and tired little feet . . .

It was a place you could only laugh about, or the squalor would break your heart. Even the bed was rocky. And that was *after* I had pieced in a new leg and tightened the mattress webs.

I was trying out a new way of making love to Helena, which I had devised in the interests of not letting our relationship go stale. I had known her a year, let her seduce me after six months of thinking about it, and had finally managed to persuade her to live with me about two weeks ago. According to my previous experience of women, I must be right on target to be told I drank too much and slept too much, and that her mother needed her urgently back at home.

My athletic efforts at holding her interest had not gone unnoticed. 'Didius Falco . . . wherever did you . . . learn this trick?'

'Invented it myself . . .'

Helena was a senator's daughter. Expecting her to put up with my filthy lifestyle for more than a fortnight had to be pushing my luck. Only a fool would view her fling with me as anything more than a bit of local excitement before she married some pot-bellied pullet in patrician stripes who could offer her emerald pendants and a summer villa at Surrentum.

As for me, I worshipped her. But then I was the fool who kept hoping the fling could be made to last.

'You're not enjoying yourself.' As a private informer, my powers of deduction were just about adequate.

'I don't think . . .' Helena gasped, 'this is going to work!'

3

'Why not?' I could see several reasons. I had cramp in my left calf, a sharp pain under one kidney, and my enthusiasm was flagging like a slave kept indoors on a festival holiday.

'One of us,' suggested Helena, 'is bound to laugh.'

'It looked all right as a rough sketch on the back of an old rooftile.'

'Like pickling eggs. The recipe seems easy, but the results are disappointing . . .'

I replied that we were not in the kitchen, so Helena asked demurely whether I thought it would help if we were. Since my Aventine doss lacked that amenity altogether, I treated her question as rhetorical.

We *both* laughed, if it's of interest.

Then I unwound us, and made love to Helena the way both of us liked best.

'Anyway, Marcus, how do you know the Emperor wants to send you to Germany?'

'Nasty rumour flitting round the Palatine.'

We were still in bed. After my last case had staggered to what passed for its conclusion, I had promised myself a week of domestic relaxation – due to a dearth of new commissions, there were plenty of gaps in the schedule of my working life. In fact, I had no cases at all. I could stay in bed all day if I wanted to. Most days I did.

'So . . .' Helena was a persistent type. '. . . You have been making enquiries then?'

'Enough to know some other mug can take on the Emperor's mission.'

Since I did sometimes undertake shady activity for Vespasian, I had been up to the Palace to investigate my chances of earning a corrupt denarius from him. Before presenting myself in the throne room, I had taken the precaution of sniffing round the back corridors first. A wise move: a well-timed exchange with an old crony called Momus had sent me scurrying home.

'Much work on, Momus?' I had asked.

'Chicken-feed. I hear your name is down for the German trip?' was the reply (with a mocking laugh that told me it was something to dodge).

'What trip is that?'

'Just your sort of disaster,' Momus had grinned. 'Something about investigating the Fourteenth Gemina . . .'

That was when I had pulled my cloak round my ears and scarpered – before anyone could inform me officially. I knew enough about the

Fourteenth Legion to put quite a lot of effort into avoiding closer contact, and without going into painful history, there was no reason why those swaggering braggarts should welcome a visit from me.

'Has the Emperor actually spoken to you?' insisted my beloved.

'Helena, I won't let him. I'd hate to cause offence by turning down his wonderful offer . . .'

'Life would be much more straightforward if you just let him ask you, and then simply said no!'

I gave her a smirk that said women (even clever, well-educated daughters of senators) could never understand the subtleties of politics – to which she replied with a two-handed shove that sent me sprawling out of bed. 'We need to eat, Marcus. Go and find some work!'

'What are you going to do?'

'Paint my face for a couple of hours, in case my lover calls.'

'Oh, right! I'll go, and leave him a clear field . . .'

We were joking about the lover. Well, I hoped we were.

II

In the Forum, life was proceeding much as normal. It was panic season for lawyers. The last day of August is also the last day to bring new cases before the winter recess, so the Basilica Julia was humming. We had reached the Nones of September and most barristers – still rosy from their holidays at Baiae – were scurrying to settle a few hasty cases to justify their social standing before the courts closed. They had the usual noisy touts out all round the Rostrum, offering bribes for cheerleaders to rush into the Basilica and barrack the opposition. I shouldered them aside.

In the shadow of the Palatine, a sedate procession of functionaries from one of the priestly colleges was following an elderly white-robed Virgin into the Vestals' House. She glanced about with the truculence of a loopy old lady who has men who should know better being respectful to her all day. Meanwhile, on the steps of the Temples of Saturn and Castor lounged throngs of sex-crazed idlers, eyeing up anything (not only female) that looked worth whistling at. An extremely angry aedile was ordering his heavy mob to move on a drunk who had had the bad judgement to pass out on the pavement sundial at the base of the Golden Milestone. It was still summer weather. There was a strong smell of hot donkey droppings everywhere.

Just lately I had been sizing up a piece of wall on the Tabularium. Having come armed with a sponge, a few deft strokes soon washed off the electioneering puff that was besmirching the antique stonework (*Supported by the Manicure Girls at the Agrippan Baths* . . . the usual sophisticated candidate). Deleting his offensive rubbish from our architectural heritage left a good space, just at eye-level, for me to chalk up graffiti of my own:

Didius Falco
For All Discreet
Enquiries + Legal
Or Domestic
Good Refs + Cheap
Rates
At Eagle Laundry
Fountain Court

Seductive, eh?

I knew what it was likely to bring in: shifty import clerks who wanted financial health checks on rich widows they were cultivating, or corner-shop barmen who were worried about missing girls.

The clerks never pay up, but barmen can be useful. A private informer can spend weeks looking for lost women, then, when he gets tired of putting his feet in wineshops (if ever), he only has to point out to the client that missing waitresses are generally found with their heads bashed in, hidden under their boyfriends' floorboards at home. This generally gets the bills for surveillance paid ultra-promptly, and sometimes the barmen even leave town for a long period afterwards – a bonus for Rome. I like to feel my work has community value.

Of course a barman *can* be disastrous. The girlfriend may be genuinely missing, having run off with a gladiator, so you still spend weeks searching, only to end up feeling so sorry for the dumb cluck who has lost his tawdry turtle-dove that you can't bring yourself to ask him for your fee . . .

I went to the baths for a spot of exercise with my trainer, just in case I did manage to land myself a case which required putting myself out. Then I looked for my friend Petronius Longus. He was captain of the Aventine Watch, which involved dealing with all types, many of them the unscrupulous variety who might need my services. Petro often sent work my way, if only to avoid having to deal with tiresome characters himself.

He was not in any of his usual haunts, so I went to his house. All I found there was his wife – an unwelcome treat. Arria Silvia was a slightly built, pretty woman; she had small hands and a neat nose, with soft skin and fine eyebrows like a child's. But there was nothing soft about Silvia's character, one aspect of which was a searing opinion of me.

'How's Helena, Falco? Has she left you yet?'

'Not yet.'

'She will!' promised Silvia.

This was banter, though fairly caustic, and I treated it warily. I left a message to tell Petro I was light in the occupation stakes, then hotfooted out of it.

While I was in the area I dropped in at my mother's; Ma was out visiting. I was not in the mood for hearing my sisters bemoaning their husbands, so I gave up on my relations (not a hard decision) and went home.

A worrying scene greeted me. I had crossed the stinking alley towards Lenia's laundry, the cut-price, clothes-stealing wash-shop which occupied the ground floor of our building, when I noticed a set of tough tykes bristling with buckles who were standing about the stairwell trying to act inconspicuous. A hard task to set themselves: the battle scenes on their breastplates were polished to a dazzle that would stop a water-clock, let alone a passer-by, and ten determined children had stationed themselves in a circle to gape at their scarlet helmet plumes and dare one another to try and poke sticks between the mighty mens' bootstraps. It was the Praetorian Guard. The whole Aventine must know that they were here.

I could not remember having done anything lately that the military might object to, so I assumed an innocent saunter and kept going. These heroes were out of their own refined environment and looking pretty jumpy. I was not surprised to be stopped at the steps by two spears slamming together across my chest.

'Steady, lads, don't snag my outfit – this tunic still has a few decades of life in it . . .'

A laundry girl barged out of the steam with a sneer on her face and a basket of particularly disgusting unwashed goods. The sneer was for me.

'Friends of yours?' she scoffed.

'Don't insult me! They must have been going to arrest some troublemaker and lost their way . . .'

They were obviously not here to apprehend anybody. Some lucky citizen in this sordid part of society was no doubt being visited by a member of the imperial family, incognito apart from the vivid presence of his bodyguard.

'What's going on?' I asked the centurion in charge.

'Confidential – move along!'

By now I had guessed who the victim was (me) and the reason for

8

the visitation (cajoling me into the mission in Germany Momus had warned me about). I felt full of foreboding. If the mission was so special or so urgent it demanded such personal treatment, it must involve the kind of effort I would really hate. I paused, wondering which of the Flavians was venturing his princely toes in our alley's pungent mud.

The Emperor himself, Vespasian, was too senior and too sensitive about status to make free with the populace. Besides, he was over sixty. At my house he would never manage the stairs.

I had crossed paths with his younger son, Domitian. I once exposed a piece of dirty work by the junior Caesar, which now meant that Domitian would like to see me wiped off the earth, and I felt the same about him. However, we ignored each other socially.

It must be Titus.

'Titus Caesar come to see Falco?' He was impetuous enough to do it. Letting the officer know that I despised official secrecy, I lifted apart the impressively polished spear tips with one delicate finger. 'I'm Marcus Didius. Better pass me in so I can hear what joys the bureaucracy are planning for me now . . .'

They let me through, though with a sarcastic look. Perhaps they had been assuming their heroic commander had lowered himself for an off-colour intrigue with some Aventine wench.

Making no attempt to hurry, since I was a fervent republican, I took myself upstairs.

When I went in, Titus was talking to Helena. I stopped short abruptly. The look I had seen the Praetorians exchange began to make more sense. I began to think I had been a fool.

Helena was sitting out on the balcony, a small affair which clung perilously to the side of our building, its old stone supports held on mainly by twenty years of grime. Although there was room for an informal type like me to share the bench with her, Titus had remained politely standing beside the folding door. Ahead of him lay a spectacular view of the great city which his father ruled, but Titus was ignoring it. In my opinion, with Helena to look at, anybody would. Titus shared my opinion pretty openly.

He was the same age as me, a curly-haired optimistic type who would never be soured by life. In my unmajestic billet here, the crusted gold palm leaves embroidering his tunic made an incongruous show, yet Titus managed not to seem out of place. He had an attractive personality and was at home wherever he went. He was pleasant,

9

and for a top-ranker, cultured to his sandalstraps. He was an all-round political achiever: a senator, a general, Commander of the Praetorians, a benefactor of civic buildings, a patron of the arts. On top of that, he was good-looking. I had the girl (though we did not declare it in public); Titus Caesar had everything else.

When I first saw him talking to Helena, his face had a pleased, boyish expression which made my teeth set. He was leaning on the door with his arms folded, unaware that the hinges were quite likely to give way. I hoped they would. I wished they would dump Titus in his splendid purple tunic flat on his back on my ramshackle floor. In fact the moment I saw him there, in deep conversation with my girlfriend, I sank into a mood where almost any sort of treason seemed a bright idea.

'Hello, Marcus,' said Helena – paying far too much attention to putting on a neutral face.

III

'Afternoon,' I forced out.

'Marcus Didius!' The young Caesar was effortlessly agreeable. Refusing to let it fluster me, I stayed glum. 'I came to commiserate about the loss of your apartment!' Titus was referring to one I had been renting just recently which had had every advantage – except that where this repulsive den somehow stayed upright in defiance of all engineering principles, the other had collapsed in a cloud of dust.

'Nice shack. Built to last,' I said. 'That is, to last about a week!'

Helena giggled. Which gave Titus an excuse to say, 'I found Camillus Verus's daughter waiting here; I've been keeping her occupied . . .' He must have known I was trying to lay claim to Helena Justina, but it suited him to pretend she was a model of modest propriety just waiting for an idle prince to pass the time of day with.

'Oh thanks!' I retorted bitterly.

Titus glanced at Helena Justina in an appreciative way that left me feeling out of things. He had always admired her, and I had always hated it. I was relieved to see that despite what she had told me, she had *not* painted her eyes as if she was expecting a visitor. She did look delicious, in a red dress I liked, with agates on slim gold hoops swinging from her ears and her dark hair simply twisted up in combs. She had a strong, quick-witted face, rather too self-controlled in public, though in private she would melt like honey in the warm sun. I loved it, so long as I was the only one she melted for.

'I tend to forget you two know one another!' Titus commented.

Helena stayed silent, waiting for me to tell His Caesarship just how well. I held back stubbornly. Titus was my patron; if he gave me a commission, I would do it for him properly – but no Palace playboy would ever own my private life.

'What can I do for you, sir?' With anyone else my tone would have been dangerous, but no one who enjoys existence makes threats to the Emperor's son.

'My father would like a talk, Falco.'

'Are the Palace clowns on strike then? If Vespasian is short of laughs, I'll see what I can do.' Two yards away, Helena's brown eyes had assumed an unforgiving steadiness.

'Thanks,' Titus acknowledged easily. His suave manner always made me feel he had spotted yesterday's fish sauce spilt down my tunic. It was a feeling I deeply resented in my own house. 'We have a proposition to put to you . . .'

'Oh good!' I answered darkly, with a moody scowl to let him know I had been warned the proposition was dire.

He eased himself off the folding door, which lurched sickeningly but stayed upright. He made Helena a slight gesture, implying that he thought she was here to discuss business so he would not intrude. She rose politely as he strode to the door, but she left me to see him out as if I were the sole proprietor.

I came in and started fiddling with the rickety door. 'Someone should tell His Honour not to lean his august person against plebeians' furniture . . .' Helena remained silent. 'You have on your pompous look, my darling. Was I rude?'

'I expect Titus is used to it,' Helena replied levelly. I had omitted to kiss her; I knew she had noticed. I wanted to, but it was too late now. 'The fact Titus is so approachable must make people forget they are talking to the Emperor's partner, a future Emperor himself.'

'Titus Vespasianus never forgets exactly who he is!'

'Don't be unfair, Marcus.'

I ground my teeth. 'What did he want?'

She looked surprised. 'To ask you to see the Emperor – to talk about Germany, presumably.'

'He could have sent a messenger to ask me that.' Helena was starting to look annoyed with me, so naturally I became even more stubborn: 'Alternatively, he could quite well have talked about Germany himself while he was here. And in greater privacy, if the mission is sensitive.'

Helena folded her hands at her waist and closed her eyes, refusing to quarrel. Since normally she fought me at the slightest opportunity, that was bad news in itself.

I left her out on the balcony and slouched indoors. There was a letter on the table. 'Is this scroll for me?'

'Mine,' she called out. 'It's from Aelianus in Spain.' She meant the elder of her two brothers. I had received the impression Camillus

Aelianus was a prick-eared young bastard I wouldn't be seen drinking with; but since I had yet to encounter him in person, I kept quiet. 'You can read it,' she offered.

'It's your letter!' I rejected her unbendingly.

I went into the inner room and sat on my bed. I knew exactly why Titus had visited us. It had nothing to do with any mission he was offering me. It had nothing to do with *me* at all.

Sooner than I expected, Helena came in and sat beside me quietly. 'Don't fight!' She looked equally gloomy as she dragged my fingers apart, forcing me to hold her hand. 'Oh Marcus! Why can't life be simple?'

I was not in the mood for philosophy, but I changed my grip to something slightly more affectionate. 'So what did your regal admirer have to say for himself?'

'We were just talking about my family.'

'Oh were you!' In my head I ran over Helena's ancestral pedigree, as Titus must have done: senators for generations (which was more than he could say himself, with his middle-class, tax-farming Sabine origins); her father a stalwart supporter of Vespasian; her mother a woman of unblemished reputation. Her two young brothers both abroad doing their civic duty, with at least one of them bound for the Senate eventually. I had been assured by everyone that great things were expected of the noble Aelianus. And Justinus, whom I had met, seemed a decent lad.

'Titus seemed to be enjoying the discussion. Did he talk about you?' Helena Justina: liberal education; lively character; attractive in a fierce, unfashionable way; no scandals (except me). She had been married once, but divorced by consent and anyway the man was dead now. Titus himself had been married twice – once widowed, once divorced. *I* had never been married, though I was less innocent than both of them.

'He's a man – he talked about himself,' she scoffed. I growled. She was a girl people talked to. I liked to talk to her myself. She was the one person I could talk to about pretty well anything, which I felt made it my prerogative.

'You know he's in love with Queen Berenice of Judaea?'

Helena gave a little smile. 'Then he has my sympathy!' The smile was not particularly sweet, and hardly aimed at me. After a moment she added more gently, 'What are you worried about?'

'Nothing,' I said.

13

Titus Caesar would never marry Berenice. The Jewish queen came with a vividly exotic history. Rome would never accept an alien empress – or tolerate an emperor who tried to suggest importing one.

Titus was romantic, but realistic. His attachment to Berenice was supposed to be genuine, yet a man in his position might well marry someone else. He was the heir to the Roman Empire. His brother Domitian possessed some of the family talents, but not all. Titus himself had fathered a young daughter, but no son. Since the Flavian claim to the purple had been principally based on offering the Empire stability, people would probably say he *ought* to look actively for a decent Roman wife. Plenty of women, both decent and otherwise, must be hoping that he would.

So what was I supposed to think if I found this prestigious character talking to my girl? Helena Justina made a thoughtful, graceful, sweet-natured companion (when she wanted to); she always had sense, tact, and a high concept of duty. If she had not fallen for me, Helena was exactly the sort that Titus should be looking for.

'Marcus Didius, I chose to live with you.'

'Why suddenly come out with that?'

'You look as if you might have forgotten it,' Helena said.

Even if she left me tomorrow, I would never forget. But that did not mean I could view our future together with any confidence.

IV

The next week was a strange one. I felt oppressed by the thought of the ghastly trip to Germany that was being held over me. It was work – something I could not afford to refuse – but touring the wild tribal frontiers of Europe was high on my list of entertainments to avoid.

Then I found myself checking the apartment for signs that Titus had been hanging around. There were none; but Helena noticed me looking, so that caused more strain.

My advertisement in the Forum first produced a slave who would obviously never be able to pay me. Besides, he was searching for his long-lost twin brother, which a second-rate playwright might view as good research but it looked dreary work to me. Next I was approached by two clerks, fortune-hunting; a mad woman who had convinced herself that Nero was her father (the fact that she wanted me to prove it was what warned me she was barmy); and a rat-catcher. The rat-catcher was the most interesting character, but he needed a diploma of citizenship. It would be an easy day's work at the Censor's office, but even for intriguing personalities I don't involve myself in forgery.

Petronius Longus sent me a woman who wanted to know if her husband, who had been married before, had any children he was keeping quiet about. I was able to tell her there were none registered. While I was at it I turned up an extra wife, never formally divorced. This woman was now happily married to a poultry chef (I use 'happily' in the conventional sense; I expect she was as angry with life as everyone else). I decided not to advise my client. A good informer answers what he has been asked – then retreats from the scene.

Petro's case brought in enough silver to have red mullet for dinner. I spent the change on roses for Helena, hoping to look like a man with prospects. It would have been a happy evening, only that was when she informed me she seemed to have prospects of her own: Titus had invited her to the Palace with her parents, but without me.

'Let me guess – a discreet dinner that will not appear on the public fixtures list? When is it?'

I noticed her hesitate. 'Thursday.'

'Are you planning to go?'

'I really don't want to.'

Her face was strained. If her respectable upper-crust family ever got wind of a possible liaison with the star of the imperial court, the pressure on Helena would become unbearable. It was one thing for her to leave home while her parents had no other plans. Given one unhappy marriage, her papa had told me frankly he felt diffident about ushering her into another. Camillus Verus was unusual: a conscientious father. Still, there must have been trouble after she ran off. Helena had shielded me from most of the barrage, but I can count the knots in a plank of wood. They wanted her back, before all Rome heard she was playing around with a hangdog informer, and satirical poets started putting the scandal into salacious odes.

'Marcus, oh Marcus, I particularly want to spend that evening with you – ' Helena seemed upset. She was thinking I ought to intervene, but there was nothing I could do about this ominous venture; rebuffing Titus could only come from her.

'Don't look at me, sweetheart. I never go where I am not invited.'

'That's news!' I hate ironic women. 'Marcus, I'm going to tell Papa I have a prior engagement which I cannot break, with you – '

She was avoiding the issue, it seemed to me. 'Sorry,' I said tersely. 'I have a trip to Veii on Thursday. I need to check out a widow for one of my fortune-hunting clients.'

'Can't you travel another day?'

'We need the fee. You take your chance!' I sneered. 'Go to the Palace and enjoy yourself. Titus Caesar is a soft piece of lard from a dull country family; you can handle him, my darling – assuming, of course, that you're wanting to!'

Helena went even whiter. 'Marcus, I am asking you to stay here with me!' Something in her tone disturbed me. But by then I was feeling so sorry for myself I refused to alter my arrangements. 'This means a lot to me,' Helena warned in a dangerous tone. 'I'll never forgive you . . .'

That settled it. Threats from women bring out the worst in me. I went to Veii.

Veii was a dead end. Somehow I expected it.

I found the widow easily enough; everyone in Veii had heard of her. She may or may not have possessed a fortune, but she was a pert brunette with sparkling eyes who freely admitted to me that she was stringing along four or five abject suitors – gents who had called themselves friends of her late husband and now thought they could be even better friends to her. One of them was a wine exporter, selling multiple consignments of foul Etruscan rot-gut to the Gauls – an obvious front runner if the wench remarried anyone. I doubted if she would bother; she was enjoying herself too much.

I myself received certain hints from the widow that I might have profited from a stay in Veii, but on the journey there I had been plagued by the memory of Helena's pleading expression. So, cursing, and by now fairly penitent, I rushed back to Rome.

Helena was not at the apartment. She must have already left for the Palace. I went out and got drunk with Petronius. He was a family man, so had strains of his own, and was always glad to make himself available for a night out cheering me up.

I came home late, deliberately. It failed to annoy Helena because she never came home at all.

I assumed she had stayed the night with her parents. That was bad enough. When she failed to show up at Fountain Court the next morning, I was horrified.

V

Now I was a real sprat drowning in fish pickle.

I ruled out any thought that Titus had abducted her. He was too straight. Besides, Helena was a strong-minded girl; she would never stand for it.

There was no way I could bring myself to turn up at the Senator's house, begging to be informed what was going on. For one thing, whatever it was, her high and mighty family would blame me.

Finding missing women was my trade. Finding my own should be as easy as picking peas. At least I knew that if she had been murdered and nailed under the floorboards, the floorboards were not mine. It was not particularly comforting.

I started where you always start: searching the apartment to see what she had left behind. Once I had tidied away my own detritus, the answer was not much. She hadn't brought many clothes or pieces of jewellery; most had now disappeared. I came across one of her tunics, mixed up with a rag-bag of mine; a jet hairpin under the pillow on my side of the bed; a soapstone pot of her favourite face-cream which had tumbled behind the storage chest . . . Nothing else. Reluctantly I came to the conclusion that Helena Justina had stripped my apartment of her own possessions and left in a huff.

It seemed drastic – until I noticed a clue. The letter from her brother Aelianus still lay on the table where it had been when she said I could see it. I read it now. At first I wished I hadn't. Then I was glad I knew.

Aelianus was the casual, idle one who usually never bothered to correspond with his family, though Helena regularly wrote to him. She was the eldest of the three Camillus children, and treated her younger brothers to the kind of old-fashioned affection that in other families had gone out of the window at the end of the Republic. I had already gathered that Justinus was her favourite; her letters to Spain were more of a duty. It seemed typical that when Camillus Aelianus heard that she had attached herself to a plebeian in a grubby

18

profession, he did write – and a letter filled with such vitriolic ranting that I dropped it in disgust. Aelianus was livid at the damage Helena had done to their noble family name. He said so with all the crass insensitivity of a youth in his twenties.

Helena, being such a family girl, would have been deeply hurt. She must have been brooding over this without me noticing. And then Titus had loomed, with his threat of disaster . . . It was like her to say nothing much. And like me, when she did finally appeal for help, to turn my back on her.

The moment I read that letter I wanted to wrap her in my arms. Too late, Falco. Too late to comfort her. Too late to shelter her. Too late for everything, apparently.

I was not surprised when a short, bitter message came for me, saying that Helena could not tolerate Rome any longer and had gone abroad.

VI

So that was how I let myself be sent to Germany.

Without Helena, there was nothing for me in Rome. It was pointless to try catching up with her; she had timed her message so that the trail was cold. I soon grew tired of members of my family making it plain they had always expected her to dump me. I could produce no defence; I had always expected it myself. Helena's father often used the same baths as me, so avoiding him became tricky too. Eventually, he spotted me trying to hide behind a pillar; he shook off the slave who was scraping his back with a strigil, and rushed over in a cloud of scented oil.

'I am relying on you, Marcus, to tell me where that daughter of mine is – '

I swallowed. 'Well, you know Helena Justina, sir – '

'No idea either!' her father exclaimed. Next thing, he was apologising for Helena as if I was the one who ought to be offended by her extravagant behaviour.

'Calm down, senator!' I tucked a towel around him soothingly. 'I've made my business out of tailing other people's treasures when they disappear. I'll track her down.' I tried not to look too worried at my lies. So did he.

My friend Petronius did his best to jolly me along, but even he was fairly amazed.

'*Abroad!* Falco, you have the brain of an inadequate catfish. Why couldn't you have fallen for a normal girl? The kind who rushes home to mother whenever you upset her, but then slinks back the next week with a new necklace you'll have to pay for?'

'Because only a girl who likes pointless dramatic gestures would fall for me.'

He let out an impatient growl. 'Are you looking for her?'

'How can I? She could be anywhere from Lusitania to the Nabataean desert. Leave off, Petro; I've had enough stupidity!'

'Well, women never travel far alone . . .' Petronius himself had

20

always favoured simple, timid fluff-balls – or at least women who convinced him that was what they were.

'Women are not *supposed* to travel. That simple rule won't deter Helena!'

'Why did she flit?'

'I can't answer that.'

'Oh I see: *Titus*!' The Praetorian Guard must have been spotted by one of his troopers when they were squatting outside my house. 'That's you finished, Falco, anyway!'

I told him I was tired of other people's optimism, then I slouched off by myself.

The next time a summons came from the Palace, ostensibly from Vespasian, I knew it must really be Titus who was plotting to remove me from the scene. I suppressed my annoyance, and made a vow to extract the largest fee I could.

For my interview with the purple I made a sartorial effort, as Helena would have wanted me to. I wore a toga. I had a haircut. I kept my lips pressed close together to hide my republican snarl. That was the most any palace could ever hope for from me.

Vespasian and his elder son were governing the Empire in effectual partnership. I asked for the old man, but the receiving official had gum in his ears. Even with a written invitation from his father, apparently it was Titus on that night's duty rosta to handle pleas, pardons and wine-bar rejects like myself.

'Wrong throne room!' I apologised, when the limp flunkey passed me in to him. 'Sir, I gather the good of the Empire will be best served by despatching me elsewhere! Rumour says your noble father has a horrible proposition I'm just dying to hear.'

Titus recognised my jibe at his personal motives. On hearing the news I might be leaving, he gave a short laugh, which I did not join. He signalled a slave, presumably to lead me to the Emperor, but then held us back. 'I've been trying to get wind of a certain female client of yours,' he admitted – too offhandedly.

'So she gave us both the slip! What did she tell you?' He made no answer; at least Helena favoured *me* with angry messages. Feeling braver, I risked sneering. 'She's travelling. Fraternal visit, apparently. She received a letter from the noble Aelianus recently, in high dudgeon over some imagined slight.' I saw no need to confuse Titus by saying it was over me.

21

Titus frowned warily. 'Surely if her brother was annoyed, avoiding him would be more logical?'

'Helena Justina's reaction would be to rush straight there.' Titus was still looking quizzical. I believe he had had a sister himself, an impeccable girl who had married a cousin and then died young in childbirth, as Roman women from good families are supposed to do. 'Helena likes to face up to things, sir.'

'Does she!' he commented, perhaps with irony. Then he asked more thoughtfully, 'Camillus Aelianus is in Baetican Spain? But surely he's too young for a quaestorship?' Would-be senators normally serve as provincial finance officials just before their formal election to the Curia at twenty-five. Helena's brother had two or three years to go before that.

'Aelianus is the son his family all think a lot of.' If Titus wanted Helena, he would need to bone up on her relatives. I described the situation for him with a familiar ease: 'The Senator persuaded a friend in Corduba to find the boy a staff position ahead of time, to give him the early benefit of experience abroad.' Judging by the way he had written to his sister, this plan to teach Aelianus diplomacy was a waste of time and cash.

'Does he demonstrate special qualities?'

I replied gravely, 'Camillus Aelianus seems well equipped for a spectacular public career.'

Titus Caesar glanced at me, as if he suspected I might be suggesting that the normal criterion for rapid advancement in the Senate was a touch of the dungheap. 'You seem well briefed!' He eyed me shrewdly, then called up an outdoor messenger. 'Falco, when did Helena Justina leave?'

'No idea.'

He muttered something to his mercury; I caught a mention of Ostia. Titus realised I had overheard. 'The lady is a member of a senatorial family; I can forbid her leaving Italy,' he told me defensively as the messenger left.

I shrugged. 'So she's taken an unauthorised holiday. Why not? She's not a vestal, or a priestess of the imperial cult. Your predecessors in office might have had her exiled to an island for displaying such independence, but Rome expected better from the Flavians!' Still, if he could find her – and I had myself already spent a day fruitlessly searching the Ostia quays – I was quite prepared to let Titus have my lady escorted back to Rome. I knew she would be handled respectfully because of her status. I also knew that Titus

Flavius Vespasianus was in for a Charybdis of trouble if he ordered it. 'Helena Justina will object forcibly to being hooked off her ship. I'll stay if you like,' I offered. 'Her ladyship in a temper may be more than your Praetorian Guard can handle without help!'

Titus made no attempt to call back his messenger. 'I'm sure I can mollify Helena Justina . . .' No woman he ever seriously wanted would be able to turn her back on him. He smoothed down the ample folds of his purple tunic, looking grand. I planted my feet apart and just looked tough. Then he demanded abruptly, 'You and Camillus Verus's daughter seem unusually close?'

'Do you think so?'

'Are you in love with her?'

I gave him a simple smile. 'Caesar, how could I presume?'

'She's a senator's daughter, Falco!'

'So people keep telling me.'

Both of us were heavily aware of his father's power and of how much authority had already devolved on Titus in his own right. He was too polite to draw comparisons between us, but I did.

'Does Verus approve of this?'

'How could he, sir?'

'Does he *allow* it?'

I said quietly, 'Helena Justina is a sweetly eccentric girl.' I could tell from his face Titus had already learned that. I wondered what he had said to her; then I wondered more painfully what she had said to him.

He moved in his seat, closing our interview. He could dismiss me from his throne room; he could order me out of Rome; but both of us were a good deal less certain whether he could exclude me from Helena's life. 'Marcus Didius, my father needs you to take a journey. I feel that would be best for everyone.'

'Any chance of Baetica?' I ventured cheekily.

'Wrong direction, Falco!' he whipped back with more relish than he should. Recovering, he murmured, 'I was hoping to entertain the lady here last Thursday. I was sorry that she would not come – still, most people like to celebrate their private feasts amongst those who are closest to them . . .' This was some kind of test. I stared at him, giving nothing away. '*Helena Justina's birthday!*' he explained, like a man throwing a double six with weighted dice.

It was news to me. He could see that.

With difficulty I restrained my instinctive reaction, which was to

23

punch his superbly barbered chin straight through his handsome teeth to the back of his Caesarly skull.

'Enjoy Germany!'

Titus subdued his air of triumph. But that was when I forced myself to accept the plight Helena and I were in. If this situation had become awkward for her, it was positively dangerous for me. And whatever scabby mission I was to be despatched on this time, it would suit Titus Caesar most of all if I failed to finish it.

He was the Emperor's son. There were plenty of things he could do to make sure that once he sent me out of Rome, I would not be coming back.

VII

I was passed through the perfumed offices of three chamberlains, lost in my own moody thoughts.

I am not completely deficient. After ten years of what I called a successful love life, a new girlfriend's birthday was something I reckoned to find out fast. I asked Helena; she laughed off the question. I tackled her father, but without his secretary's list of family feasts, he dodged the issue shiftily. Her mother could have told me, but Julia Justa had better ways of upsetting herself than by discussing her daughter with me. I even spent hours in the Censor's office searching for Helena's birth certificate. No luck. Either the Senator had panicked on the arrival of his first-born (understandably) and had failed to register her properly, or else he had found her under a laurel bush and could not call her a Roman citizen.

One thing was certain. I had committed domestic sacrilege. Helena Justina might overlook many insults, but my bumming off to Veii on her birthday was not one of them. The fact I didn't *know* it was her birthday was irrelevant. I should have done.

'Didius Falco, Caesar . . .' Before I was ready to concentrate on political matters, a major-domo who reeked of long-standing vanity and recently braised onions announced my name to the Emperor.

'That's a long face. What's up, Falco?'

'Woman trouble,' I admitted.

Vespasian enjoyed a laugh. He threw back his great head and guffawed. 'Want my advice?'

'Thanks, Caesar.' I grinned. 'At least this heartthrob didn't run off with my armpurse or elope with my best friend . . .'

We hit a small moment of stillness, as if the Emperor had remembered with disapproval who my latest heartthrob was.

Vespasian Augustus was a beefy bourgeois with a down-to-earth manner who had risen to power on the tail of a vicious civil war and then set out to prove that men who lacked flash ancestors could still own a talent to rule. He and his elder son Titus were succeeding –

25

which guaranteed that the snobs in the Senate would *never* accept them. Still, Vespasian had been struggling for sixty years – too long to expect easy recognition, even when he wore a purple robe.

'You're in no hurry to know about your mission, Falco.'

'I know I don't want it.'

'That's normal.' Vespasian humphed mildly, then told a slave, 'Let's see Canidius now.' I didn't bother wondering who Canidius was. If he worked here, I didn't like him enough to care. The Emperor beckoned me closer. 'What do you know about Germany?'

I opened my mouth to say, *'Chaos!'*, then closed it again, since the chaos had been stirred up by Vespasian's own supporters.

Geographically, what Rome calls Germany is the eastern flank of Gaul. Sixty years ago, Augustus had decided not to advance across the natural boundary of the great River Rhenus – a decision dragged out of him by the Quinctilius Varus disaster, when three Roman legions were ambushed and wiped out by the German tribes. Augustus never recovered. It was probably this throne room which he used to pace, groaning, *'Varus, Varus, give me back my legions . . .'* Even so long after the massacre I myself felt extreme reluctance to spend time where it had occurred.

'Well, Falco?'

I managed to sound impartial. 'Sir, I know Gaul and our Rhine provinces played a rich part in the civil war.'

It was the recent Vindex revolt in Gaul which had sparked everything by causing Nero's downfall. The governor of Upper Germany crushed the revolt, but on his recall to Rome after Galba claimed the throne, his troops refused to take the New Year's oath to Galba. When Galba died, Otho took over in Rome, but the Rhine legions rejected him and decided to elect their own emperor.

They chose Vitellius, then governor of Lower Germany. His reputation was as a brutal, loose-living drunk – obvious imperial material by the standards of the time. From Judaea, Vespasian challenged him. Seeking to pin down the legions in Germany who were his rival's main supporters, Vespasian contacted a local chieftain who might raise a diversion. It worked – too well. Vespasian grabbed the imperial wreath, but the rebellion in Germany ran completely out of control.

'A part which culminated dramatically in the Civilis revolt, Caesar.'

The old man smiled at my careful neutrality. 'You are familiar with events?'

'I read the *Daily Gazette*.' I matched his sombre tone. It was a bleak moment in Roman history.

26

The fiasco in Germany had had everything. At the time, Rome itself was a city torn apart, but the shocking scenes on the Rhine outdid even our own problems of panic, fire and plague. The leading rebel – a Batavian hothead called Civilis – had attempted to unite all the European tribes in some impossible vision of an independent Gaul. During the mayhem he managed to cause, a string of Roman forts were overrun and burnt. Our Rhenus fleet, which had native rowers, rowed itself over to the enemy. Vetera, the only garrison which held out with any credit, was starved into submission after a grim siege; then the troops who surrendered were set upon and slaughtered as they marched out unarmed.

While the native revolt raged up and down Europe, the mood of our own troops also deteriorated. Mutinies occurred everywhere. Officers who showed any spirit were assaulted by their men. There were wild tales of legionary commanders being stoned, making a run for it, and hiding in tents disguised as slaves. One was murdered by a deserter. Two were executed by Civilis. The governor of Upper Germany was dragged from his sickbed and assassinated. In a particularly horrific incident, the legate from the surrendering fort at Vetera was sent off in chains by Civilis as a present to an influential priestess in the barbarian part of Germany; even today his fate remained unknown. Finally, at the height of the upheavals, four of our Rhineland legions actually sold their services and we had to endure the ultimate horror of Roman soldiers swearing allegiance to the barbarians.

It sounds fantastic. At any other period it would have been impossible. Yet in the Year of the Four Emperors, when the whole Empire blazed in ruins while the imperial contenders slogged it out, this was just one especially colourful sideshow amongst the wide-scale lunacy.

I wondered glumly how the colourful Rhenus frontier was about to impinge on my drab life.

'We have Germany in hand,' Vespasian declared. From most politicians this would have been self-deception. Not him. He was a good general himself, and he attracted strong subordinates. 'Annius Gallus and Petilius Cerialis have achieved a dramatic turnaround.' Gallus and Cerialis had been sent to subdue Germany with *nine* legions. It was probably the largest task force ever sent out by Rome so success was a foregone conclusion, but as a loyal citizen I knew when to look impressed. 'I'm giving Cerialis the governorship of Britain as a reward.' Some reward! Cerialis had served in Britain during the

Boudiccan Revolt, so he would know what dismal privilege he had just won.

A lucky fluke reminded me that the esteemed Petilius Cerialis was related to Vespasian. I swallowed a witty rejoinder and asked meekly, 'Caesar, if you can spare Cerialis for higher duties, the frontier must be under control?'

'Some unfinished items – I'll come to those.' Whatever was said in public, the whole region must still be highly sensitive. Not the time for a quiet cruise downstream on a wineship. 'Petilius Cerialis held a meeting with Civilis – '

'I heard about that!' Dramatic stuff: the two opposing commanders had confronted each other in the middle of a river, both bawling across the void from the ends of a severed bridge. It sounded like some incident from the mists of Rome's heroic history that schoolboys learn about.

'Civilis has fallen unnaturally quiet since then . . .' Speaking of the rebel chief, Vespasian paused, in a way that ought to have worried me. 'We were hoping he would settle down peacefully in the Batavian homeland, but he's missing.' That did arouse my interest; I read in it a bad prophecy for me. 'Rumour says he may have travelled south. On that subject, I'd like to say to you – '

Whatever he had intended to tell me – or warn me – about the rebel Civilis never happened, because just then a curtain swung open and the official who must be the one he had called Canidius arrived.

VIII

When he shambled in, the sharp lads in glittering white uniforms who waited on the Emperor all stepped back and glared at him bitterly.

He was a real papyrus beetle. Even before he opened his mouth, I guessed he must be one of those odd cases who hang around secretariats doing jobs no one else will. No well-kept palace would tolerate him unless his contribution was unique. He wore a dingy damson tunic, shoes with one lace tied up crookedly, and a belt so poorly tanned it looked as if the cow it came from was still alive. His hair was lank, and his skin had a grey pallor that might have washed off when he was younger, but was now ingrained. Even if he did not actually smell, he looked musty.

'Didius Falco, this is Canidius,' Vespasian himself introduced us in his brisk way. 'Canidius keeps the legionary archive.'

I was right then. Canidius was a clerk with unpromising prospects who had found an offbeat job he could invent for himself. I grunted noncommittally.

Vespasian shot me a suspicious glance. 'Your next assignment, Falco, is as my personal emissary to the Fourteenth Gemina in Germany.' This time I saved myself the hypocrisy of politeness and openly grimaced. The Emperor ignored it. 'I hear the Fourteenth are in a truculent mood. Brief us, Canidius.'

The eccentric-looking clerk recited nervously, without notes. 'The legio Fourteenth Gemina were an Augustan creation, originally raised at Moguntiacum on the River Rhenus.' He had a thin whine of a voice that tired a listener rapidly. 'They were among the four legions chosen by the Divine Claudius for the invasion of Britain, acquitting themselves bravely at the Battle of the Medway, much assisted by their native auxiliaries, who were Batavians.' North Europeans from the Rhenus delta, Batavians are rowers, swimmers and river pilots to a man. All Roman legions are supported by such units of foreigners, in particular native cavalry.

29

'Falco doesn't need your Claudian anecdotes,' muttered Vespasian. 'And I was there!'

The clerk blushed; forgetting the Emperor's history was a bad mistake. Vespasian had commanded the Second Augusta at the Battle of the Medway, and he and the Second had played a celebrated part in the conquest of Britain.

'Caesar!' Canidius writhed in misery. 'The Fourteenth's roll of honour includes defeating Queen Boudicca, for which – along with the Twentieth Valeria – they were awarded the honorific title of "Martia Victrix".'

You may wonder why the Second Augusta did not win that prestigious handle too. The answer is that due to the kind of mix-up which we like to pretend never happens, the wonderful Second (my own legion as well as Vespasian's) failed to show up at the battlefield. The legions which did face the Iceni were lucky to survive. That was why any member of the Second needed to avoid the Fourteenth Gemina, honorific titles and all.

Canidius went on: 'In the recent wars, the Fourteenth's Batavian auxiliaries featured crucially. They had been separated from their parent legion and summoned to Germany under Vitellius. The Fourteenth themselves were devoted first to Nero – since after the Boudiccan Revolt he had called them his best legion – and then supported Otho. Otho brought them to Italy. This placed the legion and its native cohorts on opposing sides, and at the first battle of Bedriacum . . .' Canidius tailed off unhappily.

He was intending to fudge the issue, so I barged in: 'Whether the Fourteenth Gemina actually took part at Bedriacum is a moot point. Rather than admit they had been beaten in battle, they claimed they had not been there!'

Vespasian grumbled under his breath. He must think they were simply covering up.

Canidius rushed on again. 'After Otho's suicide, the legion and its auxiliaries were reunited by Vitellius. There was some rivalry,' the archive clerk said, with quaint discretion. He had no real grasp of what the Emperor required.

'You're leaving out the picturesque details!' I interrupted. 'Be frank! The Fourteenth's subsequent history involved squabbling and public scuffles with their Batavians, during which they burned down Augusta Taurinorum . . .' This episode at Turin placed the main question mark over their discipline.

Wary of handling a sensitive issue, Canidius raced to finish.

'Vitellius ordered the Fourteenth itself back to Britain, attaching the eight Batavian cohorts to his personal train until he redeployed them in Germany.' More politics. Canidius was looking unhappy again.

'In Germany, the Batavian cohorts promptly attached themselves to Civilis. It gave the rebellion a tremendous boost.' I was still angry about it. 'Since Civilis is their chief, the Batavians' defection should have been foreseen!'

'Enough, Falco,' rasped Vespasian, refusing to criticise another Emperor – even the one he had deposed.

He nodded encouragement to Canidius, who squeezed out: 'The Fourteenth returned from Britain again to assist Petilius Cerialis. They now occupy Moguntiacum.' He finished his tale with relief.

'Only the Upper German forts survived,' Vespasian told me crisply, 'so Moguntiacum is at present policing both parts of the territory.' Clearly while the fort where they were stationed had such a vital role, he needed to feel absolute confidence in the Fourteenth. 'My priority is to tighten up discipline and dissipate old sympathies.'

'What happens to the troops who swore allegiance to the Gallic federation?' I asked curiously. 'Which were they, Canidius?'

'The First Germanica from Bonna, the Fifteenth Primigenia from Vetera and the Sixteenth Gallica from Novaesium – plus the Fourth Macedonia from . . .' He had forgotten; it was his first sign of humanity.

'Moguntiacum,' said the Emperor. It emphasised why he wanted loyal legions there now.

'Thank you, Caesar. When Petilius Cerialis received the culprits,' the clerk informed me, 'his words to the mutineers were . . .' Canidius for the first time referred to a note tablet in order to thrill us with the exact historical detail: ' *"Now the soldiers who revolted are once more soldiers of their country. From this day you are enlisted in the service and bound by your oath to the Senate and People of Rome. The Emperor has forgotten all that has happened, and your commander will remember nothing!"* '

I tried not to sound too shocked at this enlightenment. 'We call the circumstances exceptional, and give out lenient treatment, Caesar?'

'We cannot lose four legions of crack troops,' Vespasian growled. 'They will be disbanded, stiffened up and reformed in different units.'

'These new legions will be shifted from the Rhenus?'

'No sensible alternative. The forces which Cerialis and Gallus commanded will guard the frontier.'

'It won't take all nine legions.' I could now see the options that were facing the Emperor. 'So the Fourteenth Gemina could either be sent back to Britain or stationed at Moguntiacum permanently. I believe Canidius told us it was their original home base. What's your plan, sir?'

'I have not yet decided,' the Emperor demurred.

'Is that my mission?' I like to be frank.

He looked annoyed. 'Don't pre-empt my instructions!'

'Caesar, it's obvious. They served you well under Cerialis, but were highly restless beforehand. Ever since they defeated the Iceni, the Fourteenth have become a byword for wilfulness – '

'Don't decry a good legion!' Vespasian was an old-fashioned general. He hated to believe any unit with a fine reputation could deteriorate. But if they did, he would be ruthless. 'Moguntiacum is a two-legion fort, but they are doubled up with some inexperienced troops. I need them – if I can trust them.'

'The legion was raised there,' I mused. 'There's nothing like their own interested grannies living locally to keep soldiers meek . . . Also, it's nearer than Britain, which makes supervision easier.'

'So, Falco, how do you feel about making a discreet inspection?'

'What do you think?' I scoffed. 'I was serving in the Second Augusta during the Icenean thrash. The Fourteenth will well remember how we abandoned them.' I can handle myself in a street fight, but I shied away from taking on six thousand vengeful professionals who had good reason to thumb me out of existence like a woodlouse on a bathhouse wall. 'Caesar, they are liable to bury me in quicklime and stand around grinning while I frizzle!'

'Avoiding that should test your talents,' the Emperor sneered.

'What exactly,' I queried, letting him see I felt nervous, 'are you asking me to do, Caesar?'

'Not much! I want to send the Fourteenth a new standard, to mark their recent good conduct in Germany. You will be transporting it.'

'Sounds straightforward,' I muttered gratefully, waiting to discover the catch. 'So while I'm handing over this token of your high esteem, I size up their mood and decide whether your esteem ought to last?' Vespasian assented. 'With respect, Caesar, if you are planning to sponge the Fourteenth off the army list, why don't you ask their commanding legate to report in suitable terms?'

'Not convenient.'

I sighed. 'That suggests there is a problem with the legate too, sir?'

'Certainly not,' replied Vespasian decisively. He would say that in public, unless he had firm grounds to cashier the fellow. I guessed I was supposed to produce grounds.

" I moderated my tone. 'Can you tell me something about him?'

'I don't know the man personally. Name's Florius Gracilis. He was suggested for a commander's post by the Senate, and I knew no reason to object.' There was a myth that all public posts were awarded by the Senate, although the Emperor's veto was absolute. In practice, Vespasian would normally suggest his own candidates, but he might sometimes flatter the Curia by allowing them to nominate some dumb cluck of their own. He seemed suspicious of this man – but did he fear blatant corruption, or everyday inefficiency?

I let it lie. I had my own resources for boning up on senators. Gracilis was probably the usual upper-class fool doing his stint with the legion because a military command when he was thirty formed a fixed step in the *cursus publicus*. He was bound to have been posted to one of the frontiers. Getting a legion in Germany was just his bad luck.

'I'm sure His Honour is well up to the demands of his post,' I commented, letting the Emperor know that while I was squinting at the legion he could rely on me to cast my usual sceptical eye over Florius Gracilis as well. 'This sounds like my usual complex mission, sir!'

'Simplicity!' the Emperor declared. 'While you are out there,' he added inconsequentially, 'you can apply yourself to some loose ends that Petilius Cerialis was forced to leave behind.'

I took a deep breath. This was more like it. The Fourteenth's loyalty could be assessed by any competent centurion on the spot. M. Didius Falco was being sent racing in circles after some other escaped goose.

'Oh?' I said.

Vespasian appeared not to notice my sour face. 'Your written orders will cover what's required . . .'

Vespasian rarely skimped discussing business. I knew from the airy way he ducked out of giving details that these 'loose ends' which I was inheriting from the fabled Petilius Cerialis had to be really filthy tasks. Vespasian must be hoping that by the time I read my instructions I would be safely en route and unable to quibble.

He made them sound unimportant. But these unspecified items tossed after me like party gifts were the real reason why he was sending me to Germany.

IX

It grieved me to be seen in public with a wraith like Canidius. He looked as if he had lost himself going to the bathhouse and three weeks later was still too shy to ask the way.

Still, I needed to pick his well-informed noddle. Stationing myself to windward, I led this sallow fellow to a wineshop. I chose one I rarely frequented, forgetting that the outrageous prices were why it had lost my patronage. I installed him on a bench among the desultory dice players, where he let himself be introduced to the warmth of an expensive Latian red.

'You've slung me the official spiel on the Fourteenth, Canidius; now let's hear the truth!'

The archive clerk looked uneasy. His orbit involved only the manicured version of public events. But with a beakerful inside him, he ought to give me all the grubby, hangnail stories that are never written down.

His eyes wandered slightly at the muffled sounds of commercial pleasure from the barmaids' overhead bedroom. He must have been forty, but he behaved like an adolescent who had never been let out before. 'I don't involve myself in politics.'

'Oh neither do I!' I retorted dismally.

I chewed my winecup, pondering the mess I was in. Ordered to a province on the harsh rim of the Empire, at a moment when its prospects for a civilised future were bleak. A mission so vague it was like trying to pick burs off a rumbustuous sheep. No girlfriend to comfort me. Every chance I would find a hit man lurking in some way station, with orders from Titus Caesar to make sure that that was the limit of my trip. Every chance, too, that if I ever did reach Moguntiacum, the Fourteenth Gemina would roll me into a trench like a foundation log and build their next rampart over my corpse.

I tackled the archive clerk again. 'Is there anything else I ought to know about Nero's favourite legion?' Canidius shook his head. 'No scandal or gossip?' No luck. 'Canidius, have you any idea what special tasks the Emperor wants me to do out in Germany?' Ideas were not his strong point. 'All right, try this one: what was the Emperor going to tell me about the rebel chief Civilis? He was interrupted in mid-flow when you arrived.' Hopeless.

I had wasted both patience and money. There were plenty of facts I still needed; once on location, I would have to discover the gaps – and the answers – myself.

Cursing myself for being gracious to this dim-wit, I left him with the flagon. Canidius let me pay, of course. He was a clerk.

Returning home, I brought in a loaf and some cooked sausage. Night was falling beyond my open window. The apartment block reverberated with distant knocks and cries as its occupants beat all Hades out of each other in various happy ways. The street below my balcony was full of oddly muttering voices which I preferred not to investigate. The night air brought a city cacophony of grumbling wheels, off-tune flutes, squalling cats and dolorous drunks. But I had never before noticed how intense the silence was indoors when Helena was not there.

Intense, until footsteps approached.

They were light, but reluctant – tired out by the long haul upstairs. Not boots. Not slipshod sandals either. Too long a stride for a woman, unless it was a woman I would not welcome. Too casual to be any man I needed to fear.

The feet stopped outside my door. There was a lengthy pause. Someone knocked. I leaned back on my stool saying nothing. Someone opened the door gingerly. The high-class odour of an extremely subtle unguent sneaked in and shimmied curiously around the room.

A head followed. It had sharply layered dark locks, held in place by a fillet of braid. It was a haircut you were meant to notice. It looked clean, neat, well attended, and as out of place in the Aventine as bees in a feather bed. 'You Falco?'

My own scalp began to feel dandruffy and hot. 'Who's asking?'

'I'm Xanthus. I was told you would be expecting me.'

'I'm not expecting anyone. But you can come in now you're here.'

He came in. He was sneering at the place; that made two of us. He left the door open. I told him to close it. He did so as if he was afraid he would be grappled to the floor by a pair of wild centaurs and robbed of his manhood amid much whinnying.

I gave him a rapid scan. He was a daisy. Not the usual Palace

35

messenger, with a brain as thick as his bootsoles. This one had class – in his queer way.

While I stared, the inappropriate shaving-lotion continued to make itself at home. The chin that was sporting the magic Eastern mixture had been bristling gently for about ten years. The messenger wore a white Palace uniform with gold on the hem, but the shoes I had heard on the apartment stairs were his gesture to personality: round-toed vermilion calfskin jobs that must have cost a lot of money, though they were in questionable taste. The sort of supple footgear a low-grade actor might accept in return for paying attention to a female devotee.

'Letter for you.' He held it out: the papyrus I had come to dread, solid as piecrust, and weighed down with an ounce of sombrely embossed wax. I knew it contained orders for my German trip.

'Thanks.' I sounded thoughtful. This odd bod in the lurid shoes already had me wondering. He was not all he seemed. Although that applies to most of Rome, with Titus Caesar jealously concerned about my private life I felt more nervous than usual about social frauds. I took the letter. 'Hang yourself up on a cloak-peg, in case I want to send a rude reply.'

'That's right!' he ranted bitterly. 'Give me your orders! My sole purpose is to dally on doorsteps while people read their correspondence.'

Something was wrong here. I needed to probe. 'You seem a restless sort of messenger. Are your corns worse than usual?'

'I'm a barber,' said he.

'Stick with it, Xanthus. There are fortunes to be made out of bristle for a man with a deft hand.' And other fortunes, too, for hired hacks who deftly applied sharp weapons to people's throats. I checked him over discreetly; if he was carrying a blade it was well hidden. 'Whose barber are you anyway?'

He looked thoroughly depressed. 'I used to shave Nero. He killed himself with a razor, I heard; probably one of mine. Since then they've all passed through my hands. I shaved Galba; I shaved Otho – I laundered his toupee as well, in fact!' For the first time it sounded like the truth: only a genuine barber would make so much of name-dropping eminent clients. 'After that, when he remembered to let somebody attack his fortnight's undergrowth, I even shaved Vitellius . . .'

Distrust had struck again. I rasped bleakly. 'You ever scraped Vespasian?'

36

'No.'

'What about Titus?' He shook his head. I was too old to believe it. 'Know a man called Anacrites?'

'No.'

Anacrites was the official chief spy at the Palace, and no crony of mine. If anyone at the Palace was commissioning a private extermination, Anacrites was bound to be involved. Especially if they were exterminating me. Anacrites would enjoy that.

I bit my lip. 'So how come, when a clean shave is as rare as an emerald in a goose's gizzard, an imperial razorman has been reduced to footslogging round the Aventine in his natty scarlet lace-ups?'

'Demoted,' he said (unhappily).

'To the seedier end of a delivery round? It's hardly apt. I think you're lying.'

'Think what you like. I did my best to satisfy whoever turned up under the towel, but I'm told there's no further call for my skills and since Vespasian hates waste, I'm reallocated to the secretariat.'

'Tough!'

'It is, Falco! The Flavians have a set of strong chins. I had been assigned to Titus Caesar – '

'Nice mop of curls!'

'Yes. I could have done decent work on Titus . . .'

'But the victor of Jerusalem declines to trust his handsome epiglottis to a sharp Spanish blade in the hands of a man who has previously scratched Nero and Vitellius? Who can blame him, friend?'

'Politics!' he spat. 'Anyway, I'm now shoved off to tramp through the dung in stinking alleys and struggle up endless smelly stairs bringing so-called urgent despatches to unfriendly types who don't even bother to read them when I arrive.'

The complaints did not deflect me. 'Sorry, I'm not convinced. Did Titus send you here?' The barber shook his head impatiently, but by now I knew better. 'Stop jiggling like a whore on a busy night after the races.'

'Why the heavy suspicion? I'm just a runt they have no other use for.'

They had a use for him all right.

I broke open the scroll Xanthus had delivered, only to reveal more bad news.

My orders from Vespasian had been written by a secretary whose pretty Greek lettering would make a good vase decoration, though it

37

was torture to read. While I struggled to decipher the rambling-rose script, the barber clung against one wall of the apartment. He seemed frightened of something. Possibly me.

When I had finished, I sat in silence. I was feeling bilious from the wine I had drunk with Canidius and from eating my sausage too fast. I would have been squeamish anyway. What I had to do in Germany was:

Deliver the Emperor's gift to the Fourteenth Gemina – and make a report to the Emperor.

Any fool could do that. I might even manage it myself.

Ascertain the fate of the most noble Munius Lupercus.

Who was he? I'll tell you: only the commanding legate of the legion at Vetera, the fort which had held out against the rebels to the verge of starvation before its surrendering troops were all butchered. All except Lupercus. The freedom fighters had sent *him* over the Rhine as a present to their thoroughly nasty priestess.

Attempt to curtail the activities of Veleda.

You guessed: Veleda was the priestess.

Ascertain the whereabouts of Julius Civilis –

'Oh gods!' Even with my long history of resistible commissions, this final task was unbelievable.

Ascertain the whereabouts of Julius Civilis, chieftain of the Batavians, and ensure his future co-operation within a pacified Gaul and Germany.

Vespasian had already sent two commanders-in-chief in full purple panoply plus nine trusted legions to undertake the reclamation of Civilis. Whatever the *Daily Gazette* trustingly reported from its pillar in the Forum, they must have failed. Now Vespasian was sending me.

'Bad news?' quavered Xanthus nervously.

'A disaster!'

'You're going to Germany, aren't you?' So I had intended, until I read this catalogue of impossible treats. Now the obvious thing was to head the other way. 'I really envy you,' the barber enthused, with the true tactlessness of his trade. 'I've always wanted to see something of the Empire outside Rome.'

'There are cheaper ways to be uncomfortable here. Try a hot

afternoon in the Circus Maximus. Try a bad play at Pompey's Theatre. Try buying a drink near the Forum. Try shellfish. Try women. Go for a swim in the Tiber in August if you want to catch some exotic complaint . . . Xanthus, I badly need to think. Shut up. Get out. And try not to walk your horrible scarlet footwear in my direction again.'

'Oh I have to,' he assured me smugly. 'I'm coming back tomorrow to bring the package that you have to take to Germany.'

I thanked him for the warning, so I could make sure I was out.

X

I ought to have refused this mission. I wanted to.

I desperately needed the money. It would be good – if I survived to apply for it. I was also keen to remove myself from Rome before the glances which Titus Caesar was casting in my direction led to something worse. Most of all, now that I had grown used to her lively presence in my billet, I could not bear it here without Helena.

I could have coped with poverty. I might even have faced up to Titus. Missing Helena was different. Helena was why I went on sitting sadly, in the squalor of my room at Fountain Court, unable to bestir myself even to rush to the Palatine and complain. Helena provided one pressing reason why I did want to go to Germany. I wanted to be there even if it meant enduring a European winter in a province stripped of all pretence of luxury by a barely quelled rebellion, where my own tasks ranged from the risky to the ludicrously impossible.

I had told Titus that Helena Justina was visiting her brother. I had said it because I believed it was the truth.

But I might have misled Titus slightly. Helena had one brother called Aelianus, who was studying diplomacy in Baetica. She had another called Justinus. I had met Camillus Justinus. It had been at the fort where he was serving as a military tribune, at a place called Argentoratum. Argentoratum is in Upper Germany.

Next day I made preparations. A secretary whom I cultivated at the Palace promised me copies of despatches relating to the Civilis revolt. I made my request for a travel pass and a set of official maps. Then I strolled out to the Forum, positioned myself against a pillar on the Temple of Saturn, and waited. I was looking for someone: a one-legged man. I wasn't particular which single-limbed person hopped into my orbit, so long as he met a condition: he had to have been on active service in the civil war, preferably with Vitellius.

I tried four. One was home from the East, which was no use, and

40

three were fakes who ran off on normal sets of legs when asked questions. Then I found one who fitted. I took him to a cookshop, let him order a full bowl, paid for it – then held up the order while I made him talk to me.

He was an ex-legionary, pensioned off after his amputation, which was recent, for the red-raw stump had barely healed. I use the term 'pensioned off' somewhat lightly, since Rome has never provided well for troops who become unavailable for further action without having the consideration to be actually dead. This poor fellow failed to qualify for either a tombstone or his veteran's retirement land-grant; he had limped back to Rome, where only the corn dole and his fellow-citizens' consciences stood between him and starvation. Mine seemed to be the only active conscience this week, and it seemed a normal week.

'Tell me your name and legion?'

'Balbillus. I was in the Thirteenth.'

'Did that include the battles at Cremona?'

'Bedriacum? Only the first.'

Vitellius had fought both his important battles – against Otho, whom he defeated, and Vespasian, who defeated him – in the same place: a village called Bedriacum, near Cremona. Don't find this confusing. Once he had selected a decent spot with a river view and interesting features, why should he change?

'Bedriacum will do. I want to hear about the conduct of the Fourteenth.'

Balbillus laughed. The Fourteenth Gemina tended to produce a derisive reaction. 'My lot drank with them sometimes . . .' I took the hint and procured him liquid encouragement. 'So what do you want?' He was out of the army, on the worst possible terms; he had nothing to lose from democratic free speech.

'I need background. Only recent stuff. You can omit the Fourteenth's glorious feat against Queen Boudicca.'

We both laughed that time.

'They always were a stroppy lot,' Balbillus commented.

'Oh yes. If you care to study history, the reason the Divine Claudius chose them to conquer Britain was that he needed to keep them occupied. Even thirty years ago they were disruptive. Something about serving in Germany apparently leads to mutiny!' *Everything* about it, if I was any judge. 'So, Balbillus, tell me the florid details. First, how did they react to Vespasian?'

This was a risky question, but he half answered me: 'There were plenty of mixed feelings around.'

'Oh I know. In the Year of the Four Emperors, people had to readjust their positions every time a new man took the stage.' I could not recall adjusting mine. That was because I had, as usual, despised the entire list of candidates. 'I'm assuming all the British legions viewed Vespasian as one of their own?'

Balbillus disagreed. 'A lot of officers and men in the British legions had been promoted by Vitellius.'

No wonder Vespasian was now so keen to send Britain a new governor he could trust. Petilius Cerialis must be sailing across the Gallic Strait with a brief to weed out dissent.

Balbillus tore at a piece of bread. 'There were some very strange scenes in Britain.'

I shoved an olive bowl his way. 'What happened? The scandalous version, if possible!'

'The Fourteenth told us the British governor had upset his troops even more than governors normally do.' This burst of cynical wit endeared the ex-soldier to me even more than his pathetic wound. 'He had a running feud with the legate of the Twentieth Valeria.' I had run across them in my service days. Dull, though competent. 'The war inflamed the row, the troops sided with the legate, and the governor actually had to flee the province.'

'Jupiter! Whatever happened to Britain?'

'The legionary commanders formed a committee to run things. The Fourteenth seemed rather sorry to be missing it.'

I whistled. 'Nothing of this jolly scandal got out!'

'I expect in a wild bog like Britain,' Balbillus confided sarcastically, 'unusual arrangements seem perfectly natural!'

I was thinking about my own problem. 'Anyway, this means when the Fourteenth crossed to Europe, they already had a habit of inventing their own orders? Not to mention infighting.'

'You mean the Batavians?'

'Yes, especially their escapade at Augusta Taurinorum. They were fighting under Vitellius and met up with their legion at Bedriacum, am I right?'

He savaged the bread again. 'You can imagine how before the battle we were all on tenterhooks because the renowned Fourteenth Gemina were supposed to be approaching.'

'It was a crucial engagement, and the Fourteenth could swing it?'

'Well, they thought so!' Balbillus grinned. 'They never showed.

The Batavian cohorts did fight on the winning side – they took on a group of gladiators in a clever skirmish on an island in the River Po. Afterwards, of course, they made the most of it. They paraded before the rest of us, jeering that they had put the famous Fourteenth in its place, and that Vitellius owed his entire victory to *them*.'

'So the Fourteenth felt obliged to squabble with them as publically as possible?'

'You picture the scene, Falco. They were one set of hooligans paired with another, but at Augusta Taurinorum Vitellius quartered them together – even though relations had broken down.'

'That led to the rumpus? Did you see it?'

'Couldn't miss it! A Batavian accused a workman of cheating, then a legionary who had been billeted on the workman threw a punch at the Batavian. Running street battles broke out. The whole legion joined the scrap. When we forced them apart and mopped up the blood – '

'Corpses?'

'Just a few! The Fourteenth were ordered back to Britain. As they marched out of the city they left fires alight everywhere – quite deliberate – so Augusta Taurinorum burned to the ground.'

Inexcusable – in ordinary circumstances. However, even though the Fourteenth behaved like delinquents, they had never mutinied, whereas the Batavian cohorts they hated had defected to Civilis. The Fourteenth themselves served whoever happened to be Emperor that month. Vespasian could well decide that all these buoyant heroes needed now was a commander who could rein them in.

'He'll need a fierce grip!' snorted Balbillus, when I suggested it. 'On their way home to Britain, after Vitellius got rid of them, they had specific orders to avoid Vienna because of local sensitivities. Half of the idiots wanted to march straight there. Did you know that? They would have done it too, but for others who were thinking about their careers . . .'

I noted, in the Fourteenth's favour, that wiser council had prevailed. But it all confirmed that they were not in a mood to have me turning up to say they should reconcile themselves to a future of sitting in barracks fiddling their ration allowances, instead of boasting and burning towns . . .

I gave Balbillus the price of a shave and another wine flask, then left the one-legged soldier tucking into his hot food while I went home like a respectable citizen.

I should have stayed out drinking. I had forgotten about the Palace barber. He was waiting in my room with a chirpy smile, foul cherry-coloured shoes and a large wicker basket.

'I promised!'

'Yes, you warned me.'

Cursing, I grabbed a handle and attempted to drag the basket nearer. It stuck. I braced myself against a bench and heaved. The dead weight scraped a floorboard with an ear-splitting screech of cane. I unbuckled some heavy-duty straps and we peered in at the Fourteenth's new standard.

Xanthus was startled. 'Whatever is that?'

I prefer to travel light (if I have to go at all). The Emperor had selected just the kind of trinket anyone on a long journey hates to have tossing about in his backpack. I was being sent to Germany in charge of a two-foot-high, strongly sculpted human hand. It was gilded – but under the pretentious ornamentation the object which I had to carry across Europe was made of solid iron.

I groaned at the barber. 'Depending whether the expert you ask is an optimist or a realist, this represents an open-palmed gesture of international friendship – or a symbol of ruthless military power.'

'What do you think?'

'I think lugging it across Europe will ruin my back.'

I slumped on the bench. I wondered who had helped this frail blossom carry his basket upstairs. 'Well, you've brought it. What are you waiting for?'

The dubious Palace messenger looked coy. 'Something I wanted to ask you.'

'Cough up.'

'Can I come with you to Germany?'

This fitted my conviction that Titus had him lined up to do me some mischief. I wasn't even surprised. 'I don't think I heard that correctly.'

He was absolutely brazen. 'I have my savings – I've already applied to buy my freedom. I'd love to travel before I settle down – '

'Jupiter!' I growled into the neck of my tunic. 'It's bad enough having your chin snicked while some inane fellow demands whether sir intends visiting his Campanian villa this summer, without having one of the bastards wanting to join you on holiday!'

Xanthus said nothing.

'Xanthus, I'm an imperial agent visiting the barbarians. So what, my friend, is supposed to be the point of a *barber* sharing my misery?'

44

Xanthus replied morosely, 'Somebody in Germany might need a decent shave!'

'Don't look at me!' I rubbed my palm across my chin; the stubble was fierce.

'No,' he agreed, insultingly. Nothing stopped him once he got an idea beneath that well-trimmed thatch. 'No one will miss me here. Titus wants to be rid of me.' I could believe that. Titus wanted his private knife-man firmly attached to me. All the better if I took Xanthus somewhere remote before he pulled his blade.

'Titus can spread your travel pass with fish pickle and eat it under water – I journey alone. If Titus wants to retire you from official duties, let him give you a bounty so you can set up in a booth at some bathhouse – '

'I won't be a nuisance!'

'The qualification for a career in scissors must be being born with your ears missing!'

I closed my eyes to close him out, though I knew he was still there.

I was reaching a decision. I was now convinced that Titus had decided this piece of scented buffoonery could usefully strop his razor on my throat. If I went along with it – or appeared to – at least I knew whose dagger hand to watch. Turn down this chance, and I would be forced to make myself suspicious of everyone.

I looked up. The barber must have been stretching his mental capacity too, because he suddenly asked, 'People hire you, I gather?'

'Foolish ones do.'

'How much does it cost?'

'Depends how much I dislike what they commission me to do.'

'Give me a clue, Falco!' I obliged, with a show of distaste. 'I can find that sort of money,' he snivelled. I was not surprised. Any imperial slave is well placed to garner heavy tips. Besides, I reckoned Xanthus had a banker standing him his European tour. 'I'll hire you to escort me on the same trip as you.'

'The lure of adventure!' I scoffed. 'So do I get a bonus every time I can arrange for you to be cudgelled and robbed? Double rates if you catch a nasty rash from a cheap continental prostitute? Triple if you drown at sea?'

He said stiffly, 'You will be there to advise me how to avoid the perils of the road.'

'Well my first advice is, don't take this road at all.'

My world-weariness appeared to strike him as a romantic pose. Nothing was going to put him off; he must have been ordered to come with me by persons whose orders are obeyed. 'Falco, I like your attitude. I reckon we could rub along together successfully.'

'All right.' I pretended I was too tired to argue. 'I was always a soft option for clients who enjoy being insulted twenty times an hour. I'll be taking two more days to finish my background enquiries and put my own affairs in order. Meet me at the Golden Milestone – on a journey this long, I always start from Zero. Be there at dawn with all your savings, wear more sensible footgear than those ghastly pink things, and bring your valid diploma of freedom from slavery, because I do *not* want to be arrested for stealing imperial property!'

'Thanks, Falco!'

I looked annoyed at his gratitude. 'What's another encumbrance? The Emperor's present to the army weighs a bit. You can help me transport the iron hand.'

'Oh no!' exclaimed the barber. 'I can't do that, Falco; I'll be carrying all my shaving kit!'

I told him he had a lot to learn. Though in agreeing to be lumbered with this Xanthus, I must have been suffering from brain failure myself.

PART TWO:
GETTING THERE

GAUL AND UPPER GERMANY
OCTOBER, AD 71

' *"Lukewarm! We'll be in hot water soon, though . . ."* '

Tacitus, *Histories*

XI

We made a pretty picture travelling, the barber, his trunk of emollients, the Hand in its basket, and I.

There were two ways to tackle getting there: over the Alps via Augusta Praetoria, or by sea to southern Gaul. In October both were best avoided. Between September and March, anybody sensible stays safe in Rome.

I hate ocean travel even more than I hate mountaineering, but I chose to go via Gaul. It's the route the army uses most – someone must once have worked out that it was the least dangerous logistically. Also, I had been that way with Helena once (though in the opposite direction), and I convinced myself that if she *was* going to Germany instead of Spain, she might want to revisit places which held fond memories . . .

Apparently not. I spent the whole trip scanning round for a tall, dark-haired woman throwing insults at customs officers, but there was no sign. I tried not to think of her being buried alive in an avalanche, or attacked by the hostile tribes who lurk in the high passes above Helvetica.

We landed at Forum Julii, which was comparatively pleasant. Things deteriorated when we reached Massilia, where we had to pass a night. So much for a well-planned trip. Massilia is, in my opinion, a rotten gumboil on the Empire's most sensitive tooth.

'Gods, Falco! This is a bit rough . . .' complained Xanthus, as we struggled against the tide of Spanish oil-sellers, Jewish entrepreneurs and wine merchants from all countries who were competing for a bed in one of the least disreputable inns.

'Massilia has been a Greek colony for six hundred years, Xanthus. It still thinks itself the best thing west of Athens, but six hundred years of civilisation have a depressing effect. They possess olives and vines, a brilliant harbour surrounded by sea on three sides, and a fascinating heritage – but you can't move for stallholders trying to interest you in trashy metal pots and statuettes of plump deities with funny round eyes.'

'You've been here before!'

'I've been *cheated* here! If you want dinner, you'll have to entertain yourself. There's a long road ahead of us, and I'm not going to sap my strength getting gut-rot from a bowl of Massilia shrimps. Don't start talking to any locals – or any tourists, come to that.'

The barber unhapp.iy slunk off for a bite by himself.

I settled down with a very sick oil-lamp to study my maps. One benefit of this trip was that the Palace had equipped me with a first-rate set of military itineraries for all the major highways – the full legacy of seventy years of Roman activity in central Europe. These were not merely mileage lists between the towns and forts, but decent, detailed travel guides with notes and diagrams. Even so, I would have to rely on my wits in some places. There were huge, worrying blank spaces east of the River Rhenus: *Germania Libera* . . . Endless tracts of territory where 'free' meant not only free from Roman commercial influence, but with a complete absence of Roman law and order too. That was where the priestess Veleda lurked, and where Civilis might be hiding up.

The frontier was uncertain enough. Europe was full of restless tribes constantly trying to migrate to other districts, sometimes in great numbers. Since Julius Caesar's time, Rome had been attempting to settle friendly groups of them in ways that created buffer zones. Our Upper and Lower German provinces formed a military corridor along the River Rhenus between the pacified lands in Gaul and the great unknown. That was the policy at any rate, until the civil war.

I studied my map thoughtfully. In the far north, alongside Belgica, around the Rhenus Estuary, lay the Batavian homeland, with the stronghold they called The Island. All along the river stood the Roman forts, guard posts, watch-towers and signal stations which had been built to control Germany; most of them were now neatly lined through by the scribe who had brought the maps up to date for me. Furthest north was Noviomagus, where Vespasian was planning a new fort to watch over the Batavians, but which was currently just a cross on the map; next came Vetera, scene of the grim siege. Then there was Novaesium, whose pathetic legion had defected to the rebels; Bonna, which had been overrun by the Fourteenth's Batavian cohorts amid horrible slaughter; and Colonia Agrippinensium, which the rebels had captured but spared from the flames for strategic

50

reasons (also I think Civilis had relations living there). On the River Mosella stood Augusta Treverorum, tribal capital of the Treveri, where Petilius Cerialis had roundly defeated the rebels. Where the River Moenus joined the Rhenus, lay my initial destination: Moguntiacum, capital of Upper Germany. I could reach it on a direct highway from the great Gallic crossroads at Lugdunum.

Alternatively, I could branch off the highway at a junction town called Cavillonum, and approach Upper Germany from further south. It was a good excuse to acclimatise myself to the province. I could travel to Moguntiacum and my rendezvous with the Fourteenth by water. This alternative route was no greater distance (I convinced myself) and I would hit the Rhenus most conveniently at Argentoratum, home station of a certain party whose sister I doted on.

While I was still frowning at the immense distance that lay ahead of us, the barber scuttled in looking green.

'Xanthus! Which hazard of travel has blighted your life now? Garlic, constipation, or just being fleeced?'

'I made the mistake of ordering a drink!'

'Ah! Happens to everyone.'

'It cost – '

'Don't tell me. I'm already depressed. The Gauls have a crazy standard of values. They are wine-mad, and spend like lunatics in the quest for liquor. No one who believes that a sound-bodied slave is fair exchange for one amphora of mediocre imported wine is reliable. And the vintner won't charge you less than he paid for it just because *you* were brought up to expect a flagon on the tavern table for half an as.'

'What are people supposed to do, Falco?'

'I believe seasoned travellers carry their own.'

He stared at me. I gave him the peaceful smile of a man who had probably been drinking a private supply while his companion was out being rooked.

'You want a shave, Falco?' He sounded hurt.

'No.'

'You look like a savage.'

'Then I'll merge in nicely where we have to go.'

'I heard you were a ladies' man.'

'The lady whose man I happen to be happens to be somewhere else. Get to sleep, Xanthus. I warned you that having your pretty sandals on foreign soil would involve pain and stress.'

51

'I hired you to protect me!' he grumbled, winding himself into the thin blanket on his narrow bed. We were in a small dormitory. Massilia believes in packing in the customers neck to neck, like pickle jars on a cargo boat.

I grinned. 'That's the spirit! Adventures were what you wanted. They always involve suffering.'

Just before the lamp died of exhaustion, I let him see me testing my dagger and placing it under what passed for a pillow. I think he understood the message. I was a highly trained professional. Danger was my way of life. If so much as a mouse scratched a floorboard, knifing the barber would be my instant response. Given the amount of shaving-lotion he splashed on, I would smell him coming even in the pitch-dark. And I knew where to sink my weapon for the best effect. Whatever the Palace had told him, or not told him, he must be aware of that.

His first day in Gaul had made him too miserable to try anything that night.

There would be plenty of other chances. But whenever he decided to do the dirty work for Titus Caesar, I would be on the alert.

XII

We reached Lugdunum. I won't say without incident. We had fought off a gang of village urchins who thought my basket of symbolic ironwork contained something they could sell, then I hitched a lift on a wineship and nearly dropped the Hand overboard. In fact, every time we rode away from the previous night's mansio, I ran the risk of leaving Vespasian's present for the Fourteenth behind on a shelf.

The drinking-water started to affect us at Arelate; Gallic cooking oil knocked us sideways as we were rowed past Valentia; some tricky pork laid us low for a day at Vienna; and by the time we slunk into the civic capital, the wine we had gulped down to try and forget the pork had given us splitting heads. All along the route we were playing patball with the normal autumnal quota of fleas stocking up before the winter, bedbugs, wasps, and invasive little black things whose favourite lodging was up a luckless traveller's nose. Xanthus, whose pampered skin had rarely been outside the Palace, broke out in a rash whose progress he described for me at tedious length.

So, Lugdunum. As we disembarked, I favoured Xanthus with an informative travelogue: 'Lugdunum – capital of the Three Gauls. That's as in *"Caesar divided Gaul into three parts . . ."*, which every schoolboy is compelled to know, though you barbers may escape such low points of education . . . A handsome city, established by Marcus Agrippa as a focus for communication and trade. Notice the interesting aqueduct system, which uses sealed pipes constructed as inverted syphons to cross the river valleys. It's extremely expensive, from which we can deduce that in provincial terms the people of Lugdunum are *extremely* rich! There is a temple to the imperial cult, which we shall not be visiting – '

'I'd like a chance to sightsee!'

'Stick with me, Xanthus. This city also boasts an outstation of the mighty Arretinum pottery. We'll go there for our treat. You and I will be following the grand tourist tradition of trying to take home

53

some dinnerware – at twice the cost and three times the trouble of shelling out for it in Italy.'

'Why do it then, Falco?'

'Don't ask.'

Because my mother told me to.

The samian tableware factory offered a fabulous chance to make our feet hurt tramping about all morning staring at thousands of pots, not to mention the opportunity of lashing out on presents that would make our bankers wince. The Lugdunum potters were bidding to supply the whole Empire. Theirs was the big commercial success story of our time. They were cornering the market, and their compound had that atmosphere of tenacious greed which passes for business enterprise.

Kilns and stalls stretched around the town like a besieging army, dominating normal life. Wagons blocked all the exit roads, hardly able to creak forwards under towering crates of the famous red dishes packed in straw for transit all over the Empire and probably beyond. Even in the depression that had followed the violence of the civil war, this place thrived. If ever the ceramics market slumped, Lugdunum would see widespread grief.

There were acres of workshops. Each one contained a local craftsman, most of whom were freeborn, unlike at the main factory in northern Italy, which I knew was run by slaves. My mother (who always made helpful suggestions for a present I could bring her) had informed me that Arretinum was in decline, whereas its outstation here at Lugdunum was known by discerning housewives as a source of more refined goods. They were certainly expensive, but as I gazed at the tottering stacks of dishes, jugs and comports, I acknowledged I was chasing quality. The moulds used here had crisply defined patterns or delicately sculpted classical scenes, and the finished clay was fired with great assurance to a warm, deep red gloss. I could see why these ceramics were sought after as eagerly as bronze or glass.

My mother, who had brought up seven children mainly without my father's assistance, deserved an item of decent redware, and I would have liked to buy a handsome platter to mollify Helena. I owed them both some attention. But I resented being set up. Every time I risked asking a price, I moved on again hastily.

There were no bargains. The loss-leader principle was unknown in Lugdunum. These artisans believed that if people were stupid enough to come two hundred miles upriver to inspect their fancy goods, they might as well pay the going rate. The going rate was just about as high as the potters thought they could push it, after weighing up the gemstones in your finger-rings and the nap on your travelling cloak. In my case that meant not very high – but still more than I was prepared to pay.

I burrowed around, but they all thought the public existed to be squeezed. I ended up under a trestle-table, rooting through a basket of cut-price chipped pieces.

'Those look a waste of time,' Xanthus muttered.

'I'm an auctioneer's son. I was taught that alongside the junk in the discard box sometimes nestles a treasure . . .'

'Oh you're full of homespun lore!' he grinned.

'I can spot a sound turnip – see?'

I had found a hidden serving dish that was relatively free from cracks and firing blemishes. The barber acknowledged graciously that persistence had paid; then we went to find someone to sell it to us.

Not so easy. The potters at Lugdunum certainly had their own ways of obstructing cheapskates. The lads shifting the sacks of wet clay pleaded ignorance of prices; the man carving a new mould was too artistic to barter; the stokers at the kiln were too hot to be bothered; and the craftsman's wife, who normally took the money, had stayed at home with a headache.

'Probably got it worrying how they can possibly spend all their profits!' I muttered to Xanthus.

The craftsman himself was temporarily unavailable. He and most of his neighbours had formed a surly crowd on the cart-track outside. When we came looking for him a dispute was in progress, and there was pushing and shoving. I made Xanthus hang back.

A small, angry group of potters, with wet clay on their aprons and forearms, had gathered round a spokesman who was giving rough answers to two men who appeared to be trying to force a debate. There were more beards and side-whiskers in evidence than you would find in a male gathering in Rome, but not much to choose between any of them otherwise. The two men arguing most heatedly wore the same Gallic tunics as the locals, with high collars of folded material at the throat for warmth, but over these they had European felt capes, with vertically slashed necks, wide sleeves and pointed hoods thrown back. They were both shouting fiercely, with the air of men losing a struggle. The others made loud retorts from time to time, but tended to stand back contemptuously, as if they had less need to haggle because they were in control.

Things grew distinctly ugly. A tall chap with a cleft chin and vivid sneer appeared to be the local leader. He made a sudden obscene gesture at the two men. The stouter party swung a fist, but was restrained by his comrade, a younger man with reddish hair and warts.

I had been hoping the heat would simmer down so I could buy my pot. Now it looked as if any bargains today would be sealed with bloody noses. I handed Ma's present to a local, grabbed Xanthus and made a fast exit.

'What was that about, Falco?'

'No idea. When you're travelling, never get drawn into feuds. You don't know the history, you're bound to pick the wrong side, and all that can happen is both parties will turn on you.'

'You've left your dish!'

'That's right.' It was lopsided anyway.

XIII

On the next leg of our journey things started to happen.

I was fast losing heart. Visiting the ceramics factory had served as a diversion, though one which produced its own anxieties since I had bought nothing and would be due for a drubbing back at home. Still, I gave no more thought to potters and their problems; I had troubles of my own. My real mission loomed. By Lugdunum we had put a third of the distance across Europe behind us, with the tiring sea trip from Ostia before that. Now we were on the final push, and the nearer we drew to the great Rhenus river, and to the ludicrous tasks Vespasian had set me, the more depressed I felt.

Not for the first time, I had become horrified by how far we had to journey in order to cross Europe, and by how long it was taking.

'More bad news, Xanthus! River travel's too slow. At this rate I'll hit winter before I finish my mission. I'm transferring to horseback, courtesy of my imperial travel pass, so you'll have to hire yourself a mule if you want to keep up.'

Don't imagine that Vespasian had kitted me out with the wherewithal to commandeer a horse from the state despatch stations because he wanted me to travel in comfort; he probably thought it more convenient for the Iron Hand.

The terrain looked decidedly foreign now. Instead of huge Italian villas with absentee landlords and hundreds of slaves, we were riding past modest tenant farms. Pigs instead of sheep. Fewer olive groves and thinner vineyards with every milestone. We were being held up at bridges by army supply convoys; it was definitely the approach to a military zone. Towns became a novelty. Everywhere was colder, wetter and darker than when we had left home.

As a traveller Xanthus was becoming more confident, which meant that as the idiot's nursemaid I had to be even more on guard. Explaining trivial regional habits every time we stopped to change horses was maddening. In addition, it had started to rain.

'I've been slipped some duff coins, Falco – cut in quarters and halves!'

'Sorry, I ought to have warned you: there's a long-term small-coin shortage. No need to show your ignorance by causing a fuss. Cut halves are accepted locally, but don't take any home. Assuming we ever go home.' I was so gloomy I doubted it. 'You'll adapt. Just try not to waste an as or a quadrans if you can pay with one of your larger coins, and pick up change for when we're desperate. If they run out of coppers altogether the barmaids use kisses, and when they run out of *those* . . .' I shuddered pointedly.

'Seems daft!' Xanthus moaned. A true barber. Jokes were lost on him.

Sighing inwardly, I supplied the sensible explanation: 'The army has always been paid in silver. Sesterces are easier to transport in bulk, so the Treasury never thinks of sending out a few chests of coppers for the lads to use as pocket money. There is a mint at Lugdunum, but civic pride seems to make them prefer turning out the big shiny ones.'

'I wish they'd cut their prices in half too, Falco.'

'And I wish a lot of things!'

I spoke with restraint, though I was near breaking-point. I wished it would stop raining. I wished I could find Helena. I wished I was safe in my own city, commissioned for a risk-free job. Most of all, as the barber prattled on relentlessly, I wished I could lose him.

We stayed the night in a village typical of that highway: a long skein of ribbon development with one main street devoted mostly to entertaining travellers. There were plenty of rest-houses, and once we found a clean one to dump our baggage at, there were plenty of taverns we could walk to for a change of scene. I chose one of the porticoed bars that was throwing light across the street, and we fumbled our way down into a back basement where other travellers were seated at circular tables enjoying cold meat or cheese with beakers of the local fermented beer. The scent of damp woollen cloaks and sodden boots hung everywhere as we all steamed after the day's wet ride. The bar was warm, dry and lit with reed tapers. It had a we-are-here-to-please-you atmosphere which eased the strain of travelling even in those of us who were reluctant to be eased by anything too much in case Fate made us pay a sour penalty.

We drank. We ate. Xanthus perked up; I said nothing. He called for a drink again; I jingled my purse morosely. I would be paying as usual. Xanthus found plenty of ways to squander his holiday cash, but possessed a knack of digging deep only when I let him out by himself. He had cluttered us up with souvenirs – rattling lanterns, statuettes of muscular local deities, and chariot-wheel talismans – yet somehow funding our supper always seemed to be my responsibility.

This bar was casual about payment: you settled up at the end. It was a good way to part people from more money than they had intended, though in fact when I heaved myself over to sort out the reckoning, the extortion was not too painful, considering how much the barber had eaten and drunk.

A good evening – for a man who could feel free to enjoy it.

I told Xanthus to press on ahead while I waited for the usual scramble among the staff to find coins for my change. When I emerged on the main street my tame pest had already vanished. I was in no hurry to catch up. It was a dry night, with crazy stars dotting a black sky among a few fast, high clouds. Tomorrow we would probably have teeming showers again, but I stood for a while enjoying this fierce, dry wind on my face. The street was empty at that moment. I was suffering a pang of traveller's melancholia.

I turned back into the bar, where I ordered a dish of raisins and another drink.

The room had thinned out. Feeling independent, I changed seats. This allowed me to survey my drinking companions. Men were talking together in small parties; some were dining alone. Two caught my eye because they seemed to be together yet never spoke. There was no impression of a quarrel; they simply looked even more depressed than I had been before I shook off Xanthus.

A barmaid lit a new taper on their table. As it flared, I recognised the pair; they wore high-necked tunics under blackberry-coloured Gallic wraps with pointed hoods. One was overweight and middle-aged; the other had reddish hair and a particularly florid crop of warts on his cheeks and hands. They were the two I had seen at the ceramics factory, arguing.

Had they looked more communicative I might have gone over and mentioned the coincidence. As it was, they were sunk in their thoughts and I was sleepy, enjoying my snatched period of privacy. I finished my raisins. The next time I looked up they were on their way out. Just as well, probably. I doubted if they had noticed me at Lugdunum, and in any case, they had been so angry there that they might not welcome a reminder of the scene. Tomorrow we would all

59

continue our journeys to different destinations. It was highly unlikely another chance meeting would occur.

But it did. Well, *I* saw *them*.

Next morning, half an hour out of the village, while the barber was still maundering on about where I had disappeared to for so long the previous evening, and I was ignoring the flow of complaint with my usual tight-lipped tact, we came across two tent parties of army recruits. There were no legions stationed in Gaul itself. These goslings must have been waddling towards the frontier. Now they had stopped. They were standing about the highway like spilled carrots, twenty seventeen- and eighteen-year-olds still unused to the weight of their helmets and only just discovering the drear boredom of a long march. Even the centurion in charge of them, who must have been around a bit, was inadequate for the crisis they had stumbled across. He knew he represented law and order, so he knew he had to do something. But he would rather have kept going with his eyes fixed straight ahead. Frankly, so would I.

The problem was that the recruits had spotted the bodies of two travellers lying in the drainage ditch. They had called out eagerly to the centurion, so he had had to stop. When we arrived he was not a happy man. As he had clambered down to investigate, his boot had skidded on the wet, slippery turf. He had twisted his back, soaked his cloak, and smeared mud all down one leg. He was cursing repetitiously as he tried to clean his leg with a bunch of grass. Xanthus and I reining in to watch made him even more upset. Now, whatever he decided to do about the problem would have critical witnesses.

We had ridden out north from Lugdunum, following the River Sâone on the consular highway constructed by the army as a fast route towards the two Germanies. Maintained by commissioners at public expense, it was a top-quality piece of engineering: rammed earth, then a layer of pebbles, another of rubble, a bed of fine concrete, then squared paving with a camber that would shed water like a tortoise shell. The highway rode a little above the surrounding countryside. On either side were steep ditches to provide both drainage and security from ambushers. Looking down from the road, I had a perfect view.

The keenest young lads had slithered down after their centurion. This was the best thing that had happened to them since they had left Italy. They were rolling the fat corpse onto his back. I think I was ready for what was to follow even before I had a look at his face.

It was puffed up from lying in rainwater, but I knew this was one of the two men from Lugdunum. I knew his stiffening companion, too, though he was still face down; I could see the warts on his hands. They were visible because before depositing him in the ditch-water, someone had bound his arms behind his back.

Whatever had made these two so angry, fortune had found a decisive way of helping them get over it.

XIV

The centurion tucked up the swinging, bronze-weighted ends of his groin-protector into his belt, then handed his helmet to a soldier, who held it gingerly by the carrying loop. The rain had stopped temporarily, but the officer's scarlet cloak twisted awkwardly against his silvered sword baldric, the cloak's woollen folds clinging to him with the dampness you never seem to lose when travelling. As his head lifted, I spotted weary resignation because our arrival had dispelled any plan he might have had for dragging brushwood over the bodies and hurrying off out of it.

Leaning on my horse's neck, I gave him a slight nod.

'Move the crowd on, soldier!' he called up. The recruits were so new to army life that instead of each stubbornly assuming the order was for the next man along, they all squared up to us. I stayed where I was.

'Show them your pass!' Xanthus hissed at me loudly, assuming we were in trouble – which, once he had spoken, we immediately were. I ignored him, but the centurion stiffened. Now he would want to make quite sure who we were, and if he was as thorough as he looked, where we were going, who had sent us, what we were up to out here in this wilderness, and whether anything in *our* business was likely to produce repercussions affecting him.

This seemed good for holding us all up for at least a couple of weeks. My dangerous stillness communicated itself to the barber, who subsided unhappily. The centurion glared at us.

By now I was more or less resigned to people concluding that Xanthus and I were two fancy boys out on a spree. Xanthus was unmistakably a barber – and I was just as obviously too poor to afford a personal attendant. Our horse and mules were drawn from the local stables who supplied the imperial despatch-riders, but there was nothing about the beasts to give that away. The basket with Vespasian's gift to the Fourteenth had a well-buckled, military air. My own luggage looked businesslike. Yet any hint of officialdom I managed to carry clashed heavily with the barber's daintiness. Like everyone else, the centurion assessed his Greek-looking cloak and violet tunic with saffron embroidery (it was probably a cast-off from Nero, but I had refused to enquire and give Xanthus the pleasure of telling me). The officer considered the brighter-than-life complexion, the fastidiously trimmed hair and today's shoes (hole-punched, purple-tasselled jobs). He took in the simpering, insufferable expression. Then he turned to me.

I stared back, uncombed and unperturbed. I allowed him three seconds of failing to explain me. Then I suggested quietly, 'One for the municipal police at the next town with a magistrate?' I was consulting my itinerary; I let him see it was army issue. 'We're three days past Lugdunum; Cavillonum should be only a cricket's jump ahead. That's a substantial town . . .'

People are never grateful. Offering him a let-out only made him take an interest. He turned back to the corpses. I should have ridden on, but our previous contact with the dead men gave me some sort of fellow-feeling. I dismounted and half jumped, half slid down into the *fossa* too.

I felt no sense of surprise at finding them here, dead. They had carried the marks of men in the midst of crisis. Maybe it was hindsight, but what I had seen of them had seemed to forebode tragedy.

Signs of what had done the actual damage were minimal, but it looked as if both men had been beaten to subdue them, then finished off by pressure to the neck. Their bound arms proved pretty conclusively that the killings were deliberate.

The centurion searched them without emotion while his young soldiers stood back more shyly. He glanced at me. 'Name's Falco,' I said, to show I had nothing to hide.

'Official?'

'Don't ask!' That told him I was official enough. 'What do you think?'

He had accepted me as an equal. 'Looks like robbery. Horses missing. This stout party has had a pouch cut from his belt.'

'If that's it, report their positions as you pass through Cavillonum. Let the civilians deal with it.'

I touched one of the dead men with the back of my hand. He was cold. The centurion saw me do it, but neither of us commented. The clothing of the one they had turned over was wringing wet where the brackish bog at the base of the ditch had soaked right through the material. The centurion saw me looking at that, too.

'Nothing to show who they are or where they were going! I still put it down to thieves.' He met my gaze, daring me to disagree; I smiled faintly. In his position I would have taken the same line. We both stood. He shouted up to the road, 'One of you run back to the milestone and take a note of it.'

'Yes, Helvetius!'

He and I took a run at the bank and regained the road together. The recruits below had a last poke at the bodies for bravado, then followed us; most of them floundered and fell back a few times. 'Stop fooling!' Helvetius growled, but he was patient with them.

I grinned. 'They seem up to the usual dim standard of nowadays!' He hated them, as recruiting officers do, but he let it pass. 'What's your legion?'

'First Adiutrix.' Brought over the Alps by Cerialis as part of the task force that quelled the rebellion. I had forgotten where they were based presently. I was just happy not to hear he belonged to the Fourteenth.

Xanthus was asking one of the soldiers what fort they were heading for; the lad was unable to tell him. The centurion must have known, but he didn't say; nor did I ask.

We parted company from the soldiers and rode on towards the Cavillonum junction, where I was planning to fork south. After a while Xanthus informed me, with obvious pride, that he had recognised the dead men from Lugdunum.

'So did I.'

He was disappointed. 'You never said!'

'No point.'

'What will happen now?'

'The centurion will instruct a town magistrate to collect the corpses and organise a posse to search for the thieves.'

'Do you think they'll be apprehended?'

'Probably not.'

'How do you know he was a centurion?'

'He wore his sword on the left.'

'Do ordinary soldiers carry them differently?'

'Correct.'

'Why?'

'Keeps the scabbard out of the way of the shield.' To a foot-soldier unimpeded freedom of movement could mean life or death, but such details failed to interest Xanthus.

'You know, it could have been us!' he trilled enthusiastically. 'If

64

you and I, Falco, had set out earlier than they did this morning, *we* could have had that chance meeting with the thieves.'

I said nothing. He assumed I was unnerved by the suggestion, so he rode on looking superior. It was another of his irritating habits; he could reason himself halfway through a problem, then his brain stuck.

Even if he and I had ridden out at dawn with clinking saddlebags marked 'Help yourselves' in three European languages, I did not believe that whoever killed the pair would have touched us. This was no straightforward highway robbery. There were oddities here which both Helvetius and I had spotted. For one thing, the two men from Lugdunum had *not* died that morning. The bodies were cold, and the condition of their clothing showed that they had been lying in the ditch all night. Who travels by night? Not even imperial despatch-riders, unless an emperor has died or they have details of a *very* lurid scandal involving people at the top. In any case, I had seen the victims at their supper. They had looked unhappy, but had given no impression of needing to dash on with lanterns. They had been resting as leisurely as the rest of us at the tavern that night.

No. Somebody had killed those two men, probably at the village not long after I saw them, then transported the bodies a fair distance in the dark. Perhaps if I had not lingered over my drink, I would have run into the fracas. Perhaps I might even have prevented it. At any rate, after I watched them leave the tavern they must have been sought out, beaten and throttled, then the murders disguised as a natural hazard of travelling so that no questions would be asked.

'All a bit of a coincidence, eh Falco?'

'Possibly.'

Possibly not. But I had no time to stop and investigate. The only question I could ponder as I rode through Cavillonum was, did their sad fate derive entirely from their personal business in Lugdunum – or did it have some bearing on my own task?

I told myself I would never know.

It didn't help.

XV

Argentoratum had forgotten how to welcome strangers – assuming it had ever possessed the knack. The town had hosted a huge army base for as long as Rome had taken an interest in Germany, and its good manners had suffered. This was the original home station of my own legion, the Second Augusta. By the time I had been sent out to them in Britain there had been only a few grumpy veterans with any recollection of life on the Rhine, but Rome's foothold in Britain had always seemed perilous, and in any case, we had always hoped to be posted somewhere better, so Argentoratum had always been a place whose name the men of my legion spoke with a proprietary twang.

That did not mean I could call up old favours when I made the mistake of going there.

I had passed through this hard-faced habitation before, en route to even worse places. At least the last time I had met young Camillus Justinus, who had treated me to a dinner I still remembered plus a tour of the high spots and the low life – which were neither as high as Argentoratum liked to think, nor as low as I was hoping for at the time. I had been depressed – a man in love, though one who had not yet noticed it. I wondered now if Camillus had been able to see that his stately sister (whom I was supposed to be escorting, though as usual Helena had placed herself in charge) had been busy caging me like some little pet singing finch. I looked forward to asking him, and sharing the joke. But I would have to find him first.

Big military centres have their drawbacks. At the fort you can never encounter any sentry you recognise. No friendly official from your last visit has ever stayed in post. The town is equally unpromising. The locals are too busy making money out of the soldiery to bother with casual visitors. The men are brusque and the women contemptuous. The dogs bark and the donkeys bite.

Eventually I dragged Xanthus to the front of a complaining queue at the main guardhouse. I could have registered as an imperial envoy and been poked into a billet inside the fort, but I spared myself a night of being polite to the commissariat. One of the men on guard told me all the bad news I needed to winkle out: they had no listing for the arrival here of any noble tribune's noble sister, and his honour Camillus Justinus had left Argentoratum anyway.

'His replacement came two weeks ago. Justinus had completed his tour.'

'What – gone home to Rome?'

'Hah! This is the Rhine; no one gets to escape that easily! Posted on.'

'Where's he stationed now?'

'No idea. All I know is we get the password for the night watch from some beardless little idiot fresh out of philosophy school. Last night's little gem was *xenophobia*. Today there are three sentinels in the cells for forgetting it, and a centurion's optio is striding round like a bear who just sat on a thorn-bush because he has to do disciplinary reports on his best tent party.'

No legion in Germany at present could risk mistakes by the guard. The province was under strict martial law – for very good reasons – and there was no room for idiotic tribunes who wanted to show off.

'I imagine your clever new boy is listening to a rich lecture from the legate!' I fought back my worries about Helena, concentrating on her brother. 'Maybe Camillus Justinus was deputed to one of the task-force legions?'

'Want me to make enquiries?' The gateman gave every impression he was prepared to help a tribune's friend, but we both knew he did not intend to leave his stool.

'Don't trouble yourself,' I answered with a courteous sneer. It was time to go. I was all too aware that the barber, who had been peering over my shoulder in a haze of exotic skin lotion, was starting to make a poor impression on this hard-nosed front-line legionary.

I made one last play for information. 'What's the word on the Fourteenth Gemina?'

'Bastards!' retorted the guard.

This unsophisticated parley was all I could expect. In a legionary gatehouse on a dark, wet October night, there was not much scope for light salon conversation. Behind me, two exhausted despatch-riders were waiting to register, Xanthus was looking even more indiscreet, and a very drunk venison-supplier who wanted to dispute a bill with the centurions' dining club was jostling me so closely that

I left, not wanting a fight right then, yet feeling as bruised and indignant as a barmaid at a Saturnalia feast.

I booked us into a civilian lodging-house between the fort and the river, so we could make a quick departure at first light. We went to the baths but were already too late for the hot water. Dazed by the way foreign towns draw their shutters so early, we ate a grim supper, forcing it down with acidic white wine, and were then kept awake most of the night by tramping boots. I had settled us in a street full of brothels. Xanthus became intrigued, but I told him the disturbance was just troops on a night exercise.

'Listen, Xanthus. When I go up to Moguntiacum, you can stay here if you like. I'll pick you up for the trip home when I've done what I have to for the Emperor.'

'Oh no. I've come this far, I'll stick with you!'

He spoke as if he was doing me a gigantic favour. I closed my eyes wearily and made no reply.

Next morning I tried to hitch us a ride for nothing, but no luck. The trip down the Rhenus is a highly picturesque one, so the owners of the river barges were charging equally highly for the privilege of surveying a hundred miles of its scenery.

Ours was a wineship; most of them are. We shared the slowly passing vistas with two old fellows and a pedlar. The grandads had bent backs, bald heads, and a series of mouth-watering picnics which they had no intention of sharing round. They sat opposite each other for the whole journey, talking hard, like people who have known one another for a very long time.

The pedlar, who came aboard at a small settlement called Borbeto-magus was bent too, but under the trappings of a fold-up stall and the ghastly stuff he sold. Xanthus and I were a captive audience so he soon unknotted the corners of his cloth bundles and spread his offerings on the deck. I ignored him. Xanthus immediately throbbed with crass excitement.

'Look at this, Falco!'

Since I did sometimes make a feeble attempt to save him from his stupidity, I glanced at the trash he was about to invest in now. Then I groaned. This time it was militaria. You may suppose our footslogging heroes would have had enough of kit and harness without spending their pay on more, but never believe it; this canny pedlar was doing a fine trade flogging the legionaries his sad souvenirs of ancient wars. I had seen it in Britain. I had seen it in the cartload of junk my elder brother, who had no sense of proportion, had dragged home from the exotic souks of Caesaria. Here, with nine legions along the Rhenus, most of them bored and all of them flush with imperial silver, there must be a vast scope for trading in quaint tribal buckles, worn-out weaponry and odd jags of iron that could have come off any farm implement.

The man was a native Ubian, all top lip and small talk. The lip was stretched over big buck teeth; the chat was his softening-up technique. It worked on Xanthus. Most things did. I let the two of them get on with it.

The pedlar's name was Dubnus. He was selling the usual native helmets with spikes over the ears, several bowls of 'old' arrowheads and speartips (which he had obviously gathered up last Thursday from a rubbish tip at a previous fort), a dirty drinking-cup which he swore to Xanthus was an aurochs' horn, some links of 'Sarmatian armour', half a set of 'Icenean horse-trappings', and just by the way, a collection of Baltic amber.

None of it contained fossilised insect life, but the amber was the only stuff worth considering. Naturally Xanthus passed straight on without a second glance. I said I would have bought some beads for my girlfriend if they had been matched and threaded properly. Not entirely to my surprise, Dubnus immediately produced from his unsavoury pocket three or four decent necklace strands – at three or four times the price.

We spent a tolerable half-hour haggling over the string with the smallest beads. I beat him down to about a quarter of the asking price just for the vocal exercise, then snapped up one of the better necklaces as I had intended all along. The pedlar had weighed me up cannily, but Xanthus looked startled. He did not know I had spent my childhood burrowing around the Saepta Julia second-hand stalls. I also thought it might be wise to buy a present for Helena's birthday in case I ran into her. I was missing her. It made me an easy mark for anyone hawking trinkets that showed slight vestiges of taste.

Judging that my purse was now firmly closed, Dubnus turned his whining charm on Xanthus again. He was an artist. As an auctioneer's son, I almost enjoyed watching it. Luckily, we were not sailing all the way down to the delta, or the barber would have bought up the pedlar's entire stock. He did fall for the aurochs' horn, supposedly hacked by Dubnus himself from one of the wild Gallic oxen whose savage temper is legendary . . .

'I'd really like to see one of those, Falco!'

'Just be thankful it's unlikely!'

'You ever spied one on your travels?'

'No. I'm sensible, Xanthus – I never wanted to.'

His acquisition was a fairly useful drinking-cup, which didn't spill too much down his tunic neck when he attempted to use it. He managed to polish it up to a handsome shine. I never told him that aurochs don't have twisted horns.

As the wineship floated on to our destination, Dubnus slowly rewrapped his treasures. Xanthus began to handle a helmet. Partly to rescue him before he was bankrupt (because that would mean I'd have to pay for *everything*), I took the item away from him.

It looked like army issue at first, but with differences. The modern helmet incorporates a deeper guard around the back, protecting the neck and shoulders; it also has cheekpieces and extra protection over the ears. I suspect the revised design was developed to counter damage from Celtic broadsword swipes. The original pattern had been superseded long before my time, but I was staring at one now.

'This must be quite an antique, Dubnus.'

'I call that a relic of the Varus disaster!' he confessed amiably, as if owning to a fake; then his eyes met mine and he had second thoughts. I managed to stop myself shivering.

'Where did you get it?'

'Oh . . . somewhere in the woods.' His voice faded evasively.

'*Where?*' I asked again.

'Oh . . . up in the north.'

'Somewhere like the Teutoburger forest?'

He was reluctant to clarify. I dropped to one knee, surveying his stock more attentively. He had marked me up as trouble, so he didn't like me doing it. I ignored his agitation. That worried him even more.

Now I noticed a piece of old bronze that could have come from a Roman sword pommel; clasps that resembled a set I had seen at my grandfather's house; a holder for a helmet plume – another discontinued line, now altered to a carrying loop.

'Sell a lot of these "Varus relics", do you?'

'People believe what they want to.'

There was also a blackened object I refused to handle because I guessed it was a human skull.

I stood up again.

Augustus's stepgrandson, the heroic Germanicus, was supposed to have found where the massacre had taken place, collected the scattered remains of the dead, and given the lost army of Varus some kind of decent funeral – but who believes that out in the hostile forest Germanicus and his nervous troops spent too much time offering themselves as another target? They did their best. They brought the lost standards back to Rome. After that we could all sleep with clear consciences. It was best not to think that somewhere deep in the dark woods of unconquered Germany broken weapons and other booty might still lie among unburied Roman bones.

The troops of today would buy this mouldy paraphernalia. Army lads love souvenirs that smack of manly deeds in dangerous venues. The grislier the better. If Dubnus really had discovered the old battle site, he must be coining it.

I avoided the issue by probing for my own purposes. 'So you go across the river, do you? In the north?' He shrugged. Commerce breeds daring. In any case, free Germany had never been a no-go area for the purposes of trade. 'How far do your travels take you? Ever come across the famous prophetess?'

'Which prophetess would that be?'

He was teasing. I tried not to look particularly interested, in case word of my mission ran ahead of me. 'Is there more than one sinister spinster wielding influence over the tribes? I mean the bloodthirsty priestess of the Bructeri.'

'Oh, Veleda!' sneered Dubnus.

'Ever met her?'

'No one meets her.'

'Why's that?'

'She lives at the top of a high tower in a lonely place in the forest. She never sees anyone.'

'Since when have prophets been so shy?' Just my luck. A really weird one. 'I never imagined she kept a marble office, with an appointments secretary serving peppermint tea for visitors, but how does she communicate?'

'Her male relations carry messages.' Judging by the effect Veleda had had on international events, her uncles and brothers must have busily trampled a wide swathe through the woods. It rather took the shine off her elusiveness.

The barber was wearing his excitable look. 'Is Veleda part of your mission?' he hissed. His wide-eyed simplicity was beginning to afflict me like a stitch in the side when you're running away from a mad bull.

71

'Women I can handle. But I don't do Druids!' It was a line. Two of us knew it, yet poor old Xanthus looked impressed.

I had to act fast. Our barge was approaching the great bridge at Moguntiacum; we would soon berth at the quay. I gave the pedlar a thoughtful glance. 'If somebody wanted to contact Veleda, would it be possible to get a message to this tower of hers?'

'Could be.'

Dubnus looked disturbed by the suggestion. I made it plain I was speaking with some authority, and told him not to leave town.

The pedlar assumed the air of a man who would leave town exactly when he wanted to, and without telling me first.

PART THREE:
LEGIO XIV GEMINA MARTIA VICTRIX

MOGUNTIACUM, UPPER GERMANY
October, AD 71

'. . . *above all the Fourteenth, whose men had covered themselves in glory by quelling the rebellion in Britain.*'

Tacitus *Histories*

XVI

Moguntiacum.

A bridge. A tollbooth. A column. A huddle of civilian huts, with a few handsome homes owned by the local wool and wine merchants. All dominated by one of the Empire's biggest forts.

The settlement stood just below the confluence of the Rhenus and the Moenus waterways. The bridge, which joined the Roman side of the Rhenus to huts and wharfs on the opposite bank, had triangular piers thrust out to break the current, and a wooden rail. The tollbooth was a temporary affair, about to be superseded by a massive new customs-post at Colonia Agrippinensium. (Vespasian was a tax-collector's son; as Emperor it coloured his approach.) The column, erected in the time of Nero, was a grand effort celebrating Jupiter. The huge fort declared that Rome meant business here, though whether we were trying to bluff the tribes or convince ourselves was open to debate.

My first disappointment was immediately thrust on me. I had been telling Xanthus he could busy himself setting up shop with his razors among the *canabae*. Most military establishments grow a thicket of booths, a shanty-town fringe that hogs the outer walls, offering the troops off-duty entertainment of the usual sordid kinds. It springs up when the baths are constructed outside the fortress as a fire precaution, after which breadshops, brothels, barbers and bijouteries rapidly collect – with or without licences. Then the inevitable camp-followers and the soldiers' unofficial families arrive, and soon the extramural clutter swells into a civilian town.

At Moguntiacum there were no booths.

It was a shock. We could see where they had all been cleared. The operation must have been swift and thorough. A mound of bashed-in shutters and splintered awning poles still stood nearby. Now bare ground surrounded the fort, forming a wide defensible berm from which the turf walls rose a clean eighteen feet to the watch-towers and patrol-track. Among the visible defenses I counted one more

Punic ditch than usual, and in the midfield a fatigue party was planting what the legions call a lily garden; deep pits dug in a quincunx pattern, set with sharpened stakes, then covered with brushwood to disguise their whereabouts – a savage deterrent during an attack.

The civilians had been deposited way back beyond the outer ditch, and even a year after the Civilis Revolt no re-encroachment was allowed. The impression was stark. It was meant to be.

At the fort itself, instead of the usual organised but easy-going atmosphere of an army in peacetime, we soon grasped that this army sketched in its civic role with a light hand. Its gestures to the local community were mostly obscene.

The barber and I counted as locals until we proved otherwise. When we presented our persons at the Praetorian entrance, even Xanthus stopped twittering. We had to leave our horses. There was no making ourselves agreeable to bored sentries inside the guardroom; we were detained in the square chamber between the double sets of gates, and it was plain that if our story and our documents failed to match, we would be pinned up against a wall by a nine-inch javelin-tip and vigorously body-searched.

The atmosphere upset me. The jolt reminded me of Britain after the Boudiccan affair. That was something I had intended to forget.

We were passed in, however. My docket from the Emperor aroused suspicion but worked the trick. We were eyed up, listed, given order to go directly to the Principia, then allowed through the inner gates.

I myself was ready for the size and scope of the immense interior, but even being born and bred in the labyrinthine corridors of Rome's imperial court had failed to prepare Xanthus for this. Moguntiacum was a permanent fort, and a double one at that. With two legions stationed there, almost everything was in duplicate. It was a military city. Twelve thousand men were packed inside, with enough stores, smithies and granaries to withstand months under siege – not that that had worked for the poor devils attacked by the rebels at Vetera. Within the base, the two commanding legates would occupy minor palaces designed to reflect their grandeur and diplomatic standing; the housing stock for the twelve young military tribunes who supported them would make the best villas in most Italian towns look mean; and even the commissariat buildings, where Xanthus and I were heading, were dramatic in their blunt, military way.

We came out from the cold shadow of the rampart walkway. With the guard-towers of the gatehouse looming overhead, we had first to cross the perimeter road. It was eighty feet wide. The perimeter track, which was designed to give protection from missiles as well as provide ready access to all parts of the fort, was kept well clear of obstruction. I made a mental note that the Fourteenth Gemina must take half the credit for the immaculate housekeeping, though they probably made their lesser colleagues empty the rubbish skips and sweep the roads. Stacks of spare javelins were stored handy for the ramparts, along with piles of heavy shot and field ballista bolts, but there were none of the roaming beasts or the litter of wagons that you often see. If the sacred chickens were allowed free range, it was not on this side of the fort.

I towed the barber past the endless barrack blocks: nearly fifty pairs (though I can't say I counted), each housing a hundred and sixty men in groups of ten, with a double set of centurions' quarters at one end of every block. Adequate space for the legionaries, plus more cramped quarters for their native auxiliaries – not that that applied to the Fourteenth at present, since their eight famous cohorts of Batavians had defected to the rebels . . . Vespasian would not be replacing them until I made my report.

Xanthus was already awed by the atmosphere; I merely felt a throb at re-encountering the familiar. To me the fort had a daytime, half-empty feel. Many of the troops would be in training or sweating on fatigues, others on their monthly ten-mile route march in full kit. Most of the rest would be on local patrol, and it would be no mere exercise.

'Impressed, Xanthus? Wait until the camp's full this evening! Then you will have the unique experience of being among twelve thousand men who all know exactly what they are doing!' He said nothing. 'Are you thinking of the potential in twelve thousand stubbly chins?'

'Twelve thousand flavours of halitosis!' he responded valiantly. 'Twelve thousand variations on "the girl I stuffed last Thursday". And being warned not to nick twelve thousand different wens!'

We reached the main thoroughfare. 'Xanthus, in case you get lost, try to remember the most important street is this one. It's called the Via Principalis. It's a hundred feet wide; even you can't miss the thing. Take your bearing now. The Principalis bisects the camp crossways between the Sinister and Dexter Gates, and the Via Praetoria meets it at right angles at the HQ. The headquarters always face the enemy, so as long as you can see which way the slingstones are flying in, you can orientate yourself in any fortress in the world . . .'

'Where's the enemy?' He was dazed.

'Across the river.'

'Where's the river?'

'*That* way!' I was losing my temper and wasting my breath. 'The way we came in,' I reminded him, but he was already too confused.

'So where are we going?'

'To introduce ourselves to the nice fellows of the Fourteenth Gemina.'

It was not a success. Still, I had come prepared for that.

For one thing, no job I ever undertook concluded itself that easily, and for another the XIV Gemina had *never* been nice.

XVII

The fortress headquarters were designed to overawe any wild tribes-man who dared put his nose round the Praetorian Gate. They formed the main vista as we stared ahead, and tramping closer certainly awed us.

There was one administration block in the fort. The two legions currently in post took up their quarters on either side, but they shared this edifice, which represented the fort's permanence. It was massively constructed. The façade comprised heavily colonnaded stonework on either side of a magisterial triple gate that looked straight at us down the Via Praetoria. Dwarfed, we crept in through the left-hand arch to find ourselves facing a well-tramped parade-ground that occupied more land than the forum in most provincial towns. Luckily no one was parading at the time. My timid companion would have expired from shock.

'We can't go in here!'

'If anyone issues a challenge, keep your pearly teeth clamped together and let me talk. As a general rule, while we're inside the fort don't argue with anybody wearing a sword. And, Xanthus, do try not to look so much like a lost understudy from one of Nero's theatricals . . .'

Three sides of the square were taken up by storerooms and the quartermaster's offices. Opposite, stood the basilican hall, which pro-vided a focus for the formalities of both legions. It was where we were going, so I set off straight across the parade-ground. By halfway, even I felt slightly exposed. It seemed to take us half an hour to reach the other side and I could sense enraged centurions breathing fire from all the overlooking offices. I realised how the lobster feels when the water in the cooking pot slowly starts heating up.

The Principia was enormous. It stretched the full width of the complex. Decoration was minimal; it achieved its effect through size. The central nave was forty feet wide, separated by gigantic columns from sombre aisles each half its width again. The columns supported an almighty roof whose weight it was best not to contemplate while standing underneath. On a rainy day a whole legion could be crushed in there like anchovy bones in fish pickle. The rest of the time this formidable hall stood empty and silent, guarding secrets and forming a bold tribute to the skill of the army's engineers.

Through the gloom we could see the commander's tribunal at one end. The main feature, directly opposite the entrance, was the legionary shrine.

I walked across. My boots rang on the paving. There was a lurking scent of ceremonial oil, recent not rancid. Behind a border of stone screens lay a fireproof vaulted chamber; it guarded that other religious sanctum, the underground strongbox room. Up here, in the unlocked part, they kept the portable altar for taking auguries. Around it the standards were spikily arranged.

The Fourteenth had grabbed the most prominent position for their display, their companion legion obligingly tucking itself up on one side. In the place of honour gleamed the Fourteenth's eagle and a portrait of the Emperor wreathed in purple cloth. By the dim light from remote clerestory windows high in the main hall, I could see on the centuries' standards more medals for acts of valour than I had ever seen assembled together. Predominantly honours from the Emperors Claudius and Nero, they must have been awarded for outstanding service in Britain. Naturally they also had bronze statues of their titular patrons, Mars and Victory. The other legion's standards were by contrast unadorned.

We had not come to make obeisance. I winked at the eagle who was guarding the naked set of standards. Then I wheeled Xanthus into the nearby offices. The secretariat occupied the most significant place, alongside the shrine. Since no one else wants to bother with accommodation problems, the clerks always control the fortress plan. They naturally allocate the most desirable roost to themselves.

A bald will clerk nodded us towards the lavish suite which the Fourteenth had commandeered. Things were peaceful. That could mean either the legion were a dozy, inefficient outfit, or that the day's business had already been stamped up and cleared away. Perhaps their legate was taking a siesta at his own house, and the camp prefect had a cold. Perhaps the tribunes had all snatched a day's hunting leave. I reserved judgement. So long as they were keeping full granaries, a careful weapons count and an up-to-date log of what went into the savings bank, Vespasian was not a man who would quibble at the

Fourteenth maintaining an unrushed commissariat. His interest was in results.

In the biggest room, we found two of the legion's senior men.

One, who was a non-combatant, wore a red tunic but no body armour. On a nail hung his helmet, adorned with the two horns that gave him his title of Cornicularius: head of the commissariat. In my opinion, the little horns are the legions' joke to make their chief clerks look ridiculous. His companion was a different species. A centurion in full kit, including a complete set of nine *phalerae*, the chest medallions awarded for dedicated service. He was over sixty, and his air of ingrained contempt told me this was the Primipilus, the First Spear, leading centurion. This sought-after rank is held for three years, after which lies a gratuity equivalent to middle-class status, and a passport into plum civilian jobs. Some, and I guessed this was one of them, opt to repeat their first spear posting, thereby making themselves public menaces in the way they know best. Dying in harness in some godforsaken province is a first spear's idea of a good life.

This primipilus had a short, thick neck and looked as if his party trick was killing flies with a head-butt. He had broad shoulders and his torso hardly narrowed on the way to his belt, but none of what went on below the chest was paunch. His feet were small. He hardly moved while he was talking to us, but I guessed he would be nippy when he wanted to exert himself. I didn't like him. That was irrelevant. He didn't care for me, either; that was what would count.

The cornicularius was much less impressive physically. He had a turned-up nose and a small, bitter mouth. What he lacked in presence he made up in personal venom and his ability to express himself.

When we entered, these two were tearing shreds off a soldier who had committed some misdemeanour, like asking an innocent question. They were enjoying themselves, and were ready to humiliate their victim all afternoon unless someone who disgusted them even more turned up. Someone did: Xanthus and I.

They told the soldier to sheath himself in his own scabbard, or words to that effect. He slunk out past us gratefully.

The primipilus and cornicularius looked at us, glanced at each other, then stared back at us derisively while they waited for the fun to start.

'I don't believe this!' the primipilus marvelled.

'Who let this rabble in? Someone must have bopped the gate security on their heads!'

'Those slack bastards in the First!'

'Good afternoon,' I ventured from the doorway.

'Shove off, curly!' snarled the primipilus. 'And take your garland girl.'

In my business insults are the normal convention, so I rode out the squall. I could feel Xanthus throbbing indignantly, but if he expected me to defend him in this company he could think again. I moved further in, and dumped the basket containing the Emperor's gift. 'Name's Didius Falco.' It seemed wise to be formal. I flipped my imperial passport at the cornicularius, who lifted it between one finger and thumb as if it had been found in a sewer. He let a sneer play around his tight little mouth, then shoved my tag across his table for the primipilus to laugh at too.

'And what do you do, Falco?' asked the mouth. It squeezed out his words like stuffing from a badly sewn mattress case.

'I deliver awkward packages.'

'Hah!' commented the primipilus.

'So what's in the picnic basket?' jeered his more talkative pal.

'Five bread rolls, a sheep's-gut sausage – and a new standard to mark the Emperor's personal favour to the Fourteenth. Want to take a look?'

The primipilus was the man of action around here, so while the cornicularius attended to a snag in his manicure with the stump-end of a stylus, he forced himself to approach as I unbuckled the basket straps. The Iron Hand weighed as much as a chunk of aqueduct supply pipe, but he lifted it by its thumb as lightly as an amulet.

'Oh very nice!' No one could fault the words. Only the tone was treasonous.

I kept my own voice level. 'I am to deliver Vespasian's gift to your legate in person. I also have a sealed despatch for him, which I believe contains the programme for a suitable investiture ceremony. Any chance of a word with Florius Gracilis at once?'

'No,' said the cornicularius.

'I can wait.'

'You can measure yourself for a funeral urn and pour yourself into it.'

I remarked to Xanthus pleasantly, 'This is the Fourteenth legion's famous helpfulness and charm.'

'Who's the flower with the disgusting reek?' demanded the primipilus suddenly.

I gave both sections of the military a narrow look. 'Special envoy from Titus Caesar.' I drew one finger across my neck in the time-honoured gesture. 'I haven't worked out yet whether he's a well-disguised assassin looking for someone to dispose of, or just an auditor with a fancy dress sense. Now we've got here we should soon know. Either there'll be a body count, or you'll find him peering at your daily accounts . . .'

Xanthus was so startled that for once he kept his trap shut.

The two wits consulted each other wearily. 'As we thought!' sighed the cornicularius. 'Things must be rough in Rome. Now they're sending us rejects from musical parties and bogus scum like this – '

'Steady on!' I grinned, attempting to go along with them. 'Whatever I am, it's genuine! Let's get back to the point. If Gracilis is too busy now, make me an appointment when his schedule has more space.'

Sometimes ingratiation works. Not here. '*Genuine* scum!' commented the primipilus to his crony. 'Disappear up your own arse, curly!'

'Leave my orifices out of the orders of the day! Listen, centurion. I've just lugged an Iron Hand halfway across Europe and I'm intending to deliver it. I know the Fourteenth are a blasphemous, uncultured mob, but if your legate wants his consulship he's not going to let a drill-swank and an ink-swab reject an award from the Emperor – '

'Don't get clever,' the cornicularius warned. 'You can leave the trophy, and you can leave the sealed despatch. Maybe,' he speculated with his most cheerful expression yet, 'the despatch says "*Execute the messenger*" . . .'

I ignored that. 'I'll happily ground the ironwork, but I'm going to hand the confidential orders to Gracilis himself. Do I get quarters at the fort? Your accommodation must be flush now you're light of the loyal Batavians!'

'If that's a jibe at the Fourteenth's expense,' the primipilus snorted, 'make the most of it; you won't manage another!'

I said I wouldn't dream of insulting the victors of Bedriacum, and that I'd find my own roost.

As I shoved him down the corridor outside, Xanthus whined, 'What's Bedriacum?'

'A battle where the Fourteenth escaped being called losers by the simple trick of claiming they had never arrived for the fight.'

'I thought it would be something like that. You've upset them, Falco!'

'Suits me.'

'And they know you are working for the Emperor – '

'No, Xanthus; they think *you* are!'

'What's the point of that?'

'They appreciate they have a tricky record. They know the Emperor will send someone to look them over, but they reckon I'm the dregs. So long as I behave stupidly, they'll never believe I'm the spy.'

Fortunately, Xanthus didn't ask why I was so anxious to identify someone else as the Emperor's agent.

Or what I thought the Fourteenth Gemina might try and do to whoever they thought it was.

As we reached the exit, two tribunes came from another office, arguing in a gentlemanly way.

'Macrinus, I don't want to be a nuisance, but – '

'He's incommunicado; planning one of his forays against imagined troublemakers. Remind me tomorrow and I'll get you in to see him when he has some breathing-space.'

At first I listened because I guessed they were referring to the legate Gracilis. The young man speaking was the assured and stocky type that had never impressed me, with an athletic build, square head and a burnished tint to his tight curls. The one who seemed to be protesting struck me as familiar.

He must have been twenty, but looked younger. An ordinary, boyish face. A tall, slim frame. A quiet manner but a ready smile from a wide mouth.

'Camillus Justinus!' At my cry of recognition for his companion, the first tribune reacted deftly. Coming from a senatorial family, he had had a good education: he knew Latin, Greek, mathematics and geography, how much to tip a prostitute, where the best oysters come from – and the old forum art of escaping from someone he wanted to avoid. 'Sorry, Justinus. Were you in conference?'

Helena's brother growled after the gleamingly armoured and fast-retreating back. 'Never mind. He wasn't going to oblige me. It's Falco, isn't it?'

'Yes. Marcus Didius. I heard you were posted – not to the Fourteenth I hope?'

'Oh, I don't meet their high standards! No, I was persuaded to "volunteer" for an extra tour with the First Adiutrix – they're a new outfit.'

'Glad to hear it. The Fourteenth are an impolite mob. I just brought them a trophy and they refused me a billet,' I hinted without shame.

Justinus laughed. 'Then you'd better stay at my house! Come on. After trying to wrestle sense out of this crew I need to go home and lie down in the dark.' We started to walk. 'What are you doing here, Marcus Didius?'

'Oh, nothing very exciting. Business for Vespasian. Mostly routine. One or two extra tasks to toy with in my free time – coercing rebels, that sort of stuff,' I joked. 'There's a missing legate to find, for instance.'

Justinus stopped in his tracks. He seemed amazed.

I pulled up too. 'What's up, tribune?'

'Does the Emperor have access to new kinds of Etruscan augury?'

'Something not right?'

'You flabbergast me, Falco! That was what I was trying to get straight with my oppo just now. I don't see,' he grumbled, 'how Vespasian could have known there was something fishy out in Germany in time for you to turn up here before my commander has even made up his mind that he needs to signal Rome!'

As he ran out of breath, I simply said, 'Explain?'

Camillus Justinus glanced over his shoulder then lowered his voice, even though we were crossing the empty parade-ground. 'Florius Gracilis has not been seen for several days. The Fourteenth won't admit it even to my own chief, but we in the First reckon that *their* legate has disappeared!'

XVIII

I set a warning hand on the tribune's arm. Then I told Xanthus to walk ahead and wait for us at the main gate opposite. He sulked, but had no choice. We watched him set off, scuffing his feet in the dust at first as a gesture, but soon preferring to save the turquoise leather of his nattily bethonged shoes.

'Who exactly is that?' queried Justinus in a wary tone.

'Not sure.' I gave him a stiff look, in case he thought it was a companion of my choice. 'If you want a boring couple of hours, get him to tell you why Spanish razors are the best, and the secrets of German goosefat pomade. He's a barber by trade – that's genuine. He forced himself on me as a tourist. I suspect there's a more sinister reason behind his trip.'

'He may simply have a yearning for travel.' I remembered that Helena's youngest brother had a touching faith in humanity.

'Or he may not! Anyway, I'm passing him off as Vespasian's nark.' Justinus, who must have known about my own undercover duties, or my past history anyway, smiled faintly.

As we waited for Xanthus to trot out of earshot, a slight breeze lifted our cloaks. It carried the characteristic aromas of cavalry stables, oiled leather and mass-produced stewed pork. Dust bowled across the parade-ground, stinging our bare shins. The hum of the fort reached us, like the low undernotes of a water-organ as it grinds into life: metallic hammering; rumbling carts; the clack of wooden staves as troops practised sparring against an upright stump; and the sharp cry of a centurion giving orders, raven-harsh.

'We won't find anywhere more private than here. Now Justinus, what's all this about? Tell me about Gracilis.'

'Not much to tell. He hasn't been seen.'

'Is he ill, or taking leave?'

'If so, it's highly impolite of him not to inform his senior colleague in the same fort.'

'Bad manners would be nothing new!'

'Agreed. What alerted the First to something peculiar was that even his wife, who is with him here, seems unsure where he is. She asked *my* legate's wife if there was a secret exercise going on.'

'Is there?'

'Joke, Falco! We have quite enough operational tasks without playing board-games or throwing up practice camps.'

I paused for a moment, considering him. He had spoken with a flash of authority. Last time we met he had been holding down a junior tribune's place, but now he was wearing the broad purple stripes of a senior – his legate's right-hand man. Those posts were mainly earmarked for senators designate; promotion to them while in service was highly unusual. Justinus qualified socially – he was a senator's son – but his elder brother was using up all the embalming oil. The family had long ago decided this one was destined merely for middle-rank bureaucracy. Still, he would not be the first young man to discover that the army lacks preconceptions, or to find that once away from home he could surprise himself.

'So how are the Fourteenth reacting? What do the men say?'

'Well, Gracilis is a new appointment.'

'So I heard. Is he unpopular?'

'The Fourteenth have been having a few problems . . .' Justinus was a tactful lad. The Fourteenth *were* a problem, but he glossed over that. 'Gracilis has a rather abrasive attitude. It goes down badly when a legion are in a touchy state.'

'Gracilis was the Senate's choice,' I confided, based on what Vespasian had told me. 'You know, "*Step up, most excellent Florius. Your grandpa was a friend of ours; it's your turn next . . .*" What's he like?'

'All virile sports, and shouts a lot.' We both winced.

'So let's be clear what you are suggesting, tribune. I already know the Emperor has doubts about this character, and now you say he's vanished. Has the First Adiutrix convinced itself that he has been bumped off – and by his own men?'

'Olympus!' Justinus flushed. 'That's an alarming suggestion!'

'Sounds like one you have grounds for.'

'The First is in a tricky position, Falco. We have no remit to interfere. You know how it is – the governor is away reviewing deployments at Vindonissa, so if Gracilis is playing truant, "honour among commanders" comes into play. Besides, my legate is reluctant to march in directly and demand to see his opposite, in case we're wrong.'

'He would certainly look foolish if Gracilis strolled out to greet him, wiping his breakfast porridge off his chin!' I agreed. Then, influenced by too long in a barber's company, I suggested, 'Gracilis may have had a haircut he's ashamed of and is hiding until it grows out!'

'Or he's developed an *extremely* embarrassing rash . . .' He sounded like Helena and their father, his serious air covered a highly attractive humorous streak. 'It's no joke though.'

'No.' I quashed the pang of misery his familiar laugh had roused. 'Gracilis had better be exposed, whatever crab he's caught.' I hoped it was nothing worse. Mutiny in the legions just when things were looking settled would be disastrous for Vespasian. And there were grim political implications if yet another Roman legate should disappear in Germany. 'I can see good reasons for keeping this news stitched up. Vespasian will want to plan how it is to be presented publically . . . Camillus Justinus, you don't think the Fourteenth have reported the facts, and are waiting for special orders back from Rome?'

'My legate would have been informed.'

'Oh, that's what he thinks! Bureaucracy thrives on secrecy.'

'No, Falco. Despatch-riders are still bringing "Your eyes only" messages for Gracilis. I know because my own man keeps getting asked to sign for them. Neither Vespasian nor the governor would send confidential flags unless they believed Gracilis was available.'

My sour welcome from the primipilus and corniculary was beginning to make sense. If they had simply lost their man, things looked bad for them; if he had been throttled in a hastily hushed-up mutiny, that was desperate. 'Their senior trib brushed you off pretty shamelessly; my reception was much the same. Is that what always happens?'

'Yes. All the officers seem to be covering up.' This couldn't happen on the march, where Gracilis would have to be seen in the column, but here in the fort they could run things themselves. It reminded me of Balbillus's story of the legionary commanders coolly running Britain after having driven out their governor. But the era of anarchy was supposed to be over.

'Until the next festival occasion, there's no need to produce anyone in a commander's cloak,' I grinned. 'But if there *is* a conspiracy, I've just upset the tray of drinks! I brought an Iron Hand, plus orders for its investiture with a full colour ceremony. They'll need to parade their legate then.'

'Ha! The governor will make a point of being back for that!'

Camillus Justinus had a streak of tenacity I liked. He showed real pleasure that the Fourteenth's attempts to thwart him were about to be wrecked. 'When must they hold the ceremony?'

'The Emperor's birthday.' He looked uncertain. Vespasian was too new in power to be thoroughly enshrined in the calendar. I knew (a scribe who thought informers were ignorant had noted it in my orders). 'Fourteen days before December.' We were still in October. 'Which gives you and me the rest of this month plus the first sixteen days of November to sort out the puzzle discreetly and make names for ourselves.'

We grinned. Then we set off towards the main gate. Justinus had enough character to see the possibilities. It would do him good if he could untangle this conundrum before Rome had to be involved.

I felt obligations looming. I was his sister's lover – almost one of the family. It was my duty to assist him to good fortune. Even though Justinus probably hated the thought of what his sister and I had been up to. And even though I would be landing myself with most of the work.

As we walked, falling into companionable silence, I was thinking hard. This had the smell of serious trouble. I had been chasing enough of that already. I had only been at Moguntiacum a bare hour and now there was a second senior officer missing – just one more complication to add to the *official* missing legate, the mutinous troops, the maniacal rebel chieftain and the loopy prophetess.

XIX

We picked up Xanthus and braced ourselves for the hike to the First's sector of the fort. To cover the journey with neutral conversation, I asked Justinus about his unusual promotion.

'I remembered your last command was at Argentoratum – in fact I went looking for you there. You weren't a senior then?'

'No, and I never expected to be. That was the lure that made me accept an extension to my tour. Obviously, in the long-term it's good to be able to say I held a broad-stripe position . . .'

'I hope your ambitions run to more than that on your tombstone! You must have impressed someone?'

'Well . . .' He still seemed a boy in a man's world. Big words like ambition startled him. 'My father is a friend of Vespasian; perhaps that was it.'

I thought the lad was doing himself down. People must have thought he had something to offer. Germany was not a province where they could carry dead wood. 'What's your new unit like? I don't know the First.'

'It's a legion Nero formed – with men drawn from the Misenum fleet, actually. Both the First and Second Adiutrix were put together using marines. That explains some of the tension here.' Justinus smiled. 'I'm afraid the illustrious Fourteenth Gemina Martia Victrix regard *our* outfit as a useless gang of wharfingers and matelots.'

Regular troops have always regarded marines as web-footed hangers-on – a view I rather shared. Shoving an untried unit out on this volatile frontier seemed like madness, too. 'So you're here to stiffen them up with your experience?' He shrugged in his self-deprecating way. 'Don't be so shy,' I said. 'It will all look good on your manifesto when you stand as a town councillor.'

Ten or twelve years ago, Titus Caesar had led the replacements that filled the gaps in the British legions after the Boudiccan Revolt. And now every town in the misty bogs was erecting his statue and remarking how thoroughly well liked he had been in his days as a young tribune.

It made me wonder uncomfortably if Justinus, like Titus, would one day find himself related to a reigning emperor – by marriage, for instance . . .

I wanted to ask if he had any news of his sister. Luckily we had reached his house, so I could spare myself the embarrassment.

XX

The senior tribune's house lacked its own bathhouse, but for one lad barely into his twenties who only needed space for his parade armour and the stuffed heads of any wild animals he speared in his spare time, it was an extravagant hutch. Tribunes are not famous for taking home bulky documents from the commissariat to work on, and their schedule of domestic entertainment tends to be thin. They are invariably bachelors, and not many invite their loving relatives to stay. Still, providing single officers with mansions that would house three generations is the kind of extravagance the army loves.

Justinus had enlivened the place with a pet dog. It was a scruff, not much more than a pup, which he had rescued from some soldiers who had been having fun torturing it. The dog now lorded it here, rampaging through the long corridors and sleeping on as many couches as possible. Justinus had no control over the creature, but one yap from it could make *him* sit up and beg.

'Your puppy's found a lavish kennel! I can see why so many tribunes rush to get married the minute their service ends. After so much independence, who wants the restrained parental home again?'

Marriage was another concept that made Justinus nervous. I could understand that.

Helena's brother definitely needed a crony to liven up his life. Well, I was here now. (Though Helena herself would probably disapprove of me doing it.)

Justinus decided after all that he ought to advise his legate of the lack of progress against the Fourteenth's wall of silence. While he jogged off to report, someone was sent to the fortress gate for our luggage. One of the tribune's private slaves stowed the barber somewhere appropriate, while I at last regained the luxury of a room to myself. Almost immediately I sauntered out of it, intent on a quiet look round. I noticed I had been given a good bedroom, though not the best. From that I could gauge my position: a friendly guest, but not a family friend.

My mother would have been shocked by the dust on the side-tables; my standards were not so immaculate, and I felt I could settle here. Justinus came from a family of thinkers and talkers, but the Camilli liked to talk and think with fruit bowls at their elbows and cushions at their backs. Their treasure had been sent abroad well equipped to fend off homesickness. His house was comfortable. His attendants were only so slovenly because they were unsupervised. I wrote 'Falco was here' with one finger in the bloom on a vase plinth, as a gentle hint.

It could have been worse. There were too many mice droppings and no one bothered to replenish the lamp oil, but the servants were polite enough, even to me. They wanted to avoid forcing their young lord into any stressful show of discipline. That seemed wise. If he was anything like his sister, he could summon an exotic temper and a vivid way with words.

If he *was* anything like Helena, Justinus also had a soft heart and might commiserate as I roamed about his quarters gloomily wondering wherever in the Empire his temperamental sister had hidden herself. Mind you, if he was as touchy as Aelianus on family matters, my connection with Helena was more likely to get me rolled up in a sack and flung from a heavy catapult halfway across the Rhine. So, even though I was frantic over her whereabouts and safety, I decided to keep that to myself.

I went out to the legionary baths, which were hot, efficient, cleanly run and free.

Justinus and I returned to his house at the same time. In my room someone had unpacked my togs, taking away my dirty clothes. My wardrobe was so frugal that to lose three garments for laundering had emptied my saddlebag, but I managed to find a tunic which would just pass at the dinner table here, given the dim lamps. Afterwards we stuck our noses out into the courtyard garden, but it was too cold, so we settled indoors. I felt conscious of the difference in our ranks, but Justinus seemed glad to play the good host and chat. 'Eventful journey?'

'Nothing too fraught. Gaul and Germany still seem pretty lawless.' I told him about the two bodies we had seen in the Gallic ditch.

He looked alarmed. 'Should I do something about it?'

'Relax, tribune!' I brushed aside his insecurity. 'It happened in another province and the civilian magistrate ought to deal with high-way robbery . . . Mind you, the centurion I mentioned – Helvetius – must be one of yours. He told me he was assigned to the First, though I failed to make any connection as I thought you were still in your old post.'

'The name's unfamiliar. I've not been here long enough to know them all. I'll look him out.' Expecting to recognise all sixty centurions in his legion was stretching it. I was amazed this lad had ever been promoted. He worked with all the dedication and thoroughness that are traditionally overlooked in personal character reports.

I thought he might be amused by what I had heard at Argentoratum about his successor's progress. 'Would *you* give out a password like "Xenophobia"?'

'Afraid mine are always more mundane. "Mars the Avenger", or "Pickled fish", or "The camp surgeon's middle name".'

'Very wise.'

We had a flagon. 'The wine's rather basic here . . .' Justinus was either too timid or too lazy to be rude to his wine merchant. It tasted like goat's pee (from a goat with bladder stones), but a glass in the hand helped pass the time. 'So Marcus Didius, why did you come through my old base?'

He must have known I was looking for Helena. 'Looking for you.'

'Oh that was kind!' He managed to sound as if he meant it.

'I thought you might like news of your family. They all seem well. Your father wants to buy a yacht but your mother won't hear of it . . . Have you heard from your sister recently?'

I posed the question before I could stop myself; too late to make my interest sound merely banal. Justinus whipped back, 'No, she seems unusually quiet these days! Is there something I ought to know?'

He must have heard about her choosing to eat the gritty bread at my table. Explaining our relationship was beyond me. I said briefly, 'She's taken herself off from Rome.'

'When?'

'Just before I came away.'

Justinus, who was reclining on an army-issue reading-couch, stretched slightly to ease the pressure on his arm. 'That seems rather sudden!' He was laughing, though I could see solemnity looming. 'Did someone upset her?'

'Probably me. Helena has high standards and I have low habits . . . I hoped she might have invited herself to stay with you.'

94

'No.' The reason for my keen interest still hovered unhealthily, but remained unsaid. We both felt shy of turning that boulder. 'Should people be worried?' Justinus asked.

'She's sensible.' Justinus thought a lot of his sister and was prepared to accept that. I cared about her too, and I was not. 'Tribune, as far as I know your sister made no arrangements with her banker, and took no bodyguard. She never said goodbye to your father; she completely bamboozled your mother; she surprised mine, who is very fond of her; and she left no forwarding address. That,' I said, 'worries me.'

We were both silent.

'What do you suggest, Falco?'

'Nothing. There's nothing we can do.' That worried me as well.

We changed the subject.

'I still don't know,' Justinus broached, 'how you came to be here seeking a missing legate the minute we had a problem with Gracilis?'

'Coincidence. The one I'm chasing is Munius Lupercus.'

'Olympus! That's a forlorn hope!'

I grinned unhappily.

Several of his relatives were close to the Emperor, and I felt satisfied that Justinus had inherited their discretion. I spoke freely about my mission, though I shied off mentioning the XIV Gemina. This courtesy to them was probably pointless, but I do have some standards. 'One or two challenges!' he commented.

'Yes. I've already discovered that the prophetess Veleda lives at the top of a tower, and can only be approached through her male friends. This must be to endow her with a sinister aura. Going across the Rhenus river unnerves me enough, without any theatricals!' Justinus laughed. He could. He didn't have to go. 'You seem the type who keeps up to date, Justinus. Can you tell me anything about the rebel chief?'

'Civilis has disappeared – though there are plenty of stories about his horrible habits!'

'Thrill me!' I growled.

'Oh, the most lurid anecdote has him handing over Roman prisoners to his small son as targets for arrow practice.'

'True?'

'It could be.'

Wonderful. Just the sort I enjoy taking out to a wine bar so I can

95

have a quiet word in his ear. 'Before I try to buy a drink for this civilised parent, is there anything less colourful that I ought to know?'

I knew the general background. Before the revolt the Batavians had always had a special relationship with Rome: their lands were exempt from colonisation – and therefore from taxes – in return for them supplying us with auxiliary troops. It was not a bad bargain. They got excellent pay and conditions – a vast improvement on what they could achieve by the rough-and-ready Celtic tradition of raiding their neighbours when the grain pits ran low. We acquired their nautical skills (pilotage, rowing and swimming). They were famous for being able to cross rivers in full kit, paddling alongside their horses.

Justinus plunged straight in, cogently and without floundering: 'You know Julius Civilis is a member of the Batavian royal family. He spent twenty years in Roman military camps, leading auxiliaries for us. When the recent upsets started, his brother Paulus was executed as a troublemaker by the then governor of Lower Germany, Fonteius Capito. Capito sent Civilis himself in chains to Nero.'

'*Were* they troublemakers at that stage?'

'The evidence suggests it was a trumped-up charge,' Justinus declared in his measured way. 'Fonteius Capito was a highly dubious governor. You know he was court-martialled and killed by his own officers? He had a reputation for governing greedily, but I can't tell you whether that was justified. Galba omitted to investigate his execution, so perhaps it was.' Or perhaps Galba was a geriatric incompetent. 'Anyway, Galba acquitted Civilis of treachery, but only lasted eight months as emperor, so then Civilis became vulnerable again.'

'How come?' I asked.

'When Vitellius seized power his armies called for various officers to be put to death, ostensibly for loyalty to Galba.' I remembered that nasty episode now. Quite blatantly, it had been about settling old grudges. Unpopular centurions were the main target, but I knew the troops had also clamoured for the Batavian leader's head. Vitellius ignored them and confirmed Galba's 'pardon', but it must all have left Civilis with a great bitterness against his so-called Roman allies. 'Also in that period,' Justinus went on, 'the Batavians were being sorely treated.'

'Example?'

'Well, for instance, during conscription for Vitellius, imperial agents were calling up the infirm and the old in order to extract bribes for their release from the levy. And young lads and lasses were dragged behind the tents for unpleasant purposes.'

Batavian children tend to be tall and good-looking. All Germanic tribes have a strong sense of family, so this treatment must have festered sordidly. That was why the next imperial claimant, Vespasian, had felt he could call on Civilis to help him oppose Vitellius. But far away in Judaea, Vespasian had misread the situation. Civilis co-operated at first, in alliance with a tribe called the Cannenefates. They made a joint attack on the Rhenus fleet, thereby capturing all the arms and ships they needed and cutting Roman supply lines. Vespasian was then proclaimed Emperor.

'That forced Civilis to come out in his true colours,' Justinus explained. 'He summoned all the chiefs of the Gallic and German tribes to a meeting in a sacred grove in the forest, let the wine flow freely, then fired them with powerful speeches about shaking off the Roman yoke and establishing a free Gallic empire.'

'Stirring stuff!'

'Oh, highly dramatic! Civilis himself even dyed his hair and beard bright red, then swore never to cut them until he had driven out every Roman.'

This colourful detail gave my own mission a picturesque quality I hated. 'Just the sort of ethnic madman I love trying to outwit! Did he ever shave?'

'After Vetera.'

We were silent for a moment, thinking of the siege.

'A fort like that should have held out.'

Justinus shook his head. 'I haven't been there, Falco, but by all accounts Vetera was neglected and understaffed.'

We buried ourselves in the tribune's gruesome wine, while I reflected sourly on what I had heard about Vetera.

It had been a double fort, though nowhere up to strength after Vitellius had drawn off large vexillations for his march on Rome. The remnant of the garrison put up the best show they could. Plenty of initiative. But Civilis was Roman-trained in siege warfare. He made his prisoners build battering-rams and catapults. Not that the defending legions lacked invention: they had devised an articulated grab that could scoop up attackers and toss them into the fort. But by the time they surrendered, they really had eaten all the mules and rats and were down to chewing roots and grass torn from the rampart walls. Besides, with the civil war raging in Italy, they must have felt completely cut off. Vetera was one of the most northerly forts in Europe, and Rome had other preoccupations.

A relief force *was* sent, under Dillius Vocula, but he bungled it. Civilis stopped him fairly decisively, then paraded the Roman standards he had captured around the fort at Vetera, just to add to the occupants' despair. Later Vocula did break through and raise the siege, but he found the garrison sullen. His own men mutinied, and he himself was murdered at Vetera by the troops.

The fort surrendered. The soldiers, having despatched their commander, swore allegiance to the Gallic Empire. They were disarmed by the rebels, ordered to march out of camp – and were then ambushed and cut down.

'Justinus, did Civilis have a reputation that should have led our men to expect to be betrayed?'

'I think not,' replied Justinus slowly, not wanting to pre-judge the Batavian. 'I believe they assumed that an ex-Roman auxiliary commander would honour their parole. It's said that Civilis did protest to his allies about it.'

We were silent again for a moment.

'What kind of man is he?' I asked.

'Highly intelligent. Massive charisma. Intensely dangerous! At one time most of Gaul plus several tribes from Germania Libera were supporting him, and he achieved a completely free run of Lower Germany. He regards himself as a second Hannibal – or Hasdrubal, in fact, since he too has only one eye.'

I groaned. 'So I'm searching for a tall, one-eyed prince with flowing bright red hair, who hates Rome bitterly. At least he ought to stand out in the market-place . . . Did he also,' I wondered, 'make an objection when Munius Lupercus was captured in the ambush and bundled off as Veleda's gift?'

'I doubt that. Civilis encouraged her prophetic authority. They were regarded as partners. When Civilis seized the flagship of Petilius Cerialis, he sent that to her too.'

'I'm too far gone to ask you how that disaster came about!' I had heard that our general Cerialis had his faults. He was impetuous and kept poor discipline, which led to losses he could have avoided. 'So Veleda received her personal state barge – in addition to a high-ranking Roman trussed up and delivered to her tower to use as a sex slave, or whatever! What do *you* think she did with Lupercus?'

Camillus Justinus shuddered, and would not try to guess.

★

My head was spinning. This seemed a good point to yawn a lot like a tired traveller and depart for bed.

The notes of the twisted trumpet sounding out the night watch upset me, and I dreamed I was a young recruit again.

XXI

Next day I pondered fitfully on the brain-teasers Vespasian had commissioned me to pursue. It was hard to raise any enthusiasm for this crazy selection, so I looked instead into the one problem where no one had asked me to interfere: I went to see the missing legate's wife. As I crossed to the XIV's side of the fort, I must say I felt fairly confident that the eminent Florius Gracilis would turn out not to be missing at all.

The legate's house was everything you would expect. Given that Julius Caesar, even when campaigning in hostile territory with all his resources stretched to the limit, carted panels of floor mosaic to lay in his tent in order to demonstrate Roman splendour to the tribes, there was no chance that a full-scale diplomatic residence inside a permanent fort would lack any convenience. It was as large as possible, and decorated in spectacular materials. Why not? Each succeeding occupant, his noble wife full of design ideas, would call for improvements. Every three years the house would be stripped out and refurbished to a different taste. And every extravagance they ordered came at State expense.

The residence was based around a series of courtyard gardens with long pools and exquisite fountains that filled the air with a fine, luxurious mist. In summer there must have been strident flowers; in October the impeccable topiary assumed a lonelier grandeur. But there were peacocks. There were turtles. In the morning, when I turned up with my hopeful grin, leaf-sweepers and twig-pruners were crawling over the scenery like aphids. Real aphids stood no chance. Neither did I, probably.

Indoors was a parade of frescoed reception rooms. The brilliant-white stuccoed ceilings were astounding. The floors comprised geometric mosaics with fascinating three-dimensional effects. The lamps were gilded (and screwed to the walls). The urns were immense (too heavy to run off with). Discreet wardens patrolled the colonnades, or were stationed unobtrusively among the Hellenic statuary. The salon furniture would have made my auctioneer father gnaw his nails and ask for a quiet word behind a pillar with the household steward.

The steward knew his stuff. Florius Gracilis had long ago made a smooth transition from the casual bachelor disorder in which Camillus Justinus lived to a world of constant public entertainment on the grandest scale. His residence was organised by troops of purposeful flunkeys, many of whom would have been with him for nearly two decades of hectic senatorial social life. Since high officials travel out to their provinces all expenses paid, the legate had not only brought his tortoiseshell bedheads and gold Cupid lampstands, but while he was packing he also made space for the wife. But I knew even before I met her that adding a young bride to this slick regime had almost certainly been superfluous.

My research in Rome had told me Gracilis was the normal age for a legionary commander. He was in his late thirties – still free of arthritis, but mature enough to strut impressively in the circular purple cloak. His wife was twenty years younger. In patrician circles they tend to marry schoolgirls. When alliances are being made for blunt political reasons there is a premium on the untouched and biddable. Not for men of this status the haphazard attractions that mess up life for the rest of us. Florius Gracilis had first married in his twenties, when he was aiming for the Senate. He had shed the woman as soon as it seemed convenient, then equipped himself adroitly with a new wife – this time from an even older, even richer family – about eighteen months ago. That must have been when he started looking for his legionary command and wanted to appear a man of public probity.

Maenia Priscilla interviewed me in a gold and black salon, the kind of highly lacquered room that always makes me notice where a flea bit me the previous day. Half a dozen maids escorted her, broad-browed, slightly hirsute wenches who looked as though they had been bought at the slave market as a matched set. They seemed remote from their mistress, sitting quietly in two groups and getting on with rather dull embroidery.

Priscilla ignored them. She was small. A sweeter nature might have given her a dainty air. Time and money had been spent on her, though without disguising her inbuilt surliness. She favoured a languid, catlike expression, which grew harder when she forgot to cultivate it. She was probably the daughter of some offhand praetor who only perked up when his female offspring were old enough for flashy dynastic marriages. Now she was married to Gracilis. Not much fun either, probably.

She took several minutes settling herself in a shimmer of violet flounces. She wore pearl ear-drops, amethyst-studded bracelets and at least three plaited gold necklaces, though more may have lurked in the lustrous folds that swathed her. This was her Thursday-morning set, completed by the usual battery of finger-rings. Somewhere among the tinsel was a half-inch wedding band; it failed to make its presence felt.

'Didius Falco, madam.'

'Oh really?' Sustaining a conversation was just too wearisome. My mother would have put this limp little creature on a red meat diet and had her digging turnips for a week.

'I am an imperial representative.' Interviewing an imperial envoy ought to have brightened her morning. Indeed, life in the most dangerous part of the Empire would have fascinated some girls, but I could tell Maenia Priscilla's interests rarely stretched to current affairs. A bird who had managed to avoid learning. She despised the arts. I could not envisage her busy with charitable works. Altogether, as the partner of one of the Empire's most prominently placed diplomats, she failed to impress.

'How nice for you!' No wonder the Empire had been creaking at its seams lately. I refused to react, but it was ill-judged and inexcusable. The girl possessed a mixture of schoolgirl arrogance and ignorance that was likely to cause trouble. If Gracilis didn't watch her, I gave him six months before there was a scandal with a centurion or an incident in a barrack block that had people being sent home hurriedly.

'Excuse me for invading your privacy. I need to see your husband, but he was not at the Principia – '

'He's not here either!' This time she spoke out quickly, with the triumphant edge some people use instead of wit. Her brown eyes gave me the once-over, which was fair enough since I had done the same to her. Yet she was seeing nothing, trying only to insult me.

I twitched up an eyebrow. 'You must be very concerned. Does Gracilis make a habit of vanishing?'

'The legate's habits are his own affair.'

'Not quite, madam.'

Annoyance yanked her mouth into an uglier twist. Men in shapeless sorrel-coloured tunics with woolly linings in their battered boots did not usually answer her back. (I would have liked to be kitted out

102

more excitingly, but my banker had counselled against overstretching my budget that year. Bankers are so predictable. My budget, too.)

'Your ladyship, there seems to be a problem here! A man of your husband's standing ought not to become invisible. It worries the lower orders. In fact, the Emperor might consider it politically inept . . . If Gracilis is dodging his creditors – ' I had been joking, but she let out a bitter laugh. A wild guess had struck lucky. 'Oh, is that it?'

'Possibly.'

'Can you give me a list of his debts?'

She shrugged. Gracilis had probably brought her to Germany to avoid the risk that back in Rome she might suborn his numerous stewards into letting her spend cash. Men like that keep their wives securely cut off from the household abacus. I prodded, but she seemed genuinely uninformed. I was not surprised.

'So you cannot tell me where to start looking? You have no idea where your husband may be?'

'Oh I know that!' she exclaimed archly. I bit back my irritation.

'Madam, this is important. I have a message from Vespasian for Florius Gracilis. When the Emperor sends despatches, he expects me to deliver them. Will you say where your husband is?'

'With his mistress, presumably.' She was so vapid, she did not even watch me to see the effect it had.

'Look,' I said, still trying to keep my temper, 'your domestic life is private, but however modern your views on marriage, I assume you and Gracilis follow *some* rules. The conventions are clear enough.' I stated them anyway: 'He fritters away your dowry; you eat into his inheritance. He can beat you; you can slander him. He supplies you with moral guidance and an extravagant dress allowance; you, madam, at all times protect his reputation in public life. Now try to grasp this: if I don't find him quickly, there is going to be a scandal. Whatever else, he will want you to avoid that!'

She jumped up in a jangle of atonal jewellery. 'How dare you!'

'How dares a public man have the front to disappear right under the nose of the provincial governor?'

'I couldn't care less!' cried Maenia Priscilla with her first real sign of liveliness. 'Get out of here, and don't come back again!'

She swept from the room. A gust of unlikeable balsamic perfume swirled round after her. She bounced off so angrily that an ivory hairpin shot itself from the torsion of a castellated braid in her elaborate hair, and landed at my feet.

I picked it up, then silently handed the missile to one of the waiting-women. The maids looked resigned, then gathered their trappings and followed her out.

I was not alarmed. Somewhere in the residence there would be a wizened accountant who would take a more realistic attitude to my enquiry than the petulant wife had. He was bound to know exactly which creditors he was fobbing off on a daily basis, and if I took an interest in his work, he would probably tell me.

As for the name of the legate's mistress, that would be common coin anywhere in the barracks.

XXII

During my search for information, I at one point bumbled into the legate's private gymnasium. I saw what Justinus meant about Gracilis being a sporty type: his den was packed with weights, dumb-bells, beanbags for throwing-games, and all the other paraphernalia that normally suggest a man who is afraid of seeming puny – probably because it's true. At one end of the room his spears and hunting trophies were hung on hooks. A sad Egyptian who would have been better employed mummifying kings for their meeting with Osiris sat cross-legged, engaged in taxidermy on a rather small deer. I never waste time talking to Egyptians. He could stuff a roebuck, but hearing his views on life as a timeless river of sorrows would not help me find his master. I nodded and passed on.

I finally tracked down the accountant, who supplied me with a lengthy list of disappointed wine merchants, furriers, bookmakers, stationers and importers of fine-scented oils.

'Jupiter, this man certainly does not believe in paying bills!'

'He's a little unbusinesslike,' the scribe agreed mildly. The fellow had swollen eyes and a restrained manner. He looked tired.

'Is there no income from His Honour's estates in Italy?'

'They're flourishing, but mostly mortgaged up.'

'So he's in trouble?'

'Oh, I doubt that!'

He was right. Gracilis was a senator. In the first place, teetering on the brink of financial disaster was probably second nature, so unlikely to worry him. Marrying Maenia Priscilla must have given his collateral a fillip. In any case, he came equipped with massive clout. To the small tradesmen of a remote provincial town, his lordship must be untouchable. A few adroit business fiddles would soon get him out of any temporary squeeze.

'Can I take it you have no idea then why your master might have disappeared?'

'I was unaware of any mystery.'

'He left you no instructions?'

'He's not renowned for forethought. I thought he was off on business for a few days. His bedchamber slave is absent too.'

'How do you know that?'

'Heard the man's girlfriend bemoaning the fact.'

'She works in the house?'

'She's a barmaid at the Medusa, near the Principia Dexter Gate.'

I took away the names of both the creditors and the slave's girlfriend scratched on my pocket memo tablet. Its wax had hardened up through lack of use, a sure hint that it was time to do some work.

'Tell me something else: is your master a ladies' man?'

'I couldn't possibly comment.'

'Oh, stretch a point!'

'My sphere is purely financial.'

'That needn't be unrelated to what I asked! His funds could be tight as a result of expensive mistresses . . .'

I let him stare me out. We both knew I would find other sources eager to supply me with the sordid facts.

I left the residence with a light step. Having clues always gives my optimistic side a boost.

I then made the mistake of pushing my luck again with the high-handed XIV Gemina.

Prefect of the camp was never a post in the traditional republican legion. As with so much else, I reckon the old republicans got it right. Nowadays these prefects wield an undue influence. Each legion appoints one, and they have a wide range of responsibilities for organisation, training and kit. In the absence of the legate and senior tribune they take command, which is when things become dangerous. They are drawn from the pool of first spears who are resisting retirement, which makes them too old, too pedantic, and too slow. I don't like them on principle. The principle being that it was a camp prefect whose obtuse behaviour destroyed the Second Augusta's reputation in the British Revolt.

At Moguntiacum there was just one, responsible for the whole fort. Since the Fourteenth were the only experienced legion stationed there, he had been supplied by them.

The camp prefect occupied an office whose oversized proportions must have appealed to his underdeveloped personality. I found him in it. He was reading scrolls and writing busily. He had made his nook deliberately spare. He used a folding stool with a rusted iron frame and a campaign table that looked as if it had served at Actium. It was supposed to give the impression that he would have preferred to be on active duty in the field. In my view, if Rome was to sustain any military reputation, men like this had to be kept in camp – gagged, bound and bolted to the floor.

'Sextus Juvenalis? I'm Didius Falco. The envoy from Vespasian.'

'Oh I heard some worm had poked its head out of a hole on the Palatine!' He wrote with a quill. He would.

Setting down the quill, meticulously balanced on the ink-pot in a way that prevented drips, he bounced at me: 'What's your background?'

I assumed he didn't want to hear about my aunties in the Campagna. 'National service in the usual stinking province, then five years as a scout.'

'Still in uniform?' Army life was his only social yardstick. I could imagine him boring everyone rigid with his stubborn theories that traditional values, antique equipment and dreadful old commanders whose names no one had heard of were unsurpassed by their modern equivalents.

'Self-employed now.'

'I don't approve of men who leave the legions before time.'

'I never supposed you would.'

'National service lost its glint?'

'I copped a tricky spearhead wound.' Not as tricky as all that, but it got me out.

'Out of *where*?' he persisted. He should have been an informer.

'Out of Britain,' I admitted.

'Oh we know Britain!' He was eyeing me narrowly.

I braced myself. There was no escape. If I dodged any more he would guess anyway. 'You know the Second Augusta then.'

Sextus Juvenalis barely moved, but contempt seemed to flood his features like new colour in a chameleon. 'Well! You were unlucky!' he sneered.

'The whole Second were unlucky – in a certain camp prefect called Poenius Postumus!' Poenius Postumus was the imbecile who had ignored orders to join battle against the Iceni. Even we never really knew what his motives were. 'He betrayed the Second just as much as the rest of you.'

'I heard he paid for it.' Juvenalis lowered his voice a semitone, overcome by horrified curiosity. 'The word was, Postumus fell on his sword afterwards. Did he *fall* – or was he dropped?'

107

'What do you think?'

'Do you know?'

'I know.' I was present. We all were. But what happened on that angry night is the Second Augusta's secret.

Juvenalis stared at me as if I were a guardian at the gates of Hades with a downturned torch. He rallied soon enough, however. 'If you were with the Second, you'll need to tread carefully here. Especially,' he added heavily, 'if you are Vespasian's private agent!' I put up no attempt to quibble. 'Or is it your fancy companion?'

'So people have noticed Xanthus?' I smiled quietly. 'I honestly don't know his role. I prefer not to.'

'Where did you acquire him?'

'An unsolicited gift from Titus Caesar.'

'Reward for past services?' the prefect sneered.

'I suppose it could be for future ones.' I was ready to tighten the ligature: 'You're the best man to make excuses for the Fourteenth. Let's talk about Gracilis.'

'What's to say?' Juvenalis queried in a light tone. He appeared to be taking the reasonable line. I was not fooled.

'I need to see him.'

'It can be arranged.'

'When?'

'Soon.'

'Now?'

'Not immediately.'

I shifted restlessly. 'October in Upper Germany is hardly the time or place for legates to be snatching unofficial holidays.'

'He doesn't ask advice from me.'

'Perhaps he should!' Blatant flattery was also a failure. Camp prefect is an immodest rank; he thought it was his due. 'Maybe taking advice is not your legate's strong point. I hear he's been making himself unpopular.'

'Gracilis has his methods.' He defended his commander loyally. Nevertheless, I saw the flicker behind the prefect's eyes – annoyance at the legate's abrasive attitude.

'So is he off with a woman, or moonlighting from the bailiffs?'

'Official business.'

'Tell me. I'm official too.'

'It's officially secret,' he jeered. He knew I had no comeback. Men like that can judge your status from the way you lace your boot-thongs. Mine must have been twisted the wrong way.

'I have my orders, Prefect. If I can't carry them out, I may have to send a query back to Rome.'

Juvenalis let a thin smile play on his lips. 'Your messenger won't leave the fort.' I was wondering how much I could remember of the smoke-and-bonfire semaphore code when he forestalled me contemptuously: 'You'll find the signal station out of bounds.'

'And I don't suppose Moguntiacum keeps carrier pigeons?' I gave way with an air of grace I didn't feel. But I preferred not to find myself in the tiny cells beside the main gate, rationed to one bowl of barley gruel a day. I changed tack. 'I was sent here to take political soundings. If I can't get a briefing from Gracilis, I'll have to pick your brains instead. What's the mood among the local tribes?'

'The Treveri were roundly beaten by Petilius Cerialis.' Juvenalis ground it out in a tone which implied he was too long in the tooth to be openly obstructive, though he could easily spoil my mission if he decided to.

'At Rigodulum? The Twenty-first Rapax did well for Cerialis there!' I replied, jibing at the Fourteenth's less notable contribution.

Juvenalis ignored it. 'The tribes have gone back to earning their living and keeping their nasty heads down.' This was unexpectedly helpful. No doubt he was hoping I would go out into the local community and offend someone there, to save him the trouble of smacking me senseless.

'What are the staple industries hereabouts?'

'Wool, shipping on the river – and ceramics,' Juvenalis informed me, striking a chord with that last one.

'Cloaks, boats and pots! Didn't the rebel leader Civilis have family contacts in this area?' I asked. 'I'm told his wife and sister stayed at Colonia Agrippinensium during the revolt.'

His face set. 'The Batavians come from the north coast.'

'Spare me the geography lesson, Prefect. I know their habitat. But Civilis has made himself scarce from The Island and that whole region. I have to find him – I wonder if he's been back south?'

'Funnily enough,' Juvenalis replied, with some sarcasm, 'we do hear of him being sighted from time to time.'

'Really?'

'It's just rumour. He had a certain mystique among his people. When men like that die or disappear, you'll always find fake versions.'

He was right, up to a point. In the early days of the Empire, impersonators of tyrants were a constant phenomenon: Caligula, for instance, was continually being reborn among crazy supporters in exotic eastern states.

'So you reckon these rumours of local sightings are all moonshine?'

'He's a fool if he comes anywhere near the Fourteenth!' The defection of their Batavian cohorts obviously rankled sorely.

'Do you send out patrols to investigate?'

'They find nothing.'

I thought that did not necessarily mean there was nothing to find. 'What are the chances rebellion will flare again among the tribes?' Juvenalis did not regard it as a function of his appointment to give political briefings, so I let myself speculate: 'It's the old joke still. If a Greek, a Roman and a Celt are shipwrecked on a desert island, the Greek will start a philosophy school, the Roman will nail up a rota – and the Celt will start a fight.' He glared at me suspiciously; even as a joke it was too metaphysical. 'Well, thanks – ' I never finished, for the door opened.

I should have expected it.

Whether by coincidence, or, more likely, in response to a conspiratorial grapevine, several of the Fourteenth's men of influence were joining us. As I skewed round to inspect them, my heart sank. They all had a grim air of purpose. Among them I recognised Macrinus, the gilded senior tribune I had seen arguing yesterday with Justinus, my antagonist the primipilus, at least three other dour-faced centurions, and a sturdy, silent man whom I guessed was their specularius, a post I had held once myself, when I had first carried out undercover assignments and studied interrogation – along with all the unkind techniques that speed it along.

I knew what the presence of this sinister individual would have meant in my day. Still, perhaps things had changed.

XXIII

I was seated on a stool. They gathered round. The space became too cramped for me to rise. The small room grew warmer and darker. I heard a soft chink of bronzes on a groin-protector, too close for comfort behind my left ear. It was impossible for me to turn and see what movement had caused the noise. The tribune and the centurions stood with their hands resting on their sword pommels.

I could feel the power that formed within a long-established legion. Messages passed with no visible effort. Councils of war almost summoned themselves. Internal conspiracies would be unbreakable by an outsider, and the men came equipped with menace like bear cubs – murderous from birth.

Since it was his office we occupied, the prefect retained the initiative. None of the other centurions spoke.

It was the tribune who started, however. The gilded Macrinus ran his free hand through his hair in a habitual gesture that emphasised the natural glints. 'We have had a complaint from the legate's wife about an intruder.' His cultured tones expelled the syllables as distinctly as if he had been spitting out seeds. He was a handsome, lazy-eyed, conceited hunk. I could imagine Maenia Priscilla scuttling with her troubles to this one. He was her own generation, her own rank. If she wasn't already going to bed with him, I bet she wanted to.

'A most gracious lady,' I murmured. He was daring me to call their legate's wife a spoiled little cat. They all were. I could see the prefect's fingers twitching for his quill, longing to write out a charge for disrespect.

'Dogs like you call our tribune "Sir"!' Juvenalis spat.

'Sorry, sir! I did apologise for intruding. I had thought the noble Florius Gracilis might be at home with a cold.'

'The residence is out of bounds.' Camp prefects adore drawing demarcation lines. 'Use the proper sources!'

'The proper sources had proved unforthcoming, and I have duties for the Emperor.' Once again I was aware of a worrying movement behind me.

The tribune burst out irritably, 'Who is this inquisitive slob?'

'A pest called Didius Falco,' the prefect announced. 'He's an ex-ranker from the Second Augusta. We ought to pass *that* news along the lines with the watchword.' I suppressed a groan. He had ensured that not a man in the legion would talk to me – and was probably preparing for me a worse fate than that. By curfew tonight I would be a soft target for every drunken muscleman who wanted to show off to the boys. 'Now he works for Vespasian – as you would expect.' The allusion to the Emperor's former command of the Second in Britain sounded as caustic as Juvenalis could make it without disloyalty to his service oath. 'But that's all right,' he assured the gathering. 'He's not here to bother us. This idiot is going to annoy the locals searching for their rebel chief. *He thinks he's going to tame Civilis!*'

No one laughed at the joke.

I sighed quietly. 'I am, as it happens, charged to find a missing legate, but it's Munius Lupercus, so the trail's cold . . . Lads, I read your message. Members of the Second are *persona non grata* with your notable selves. I'll go.'

There was silence, but a shift in the light and colder air behind my shoulders told me the armed wall had parted. I stood up. They continued to crowd me, so I blundered against the stool as I turned. I felt surprised that no one jumped me. They meant me to be. They all enjoyed my nervousness, but they let me leave. Someone kicked the door shut. I expected to hear laughter, and when none came that was worse. I walked out on to the parade-ground, where bright autumn sunshine from low on the horizon streamed uncomfortably in my eyes.

No one had touched me. But I felt as if I had been thrashed with knotted ropes by the entire legion at a ceremonial punishment parade.

XXIV

These cheerful events had taken up enough of the morning for me to stroll back to the tribune's house, where we had agreed to meet for lunch. 'I'm taking you out – I owe you a drink. There's a tavern called the Medusa that's been recommended to me . . .'

Justinus looked alarmed. 'Nobody I know drinks there!'

I admitted that that was probably because his friends were much too cultivated types, then explained my reason for going. Justinus enjoyed being part of the investigation, so overcame his qualms. As we walked he enquired after progress.

'I just had another encounter with the Fourteenth. They claim their man is away on official business, which is hard to disprove. But something is up. They overreact preposterously.'

I warned him about the Fourteenth's ominous attitude towards me. Justinus was too young to remember detailed events of the British Rebellion, so I had to relate the whole sorry tale of how the Second Augusta had been deprived of glory. His face fell. Apart from having a marked man for a house guest, he was probably as unimpressed as most people were by my legion's contribution to history.

The Medusa was less attractive than I had hoped, though not so fusty as I had feared. It had the air of an all-night establishment that by day was only half awake. In fact, *nowhere* in Moguntiacum was open all night; the Medusa's sleepy atmosphere at lunch-time was simply the result of being slackly run. The tables lolled against peeling walls like fungi clinging to ancient trees, and the winejars were grotesque misshapes from an inefficient pottery. It was full of boorish soldiers and their shifty hangers-on. We ordered the meal of the day, on the premise that it might be prepared freshly – a vain hope.

It was just about warm enough to take a table outside in the fresh air.

'Ah, meatballs!' exclaimed Justinus politely when the food came. I could see him fast losing interest. 'Looks like rabbit . . .' In fact, the eats seemed to be the crudely minced remains of a worked-out, broken-down pack-mule that had died of grief and mange.

'No need to worry what they may have used for flavour, as there doesn't appear to be any . . .' The thought crossed my mind that my companion's noble mother, Julia Justa, who already had a low opinion of what I had done to her beautiful daughter, was unlikely to form a kinder view of me if I finished off her son in a dive like this.

'You all right, Falco?'

'Oh, I'm fine!'

Tribunes were a rarity here. The landlord had served us himself. He probably thought we were inspecting him – a task neither of us liked to face too closely. After a while he sent a barmaid to ask whether we needed anything. It was a question which had nothing to do with food or wine.

'What's *your* name?' I asked, pretending to go along with it.

'Regina.' At this Justinus twitched excitedly, though not for the reasons she thought. (He knew from me that Regina was the name of the girlfriend of the missing legate's missing slave.)

'A queen!' I exclaimed to Justinus, so archly it was unbelievable. She loved it. I ordered another half-flagon, and told her to bring an extra beaker for herself.

'She doesn't seem to mind entertaining us,' Justinus murmured while she was fetching them. He seemed anxious that we might be treading on dubious moral ground by seeming to encourage her. My scruples about the Medusa were purely practical. I was only afraid we had risked eating those sordid rissoles while following a false lead.

'Entertaining us is her job, and it doesn't rule out a pretty complicated private life off duty. I'll talk to her,' I added, switching into Greek as the girl came back with our wine. 'Let me tell you some rules for living, lad: never play board-games for money with strangers; never vote for the favourite candidate; and never trust a woman who wears an ankle chain . . .'

'You're the expert on women!' he replied wryly, in Greek that was more confident than mine. He had, at any rate, enough fluency to be rude without much effort.

'I've been fended off by a fair number of barmaids, certainly . . .' Switching back to Latin, I joked with Regina; 'Men's talk! His Honour was complaining about me ruining his sister.' The dozy girl had forgotten a beaker for herself; she flashed a meaningless smile and trotted off again.

Justinus kept his eyes on his bowl of rissoles (which certainly looked as if they needed cautious reconnaissance) as he continued in that lightly inflected, challenging Greek of his. 'As a matter of fact, Falco, I would like to ask if this business of yours with my sister is serious?'

My jaw set. 'It's as serious as I can make it.'

He looked up. 'That says nothing.'

'Wrong, tribune. It says what you really want to know: no harm will ever come to Helena from me.'

Our barmaid returned again.

Regina sat down, allowing us to go on talking among ourselves. She was used to men of commerce who finished their own business before trading with her. She seemed amenable to anything, in fact.

Justinus and I both let our previous conversation drop.

I ate as much as I could tolerate of the tasteless stew, then rinsed my mouth with wine. I smiled at the girl. She was a squat, flat-chested moppet with short red hair. Her shorn bob had curls of the 'assisted' type much favoured by girls who serve up drink with less useful commodities. She wore a fairly clean white tunic and the usual glass-bead necklace and cheap serpentine rings, as well as the inevitable ankle chain I had referred to earlier. Her attitude seemed servile, but with suggestions of a defiant streak. Back in Rome I had a bunch of hard, contemptuous sisters. Regina reminded me of them. 'Regina, do you know a bedchamber boy called Rusticus?'

'Maybe.' She was the type who avoided answering questions on principle.

'You know who I mean?'

'He works in the fort.'

'For one of the legates. Don't worry – there's no trouble!' I reassured her quickly. 'I heard you were good friends with Rusticus.'

'I may have been.' I thought I saw her confident blue eyes darken sullenly. Maybe she was frightened. Or perhaps it was something more furtive.

'Do you know where he is?'

'No.'

'Has he gone away somewhere?'

'What's it to you?' she demanded.

'I'd very much like to find him.'

'Why?' I was about to explain my search for the legate when she fetched out angrily, 'I haven't seen him for ages. I don't know where he is!' She jumped to her feet. Justinus, taken aback, pushed his stool away from the table with a screeching skid. 'What do you want?' Regina shouted. 'Why have you started pestering me?'

Other customers – mostly soldiers – glanced over in our direction, though without much interest. 'Steady on, Falco,' Justinus interrupted. The girl rushed indoors wildly. 'Yes, barmaids do seem to be your speciality!' Justinus scoffed. He glared at me reprovingly, then followed her inside the tavern.

'That's Regina!' one of the soldiers grinned.

'Scratchy?'

'Gets het up over everything.'

I left payment on the table, sauntering nearby until the tribune reappeared. 'I'm glad to see you in one piece! I gather her temper is legendary. She loves screaming and bursting into tears at innocent customers. For an encore she'll throw an amphora at your head. If you're unlucky it's a full one . . . Have you been drying her tears, or just trying to dodge?'

'You're too harsh, Falco!'

'She expected it.'

'Oh really?' Justinus muttered through his teeth. 'Well, I found out what we wanted without bullying the girl. It's quite simple. She and the slave Rusticus had a lovers' tiff. She doesn't see him any more.'

'What about the legate nipping off?'

'All she knows is she heard some mention that her boyfriend's master might be planning a few days away. She wasn't told why or where.'

'That's fine, if it's true.'

'Why should it not be?'

'She's a girl in a bar, you're a stranger, and I know when I've just seen a lying little strumpet who has something to hide!'

'Well *I* believed her.'

'Good for you,' I said.

We strode back towards the gate of the fort. Justinus still pretended to be angry, but his good nature was overcoming it. I shook my head and laughed softly.

'What's so funny?'

'Oh . . . there's a traditional method of extracting information where first you send a cruel brute who upsets the suspect, then his mild and friendly partner goes in and comforts them until they open their hearts.'

116

'It appears to be effective,' Justinus commented, rather stiffly.

'Oh yes!'

'I still don't see the joke.'

'It's nothing.' I grinned at him. 'Only the "soft" partner is *supposed* to be a fake!'

XXV

Back at the house news awaited us. 'A woman came asking for you, Marcus Didius.'

I laughed. 'That kind of message needs a careful approach!' Justinus looked prim. If I wanted to look a reliable friend to Helena, flippancy was a bad response. We were having too much banter of barmaids and not enough of the dull bombast that prevails among senators. Still, I couldn't help it if he wasn't used to me. His sister was, and she had made her choice. 'Who is this matron?'

'Julia Fortunata, Marcus Didius.'

I saw Justinus start at that. I raised an eyebrow. 'Let me guess – is she connected with Gracilis?'

'So you've heard something?' murmured the tribune. In front of his servants he was being discreet.

They were not my servants. 'Maenia Priscilla mentioned to me this morning that Gracilis flaunts a mistress somewhere. Is this her? Coming to the fort in such a public way seems strange – I wonder what she wants so urgently? Do you know where she lives?'

'I believe so,' Justinus replied, still cautiously. 'They say Gracilis has established her in a villa not far away . . .'

I told him that if he had a free afternoon he could come with me for the entertainment. He hesitated. Then he shouted for a slave to fetch both our cloaks.

We had to ride out through the Decumana Gate and go south. Once we had turned down the incline outside the gate, peace descended. Apart from the broad curve of the waterway, the square fort behind us remained the most prominent feature of the landscape, which, unusually in this section of the river, lacked the dramatic crags and rocky narrows that occur downstream. Here it was mainly low ground, sometimes broken by natural or man-made mooring creeks, though it was obviously not marshy. There were large trees, which frequently hid the Rhenus and Moenus from view.

118

Justinus took me by the road that enabled me to admire the Drusus Monument – a pleasure I did not let detain us long. Memorials to long-dead establishment heroes fail to excite me. I hardly glanced at it.

A mile or so further on stood a fortlet guarding a small village which Justinus told me regarded itself as the official Moguntiacum *canabae*. Julia Fortunata was renting a place just this side of the settlement. For a woman of standing it was only just safe. The Rhenus lay within sniffing distance. However, heading upstream to Argentoratum and Vindonissa, there was a military road parallel with our bank of the river, and the guard post afforded first-instance protection if trouble ever flared.

It was a villa farm with a basically Roman look, despite the usual provincial differences of layout, and a much-reduced scope from the vast estates of Italy. We entered by a small grassy path that ran between the barn and a duck pond, passed some apple trees, took a detour by an empty byre, avoided a loose pig, then came to a colonnaded house.

Indoors there was a square, Germanic hall with a central hearth where the milder Mediterranean climate would have allowed an open atrium with a pool. Julia Fortunata had imposed deliberate Roman style: drapery in sophisticated colouring, scroll-ended couches, well-placed statuettes of Greek runners and wrestlers, a side-table with a small library of scrolls in silver canisters. There were touches of drama too: sudden swags of purple cloth and multiple bronze acanthus-leaf lamps.

When she appeared, even though we knew she had been anxious to see me, she gave me her hand calmly and formally. This one would have made a proper wife for a highly placed official, had fortune not made her background good, but not quite good enough. While the young bride Maenia Priscilla possessed money and arrogance, Julia had to settle for culture and breeding. She lacked the social benefits that in Rome were conferred by a family of famous ancestors and decades of accumulated cash. She could have married a customs officer and been queen of some small town for life, but what strong-willed woman wants to be dragged down to dull respectability?

If Gracilis was the age I thought – late thirties – then Julia Fortunata must be older by at least enough to show. Justinus had told me their arrangement was known to be of long standing: it had survived the legate's first marriage, and looked ready to outlast the present one. Julia Fortunata travelled with Gracilis on all his postings. Wherever he arrived in Italy or Europe, it was understood that the lady would turn up, settle herself within visiting range, and provide whatever she customarily provided. The set-up had long ago ceased to be scandalous. It seemed a poor life for her, particularly if, as I had deduced, Florius Gracilis was a pathetic man. But sophisticated women pay that price for a senatorial link.

She was fairly tall, and dressed in subdued greyish-mauve material. No real beauty. An angular face, a neck that showed its maturity, and the ankles she crossed as she seated herself to talk to us were hideously bony. She had style, though. Graceful hands arranged her stole. An elegant carriage. Composure when meeting men. She was that rare goose, an independent matron – determined, self-possessed and chic.

'Madam, I'm Didius Falco and this is Camillus Justinus, senior tribune of the First Adiutrix.' As he moved in her social circle, I was willing the tribune to take the lead, but he held back and stood beside me as an observer. Julia Fortunata glanced between us: Justinus in the crisply pleated white tunic and broad purple stripe, quieter and more serious than most of his rank; me ten years older in fact and a hundred in experience. She elected to deal with me.

'Thank you for returning my visit so promptly.' Her voice was refined and assured. It matched perfectly the strong taste of her muted robes and her jewellery, which was sparse but striking – a bold bracelet of Middle Eastern origin, and two huge beaten-gold discs of earrings. Even her sandals had an interesting design. She was a woman who chose things for herself, and liked a touch of the unusual. 'You are conducting some sort of enquiry?'

I made a gesture of assent but gave no details. 'You called at the fort today? I admit I was surprised.'

'It was urgent. I presume that if you are investigating something that affects my old friend Florius Gracilis, you will welcome any help.'

I attempted to unsettle her. 'Maenia Priscilla thinks he may be with you.'

'Can Maenia Priscilla *think*?' It flashed out like a bright flood of spilt wine, making us jump. 'I'm afraid he's not here.'

I smiled. I could see what might attract him. You knew exactly where you were in this establishment. 'Have you known him long?'

'Ten years.' A slight dryness in her tone acknowledged that we could regard it as more than a nodding association.

I did try to be specific. 'And what are relations between you?'

'Cordial,' she said, in a firm tone.

I let it go. No point being crude. We all knew the tally. 'Julia Fortunata, I am an envoy from Vespasian. I was sent to Upper Germany on another matter, but any odd circumstances that occur while I am here may be related, so they need investigation. You are correct: I should welcome any information about the whereabouts of Gracilis. You may speak completely frankly.'

For a moment she was silent, candidly considering me. I rode out the scrutiny. She reached a verdict and gestured us to a seat.

She had planned what to say. It came out with little prompting and in a concise form. Gracilis had definitely vanished. His friend Julia was extremely concerned. She had asked to see me because she felt that 'other elements' were either taking the matter too lightly, or knew something and were involved in a cover-up. It was inconceivable that he should go off somewhere without mentioning it to Julia in advance.

'Does he even discuss military matters?'

'Within the proper bounds of course.'

'Of course,' I said. At my side the upright Justinus made an effort to control his disapproval. 'Tell me, did he have any worries?'

'Gracilis is extremely conscientious. He frets over everything.' A fidget, eh? A man who harried his men and aggravated his wife no doubt, though probably his mistress of ten years had learned to ignore the agitation. Perhaps, I thought, Julia Fortunata's role in his life had always been to calm him down and boost his morale.

'What most recently? Can you give me examples?'

'Since we came to Germany? In general terms, the political situation. He feared that Petilius Cerialis may have been posted away to Britain prematurely; that subduing the rebels may still be only half complete. He sensed further trouble brewing.' She discussed politics like a man. I wondered if Gracilis was really so fluent himself, or whether he relied on his mistress to frame his thoughts. Yet now, as she described him evaluating the situation as a local commander should, I had for the first time some sense of this man acting with authority. She certainly did well by him.

'What were his relations at the fort?'

'He was very conscious that the Fourteenth legion possessed most of the experience and were to a great extent carrying their colleagues.' She made a slight gesture of apology to Justinus for disparaging the First; her sensitivity was something we had come to expect. Justinus grinned back ruefully.

121

'Anything else? Money worries?'

'Nothing abnormal.'

'Problems with his wife?'

'Oh, I think Gracilis can handle that one!' Once again she had permitted herself a faintly bitter and contemptuous note, though it was well controlled. Julia Fortunata knew her position was one of strength.

'*Other* women?' I suggested lightly. She said nothing, reprovingly. 'So what has he been most preoccupied with? Anything to do with the rebels, for instance?'

'He did discuss with me a theory that the chieftain Civilis would refuse to accept defeat and might try to rally support again.'

'Any evidence?'

'Nothing firm.'

I smiled. 'Had he decided to do something about it?'

'He would like to finish the task Petilius Cerialis left behind. Gracilis is ambitious, naturally. Dealing with Civilis would enhance his status in Rome and win the Emperor's gratitude. As far as I know he had nothing to go on, however.'

To an envoy who also needed enhanced status and imperial thanks, that was reassuring news! 'Does the legate's interest extend to Veleda?'

'He never mentioned her.' It sounded like loyalty. The legate was probably as fascinated by the famous prophetess as any other man.

'So he had taken no action, and as far as you know he had no immediate plans?'

'The legate was on guard for trouble. It's all I can say. Other than that,' she said emphatically, as if she felt she had given us sufficient information for professionals to act upon, 'Florius Gracilis takes a close interest in everything that affects the fort, from the quality of the grain supply to the franchise for the bowls which his soldiers eat it from!'

I grew thoughtful. 'There must be a large number of supply contracts being renegotiated after all the commotion of the civil war?'

'Yes. As I said, Gracilis likes to involve himself closely in the details.' I bet he did!

'And how do the contractors regard him?'

'I would have thought that was obvious!' Julia Fortunata replied acerbically. 'The successful ones applaud his judgement; those who lose the work tend to grumble.'

I felt a prickle of excitement. I wondered if any contract winners ever gave the legate more material thanks than praise – or if any of the losers accused him of being less than fair . . . I had to phrase it discreetly: 'Are you aware of any recent problems with commercial deals that might have a bearing on the legate's disappearance?'

'No.' I think she knew what I meant. 'He left no clues at all.'

I felt Julia's concern for him went much deeper than her measured tones suggested, but she was too proud, both in her own right and on behalf of Gracilis, to display anything other than this cool self-control.

I allowed her to close the interview. She promised to be in touch if she thought of anything else that would help us. She was the type who would continue to ponder what had happened to her lover until she knew the answer.

I hoped it would not be the one she dreaded. I would probably despise him, but I liked her.

As we rode back to Moguntiacum, Justinus asked, 'What's your verdict?'

'A woman of strong character tied up with a man who lacks it. The usual, as your caustic sister would say!'

He passed over my reference to Helena. 'Did that get us anywhere at all?'

'It may do. My bet is something to do with Civilis.'

'Really!'

'Well, either it's that, or His Honour has embroiled himself in a cavalry-fodder fiddle or unwise scheming with the ceramic contractors. As a matter of national pride, I'd rather he's being held hostage by a dangerous rebel than just learn eventually that the fool has got himself bopped on the head with a redware porridge pot!'

Camillus Justinus grinned in his slow, appreciative way. 'I think I'll go for the pot,' he replied.

XXVI

Justinus was duty officer for the night watch, so we spurred back towards the fort as dusk drew in. Nearer to, I asked him to take my horse on while I peeled off to familiarise myself with the locale. In sight of the gate he left me to mooch about on foot.

I tramped around, exploring. The fort was set back a lengthy step from the busy wharves on the waterside, so I left those. Most civilian life sheltered behind the fort, where a competent-looking aqueduct brought water in. On the far side, some way from the military base, lay a customs post and the Jupiter Column, which paid civic lip-service to the Palatine. I made up my own version of the usual painful stuff: *Long life to Nero, companion of the Olympian Gods, say the citizens of our town (ardently hoping Nero will invest us with a theatre).* They must have mistimed it, because there was no theatre that I could find.

From its vantage point on slightly higher ground, the fort commanded a wide view downstream as the river curved away and widened after its junction with the Moenus. I took the road to the bridge, then tramped across. Only then did I really appreciate how wide the Rhenus is. It made the Tiber seem like a minnow stream meandering through watercress beds. A guard post had been thrown up on the far side, large enough to have its own name: Castellum Mattiacorum. Now I was standing in Germania Libera.

At first it felt just the same as the Roman side. The atmosphere was less alarming than the lawless immigrants' quarter of the Transtiberina in Rome. But this was not the Transtiberina, and nor – for me – was it really safe. A Roman watch-tower this side of the river was an extreme rarity. Standing as it did at the head of the great trade route that followed the course of the Moenus into the interior, this one existed only as a gesture. I had taken my first tentative step beyond the frontiers of the Empire. Behind me the lights of Moguntiacum twinkled faintly in neat rows. Ahead lay hundreds or thousands of uncertain miles, inhabited first by tribes who openly despised Rome, then by other tribes we Romans had never yet encountered in lands whose existence and features no one in my world even knew. On this rather drear evening, with night falling early, the sense of vast-scale European geography suddenly made me feel mournful and far from home.

The guard post was surrounded by a relaxed group of civil dwellings. On the water's edge I found a tavern with fewer customers and higher standards than the Medusa, where I could sit and watch the solemn flow of the Rhenus and the last ships homing in at nightfall.

I was thinking about my mission. Although developments were slow, I was beginning to feel much more assured of my role here – and aware of new drawbacks. I had a distinct sense of having discovered a rival. If Florius Gracilis had made it *his* mission to reclaim the chieftain Civilis – and whatever Julia Fortunata believed, that could well include a similar yearning to dispose of Veleda, too – I hoped he failed. Otherwise I could end up stuck in this backwater, a thousand miles from home and who knew how far from Helena, robbed of my task for the Emperor, and with it any chance to earn some cash. Vespasian was a snob. He would much rather handsomely reward a senator than find himself forced to hand out a few grudging sesterces to me.

It certainly seemed possible that Gracilis had dashed off on a search. Maybe for once he had deemed it too secret to enlighten the forceful Julia. Maybe he had even felt a need to strike out independently. The Fourteenth must be aware of what he was up to. It followed that once I let them know why Vespasian had sent me, they would have a double reason to act innocent, then interfere with my own plans. New broom or not, they would support their commander. And Gracilis himself was bound to consider this mission more suited to his elevated status rather than flung away on me . . .

Tough luck, legate! If this was a race, then M. Didius Falco was determined to win.

I had no idea how. But mere technical details can be worked out any time. All a hero needs is grit.

Satisfied with the day's progress, I enjoyed my drink. The night was calm. The atmosphere along the waterfront was pleasant and businesslike. Now I was thinking about women: barmaids, officers' wives, mistresses . . . and finally a woman it was a more creative pleasure to dream about: Helena.

That led me again into wondering where she was. Despondent, I made the dark trek home.

On the home side of the river, the provincial tradesfolk were promptly closing up, which reminded me that in four or five hours I might feel sleepy myself. If Argentoratum had been quick to draw its shutters, Moguntiacum made them look like degenerate owls. When the first man yawned in Moguntiacum, the whole town disappeared to bed. By the time a cosmopolitan Roman was just starting to feel hungry and ready for his evening's entertainment, the eating-spots here had up-ended benches on all the tables and the besoms were sweeping out lingerers. Anyone who left too slowly risked having his tunic pinched in the folding door as it slammed shut.

I crept through the sober streets hoping no one would notice me roaming about. I didn't want them to be shocked.

At the fort I hit a snag.

'Password?'

'How should I know? I'm just a visitor.' In Germany a year after the rebellion rules were rules. It was sound practice – and a thorough menace to free-and-easy types like me.

Luckily the guard party belonged to the First and wanted to help. If they had been assigned from the Fourteenth I would have had to camp out all night.

I remembered my discussion with Justinus. ' "Mars the Avenger"?'

'Try another.'

' "Pickled fish"?'

'Yesterday's.'

'Oh Hades – what about "The camp surgeon's middle name"?'

'Spot on,' said the sentry, though he failed to readjust his speartip from its dangerous aiming point, dead centre on my throat.

'So what's the problem, soldier?' I croaked wearily.

'What is it?'

'What's what?'

'What,' he enunciated clearly, 'is the camp surgeon's middle name?'

The Fourteenth were right: the First Adiutrix were a gang of crass deck hands and rigging monkeys, with brains as dense as cork.

I got in eventually. Anyone who has bluffed his way into a brothel on the Via Triumphalis while attempting to rescue a fake virgin from Cyrenaïca – and got out again without losing his sense of humour or something worse – can deal with the simple-minded gateman of a frontier fort.

Fuming, but fighting it back in case anyone embarrassed me by asking what the matter was, I stepped out briskly for my billet. There was a good chance that if I failed to turn up by dinner-time, Camillus Justinus would go out to eat with his fellow-officers, leaving me to make the best of yesterday's bread rolls. I lengthened my stride, oblivious to everything but my traditional obligation as a guest to eat my host out of house and home.

The ambush was lying in wait for me four strides from the tribune's door.

XXVII

Three of them. A trio of soldiers wandering down the Via Principalis in a sweet reek of recent barley beer, sufficiently affected by the drink to become dangerous, but not drunk enough for me to handle on my own.

At first I thought they were just clumsy. They had lurched in my path, causing me to pull up short, like lads who were just too bad-mannered to notice my presence. Then they stumbled apart and regrouped: one either side of me, one behind.

Experience gave me an instant's warning that saved my life. I missed sight of the personal dagger, but registered the arm movement. I swung away sharply, crashing aside another assailant, but grabbing him to me like a bolster. For a moment he provided a human shield as I spun on the spot. His bristles scraped my cheek; his sour breath was disgusting. The moment of safety passed – he posed a greater threat if he went for me at close quarters. Loosening my grip would be fatal, but holding on was so bad I nearly opted for a one-way ferry ticket across the Styx.

He jerked free. Somehow I sensed what was in his mind and seized the chance to scramble half backwards. There was a house wall fairly close behind me, which offered slight protection. Instinct said to huddle close, but then I would be lost if they all rushed me at once. I managed a shout – not loud enough. After that I was too busy. There were plenty of personnel in the vicinity, but this incident was being nicely choreographed to look like nothing in particular. Who expects to see a mugging outside the officers' quarters? Come to that, who expects to be mugged?

Me, was the answer. Anywhere and everywhere I prepared myself for the worst. Thank the gods, these thugs had assumed I was whistling homewards in a trance. They had planned to catch me out completely, but found themselves surprised.

Quickly, I tried to take stock. I could see – there was a broad bar of light from an unshuttered first-floor window in the tribune's house.

Right at the start a shadow had wavered across that light from someone moving in the room behind. I glanced up, hoping to attract attention, but now there was no sign of life.

My own knife was safely in my hand. Letting me get it had been a bad mistake. I was breathing hard with the shock of the first assault, but I was upright and mobile. Even so, the prospects looked gloomy. Every time I made a dagger feint, I tried to edge closer to the tribune's portico. I stood little chance of reaching it. Every time one of *them* made a feint, I was at risk from the others while I parried. At least they stuck with their daggers – drawn swords would arouse too much public interest. As we sidestepped in all directions they were still laughing and nudging one another so that it would look like good-humoured jostling. I had no time to rouse help.

I had made it one stride nearer the door, but was trapping myself in a tighter wedge between two of them and the wall, while the third soldier guarded against flight the other way. It was time for some fast talking, but my mouth dried so that I couldn't speak.

Almost without planning it, I lunged at the single man, then changed direction and tackled the other two ferociously. Blades clashed with a screech that hurt my eye-teeth; sparks flew. I was working so hard I hardly noticed that in the remote depths of the tribune's house a woman's voice cried out. I barged an arm skywards, and heard steel skidding on masonry behind me. Light from above increased. I glimpsed faces more clearly. Another shadow came and went, but I was too preoccupied to shout.

My own dagger went home somewhere, but awkwardly. I wrenched my shoulder retrieving it as one of my two men cursed and hopped on the spot. Events were becoming too public; the second mugger was all for scarpering. The third had more guts – or less wits. He sprang at me. I roared with annoyance. Then, just as I had enough to do dealing with all three at once, the tribune's door burst open. Someone stepped out, framed in black by the light behind. Wrong build for Justinus; too slight for his guards. Whoever he was, a trimly sinister shadow came gliding out of doors.

Defending myself against my attackers as they put up a last furious struggle, I could hardly take in what happened. The shadow stepped straight past me, met one of the soldiers and pulled his head back with a disturbing action. The soldier folded noiselessly, and dropped to the ground in a manner that was unmistakable. There was a moment of stillness. The two survivors ran for it with the speed of troops who knew what they had witnessed. I knew too, though it was difficult to comprehend.

No time for pursuit. I was too winded, anyway. The tribune's guards now rushed out with torches, followed by Justinus. Chaos and commotion raged, then sank in a sickly diminuendo as light revealed the dead man.

It was a horrific killing. The amount of blood was unbelievable. The soldier's head had been nearly severed from his body by a blade sharper even than military steel.

I turned to the man who had done it. He stood motionless, the weapon still held in a workaday grip. One of the tribune's guards made a feeble attempt to remove it, without achieving much – his nerve failed. Another raised a flare slowly, as if afraid of revealing something supernatural.

No such luck. All we saw were the glazed and manic eyes of a tourist whose latest adventure had left him startled at his own bravado and ingenuity.

'*Xanthus!*'

Oh dear. Now someone was going to have difficult questions to answer before the hapless world-traveller was given back his passport and allowed to go home.

XXVIII

He still saw me as his protector, and turned to me with a worried bleat. I left him with the razor – he seemed to know how to handle it. 'I won't ask how many times you've done that before!'

'No, better not.' His voice sounded matter-of-fact, but I could see he was in shock.

'I always thought you'd been sent to assassinate me. Turns out I'm in more danger from my own past history . . .'

'I think I want to go home, Falco.'

'You're all right.'

'No, I wish I was in Rome.'

Justinus was taking charge. He had examined the scratched identity marks on the dead man's sword scabbard. 'One of the Fourteenth's hooligans . . .' He told one of his guards to fetch their senior tribune. 'Be discreet. Try to bring Aulus Macrinus by himself. I don't want their whole bloody legion turning up in high dudgeon.' He came to help me deal with the barber. 'Don't worry, Xanthus. You'll have to be interviewed by my commander, but that should be the end of it.'

'You sound confident!' I muttered in an undertone. 'Are you happy about explaining to your notoriously sensitive colleagues how one of their number came to be wiped out like this on the First's side of the fort?'

'I'll find something to tell them.' He responded well in a crisis. His eyes were bright with intense excitement, but he was planning coolly. His self-control calmed others in the vicinity too. 'Marcus, be prepared. *Some* things are worse than you think!' After teasing me with this mystery, kindness filled his voice. 'Let's move this poor fellow away from here . . .'

Xanthus had started trembling slightly. He stood transfixed by the corpse; nudging him indoors would need tact. In fact we all found it hard to avoid staring at the scene.

While we were still in the street, the guard returned with Macrinus.

Even his aristocratic sneer paled slightly when we stepped back and let him see why he had been summoned.

'Is that one of ours? Dear gods, Camillus!'

'Aulus, hear the explanation – '

'It had better be good!'

'Don't threaten us!' snapped Justinus, with surprising force. 'There's no argument. I have a reputable witness. Three of your rankers set on Falco – '

'A drunken prank.'

'No! It was unprovoked *and* planned. They had been dawdling outside my house for half an hour – my witness noticed them. And much more than a prank, Aulus! The night could have ended nastily – '

'I'd say it did!'

'The alternative was for my guest to be fatally stabbed.'

In the face of this, the Fourteenth's man pulled himself up. 'If what you say is true, the culprits will be found and disciplined. But I'm protesting about the secretive way this has all been handled. I don't care for the way you had me brought across here alone. I want my own observers present, I want one of my centurions to take notes at the scene of the crime – '

As he soared off into complaint, I broke in: 'There will be no cover-up. But no one wants another riot like your legion's public rumpus at Augusta Taurinorum!'

Macrinus ignored me. 'Who did it?'

'The barber.'

That set him back. We could see him remembering how Xanthus had been called the Emperor's hit man. We all stared at Xanthus. As a hit man he looked pretty meek.

'Some of us are going to feel uneasy the next time we need a shave,' I said. A fine spray of the dead soldier's blood disfigured the crisp white linen of the barber's tunic. As usual, he was turned out so smartly that away from the court his brilliant presence became embarrassing. The stains were doubly disconcerting, as if he had been careless during a routine shave.

'In my job,' he answered quietly, 'a man can become a target for abuse quite easily. I've had to learn how to defend myself.'

'That's no excuse for murdering a soldier!' Macrinus barked. He had no finesse.

'The soldier,' I pointed out rationally, 'had no excuse for trying to murder me!'

At this stylish rebuke he condescended to subside. It was apparent that Justinus intended to take control of any necessary enquiry, which, since the crime had occurred within the First's jurisdiction, was his entitlement. Macrinus grumpily fell back on one last jibe: 'You mentioned a witness. I hope it's one we can rely on!'

'Perfectly,' Justinus answered, with a faint impression of gritting his teeth.

'I think I must insist on knowing who.' Macrinus had sensed a joke, but was too crass to withdraw.

'My sister,' Justinus told him placidly.

I winced. He had been right earlier when he had teased me. Things certainly were worse than I had realised: Helena Justina was here.

We glanced up at the window above us. She was still standing there, as she must have been during some of my fight. Her face lay in darkness. Her unmistakable figure, the outline of her smoothly upswept hair and even the elegant pendant drops of her earrings sent down a perfect, elongated shadow that reached the corpse, hiding its ghastly wound in decent shade.

The tribune Macrinus straightened up, smoothed back his crisp, curly locks, and produced a salute suitably emphatic for a tribune who thought a lot of himself greeting the only unmarried senator's daughter this side of the Alps.

I was wearing the wrong boots for heel-clicking. I waved at her, grinned at her brother, and strode indoors.

XXIX

'Fighting again, Falco?' Mild medicine from her.

She was in long-sleeved wool, with rather sombre jet earrings. Her dark, silky hair had been caught up in combs either side of her head, perhaps with more care than usual, and I could detect her perfume from two strides away. But after travelling, or possibly after seeing me attacked, she looked washed out and tense.

I was not in the mood for pleasantries. 'I gather it tickled you to watch me suffering?'

'I sent people to help.'

'You sent me a barber!'

'He seems capable.'

'You weren't to know that – I don't think he knew himself.'

'Don't quibble. He was the first person I found . . . You kept us waiting for dinner!' she grumbled, as if that settled it.

I threw back my head and commented to the gods, 'Well, things seem to be normal again!'

We always sparked like this after spending time apart. Especially when we met again with strangers watching us. For me, it held off the moment when I had to admit to missing her. For Helena, who knows? At least now she had spoken to me there was a spark in her eyes that I didn't object to seeing there.

Her brother had brought Xanthus indoors and was shepherding us all into a reception room. He had refrained from suggesting that his tribunal colleague come and be introduced to the noble newcomer, so watching Macrinus showing off was one horror we were spared. Xanthus was kept with us to be applauded and cosseted after his ordeal.

We found ourselves in the dining-room. A meal lay ready, which had obviously been set for some time. At this point I felt prepared for formalities. I would have marched over and kissed Helena's cheek, but she plonked herself decisively on her brother's dining-couch.

Unless I offended Justinus by invading the host's eating space, she was out of reach. It annoyed me. Failing to greet her made it look as if I didn't care.

I excused myself to clean up – some blood, but mostly dirt. When I returned I had missed the hors-d'oeuvres (my favourite course) and Helena was regaling the company with outrageous stories of her journey. I ate in silence, trying not to listen. When she reached the part about the wheel coming off her carriage and the chief of the mountain bandits kidnapping her for ransom, I yawned and went to my room.

An hour or so later, I re-emerged. The house had fallen quiet. I searched its bowels until I found Xanthus, lying on his bed and writing up his diary. I knew from travelling out with him that he was keeping a richly boring travelogue.

'At least "the day I killed the soldier" should keep your grand-children enthralled! And here's another excitement: this is going to be the night when you give me a proper shave.'

'You going out?'

'No. Staying in.'

He had rolled to his feet and was unpacking his gear, though mildly unimpressed by the bonanza I was offering. Wine at dinner had calmed him down to the point of utter silliness. 'Has a brush with death made you vow to dedicate your stubble to the gods in an alabaster pyx, Falco? I'm not sure they make vases big enough!' I let him sit me down and envelop me in a fine cambric wrap, but I ignored the joshing. 'What does sir prefer – depilatory liniment? I use a nice white vine paste. I never recommend my gentlemen to try the weird stuff like bat's blood – ' He was enjoying himself more than I reckoned to tolerate.

'A razor will do.' Superstition made me hope he would change to a different blade from the one that he had used earlier.

'Sure? I can do you ground pumice or individual tweezing just as easily. My word, you've been neglecting yourself. It's probably best to try and burn this off with bitumen!' I *think* the last one was a joke.

'Whatever will have the smoothest result. And I want a haircut as well – but leave some curl. Just trim off the worst shagginess . . .' Xanthus put an engraved copper mirror into my hand, like somebody keeping a baby quiet with a rattle. I carried on describing what I wanted, even though I knew barbers never listen. A private informer needs to possess some stubbornness.

'Jupiter, Falco! Who are you trying to impress?'

'Mind your own business.'

'Oh!' Xanthus spat on his whetstone. '*Oh, I see!*' Even he caught on eventually. His normal eagerness to please turned into the ribaldry I met everywhere on this subject: 'You'll have your work cut out there!' Quite often that was Helena Justina's line too, I remembered pessimistically. 'This calls for my Norican steel . . .'

I wanted the best, so was unable to quibble. But I felt pretty sure that the Norican steel was what he had used to cut my attacker's throat.

To his credit, he made the best of the unpromising material I had placed at his disposal. I had never been shaved so closely, nor with so little discomfort, and even the haircut just about fitted the style of subdued dishevelment with which I felt most at home. After years of delicately gauging the wishes of emperors, Xanthus could judge his client as nicely as you'd expect in a barber who would be sent to the public strangler if he snipped a wrong curl.

As it turned out, he might have spared himself the trouble. Still, I dare say it was not the first time he had spent hours preparing someone for an assignation that flopped.

With a stinging chin and in a fug of disconcerting unguents, I quietly admitted myself to what I knew was the best guest-bedroom. I kept telling myself that everything would be all right once I had cornered Helena on her own and treated her to my adoring attentions. I could hardly wait to see her. I had a fairly pressing need to re-establish normal relationships.

No such luck. There was a taper, but the large room lay half in darkness. I stood for a moment, adjusting to the dim light and trying to think up a suave line of conversation if my beloved was reclining on swansdown and reading a light ode or two while she waited impatiently for me . . . No point: there was no Helena. The high bed with its tortoiseshell frame, fringed coverlet and engagingly carved footstool stood empty. Instead, a small hunched figure lay snoring on a lower couch – presumably a slavegirl she had brought to look after her.

So much for me! No chance of a passionate reunion with a servant looking on! I could remember when she *never* let a slave stay in her room at night if I was in the vicinity.

I stepped back. Closing the door, my pent-up emotion gripped me. She must have known I would come. She must be keeping out of the way deliberately. Chatting with Justinus. Frightening that simple soul with her tales of broken wheels and brigands. Chewing over family business. Putting his career to rights. Anything that would avoid having to face me, angry at the way she had disappeared from Rome, yet badly wanting to go to bed with her.

I decided to take my outrageously barbered person out on the town and get as drunk as possible.

Indignation carried me as far as the front door. Then I remembered that Moguntiacum had small-town, small-minded habits. There was nowhere open for entertainment, except for the usual places too sordid to contemplate. Besides, the prospect of trying to work tomorrow with a head like a sack of oatmeal after a night gossiping inanely with some drab in a tavern when I had hoped to spend it with Helena, became too hard to bear. I sat in the tribune's garden for a while, feeling miserable, but Justinus was no devotee of landscape and it was a poor spot to sulk in. His dog found me and climbed alongside on the seat to chew at my tunic hem, but even the bench had damp moss on it and he soon jumped down and snuffled off into the darkness. I too slunk away to my room.

I had my back to the door. I had just pulled off my tunic (a clean one; too good for sleeping in) when someone came in.

'As nice a view of a nude wood sprite's back as I ever had the privilege to glimpse!'

Helena.

Having been attacked once that day, I spun round jumpily. Helena's warm appraising eyes were smiling as I lowered my handful of tunic in an attempt at decency. Her smile always had an irresistible effect on me.

'This is a private room, lady.'

'Good!' she said. I could feel my face colouring, but applied a scornful expression; it only encouraged her. 'Hello, Marcus.' I said nothing. 'I thought you wanted to see me?'

'What gave you that idea?'

'A strong scent of lotions in my room.' She sniffed. I cursed Xanthus. He had doused me in pomade until a bloodhound could have tracked me all the way from the Gallic Strait to Cappadocia.

Helena tipped her head to one side, watching me. She was leaning on the door behind her, as if to stop me escaping. My jaw set. 'How's Titus?'

'How should I know?'

'So what brings a stylish young lady to this wilderness?'

137

'Someone I follow about.' Helena had the knack of making her most illogical action sound like a rational response to some crazy slight from me.

'You left me!' I accused her, in a low tone.

'And how was Veii?' Her well-bred voice had a sarcastic note that dried my mouth like grape skins.

'Veii's a dump.' Suddenly, for no obvious reason, I felt tired.

'Are the widows attractive?' As I expected, it sounded like fighting talk. Now I knew why I felt defeated.

'Some of them think so.'

'I was talking to one,' Helena said crisply. 'She implied that your trip to Veii was a wild success.'

'The widow's a liar.'

Helena looked at me. She and I were friends for a good reason: we knew one another well enough to be able to pick a resounding fight, yet we both knew how to appeal for a truce. 'That's what I tell myself,' she answered quietly. 'But why, Marcus?'

'Jealous that I refused her and went home to you. What were *you* doing in Veii?'

'Trying to find you.'

Somewhere between us the quarrel died. 'You've found me now,' I said.

Helena Justina came across the room. She had a purposeful air I was not quite ready for, though I would be. 'What's on your mind, lady?'

'Nothing you won't like . . .' She tugged the tunic from my hand.

For pride's sake I tried to bluff it out: 'I warn you, I hate forward women – '

'Wrong. You like a girl who looks as if she knows exactly what you're thinking, and doesn't care . . .'

All the same, uncertainty flickered. She stepped back. I stepped after her.

I could feel her physical warmth even before her bare arms came through mine. She must have changed from the woollen dress I had seen earlier to a lighter one. If I undid two brooches, the flimsy material would drift to the floor, leaving all of her available. They looked like brooches with easy clasps. I put my hands on her shoulders, as if undecided whether to hold her off or hold her closer. My thumbs found the clasps automatically.

Helena started to pull away from me. It brought us effortlessly to the bed. 'Don't look so nervous, lady!'

'I don't frighten that easily.'

'You should do . . .'

'Oh stop pretending to be tough!' Helena knew most things about me, and what she didn't know she guessed. 'You're not a thug; you know how to be affectionate . . .' I felt affectionate all right. I felt so affectionate I could think of nothing else.

We landed on the bed. I let her take charge. She always liked organising. Tonight I liked whatever she liked. Today had posed enough problems. Now I had Helena Justina in my arms, in the friendliest of moods; I had everything I wanted, and was prepared for anything.

She was making herself comfortable, arranging the bedclothes, taking off her earrings, unfastening her hair, killing the lamp . . . 'Relax, Marcus!'

I relaxed. I relaxed utterly. All the anxieties in my hectic brain grew calmer. I hauled Helena closer still and sighed heavily while my hands travelled slowly over the familiar shape of her, reacquainting themselves with her secrets. I held her, and closed my eyes in gratitude. Then I did the only thing a man could be expected to do in the circumstances.

I went to sleep.

XXX

Most of the night had passed. I woke in a sweat, realising what I must have done.

'Pleasant nap?' She was still there anyway.

'You told me to relax . . . I'm awake now,' I said, trying to make it sound meaningful.

Helena merely laughed at me, and snuggled against my shoulder. 'Sometimes when I'm trying to make friends with you, I feel like Sisyphus pushing his rock up the mountain.'

I laughed too. 'Just when he's shoved the thing up farther than ever before, he gets a terrible itch on the shoulder that he's compelled to scratch . . . I know.'

'Not you,' she disagreed. 'You'd find some clever way to poke a wedge under the rock.'

I loved her eccentric faith in me.

I rolled over suddenly, seizing her in a domineering hold. Then, as she stiffened, expecting something fierce, I kissed her so gently she was overcome. 'Sweetheart, you are the one person who will never need to worry about making friends with me.'

I smiled into her eyes. She closed them. Sometimes she hated me to see how deeply she felt. I kissed her once more, making a deliberately thorough job of it.

When she looked at me again her eyes were richly brown, and full of love. 'Why did you run away from the dinner table, Marcus?'

'I hate stories where dangerous bandits are grabbing women I care about as hostages.'

'Ah, the bandit was a sweetie!' she teased softly.

'I bet you handled him.'

'I have some practice with curmudgeons who think they know all about women!' she mocked, but she was stretching beneath my weight so invitingly I could hardly concentrate. Helena grew still. '*Do* you care about me?'

'I do.'

'Did you miss me?'

'Yes, my darling . . .'

As I set about the pleasant task of showing her how much, she murmured restively, 'It's starting to get light, Marcus. I ought to go.'

'I don't think I can allow that . . .'

For a moment longer I could tell she was unhappy. I pressed on, letting her know it would have to be all her decision if she wanted us to stop. Then she forgot about the proprieties of living in her brother's house, and was all mine again.

XXXI

Light had worked round a stout northern European shutter to reach my comfortably untidy bed. We had not been asleep long this time, since we were still locked close in a way that made sleep fairly difficult.

'Thank you, lady. I needed that.'

'So did I.' For a modest girl, she could be very direct. Having grown up among women whose shameless behaviour was rarely matched by honesty in bed, it always startled me.

I kissed her. 'What am I supposed to say to your brother?'

'Nothing. Why should you?' That was more like what I expected in a girl: totally unhelpful. She smiled. 'I love you, Marcus.'

'Thank you – but are you going to forgive me for not celebrating your birthday?' It now seemed safe to broach the issue.

Good timing, Falco: she wanted a fight about it, but her sense of fairness won. 'You didn't know it was my birthday.' She paused. 'Did you?'

'No! You should know that . . .' I leaned across, then, after a slight delay caused by her sweetness and nearness, I fetched out the amber necklace I had bought on the wineship from Dubnus the pedlar.

That reminded me – I had to do something about Dubnus. Why do crucial thoughts always interrupt at such inconvenient moments? I had been happily forgetting the Ubian scavenger, not to mention my plan to use him in my search for Veleda. With Helena Justina here in my arms, going into the barbarian forest was a prospect I now found unbearable.

I let Helena inspect the glimmering skein of beads, then fastened it around her neck. 'Suits you – especially with nothing else on.'

'That should cause a sensation when I'm next asked to a dinner party! It's lovely . . .' The sight of Helena wearing nothing but her birthday present encouraged me to further reconciliation, especially as I had managed to keep our physical union intact even when stretching sideways to my bedside table. 'Marcus, you ought to be exhausted – '

'I had a good night's sleep.'

'Are you afraid you might have forgotten how to do it?' she taunted wickedly, but accepting my attentions. Helena knew how to be gracious after she had received a well-chosen necklace of daunting cost. 'Or had you just forgotten how good it is?'

'Forgotten? Sweetheart, when you leave me pining, the problem is that I remember all too well.'

For some reason this manly reassurance worked on Helena so well she responded with what might have been a sob, though it was well muffled. 'Oh hold me – touch me – '

'Where?'

'There – anywhere – *everywhere*.'

Nearby in the house something fell over with a loud crash.

Something large. A statue of museum proportions, or an immense vase.

No one squealed. But after a second, we heard small desperate feet scampering.

'That's a child!' I was amazed.

'Oh Juno, I forgot – ' Helena reached the door first. The child was fleeing down the long corridor, leaving the giant shards behind. Unluckily for her, she had fled towards us.

What she had pushed over was a dramatic, two-handled vessel that was trying to pass for a middle-period Hellenic black-figure wine crater. It almost succeeded, but I had been trained by experts and I knew a fake, even when it was the kind of high-class fake that has better workmanship than the original (and costs more). It had been displayed on the plinth where I had once written *Falco was here* in the dust to annoy the tribune's servants. The crater had been big enough for a Treasury clerk to bury his savings in, and was probably the most expensive item Camillus Justinus possessed. The first piece in his lifetime collection, possibly.

'Stop! Stand still at once!'

Helena Justina could fix me in my tracks when she wanted to; she had no trouble with an eight-year-old. It was, however, the culprit who demanded: 'What are you doing there?' The rude defiance seemed familiar.

'Escaping from you!' I growled, for this must be the unwelcome soul I had observed snoring in Helena's bedroom earlier. I strode to the remains and picked up a curved fragment. Odysseus with a jutting spade beard was enjoying being tempted by some female; she had a tantalising ankle, but the rest of her was broken off.

I turned back angrily and surveyed the infant. She had a plain face and a petulant expression, with five or six thin little plaits tied together with a skinny rag on top of her head. My brain struggled to pin down which pot-bellied little disaster this was, and what relationship she bore to me. For it was one of ours all right. The gods only knew how she came to be in Upper Germany, but I could spot a member of the rampant Didius clan even before the wail of, 'I was only playing – it fell over on its own!'

She was hip-high, wearing a tunic that ought to have been decent, though she managed to have it hitched up so her bottom showed. That settled it; I knew her parentage all right. Augustinilla. An elaborate name, but a very straightforward personality – dumb insolence. She was my most hated sister Victorina's most objectionable child.

Victorina was the eldest in our family, the bane of my childhood and my worst social embarrassment since then. As a child she had been a tough little tyke with a constant runny nose and her loincloth at half-mast around her scabby knees. All the local mothers had warned their children not to play with us because Victorina was so violent; Victorina made them play with her anyway. When she grew up she played only with the boys. There were plenty. I could never understand why.

Of all the naughty children who could have walked in on my tender reunion with Helena, it had to be one of hers . . .

'Uncle Marcus has got nothing on!' The reason was that the tunic Helena had plunged into as she rushed to the door was mine. With a good amber necklace it looked highly incongruous, increasing the impression that a Bacchanalia had been occurring in my room. The child's accusing eyes went to Helena too, but there she had better sense than to comment. Presumably Augustinilla had witnessed at close quarters how Helena Justina had dealt with the wild bandit chief.

I took up an athletic pose; a mistake. Flashing the oiled muscles of a handsome physique may succeed in a sunlit stadium within sniff of the Mediterranean, but in a dim domestic corridor halfway across Europe being unclad only makes you feel cold. In a dark mood, I waited for Helena to utter the traditional imperative: 'She's your niece; you deal with her.'

144

She said it, and I issued the traditional rude reply.

Helena tried not to let the child see she was annoyed. 'You are the head of the Didius family, Marcus!'

'Purely notional.'

Being head of our family was so punishing that the real claimant to the title, my father, had abandoned his ancestors and completely changed his identity to avoid the ghastly task. Now the role fell to me. This explains why I was no longer on speaking terms with my papa the auctioneer. It may even explain why I myself had felt no qualms about entering a profession which most of Rome despises. I was used to being cursed and treated with contempt; my family had been doing that for years. And being a private informer had the great advantage of taking me undercover or right away from home.

Perhaps all families are the same. Perhaps the idea that paternal power holds sway was put about by a few hopeful lawmakers who had no sisters or daughters of their own.

'You brought her; you can have the joy of beating her,' I said coolly to Helena. I knew she would never strike a child.

I strode back inside my room. I felt depressed. Since we were not married there was no reason for Helena to take notice of my relatives; if she did, it boded the kind of serious pressure I had come to dread.

Sure enough, after a few rapid words, followed by a surprisingly meek reply from Augustinilla, Helena came in and began to explain: 'Your sister is in trouble – '

'When was Victorina ever out of it?'

'Hush, Marcus. *Women's* trouble.'

'That's a change; her trouble is usually men.'

I sighed and told her to spare me the details. Victorina had always been a moaner about her insides. Her wild life must have strained her system intolerably, most of all after her marriage to an inane plasterer who in his ability to father horrid children in rapid succession outshone every rodent in Rome. I would never wish surgery on anyone, however. Let alone those painful, rarely successful businesses with forceps and dilators that I vaguely knew were inflicted on women.

'Marcus, the children were being parcelled out to give your sister a chance of recovery, and in the lottery you won Augustinilla . . .' Some lottery – a blatant fix. 'No one knew where you were.' That had been deliberate.

'So they asked you! Augustinilla is the worst of the bunch. Couldn't

Maia take her in?' Maia was my one half-likeable sister, which worked against her whenever problems were being handed out by the rest. Her amiable nature meant she was frequently leeched on even by me.

'Maia had no more room. And why should Maia always have to be the obliging one?'

'That sounds like Maia talking! I still don't understand. Why ever did you have to bring the nipper here?'

'What else could I do with her?' she snapped crossly. I had a few suggestions, but sense prevailed. Helena scowled. 'As a matter of fact, I didn't want to admit to other people that I was running around Europe after you.' She meant that she had refused to say she was storming off after we had had a fight.

I grinned at her. 'I love you when you're embarrassed!'

'Oh shut up. I'll take care of Augustinilla,' she assured me. 'You have enough to do. Justinus told me about your mission.'

I sat on the bed, cursing morosely. With one of Victorina's badly brought-up brats on hand, I would certainly not be staying around the house. Helena, of course, would be at home, like a decent Roman matron. Even my lady's wild flights of freedom would have to be constricted inside a military fort.

Helena squashed in beside me while she swapped my tunic for her own. As she pulled her gown over her head, I fondled her in a desultory way.

'Talking to you is like interviewing a centipede for a job as a masseur . . .' Her head popped out. 'How's your mission?' she enquired, checking up on me.

'I've made some progress.' It was my turn to start dressing and Helena's to make overtures, but she failed to take up the opportunity, even though I was repossessing my tunic as languidly as possible. Evidently I had had my fun. The passion which Augustinilla had interrupted would not be resumed today.

'How much progress, Marcus? Solved anything?'

'No. Just acquired new tasks – tracing a missing commander no one even knew about . . .'

'This ought to be an ideal location for tracking down suspects – a fort, I mean. You have a closed community.'

I laughed bitterly. 'Oh yes! Only an enclosed community of twelve thousand men! He's offended his whole legion, not to mention having a hostile wife, an interfering mistress, numerous creditors, people in the local community – '

'What people?' Helena demanded.

146

'He's been trying to trace the rebel I'm pursuing myself, for one thing.' She didn't ask for details about Civilis; Justinus must have filled her in last night. 'And he was apparently involved in wrangles over some military franchises.'

'That sounds like something that could easily have gone wrong if he mishandled it. Which franchises?' she asked curiously.

'Not sure. Well, pottery, for one thing.'

'Pottery?'

'Red tableware presumably.'

'For the army? Is there a lot at stake?'

'Think about it. In every legion six thousand rankers all needing cereal bowls and beakers, as well as cooking pots and serving platters for each ten-man tent. On top of that, full formal dinner services for the centurions and officers, plus the gods know what for the provincial governor's regal establishment. The legions reckon to do themselves nicely. Nothing will suffice for the army but the best-quality gloss. Samianware is strong, but it does break with rough handling, so there will always be repeat orders.'

'Does it have to be brought all the way from Italy or Gaul?'

'No. I hear there is a local industry.'

She seemed to change tack. 'Did you find your mother's comport?'

'Was it a comport she wanted?' I asked, innocently.

'You didn't buy one!'

'You guessed.'

'I bet you never even looked!'

'I looked all right. They were too expensive. Ma would never have wanted me to spend so much.'

'Marcus, you're dreadful! If there's a local factory,' Helena decided, 'you'd better take me to buy one for her. Then while I'm choosing your present, you can look around for clues.'

Helena Justina never wasted time. Left to my own devices I could have frittered away half a week helping her brother with his formal enquiry into the soldier's death. Instead, Justinus was on his own. I did manage to speak to him briefly on another subject, though, asking him to have the pedlar found and put in a holding cell.

'What has he done?'

'Leave that blank in the warrant. I just need ready access. It's for what he's *going* to do.'

By then Helena had enquired where the best ceramics in Moguntia-cum were to be had, and almost before I had managed to snatch breakfast I found myself escorting her sedan chair out of the fort. I did not entirely object. I still had to mention to Justinus that my niece had destroyed his wine crater, and ways of explaining the disaster were slow to suggest themselves.

Helena and I left the fort in the late morning. Autumn was making its presence felt: a chill still freshened the air several hours after dawn, and moisture clung to the sere grasses along the roadside. Spiders' webs were everywhere, making me blink whenever my horse passed under low branches. Helena looked out of her sedan chair laughing, only to brush away filaments that caught in her own eyelashes. Well, it was an excuse to stop, so I could help.

The pottery quarter at Moguntiacum was a lesser affair than the vast compound Xanthus and I had visited at Lugdunum. There were clear signs that the German enterprise was struggling to compete against its rivals in Gaul, who had backup from the original factory at Arretinum to lend them extra clout. Here the craftsmen were unsupported by the parent industry. Their goods on display were just as fine quality, yet the potters seemed surprised to see customers. The biggest workshop was actually boarded up.

We found one nearby that was open. It was owned by a certain Julius Mordanticus. Many provincial Celts adopt aristocratic names like Julius or Claudius. After all, if you are trying to advance yourself, who chooses to sound like a cheap artisan? Hardly a second-generation Romanised tribesman anywhere in the whole Empire answers to *Didius*, apart from one or two youngsters with extremely pretty mothers who live in towns which my elder brother Festus once passed through.

Helena had soon bought an impressive dish for Mother – at a price which made me wince only slightly, moreover. She then made friends with the potter, explained that she was visiting her brother the tribune, and soon led the conversation round to the legions in general. She was refined, gracious – and deeply interested in his livelihood. The potter thought she was wonderful. So did I, but I fought it back. Once I had paid for his dish, I leaned against a wall, feeling surplus.

'I expect you do a lot of trade with the fort,' Helena said.

'Not as much as we'd like these days!' The potter was short, with a wide, pale face. When he talked he hardly moved the muscles of his mouth, which gave him a wooden appearance, but his eyes were intelligent. His remark to Helena had been forced out by strong feelings – his normal nature seemed more cautious. He wanted to let the military subject drop.

I hauled myself away from the wall as Helena chatted on. 'I confess I didn't know samian ceramics were made in Germany. Is your speciality confined to Moguntiacum, or does it go further afield, among the Treveri?'

'The whole area from Augusta Treverorum to the river produces samianware.'

'I should think you do well?' she suggested.

'A bit of a slump lately.'

'Yes, we were looking at your colleague's stall – the one that's boarded up, belonging to Julius Bruccius. Is that due to the depression, or is he off on an autumn holiday?'

'Bruccius? A business trip.' A shadow crossed his face.

I had a nasty premonition as I interposed: 'Would that have been to Lugdunum by any chance?'

Helena Justina immediately retired from the debate and seated herself quietly. The potter, too, had noticed my tone. 'I came through Lugdunum on my way out to Germany,' I explained to him levelly. I breathed slowly, screwing my mouth. 'Would Bruccius be a thickset man in his forties, travelling with a younger fellow who has red hair and a fine crop of warts?'

'His nephew. Sounds as if you saw them somewhere along the way.'

Julius Mordanticus already looked worried. His friends' overdue return must have prepared him for bad tidings, but possibly not as bad as this. I kept it brief. When I told him about the quarrel I had witnessed at Lugdunum, then how I had later found the two bodies, he cried out in protest and covered his face.

Helena brought him a wicker chair. We sat him in it and I stood with one hand on his shoulder while he struggled to accept my news.

XXXII

'*Tiw!*' He spat out the Celtic name for Mars. 'Bruccius and his nephew murdered in Gaul . . .'

'I'm sorry,' I said. 'It's not much help, but there was a centurion at the fort who was going into Cavillonum to report the bodies to a local magistrate – he could tell you who is in charge and what transpired. The magistrate ought to have arranged funerals, for one thing. When Helena and I go back I'll find the centurion and send him here to speak to you. His name is Helvetius.' Julius Mordanticus nodded dully. I had been talking in order to give him time to compose himself. Now that he seemed calmer I asked carefully, 'Have you any idea who might be behind the deaths?'

He answered at once. 'Those self-seeking bastards at Lugdunum!'

I was not surprised; I had seen that Lugdunum had a great deal at stake in this industry. I felt obliged to warn him: 'Your accusation may be hard to prove.'

'If they show their faces here, we won't need proof!'

'I didn't hear that! Would you tell me what it's all about?'

Mordanticus had decided we were sympathetic; the whole story flooded out: 'Things are not easy nowadays. Trade has been bad. We rely on the military to keep us in business, but with all the recent troubles . . .' He tailed off for a moment. Helena and I avoided prying into local sympathies, but he sensed us holding back politely. 'Oh we were on the side of Rome, I can assure you. There is a close relationship between our town and the fort.' He spoke didactically, like a local leader who has to justify some peculiar festival by a neat reference to history. 'Keeping the legions here on the Rhenus is entirely in our interest. The Roman general Petilius Cerialis put it correctly when he arrived: Rome occupied this region at our forefathers' invitation when they were being harried by other tribes looking for new territory. If Rome leaves, the tribes from east of the Rhenus will sweep in and take everything.' All the more so, presumably, because these tribes on the west bank were now regarded as collaborators.

'There is no love lost between you?' Helena prompted.

'No. Civilis and his sort may have sounded off in the name of liberty, but they care no more for us than their ancestors cared for our fathers and grandfathers. Civilis wants to be king over the richest nations in Europe. His people would like to leave the Batavian marshland and move into lusher pastures here. The only German independence they believe in is their own freedom to push in wherever they fancy.'

I thought this was one-sided. For one thing, my research in Rome among despatches about the rebellion had told me that Augusta Treverorum, the nearest tribal capital, had produced Julius Tutor and Julius Classicus, two of the most hotheaded rebel leaders after Civilis, so feelings ran higher here than our friend wanted to admit. But I didn't blame Mordanticus for taking the convenient view.

I changed the subject. 'What I saw happening at Lugdunum smacked of commerce rather than politics. I gather there is a strong professional rivalry between you and the Gauls. Is it all to do with your military trade?'

He nodded, albeit reluctantly. 'A big question mark hangs over who will win the contract for the new legions at the fort. Lugdunum itself is under threat from a big consortium in southern Gaul. Bruccius and I had been trying to persuade the new legate to re-award the franchise locally.'

'That legate was Florius Gracilis?'

'The same. The other man takes a much less prominent role.'

'Yes, his troops were recruited from the navy, and are rather diffident. So, your people held the franchise previously, when the Fourth and the Twenty-second were the legions based at the fort?'

'With reason! Our produce matches the quality of Italy or Gaul, and obviously distribution is easier.'

If there was suitable clay here, Rome would naturally have encouraged a local industry, setting it up with official finance, no doubt, during the old campaigns under Drusus and Germanicus. Having established local production and persuaded people to make working for the legions their livelihood, it would then be hard to turn elsewhere. But Rome had never had much love of sentiment.

'How do your prices compete?' I asked.

He looked reproving. 'For a tender with the legions, our prices are set right! Anyway, we have no transportation costs. I refuse to believe Lugdunum can undercut our bid.'

'Unless they cheat! Was Gracilis sympathetic?'

'He never answered us directly. I felt our pleas were making no impression on the man.'

I frowned. 'Had he been got at?' Mordanticus shrugged. He was the kind of ultra-cautious businessman who never commits himself to speaking ill of those he may be forced to deal with at a later date. It looked to me as if he would have to take a more robust line. 'Let's face it, Mordanticus,' I insisted. 'Florius Gracilis would have come out through Gaul this spring by the same route that I took. He has a young wife who probably wanted new dinner-party dishes and would have dragged him to the factory site at Lugdunum. He could easily have been nobbled by your rivals before he even arrived here. You know it, don't you? The big boys at Lugdunum had stitched the legate up.'

Without directly answering, Mordanticus said, 'The potters here decided to make a last effort to sort things out, and Bruccius was elected spokesman for all of us. We sent him over to Lugdunum to try and reach a compromise. There's business for everyone. Those bullies in Lugdunum are just greedy. They already have a roaring trade in Gaul, all the legionary orders for Britain, plus Spain. They export from their southern ports all round the Ligurian Gulf and the Balearic Coast.' He spoke like a man who had eyed up the commercial possibilities carefully himself. 'They were always bitter that we were right here on the spot. After the rebellion, they saw their chance to muscle in.'

'So, it seems likely that Bruccius and his nephew did what they could there, but received no help. Things looked to me on the verge of violence, but your friends showed no physical damage when I saw them having supper the night they were killed. They must have given up on the Lugdunum mob, and were coming home with the bad news. Mind you,' I said thoughtfully, 'it means the question of who gets the franchise cannot be settled yet.'

'Why do you say that?' enquired Helena.

'No point murdering two people if Lugdunum felt confident the future trade was theirs. It's my belief the potters from Gaul felt Bruccius could be far too persuasive. With the Rhine legions right on his doorstep and the relevant legate within daily reach, he and his colleagues could pose a serious threat. That was why Lugdunum wiped him out. Somebody tracked him and the nephew far enough to deter any magistrates from making a connection, and then killed them in a spot where they might never be identified at all.'

'But why?' asked the potter. 'It still leaves plenty of us here.'

'Mordanticus, for the oldest motive in the world! Killing two of your number – or better still, having them totally disappear – will intimidate the rest.'

'No chance!' Mordanticus declared with a set face. 'We shall never give up, or let them get away with it!'

'You're a strong-willed man, but I warn you, some people will soon quaver at bullying. Don't forget there are potters with wives who don't want to be widows. Potters worried about the fate of large families if their breadwinner vanishes. Potters who just feel life has more to offer than a long-drawn-out feud which they may never win.'

'It's criminal!' raged Helena. 'Rome shouldn't even appear to sanction business methods of this type. The legate ought to show his disapproval by barring Lugdunum completely, then awarding to Moguntiacum every franchise that's available!'

I smiled at her for becoming so passionate. 'From what I've heard about Florius Gracilis, we can't rely on him for a high moral tone. I know he's desperately short of cash.'

'You mean he's taking bribes?' Helena's parents' attempts to give her a sheltered life had been partially successful. But since meeting me she had learned enough not to be surprised at any suggestion. 'Is Gracilis *corrupt*, Falco?'

'That would be a grave charge. I'm not making it.' Not at this stage, anyway. I turned to the potter. 'Julius Mordanticus, I work for the Emperor. Your problems ought not to be my business, but they may overlap with what I came to do.'

'Which is what?' he asked curiously.

I saw no reason to hide the truth. 'Principally, to liaise with Civilis. His current whereabouts are unknown, but I believe the legate may be searching for him. On the other hand, Gracilis could have gone after Veleda, the Bructian prophetess.'

'If he has crossed the river, he's a fool!' Mordanticus looked at me as if I was mad merely for suggesting it.

'Don't say that. I may soon have to cross the river myself.'

'You're in for a wild time, then. And I should say it's death for Gracilis.'

'He may be travelling incognito.'

'A Roman official is pleading be spotted. Is this something to do with the franchises?' Mordanticus demanded, single-mindedly.

'No, it's all about political glory for Florius Gracilis. But it means you and I have a shared interest. I don't like to make promises, but if I ever run across him I may well find an opportunity to discuss your franchise problem, and I may just make him believe that I am speaking for Vespasian.' For some reason, the Emperor's name carried weight. In a town that could compliment Nero on a civic column I should have expected it. Mordanticus looked as grateful as if I was signing his precious pots contract myself. 'Can you help me to arrange a meeting, Mordanticus? Do you know anything about the legate's recent movements, or even where I might find Julius Civilis himself?'

The potter shook his head, but promised to make enquiries. He still looked dazed. We left him to break the news of what had happened to his two colleagues. I did not envy him. He had told me there were young families involved.

XXXIII

I took Helena Justina to see the Jupiter Column so that I could talk to her in privacy. At least, that was my excuse.

We walked solemnly round, pretending to admire the four-sided obelisk which had been set up by two ingratiating financiers on behalf of the local community. It was a decent enough monument, if you like salutations to Nero. It pictured the usual plaques of Olympian deities: Romulus and Remus showing that having a peculiar mother need not hold a man back; Hercules doing his demigodly stuff with his usual hairy panache; and Castor and Pollux watering their horses, one each side of the column as if they were not on speaking terms. Up aloft stood a huge bronze of Jupiter Best and Greatest, all beard and big sandals, and wielding an extremely snappy thunderbolt that would be a hit at any fashionable soirée. The location of this edifice was too public for me to grab Helena in a clinch, though she knew that had been in my mind. I thought she looked disappointed. Since it was at least three hours since I had last touched her, I was too.

'I'll have to row you down the river with a picnic,' I murmured.

'Juno! Is that safe?'

'All right, I admit Germany isn't the place to come to at the moment if you fancy a quiet autumn cruise.'

'But *you* are going downriver, aren't you?' She asked it in an intensely level voice, which I recognised as anxiety.

'Looks as if I shall have to, my love.' She was upset. I hated that.

I had put Helena in a quandary. She never tried to dissuade me from work. For one thing, she was keen for me to earn enough money to buy myself into the middle rank so that we could be married without a scandal. To achieve that I needed four hundred thousand sesterces – an outrageous sum for a dusty lad from the Aventine. The kind of cash I could earn only by doing something illegal (which, of course, I could *never* contemplate) or something dangerous.

'Anyway,' she said brightly, 'you came out here on political business, but you seem to have stumbled into a straightforward ceramics war.'

'It looks like that.'

Helena laughed. 'When you agree so meekly I usually discover you mean the opposite.'

'True. I think the ceramics troubles are an incidental problem.' However, if I could help out the potters while achieving my own ends, I would. 'These potters have found themselves facing the usual administrative mess. The tendering process has been bungled by an idiot who is paid enough by the state to know better. It goes on everywhere. To have Florius Gracilis involved in that, and also poking his nose into what Vespasian sent me out here to negotiate with Civilis, is just my hard luck.'

But the last thing I wanted if I was going into a danger area was some senatorial buffoon who had shown himself unfit to handle even a routine kitchenware contract travelling the same route. Especially if, as now seemed likely, he reached the trouble spot ahead of me and started blundering about, making tribal sensitivities far worse.

'Do you ever have good luck, Marcus?'

'Only the day I met you.'

She ignored that. 'You were talking about Civilis. How do you intend to find him?'

'Something will turn up.'

'And what about the priestess?'

'Veleda?' I grinned. 'Justinus told you that one too, eh?'

'Sounds like another widow in Veii story,' Helena grumbled sarcastically.

'That's all right, then; I can handle her.'

Helena Justina called me a philandering gigolo; I told her she was a cynical witch with no concept of trust or loyalty; she thwacked me with the heavy end of her beaded stole; I trapped her against the column's plinth and kissed her until I had her more or less subdued and myself highly excited.

'I will not ask,' she said when I sadly released her before our sophisticated Roman behaviour caused a public outcry, 'what your plans are for discovering the fate of the legate from Vetera. I know he disappeared somewhere on the far side of the river.'

'He was being forwarded to Veleda as a goodwill gift.'

Helena shuddered. 'So that definitely means you have to journey into Germania Libera?'

'I won't go if you don't want me to.'

156

Her serious expression became even more intense. 'Don't say that – don't ever say it – unless you really mean it, Marcus.'

I always had to be straight with Helena. 'All right, I'll promise I won't go if I can solve the puzzle in any other way.'

'Oh you'll go,' she answered. 'You'll go, and you'll solve it and that ought to provide some comfort for the poor man's family at least. It's impossible, therefore, for me even to try to veto your trip.'

I could not have cared less for the feelings of the family of Munius Lupercus, who had been a rich senator in a career posting and who was probably as objectionable as the rest of that type. But when Helena spoke with such certainty I could never dispute the issue, so I kissed her again and took her home instead.

At the fort we found my niece Augustinilla terrorising the sentries at the Praetorian Gate. Luckily, they were so relieved to be rescued that they let me carry her off under one arm while she screamed abuse at all of us.

XXXIV

The rest of the day passed quietly. Justinus had found out about his broken urn, and his reaction was to disappear from the house. He was deeply annoyed, but too polite to say so.

'That brother of yours is going to spend his life being put upon.'

'I thought he was making his feelings clearly felt!' Helena was the same type, another vanisher when upset.

Before dinner I made Augustinilla go up to the tribune and apologise. Since no one had ever made her apologise for anything before, she went through it with a fresh pathos that worked on him in the same way as the distressed puppy he had rescued. While she gazed at him with adoring eyes, his protective urge rose. It was Augustinilla's first experience of a rich young man in an impressive uniform; I could already see her mother coming out in her.

Schoolgirl passions apart, I reckoned Camillus Justinus, with his quiet looks and reserved manner, could wreak more havoc than he knew. Women like someone deep. Someone sensitive. (Someone who looks as if he will pay large bills without arguing.) Justinus gave the impression he needed a nice girl with a generous attitude to bring him out of himself. Back in Rome, if we were to put those thoughtful brown eyes around a few dinner parties, he might find nice girls – and equally helpful older women – bringing him out of himself three times every week.

At Moguntiacum he only had to avoid an eight-year-old who had convinced herself he looked like a young Apollo. So far, Augustinilla was too much in awe of his status to start writing his name on walls. By the time she plucked up courage to leave lovelorn notes beside his breakfast bowl, the European winter would have frozen all the ink and spared him that.

The next day began with two messages: the legate's mistress said her servants thought Gracilis had been frequenting the company of potters. And the potter was telling me there was a mistress in the case.

'This is all pleasingly circular!' I murmured to myself.

I assumed the mistress was telling me about the potters at Moguntiacum. The potter, however, meant a *different* mistress – his message stated that. I sent Julia Fortunata a politely grateful letter to say I would follow up her information when I could. Mordanticus seemed the best bet for a visit.

Before I went I looked out the centurion Helvetius, whom I had last seen near Cavillonum. He was easy to locate, bawling orders wearily as he tried to drill the ham-fisted, bandy-legged, splay-footed, pigeon-brained band of ugly-mushed recruits whom I had seen him marching through Gaul. (His own descriptions.) It was his task to teach these ideal specimens how to run, ride, swim, vault, wrestle, fence, throw javelins, cut turves, build walls, plant palisades, aim catapults, form a testudo, love Rome, hate dishonour, and recognise the enemy: 'Blue skin, red hair, checked trousers, lots of noise, and they're the ones hurling missiles at your heads!' He had to weed out the lads who had cheated on the eye test and relocate them as hospital orderlies. He had to discover who couldn't count, or write, or understand Latin, then either teach them or send them home. He had to nurse them all through crying for their girlfriends, or their mothers, or their ship (the First Adiutrix was still taking navy cast-offs) or their favourite goat (second sons from farms had always formed the backbone of the legions). He had to keep them sober and keep them from deserting; he had to teach them table manners and help them write their wills. So far he had just managed to harry them into forming straight lines in three ranks.

Helvetius gladly abandoned this depressing schedule and took time to talk to me.

'Didius Falco.'

'I remember you.'

'Thanks! I like to believe I have an impressive personality.' It could only have been our first meeting at the side of the ditch that he recalled so piquantly. We spent a few moments recollecting it. 'That's why I want to see you.'

'I guessed as much!'

He was one of the impassive breed. Long years of service had taught him to expect the worst, and that nothing was ever worth getting excited about. He had very dark brown eyes, as if his origin was southern, and a face like an ostler's old rubbing-down cloth: deeply creased, stiff with use, and worn to a shine. His air of disil lusionment was as weathered as his features. He looked a sound, utterly reliable officer.

I told him that the tribune Camillus had agreed he could be excused normal duties for a spot of goodwill effort in the local community. Helvetius was happy to visit the potter, so I took him out to the factory area with me.

It was another chilly morning, though a pallid sun was trying to burn away the mist. The changing season added to my sense of urgency. I explained to Helvetius that I would probably need to go across the river soon, and that I wanted to get the journey over before winter set in. The last thing I needed to face was being stuck in barbarian territory when the European snows came down.

'Bad enough at any time,' he said grimly.

'Have you done it?'

He didn't answer immediately. 'Only when some daft tribune fancied a boar-hunt in a more exciting locality.' Not Camillus Justinus, presumably. No one would call *him* daft.

'Naturally a young gent in senatorial stripes doesn't want to risk the *real* excitement of leaving his escort behind . . . Did you meet any trouble over there?'

'No, but you have the distinct feeling that you're lucky to reach home again without running into some liveliness.'

'Some of us have a suspicion the Fourteenth's legate may have gone across.'

'Gracilis? Whatever for?'

'Searching for Civilis – or Veleda, possibly.'

Again there was a slight silence. 'Didn't think he was the type.'

'What type would you call him, then?' I asked.

Helvetius, who was a true centurion, only chuckled into his beard, which was a richly curling military one. 'He's a legate, Falco. The same horrible type as them all.'

Just before we reached the potteries our conversation returned warily to the two dead men. Helvetius asked my particular interest. I described how I had been drawn in by seeing the quarrel at Lugdunum. He smiled slightly.

I wondered why he was curious. His face set, with a stillness that implied his mind was somewhere else – somewhere else by a long way. After yet another pause, however, just when I thought he had no comment, he suddenly spoke: 'I said nothing when we came across the bodies, because I didn't know you, Falco. But I had seen the men before, alive, myself.'

'Where was that?'

'Same as you: Lugdunum.'

'Were you there on official business?'

'Should have been. The army can be efficient! Our commander had a brainstorm and made my one journey serve two – well, three – purposes: home leave, recruiting manpower, and then a site visit to check out the ceramics tenderers. That was the plan, anyway.'

'So what happened?' I could guess.

'I turned up, but taking notes about suppliers was a waste of time. His Excellency Gracilis had been there before me and had swept up the whole business himself on behalf of all the legions in Upper and Lower Germany.'

'Fancy!' I marvelled. 'Some responsibility!'

'Some haul, if he was on the take!' Helvetius must have drawn his own conclusions.

'Careful, centurion! And the two local potters?'

'Like you, I saw them there having a right barney.'

'In a crowd?'

'No, just with a sneering beanpole and a couple of hangers-on. I spotted Lanky later as well.'

'Oh?'

'On the road. The day before we found the stiffs in the ditch.'

Now that was a detail I found most interesting. I remembered the sneering Gaul, but I must have missed him while travelling. Things looked black for Florius Gracilis. I told Helvetius we would keep this to ourselves for the time being. He looked at me askance. 'Were you sent out here to compile a dossier on graft?'

It was beginning to look that way.

At the pottery I made the introductions, then left Helvetius to discuss how he had reported the deaths at Cavillonum. There hadn't been much interest from the magistrate, needless to say. Helvetius was sufficiently discreet to disguise that while speaking to the dead men's friend, but I could tell what must have happened – and not happened – from his tone.

I left them together, still talking over Bruccius and his nephew, while I roamed around yearningly looking at samianware. When Mordanticus came out he asked whether anything particular had caught my eye.

'All of it! You create a stylish platter.' This was not mere ingratiation: his pottery was fired with a satisfying colour; it had tasteful patterns, a pleasing gloss, and a good balance in the hand. 'I'd set myself up with a decent dinner service, but the problem is a distinct lack of collateral.'

'How's that? I assumed you had a rich girlfriend!' The way he spoke made the joke acceptable even to a touchy swine like me.

For once I went along with it. 'Ah, it's her father who owns the lush estates on the Alban hills. If you were him, would you let the fruits of your vintage pass into the grip of a lout like me?' Besides, I had my pride.

It was not simply the hope of possessing Helena that drove me into these mad missions for the Emperor. I had a dream of one day living without squalor. Living in my own quiet house – a house surrounded by vine-covered walkways, luxurious in space, and full of light to read by. A house where I could age an amphora of decent wine at the right temperature, then drink it philosophising with my friend Petronius Longus beside a maplewood table laid with Spanish linen – and, maybe, samian winecups, if we were tired of my chased bronzes with the hunting scenes and my gold-flecked Phoenician glass . . .

I dragged the conversation to more useful gossip. 'Thanks for your message. What's this about a woman? Julia Fortunata is going to be put out if Gracilis has been two-timing her – not to mention the rumpus he can expect from the tight-buttocked little wife!'

'Well, I don't know anything definite . . .' Mordanticus looked embarrassed. It was pleasant to witness how respectfully the provinces regarded Rome: he was almost ashamed to confess that one of our high-ranking officials had let down the Roman moral code. 'I hate to destroy the man's character – '

'No need for you to end up in court on a slander charge,' I prompted. 'Just tell me what you've found out, and I'll draw the defamatory conclusions for myself.'

'Well, one of my colleagues was once asked how Florius Gracilis could contact a woman called Claudia Sacrata.'

'Is that significant? Should I have heard of her?'

Again he looked decidedly awkward. 'She is a Ubian, from Colonia Agrippinensium.' He studied a beaker as if he had just noticed that its handle was affixed crookedly. 'Your general Petilius Cerialis was supposed to have had an intrigue with her.'

'Ah!'

I had an impression of Cerialis; so far women did not come into it. In Britain he had commanded the Ninth Hispana legion. When the Boudiccan Revolt flared, he had made a desperate dash to help but was ambushed by the tribes in a forest – meaning he must have been rushing along without proper scouts ahead of him. Petilius lost a large contingent of his men and only just escaped with a few dregs of cavalry. The remnants of the Ninth took part in the final battle against the Queen, though unlike the Fourteenth and the Twentieth they were not honoured by Nero afterwards. By all accounts, the general's more recent campaign to recapture Germany from Civilis had featured similar ill-considered incidents, from which the general himself had somehow escaped – always in time to take part in the winning engagements, and always keeping his good reputation intact.

I said with a deadpan expression, 'A Ubian temptress was not widely featured in the official accounts of his victories.' Perhaps because Petilius Cerialis wrote the accounts himself.

Mordanticus realised I was teasing, but did not quite know how to react. 'There was probably nothing in it . . .'

'I'm disappointed! But why should our own Florius Gracilis be visiting this beauty? Consoling her loneliness, now that Cerialis has popped off to Britain? I suppose he couldn't have taken her. Installing his Ubian bundle in the provincial governor's palace in Londinium would soon get back to Rome and cause a stir.' Having won his province, Petilius Cerialis would now be looking forward to a consulship. He was related to the Emperor – through *marriage* – and the Emperor was widely known to hold strictly old-fashioned views. Vespasian himself kept a long-term mistress now that he was a widower, but people seeking appointments from him dared not risk such a luxury. 'Do the Ubians have close links with the Batavians?'

Julius Mordanticus was writhing with unhappiness. 'That's difficult to answer. Some allies of Civilis punished the Ubians very heavily for their pro-Roman sympathies, but by the end some of them were battling against the Romans with him . . .'

'A right tangle! Did Claudia Sacrata know Civilis?'

'Possibly. He has relations who were living in Colonia Agrippinensium.'

'Which could explain why Gracilis has gone to see her. He knows this woman has had connections with high political circles on both sides, so she might know where Civilis can be found?'

'Perhaps.'

'Alternatively,' I suggested more facetiously, 'not content with the

163

official mistress he brought from Rome, our trusty legate Florius Gracilis is looking for an *unofficial* one – and Claudia Sacrata fits. Perhaps a liaison with Claudia Sacrata is the traditional perk for men in purple cloaks on tours of duty in Germany? Perhaps her address is handed on with their initial briefing reports. Which only leaves one question. Mordanticus: since I'm just a low weevil, who will give Claudia Sacrata's address to *me*?'

The potter was not prepared to comment on her status; but he told me where to find the woman.

That only left one other question: how could I explain to Helena Justina that I was disappearing to visit a general's courtesan?

PART FOUR:
A TRIP DOWN THE RHENUS

FROM UPPER GERMANY TO VETERA
October-November, AD 71

'Their commander . . . was saved by a mistake on the part of the enemy, who made haste to tow away the flagship, thinking that the commander was aboard. Cerialis in fact spent the night elsewhere (according to general belief at the time, because of an intrigue with a Ubian woman called Claudia Sacrata).'

Tacitus, *Histories*

XXXV

It caused less strain than I feared. That was because Helena decreed Colonia Agrippinensium to be a place she was dying to see. I went along with it, for reasons of my own.

My hope of some peace with Helena was thwarted. First her brother insisted that we take Augustinilla. Apparently he was reluctant to be left on his own at the fort with a lovesick little maid.

Then Xanthus eagerly joined the excursion. He was still suffering a serious reaction from having killed the soldier. He said it had made him think seriously about life. He liked Germany, and wanted to settle there – he could see plenty of scope for his hairdressing skills. Moguntiacum was too military, however, so he wanted to look for another town which might offer a more refined welcome to an ambitious former imperial slave. I told him flatly he could not come with me beyond Colonia, but he said that suited him.

We had the tribune's dog, too. It had bitten an armourer, so had to be removed from the fort fast.

So much for a gentle river cruise alone with my girl.

Despite the entourage, shipping north on an official fleet vessel was a joy: past jutting crags and green pastures, small quays and local moorings, outcrops of rocks and rapids, and slanting upland terraces where the new wine industry was establishing its vineyards for light, pleasant wines, some of which we tasted as we went. We dreamed on deck, watching the ducks floating downstream among occasional spars of driftwood, then heaving themselves out of the water to fly back and start again. Low barges, laden with every conceivable item, sailed down in twos or threes, then were rowed or dragged back the other way. It seemed a satisfying life. What was more, the merchants who plied their trade along this waterway were visibly affluent. With Helena beside me, I could have stayed for ever, becoming a happy river bum and never going home.

'What's in your mighty baggage pack?' Helena demanded.

167

'Scrolls to read.'

'Poetry?'

'History.'

'As in Thucydides?'

'As in Great Cock-ups of Modern Times.'

Helena glanced round to see if Augustinilla was in earshot of this irreverence, but saw my niece was too busy trying to find ways of falling off the boat. She laughed. 'Why the interest?'

'Research for my various projects here. An archivist in Rome copied out some despatches about the rebellion for me.'

Now that Helena knew what I was carrying downriver, there was no point in hiding it. I excavated the basket, and was soon absorbed in Rome's sorry exploits while trying to dislodge Civilis. The more I read about the campaign, the more I cringed.

All too soon we had surged past the conjunction with the River Mosella at Castrum ad Confluentes, experienced Bingium and Bonna (both still heavily scarred and burnt, but with new ridge-poles rising), and reached our goal.

Colonia Claudia Ara Agrippinensium tried hard to live up to its overpowering titles. Founded by Agrippa (as Ara Ubiorum), it was renamed after herself by his daughter, the forceful wife of Germanicus whose domineering reputation still had the power to make brave men feel queasy. It was the officially sanctioned shrine of the Ubii and the provincial capital of Lower Germany. It also boasted the main Roman tollpost on the river and the headquarters of Rome's Rhenus fleet, guarded by a small fort.

A well-laid out, opulent provincial city served by a military-built aqueduct and home to a large colony of retired veteran soldiers, Colonia's close links with Rome had ensured there were difficult decisions during the rebellion. At first the citizens had stayed loyal to the Empire, refusing to join Civilis and placing his son under arrest – though in 'honourable' custody, in case matters swung. Only when the situation became desperate were these cautious worthies forced to heed the call from their fellow-tribesmen to acknowledge their German heritage, and even then their alliance with the freedom fighters had its equivocal aspects. They managed to negotiate their own terms with Civilis and Veleda, since by then they were holding more of the Batavian's relations under house arrest, and they were wealthy enough to send the forest priestess the kind of gifts that pacify. Careful juggling helped the town to survive without being sacked by either side. Then, as soon as Petilius Cerialis began to make headway,

168

the good folk hereabouts appealed to him for rescue and allied themselves with Rome again.

They knew how to run their municipal affairs with grace. I felt that it was a safe place to bring Helena.

We arrived fairly early in the day. I dumped my party in a lodging-house near the prefecture, telling Xanthus he was the man in charge. Helena would soon disabuse him.

Refreshed by the river trip, I went out to make enquiries about Claudia Sacrata. I had promised Helena not to dally, but the door I chose to knock on turned out to belong to the general's ladyfriend. For her servant, a male Roman face was enough of a credential, so although I merely asked for an appointment, he whisked me in to see her straight away.

This was a modest town house. Its provincial decorator had tried hard, but had been stuck with painting frescos of what he knew. Jason discovered the Golden Fleece beneath a holly-bush in a thunderstorm. Battle scenes rolled darkly below a frieze that only came to life when crossed by a skein of Rhineland wild geese. Venus, in the local Ubian costume of high-necked dress and wimple, was wooed by Mars in a Celtic felt coat. She looked like a market-trader, and he seemed a shy, rather paunchy chap.

The servant took me to a reception room. I was met by bright colours and gigantic couches with hugely padded cushions where a tired man could flop and forget his troubles. The reds were too earthy, the stripes too broad, the tassels far too fat. The total effect was reassuringly vulgar. The men who came here relied on strong-minded wives for taste, and they probably never noticed interior-design effects. They required somewhere clean and comfortable pervaded by scents of beeswax polish and gently stewing broth, somewhere which held basic recollections of their childhoods, in Italy. It was the kind of house where the bread would be served in roughly chopped hunks that tasted like ambrosia infused with hazelnuts. The music would be dreadful, but people would be laughing and talking so loudly they would not care . . .

I found Claudia Sacrata seated in a long chair, as if she was expecting visitors. She was no ravishing seductress, but a dumpy, middle-aged woman whose bosom was trussed so firmly it might have acted as a serving tray. Her grooming was careful. She wore a Roman dress in oatmeal and ochre, with fastidiously folded pleats on her shoulders where her stole was pinned with a large Indian ruby brooch that blazed *Present from a Man!* In appearance she reminded me of a slightly old-fashioned, good-hearted aunt tricked out to make a show in front of the neighbours at a Floralia parade.

'Come in, dear. What can I do for you?' The question could have been simple politeness . . . or a commercial bid.

I played everything straight. 'My name is Marcus Didius Falco; I am a government agent. I should be grateful if you would answer a few questions.'

'Certainly.' Of course, it didn't guarantee she would answer them truthfully.

'Thank you. I hope you don't mind if I start with you? You are Claudia Sacrata, and you keep a welcoming house. Do you live with your mother?' We both understood this euphemistic phrase.

'My sister,' she corrected. It was the same flimsy veil of respectability, though I noticed no chaperone ever appeared at our interview.

I plunged straight in: 'I believe you once shared the confidence of His Excellency Cerialis?'

'That's right, dear.' She was the type who liked to catch people out by admitting the unthinkable. Her shrewd eyes watched me while she tried to deduce what I wanted.

'I need to acquire some sensitive information, and it's difficult finding people I can trust.'

'Did my general send you?'

'No. This is nothing to do with him.'

The atmosphere changed. She knew I was investigating someone; if it had been His Excellency, she had intended to slap me down. Now she saw her most notable client was in the clear; her tone became proprietary. 'I don't mind talking about Cerialis.' She gestured me to a couch. 'Make yourself more at home . . .' Home was never like this.

She rang a bell for a servant, a nippy lad who seemed to have answered quite a few bells in his time. After surveying me coyly, she gushed, 'A hot-spiced-wine man, I should say!' Outside my own home I hate the stuff. To encourage good relations, I agreed to be a man who drank hot spiced wine.

It was a rich liquor, served in magnificent cups, with the spices rather overdone. A consoling warmth flooded my stomach, then seeped into my nervous system making me feel happy and safe, even when Claudia Sacrata cooed 'Tell me all about it!', which was supposed to be my line.

'No, you tell me,' I smiled, implying that women who knew what they were doing had tried to undermine me before. 'We were discussing Petilius Cerialis.'

'A very pleasant gentleman.'

'Bit of a reputation as a hothead?'

'In what way?' she simpered.

'The military way, for instance.'

'Why do you think that?'

This was a silly dance. However, I deduced that if I wanted information, talking about her precious Cerialis was the price I had to pay. 'I've been reading about his battle at Augusta Treverorum, for one thing.' I was sipping my hefty winecup as demurely as I could. If Cerialis wore his epaulettes in the usual style, he had bored everybody silly with the story of his big fight.

Claudia Sacrata posed and considered. 'People did say at the time that he made mistakes.'

'Well, you can look at it two ways,' I conceded, playing the friendly type. There was, in fact, only one way *I* could look at it. Petilius Cerialis had stupidly allowed his opponents to concentrate in large numbers while he had been awaiting reinforcements. That had been dangerous enough. His famous engagement was a shambles, too. Cerialis had built his camp on the opposite bank of the river from the town. The enemy arrived very early in the morning, crept up from several directions, and burst into the camp, throwing all into confusion.

'I understood,' Claudia defended him with solid loyalty, 'that it was only the general's brave action that saved the situation.' So that was his story.

'Undoubtedly.' My work demands a shameless ability to lie. 'Cerialis rushed from his bed without body armour, to discover that his camp was in turmoil, his cavalry were fleeing, and the bridgehead had been taken. He grabbed the fugitives, turned them round, retook the bridge with great personal courage, then forced his way into the Roman camp and rallied his men. He salvaged everything and finished the day by destroying the enemy's headquarters instead of losing his own.'

Claudia Sacrata wagged her finger. 'So why are you sceptical?'

Because the other assessment was that our troops had been led pathetically; the enemy should never have been able to get so close undetected, the camp had been inadequately guarded, the sentries were asleep, and their commander had absented himself. Only the fact that the tribesmen had been intent on grabbing plunder had averted complete disaster from our dashing general.

I restrained my bitterness. 'Why was the general not sleeping in the camp that night?'

The lady responded calmly. 'That I can't say.'

'Did you know him at that point?'

'I met him later.' So even before their intrigue started, he had preferred the comforts of a private house.

'May I ask how your friendship came about?'

'Oh, he visited Colonia Agrippinensium.'

'Romantic story?' I grinned.

'Real life, dear.' I guessed she regarded selling sexual activity as no different from selling eggs.

'Tell me?'

'Why not? The general came to thank me for my part in undermining the enemy.'

'What had you done?' I imagined some brothel intrigue.

'Our city was looking for a way to re-establish its ties with Rome. The town councillors offered to hand over the wife and sister of Civilis, plus the daughter of one of the other chiefs, who had been kept here as securities. Then we tried something more useful. Civilis, still confident, was placing his hopes in his best forces, warriors from among the Chauci and Frisii, encamped not far from here. The men of our town invited them to a feast and plied them with lavish food and drink. Once they were all completely stupefied, they locked the doors and set fire to the hall.'

I tried not to display too much shock. 'A friendly Germanic custom?'

'It's not unknown.' The most chilling part was her matter-of-fact tone.

'So when Civilis learned that his crack troops had been burned alive, he fled north, and Petilius Cerialis rode gratefully into Colonia . . . But what was your part, Claudia?'

'I provided the food and drink for the feast.'

I put down my winecup.

'Claudia Sacrata, far be it from me to pry, but can you tell me something – ' This oddly comfortable yet insensitive woman was upsetting me. I studiously changed the subject. 'What's the true story about losing the general's flagship?'

She smiled and said nothing.

It had been another stupid incident. I told her what I already knew

172

from my research. After an unsuccessful period of campaigning in northern Europe, where Civilis and the Batavians had engaged him in guerilla warfare around the marshes of their homeland and had seemed set to fend off Rome indefinitely, Petilius Cerialis had taken a breather (his favourite kind of action) and gone to inspect some new winter quarters at Novaesium and Bonna, intending to return north with a much-needed naval flotilla. Yet again discipline was poor; yet again his pickets were careless. One dark night, the Germans crept in, slashed the guy ropes, and wreaked havoc while our men were fumbling under their collapsed tents and running about the camp half dressed and terrified. They had no one to rally them, because, of course, yet again Cerialis had slipped off elsewhere.

'Then the enemy towed off the flagship, Julius Civilis believing the general to be aboard.'

'His mistake!' Claudia agreed purringly.

'Sleeping out of camp again?' I tried not to sound critical.

'Evidently.'

'With you, as people said?' I was having great trouble imagining this.

'You really can't expect me to answer that.'

'I see.' With her.

'You said your enquiries had nothing to do with Petilius, so why all these questions about past events?' I was pushing matters further than she liked now.

'I'm a sucker for lively background.' I was hoping my interest in Petilius might appear to threaten him, so that she would try to deflect me with the information I really wanted. But she was tougher than she seemed. Any impression of foolishness hid a shrewd business sense. 'What happened to the flagship in the end?'

'At daybreak the rebels all sailed away in the Roman ships. They towed the flagship into their own territory as a present for their priestess.'

'Veleda!' I let out a low whistle. 'So if Cerialis was with you that night, you saved his life.'

'Yes,' she agreed proudly.

'If he had been aboard – ' As he should have been. ' – his fate would have been gruesome. The last Roman officer the rebels sent to Veleda has never been heard of since.'

'Terrible!' she agreed, with conventional sympathy.

'That's my mission,' I told her. 'He was a legionary legate. I have to find out for the Emperor and his family what unkind fate befell him. I doubt you would ever have met this one; he was stationed at Vetera, a long distance from here – '

'Munius Lupercus?' She sounded surprised. 'Oh you're wrong there, dear,' declared the imperturbable Claudia. 'I knew Munius *very* well.'

XXXVI

I sighed inwardly, I tried to shift position on the cushions beneath me, but they gripped me with embarrassing suction. When Claudia Sacrata told a man to make himself comfortable, she didn't intend him to prise himself free without the aid of a building-yard fulcrum.

I had brought myself to the home of a woman who knew everyone. Names were dropped here like water drips around a fountain. Gossip was the common language. I was sitting, on an aching bottom, at the centre of a social spider's web which might be anchored to any point in Europe.

'You knew Lupercus?' I croaked. I hate to be repetitive, but I was in no condition for more sinuous oratory.

'Such a nice man. Very genuine. Very generous.'

'I'm sure! You have a wide circle of acquaintances.'

'Oh yes. Most of the boys from Rome pass through here at some time. I am famous,' stated Claudia complacently, 'for my hospitality.'

That was one word for it.

'A woman of influence!' I threw my next dice with a casual air. 'How are you on the incumbent of the legio Fourteenth Gemina?'

She seemed equal to anything. 'Would that be Priscus? Or the new one, Gracilis?' Apparently both had hung up their armour on her cloak-peg.

'The new man.'

'I've met him once or twice.'

'Nice man?' I hazarded before I could stop myself.

'Oh very!' She took it at face value, luckily. Her sense of humour – assuming she had one – would be jolly and obvious, rather than my twisted kind.

'Has Gracilis visited you recently?'

Whatever else he indulged in here – and it was best not to speculate – Gracilis must have been asking the same questions as me. She answered with a knowing wink I could hardly tolerate: 'I believe he did!'

'I expect he had a good explanation for turning up here?'

She laughed. It sounded unattractive and I noticed she had several teeth missing. 'Something about a hunting trip . . .'

'That old line!'

'Oh he must have meant it, dear – a group of Gauls were taking him.'

Gauls? I already had my hands full with the German interest. This new complication was more than I liked while my brain was infused with aromatic wine.

'What was he after?' Apart from pipping me in the search for Civilis and Veleda.

'Wild boar, I believe.'

I tried a different tack. 'People at Moguntiacum are worried about what's happened to his bedchamber slave. Has Rusticus gone along on this Gallic safari to keep his master well groomed behind the spear?'

'There was no one like that with him.'

I decided not to ask any more about the Fourteenth's infernal legate. I would only find myself trying to track down some pitiful runaway slave who might simply have seen his master's absence from home as a chance to make a break for it.

I gave in, smiling. Claudia was pleased to see she had defeated me. So pleased that she condescended to add, 'The Gauls were paying for *everything*.'

I had to know. 'I hate to be pedantic, but you do mean they were treating Florius Gracilis to his visit here to you?'

She assented without speaking.

I had him now. If the Fourteenth Gemina's legate was being trailed around on an extended sweetener of this kind, Vespasian would swipe his name off the list of officials before anyone could blink.

'What sort of Gauls were they?'

'Potters,' said Claudia.

I wondered why she had chosen to inform on this client in particular. Germanic rivalry with Gaul? Annoyance at the blatant way her services had been offered for bribery? I decided it was the commercial dishonesty. Claudia being a businesswoman herself, she would naturally hate fraud.

'I won't embarrass you by prying further. Look, we were talking about Munius Lupercus. The war was a long time ago, and I'm struggling to find leads. I'm even faced with the prospect of going across the Rhenus to follow his route as a captive. Does your useful

176

network of contacts extend to the other riverbank? You won't have met the prophetess – '

I should have known better. 'Veleda?' cried Claudia Sacrata. 'Oh I know her!'

A faint mood of exasperation coloured my tone: 'I thought she was incommunicado? I heard she lived above the treetops, and that even the ambassadors who went from Colonia to negotiate terms with her had to send messages via the men in her family.'

'That's right, dear.'

A dreadful thought struck me. 'Did you take part in the Colonia embassy?'

'Of course,' murmured Claudia. 'This is not Rome, Marcus Didius.' That was certainly true. German women obviously liked to be at the front of things. It was a terrifying concept to a traditional Roman boy. My upbringing was outraged – yet fascinated too. 'I have standing in Colonia, Marcus Didius. I am well known here.'

I could guess what ensured her prominence – the universal status badge: 'You are a wealthy woman?'

'My friends have been kind to me.' So she had creamed the tops off some handsome Forum bank accounts. 'I helped choose the presents for Veleda; I provided some of them. Then I fancied seeing foreign parts, so I travelled with the ambassadors.' She was as bad as Xanthus. The world must be full of intrepid idiots trying to catch some fatal strain of alien marsh fever.

'Let me guess . . .' I was grinning despite myself. 'The men might have had to follow the rules that preserve Veleda's sanctity; *you*, however, somehow wangled a woman-to-woman chat? I suppose the venerated wench has to pop down from the tower some time – to wash her face, let's say?' This arch description seemed to fit the discreet atmosphere of Claudia's house, where Jupiter, the guardian of strangers, must have his work cut out protecting people desperate to find a polite phrase for asking their way to the latrine.

'I did my best for her.' Claudia Sacrata looked sad. 'You can imagine the life the poor girl leads. No conversation; no society. The menfolk who guard her are a feeble lot. She was badly in need of a chin-wag, I can tell you. And before you say anything dear, I made a point of asking about Lupercus. I never forget my boys if I find a chance to do one of them a good turn.'

That angered me. 'A man's death in foreign territory is no subject for gossip! Was Lupercus someone you giggled over in the Bructian groves? Did she tell you what she'd done with him?'

'No,' replied Claudia crisply, as if I had impugned all womanhood.

'Not fit for civilised ears? What did she do – hang his head up for a lantern, sprinkle his blood on her private altar and stick his balls among the mistletoe?' Rome, horrified for once by practices even more barbaric than we could devise ourselves, had outlawed those rites in Gaul and Britain. But that gave no protection to anyone trapped outside our frontiers.

'She had not seen the man,' replied Claudia.

'He never reached the tower?'

'Something happened on the way.' *Something worse than what would have happened had he arrived?*

'What was it?'

'Veleda couldn't say.'

'She must have been lying.'

'Veleda had no reason to do that, dear.'

'Evidently a nice girl!' This time I allowed my irony to grate ferociously.

Claudia was looking at me with her mouth turned down. When she spoke again, there was a hint of complaint: 'I've given you a great deal of my time, Marcus Didius.'

'I appreciate that. I'm finishing now. Just answer this: have you ever been in contact with Julius Civilis?'

'We met socially in the old days.'

'Where is he now?'

'Sorry, dear. I thought he went back to The Island?'

For the first time, her answer sounded disingenuous. I decided she knew something. I also realised that squeezing Claudia Sacrata once she had clammed up was too daunting for me. She looked like a loose ball of duck down, but her will was formidable. I had also run up against an unshakeable tribal clannishness.

It was hopeless, but I flogged on anyway. 'Civilis has disappeared from The Island. He could well have made his way south again, hoping to re-establish his old power base. I heard he was back among the Ubii and Treveri,' I started factually, 'and I feel it may be true. His family lived in Colonia.'

'That was when Civilis was attached to the Roman forts.'

'Maybe, but he knows this area. Any suggestions where I can make enquiries?'

'Sorry,' she repeated. I was one Roman who must have ceased to be a nice boy.

We were closing the interview. Claudia's good nature reasserted itself as she asked again if there was anything she could do for me. I told her I had a girlfriend waiting who believed I had just stepped out of doors for a basket of bread rolls.

'She'll be anxious!' Claudia reproved me prudishly. She provided comfort for married men away from home, but wrecking relationships on her doorstep was a proposition that deeply offended her. 'You must hurry back at once.' She led me to the door herself – a formal courtesy of the house. No doubt when she was letting out a general, she liked her neighbours to spot the purple. They would be less impressed by today's cheap visitor.

'So how do I find Veleda?' I asked. 'All I know is she lives among the Bructeri. They're a far-flung tribe.'

'I'm hopeless at geography. When I went we travelled by river.' She meant the River Lupia.

'And she lived in the forest?' I already knew, but facing it made me freeze. Veleda lived in the area all Rome hated to contemplate, where Roman hopes of controlling the eastern tribes had been obliterated so hideously. 'The Teutoburger forest? I wish it was anywhere but there!'

'You're thinking of Varus?' For a mad moment I thought she was about to tell me that Quinctilius Varus and all his three lost legions had been her boys. She was mature, but not *that* cheesy. 'The free Germans still boast about Arminius.' They would be doing that for a long time. Arminius was the chieftain who had destroyed Varus; who had liberated Germany from Roman control; and whom Civilis was now openly trying to emulate. 'Be careful, Marcus Didius.'

Claudia Sacrata spoke as if I needed a trepanning operation – a hole drilled in my head to relieve the pressure on my brain.

XXXVII

'You were out a long time,' grumbled Helena. I told her why. It seemed best, in case one of Claudia Sacrata's wide circle in Colonia later let slip the information. Helena decided I had vanished intentionally. 'And have you been drinking?'

'Had to be sociable. I declined the nibbles she usually serves to her Roman boys.'

'How restrained! You're not the salon type – did being sociable work?'

'I heard some lurid gossip. She confirmed that Florius Gracilis is running one step ahead of me in searching for the rebel leaders. He's also deep into selling favours, and disguising it as an autumn hunting trip. The only useful fact I suspect she knows – where I could look for Civilis – was the one thing she deliberately held back.'

'What happened to your persuasiveness?'

'Sweetheart, I have nothing to offer a woman who is used to being coerced by men with top-level public salaries.'

'You're slipping then!' said Helena, more sharply than usual. 'By the way, I fetched the bread myself. I realised you'd gone off somewhere working, and I thought you might forget.' She gave me a consoling wholegrain roll. I ate it gloomily. The effect on Claudia Sacrata's spiced wine was negligible. I still felt drunk, in the dire way that afflicts you when you are also in disgrace. 'Marcus, I've hired a Ubian waiting-woman to help me when you have to go away. She's a widow – the troubles, you know. She had a daughter the same age as Augustinilla. I'm hoping a little friend who has been brought up more strictly might be a good influence.'

I was not ready to think about going away. 'Good idea. I'll pay.'

'Can you afford it?'

'Yes.' She gave me one of her looks. She knew I meant no.

As if to confirm her information two small heads came round the door just then and stared at me. They were as plain-faced as each other, a well-browned bun with eyes like burnt raisins, and a round

180

dollop of pale unleavened dough. They both looked like trouble. The one with the flaxen pigtails demanded of the dark one with the topknot, 'Is that him?' She had a faint lisp, a German accent, and about six times the intelligence of my niece.

'Either get out,' I growled, 'or come in properly.'

They came in, and stood half a stride away, jostling shoulders and giggling. I felt like a hippopotamus in a seedy menagerie – the one with the reputation for making unpredictable rushes at the bars.

'Are you the uncle who is an enquirer?'

'No, I'm the ogre who eats children. Who are you?'

'My name is Arminia.' I was not in the mood for infants who had been named after heroic enemies of Rome. Arminia and Augustinilla were still egging one another on to see if they could make me charge out of my cage. 'What are you enquiring about in Colonia, please?'

'State secret.' They both went off into shrieks.

'Don't listen to him,' decreed Augustinilla. 'My mother says he couldn't find his own belly button. Everyone in Rome knows Uncle Marcus is a *complete* fake.'

Looking highly superior they stalked off hand in hand.

'I see they've palled up well,' I commented to Helena. 'Clearly there are no ethic barriers between horrid little girls. So, we now have not one uncontrollable schoolgirl underfoot, but two.'

'Oh Marcus, don't be such a pessimist.'

Things continued to deteriorate. Helena's brother Justinus arrived at our lodging-house. He would have been a welcome visitor, but he came about a week too soon. He was greeted madly by his little dog, who then ran in and peed on my boot.

Before leaving Justinus at the fort, we had arranged for him to follow us to Colonia, bringing with him the pedlar Dubnus, whom I wanted to use as a guide among the Bructeri. He was only supposed to follow after trying to persuade his legate to release some troops to come across the river with me. Arranging the escort had been expected to delay him. I was startled, therefore, when he burst in on our first evening.

'What's this? Your ship must have rowed the whole distance at double stroke to bring you here so soon! Tribune, I hate surprises. They rarely mean good news.'

Justinus looked sheepish. 'A letter came for Helena. I thought I ought to bring it here as soon as possible.' He handed it over. Both she and I recognised the Palace parchment and seal. Justinus evidently expected her to break the wax eagerly, but she held it on her knee and looked morose. A similar expression was probably afflicting me. 'It caused quite a stir at the fort,' he protested, when he saw her ignoring it.

'Really?' enquired Helena, with her own brand of chilling disdain. 'I keep my correspondence private normally.'

'It's from Titus Caesar!'

'I can see that.'

She was putting on her stubborn face. In kindness to her brother I said, 'Helena has been advising him about a problem with his aged aunt.' She shot me a look that would have skinned a weasel.

'Ah . . .' Justinus could detect an atmosphere. He had the tact to believe my bitter joke. 'I'd better be off now, Marcus Didius. I need a bathe. We can talk properly another time. I'm staying at the Rhenus fleet fort.'

'Did you manage to get me an escort?'

'You've been assigned a centurion and twenty men. Rather inexperienced, I'm afraid, but it was the best I could do. I told my legate you were official, in fact I invited him to meet you, but if you're undercover for the Palace he prefers to stand aloof and let you get on with it.'

I preferred to stand aloof from this mission myself. 'Old-fashioned, eh?'

'Forays across into the east are not encouraged nowadays.' He meant Rome was in enough trouble in the territory it held, without stirring up the eastern tribes.

'Suits me. I hate formalities. Thank him. I'm grateful for any support. Did you bring the pedlar too?'

'Yes. I warn you, though, he's protesting volubly.'

'Don't worry. I came across Gaul with a chattering barber. I can manage anything after that.'

Justinus kissed his sister and disappeared with alacrity.

We sat apart in silence. In the circumstances I thought it was her turn to speak. Helena generally ignored whatever I thought.

After a moment I muttered, 'I'd kiss you too, but it seems inappropriate with a letter from the Emperor's son lying in your lap.' She made no answer. I wished she would jump up and burn the thing. I remonstrated steadily: 'Helena, you had better open that document.' Refusing would make the tension far worse, so she slowly broke the seal. 'Shall I go out while you read it?'

'No.'

She was a fast reader. Besides, for a love letter it was foolishly brief. She read with an expressionless face, then rerolled it tightly, gripping the scroll in her clenched fist.

'That was quick.'

'More like an order for new boots,' she agreed.

'He's known as a poor public speaker, but a man in his position ought to be able to prime a jobbing poet to scribble a few hexameters to salute a lady . . . I would.'

'You,' murmured Helena, so quietly it scared me witless, 'would write the hexameters yourself.'

'For you I would.'

She was very still. There was nothing I could do for her.

'It would take me a few thousand lines,' I warbled on miserably. 'You might have to wait a month or two while I polished them properly. If *I* was asking you to come home to me, I'd want to tell you everything . . .' I stopped talking. If Titus had offered her the Empire, Helena Justina would be needing to think. She was a cautious girl.

I was trying to convince myself that whatever Titus had to say, it must so far be unofficial. If he was making any serious proposition, their two fathers would be negotiating. Even among emperors – *especially* among emperors – there are ways these things have to be done.

'Don't worry.' Helena looked up abruptly. It was always the same. Whenever I had reason to be worried about her, she tried to quash it by worrying over me. 'Nothing is going to happen, I promise you.'

'Has the great man asked his question?'

'Marcus, as soon as I reply – '

'Don't,' I said.

'What?'

'Don't reply yet.'

At least if any disaster happened to me, Titus Caesar would look after her. She would never lack anything. And the Empire's gain would be immense. A Caesar who reigned in partnership with Helena Justina might work incomparable deeds. Titus knew that. So did I.

I ought to set her free. Some people might say that once I reached Germania Libera I had a real duty to vanish in the woods. In the whimsical moments when I cared about Rome, I even thought that myself.

She was strange. Instead of demanding what I meant, she rose, came across to me, and then sat in silence beside me, holding my hand. Her eyes brimmed with tears she was too stubborn to shed.

She knew, of course. I wanted her myself. Even while I was crossing the Styx in Hades, I would be squabbling with the ferryman and trying to fight my way back off the boat to return to Helena. I only wanted to safeguard her future in case I would not be there.

She knew the rest, too. Going across the river would be stupidly dangerous. History was against me. The free tribes were implacable enemies of everything Roman. And I knew from Britain how the Celts treated their enemies. If I was captured I could expect to be denied diplomatic immunity. My skull would be speared up in a niche outside a temple. What happened to the rest of me before they swiped my head off was likely to be more degrading and more painful than I could bear to contemplate. I did not ask how much Helena knew of all this, but she was well read.

When I fell for Helena Justina, I had vowed I would never expose myself to serious risk again. There had been plenty of tricky exploits in my past, most of which I would never even hint at to her. But a man grows older. He learns that other things matter. She could guess I had a horrific career behind me, but she believed that telling her I loved her meant my daredevil days were over. Nobody could blame the girl; I had made the same assumption myself.

Now I looked like one of those madmen for whom danger is an addiction. Helena's plight seemed as bleak as if she had shackled herself to a drunkard or a fornicator. She must have told herself everything would change under her influence, but now she saw it never could . . . Still, I knew I was different. This was just one last attempt to acquire a decent bounty from the Emperor, all so that I could win her.

One last throw . . . I suppose all madmen tell themselves that.

'Cheer up,' she said. Her manner was brisk. 'Come along, Marcus. Let's give Claudia Sacrata another scandal for her portfolio. How about introducing your pet senator's daughter to the general's lady-love?'

XXXVIII

There was a scarlet cloak on the hall peg. Helena and I exchanged a glance, trying not to giggle. Claudia Sacrata came out to us. Tonight she had on a crooked garland and a dress in tones of melon seed and grape skin. A heavy hand with the mercuric paint had produced the bright-eyed effect which women think men regard as youthfulness (as many men do). Pan-pipes whootled behind her, cut off abruptly by a closing door – closed by someone else. Claudia led us to a different room. When she left us again for a moment, Helena muttered, 'Looks as if we may have caught a senior officer with his breastplate hooks undone.'

'Make the most of the occasion. I reckon we won't be staying long.'

'Where's she gone? Has she nipped back to give him a Greek novel to read while she deals with us?'

'He may be skittering out through the garden gate with only one greave on his shins . . . Have I ever told you my friend Petronius says every time he raids a brothel he discovers the aedile who issues brothel licences hiding in a blanket chest? Big-name prigs are incorrigible.'

'I expect,' said Helena Justina soberly, 'the strains of office necessitate the therapy.'

She had been married to an aedile once. I hoped he had spent all his free time in blanket boxes, and not with her.

Claudia Sacrata returned.

'I've brought someone who's dying to meet you . . .' I introduced my aristocratic escort. Whatever masculine ranks Claudia had entertained, it must be the first and perhaps the only time a senator's daughter would sit in her house. For this trophy she would have let us interrupt even her general.

Helena had dressed carefully, bearing in mind that her white dress with its little flowerbud sprigs, the shading of her cheeks, the fringe of her stole, her hooped seed-pearl earrings and the amber necklace

185

I had given her would be all the rage in Ubian society for the next ten years.

'What a lovely girl, Marcus Didius!' cried Claudia, mentally making fashion notes. Helena smiled graciously. That smile was also going to feature in scores of Colonia dining-rooms.

'I'm glad you approve of her.' This glib retort earned me a bruising from the lovely girl's attractive beaded shoe. 'She has her wild side, but I'm slowly taming her . . . Don't judge the manners in Rome by this one's impetuous behaviour. The girls there are all mumbling violets who have to ask mother's permission for *everything*.'

'You have your hands full!' Claudia confided to her ladyship, with a meaningful look at me.

'We all make mistakes,' agreed Helena. They both studied the object of their scorn. For escorting Helena into Colonia I too had dressed carefully: tunic, belt, boots, boot linings, cloak, saucy grin – the same scruffy rig as usual.

Our hostess was obviously wondering how a smart young woman like Helena could have let herself fall down so badly. Anyone could see she was highly refined (a prime candidate for disgracing herself on a portico), yet strongly sensible (and therefore more likely to give me a sturdy kick through the nearest victory arch). 'Are you married, Helena?' Claudia explored. She entertained no possibility that Helena Justina might be married to me.

'I was.'

'Dare one ask . . . ?'

'We divorced. It's a popular hobby in Rome,' Helena said in a light tone. Then she changed her mind and added frankly, 'My husband's dead.'

'Oh dear. How did that happen?'

'I never heard the full details. Marcus knows.'

I was angry at the interrogation. Helena handled it calmly and proudly, in her usual public style, but privately the subject always upset her. I told Claudia Sacrata in a cold voice, 'There was a political scandal. He committed suicide.'

My tone must have clearly stated that I wanted the matter dropped. Claudia's gaze sharpened thrillingly, as if she was going to demand, '*Sword or poison?*', but then she turned to Helena. 'He looks after you anyway.' Helena lifted her eyebrows, which were fined to an elegant crescent and almost certainly coloured, though their enhancement was delicate. Claudia Sacrata hissed, 'He means to spear me to the ceiling if I probe!'

186

Helena gave a demonstration of how a well-bred woman should simply ignore unpleasantness. 'Claudia Sacrata, I understand you are a pillar of Ubian society? Marcus Didius tells me you are his one hope of tracing Civilis.'

'Afraid I couldn't help him, dear.' In front of Helena, Claudia Sacrata now regretted that. She wanted to be seen as a public benefactor. 'The person who would have known was his sister's son, Julius Briganticus. He loathed his uncle and always stayed loyal to Rome, but through family information he could always be relied on to know where Civilis was.'

'Can Falco get in touch with him?'

'He was killed, campaigning with Cerialis in the north.'

'What about the rest of the family?' Helena persisted.

Claudia Sacrata had obviously taken to her. Details that had been denied to me gushed out. 'Oh, Civilis had a mob of relations – his wife, several sisters, a daughter, a son, a whole clutch of nephews . . .' I was starting to feel this Civilis must be a sympathetic character. The Batavian's family sounded as terrible as mine: too many women, and the men at each other's throats. 'They won't talk to you,' Claudia continued. That sounded like my relations too. 'Most were fierce proponents of the free Gallic Empire. Civilis actually had his wife and sisters with him behind the lines on occasions, and all his officers' families – the way warriors did in the old days.'

'With a picnic?' I pondered facetiously.

'To encourage them in battle, dear.'

'And discourage slacking!' snapped Helena. I could imagine her parked on a wagon at the rear of the army, shouting harangues that would terrify the enemy and egg on her own incompetent menfolk. 'When they aren't being spear fodder, Claudia, don't they live around here?'

'They did. Civilis and other leaders even met in their houses to plot. That was way back though, when Colonia wanted nothing to do with his revolt. None of his clan show their faces now. There's too much bitterness. Civilis had the Ubians raided by neighbouring tribes; his friends from the Treveri besieged Colonia; and he was known to be in a strong mind to sack and plunder us.'

'So where would he go?' Helena pondered. 'If he wanted to hide up in this area which he knows so well, but avoid the Ubii, who would turn him straight over to Rome?'

'I don't know . . . Maybe among the Lingones, or more likely the Treveri. The Lingon leader – ' Claudia chortled suddenly. 'That's a funny story. His name is Julius Sabinus, and he was a great boaster, though completely bogus. He used to claim that his great-grandmother had been a beauty who seduced Julius Caesar.'

I muttered, 'Nothing to boast about!'

'Pardon, dear?'

'It was easily done.'

'Ooh Marcus Didius! Anyway, Sabinus was full of pretentions, but Helena, as soon as Cerialis came, he panicked. He set fire to his farmhouse to make it look as if he had committed suicide, and then slithered out. His wife Eponnina is hiding him. Everyone knows, but we don't mention it. No one can believe he won't come crawling out with a red face and straw in his trousers. Still, the way things are going, he could be battened up for years.' It was a good story – and it gave me an interesting clue to the anxieties that might also be besetting my quarry, Civilis. 'Anyway, dears, Civilis won't have any truck with such a coward. He's more likely to break bread with Classicus.'

'Who's that?' asked Helena.

'A leader of the Treveri. The one who made Colonia join the rebels temporarily. He executed some of the Roman tribunes at Moguntiacum, too, for refusing to swear allegiance to the German alliance.'

'Young men you knew?'

'One or two.' As always Claudia said it impassively, but perhaps she did care. She looked older tonight, and tired of gaiety.

'I'm sorry – I interrupted you.'

'Well, I mentioned Classicus. After my general defeated the Treveri, their chief went home and brazened it out. He lives in retirement. The Romans allow him to remain on his estate.'

'We promised there'd be no reprisals,' I confirmed. 'We know where he is. One wrong step and he's outlawed. Would he risk breaking his parole by sheltering Civilis, though?'

'Not openly. But he might make a hideaway discreetly available. Yes,' Claudia decided, convincing herself. 'Augusta Treverorum is your best hunting-ground, Marcus Didius.'

That may have been so, but it was no use to me, now I was braced to investigate Veleda. The capital of the Treveri lay over a hundred miles to the south-west – well into the province of Belgica – whereas my route lay a long way north and east. Even Vetera, where I planned to make a start searching, lay nearer. If Civilis was lurking in Augusta

Treverorum, he would have to wait to have his hiding-place disturbed by me.

We had extracted more information from her, but I felt it was drying up. 'It was good of you to see us, but we'd best be on our way. Past experience tells me Helena's hot-rodded ringlets are about to droop . . .' Her new waiting-woman had helped her create a circlet of curls that fringed her face; I had been worried by the smell of singeing while it was going on.

'Yes,' she agreed sweetly. 'If that happens, panic will ensue.'

As we rose, Claudia asked, 'Where to next, then, Marcus Didius?'

'Nothing for it but a foray on to the eastern bank.'

'Germany – where the warriors have always been regarded as the fiercest in the world,' Helena said.

I smiled gently. 'I expect they have a sentimental side.'

'And the women are worse,' she tossed back.

'I'm used to furious women, love.'

She turned to Claudia. 'Is Veleda young or old?'

'Young enough.'

'Is she beautiful?'

'Men probably think so,' snapped this courtesan of legates and generals, as if mere beauty was no compliment.

She led us out. I saw her silvered eyes gleam when she found that Helena had been brought in a cedarwood sedan. She made a great fuss of putting Helena inside it, arranging her silk stole artistically and lighting our lanterns with a taper so that the neighbours would be treated to the full effect. Then she patted Helena's shoulder. 'Don't worry about Veleda. You can run rings round her.'

'I won't be there!' Helena Justina answered miserably.

XXXIX

As we approached our lodging-house, two small figures dashed away in the gloom. They must have been lying in wait for our return, but lost their nerve and scarpered. It was my niece and her small friend. I called after them angrily, but they ignored my shout.

Justinus was back. He was still hoping to hear what was in the letter from Titus. Helena still refused to refer to it. He then told us he had volunteered to come with me as far as Vetera. I wondered if he was really booked for the whole adventure, but neither he nor I discussed it in front of Helena. As it was, she took me aside for a few strong words about protecting him, and then dragged him off for more about looking after me.

The children had slunk back.

'Listen, you two, I want this understood: the women of my household do *not* leave home after dark!' It had the usual effect of peals of laughter, and was forgotten immediately.

The Ubian widow, a silent type who seemed capable enough, was trying to put the pair to bed. Augustinilla started snivelling. Arminia was in the same tired state, but took the opportunity to stare at the fuss her friend was making as if amazed to see someone be such a bad girl. I fought back my annoyance as Helena said crossly, 'Marcus, stop shouting. There isn't any point. She's just an exhausted child, dumped with strangers and taken far away from home. Her tooth hurts, and her doll's broken.' My niece's face was flushed and swollen unattractively, and the doll she always clung to had an arm missing.

I had been trying to avoid knowing about this, since I would rather be asked to pull out one of my own teeth than a child's. Luckily Augustinilla refused to open her mouth for me to look. 'That saves me a bite! Right. We'd better hold a dolly's funeral and burn her tastefully!'

'Shut up, Marcus. Augustinilla, Uncle Marcus is going to mend her. Give him the pieces, or he can't do it for you.'

'He won't be able to do it; he's no use . . .'

I groaned quietly. I'm not completely heartless. I felt sorry for the doll at least. But I had already spied out that the droopy object had jointed terracotta limbs of a kind I knew to be a real swine to mend. 'I'll try – but don't call me a murderer if she disintegrates. And if anyone says *"You're all heart, Marcus,"* I'm going to leave home.'

Helena muttered savagely, 'I thought you were leaving anyway!'

'No, lass. My permit's not signed yet.'

Mending the dolly took an hour and a half. I do not exaggerate.

Justinus had given up any hope of civilised conversation, let alone dinner. He left us early in suppressed bad language. The children sat wrapped in blankets, watching me. Helena and the Ubian woman ate a snack together and refrained from speaking, as if I was the type of workman who might at any moment explode irrationally. They had sausage. I had to decline, to avoid getting greasy hands.

As usual, the ball joint suddenly sank back into its socket perfectly easily. Everyone else exchanged glances as if they wondered why we had had to have so much swearing and wasting of time. Augustinilla shot me a hostile look, snatched the doll to her flushed cheek and went to sleep without a word of thanks.

I was feeling tense. 'Let's go out,' I growled at Helena.

'I thought your womenfolk were gated after curfew.'

'I need to be away from other people.'

'So why am I coming?'

I touched her neck briefly. 'You need to be with me.' I unhooked a lamp and swung out of the house, while Helena scrambled for the outer garments we had both been wearing earlier, then followed me.

'Thank you for doing that,' Helena ventured as I grabbed her hand while we walked. 'You have enough on your mind . . .'

I grunted. 'No point risking my neck unless it's for a world where children can believe magicians will always mend their broken toys.' It sounded trite. I found that comforting. No point being a hero unless you get to spout banal rhetoric.

'Her tooth really is bad, Marcus. Would you object if I took her to a healing shrine?'

I said no, provided every attempt was made there to drown Augustinilla in a sacred spring.

I took us along the river front. I managed to find a garden. It was almost the middle of October, but we could smell roses, though we couldn't see where they were. 'They must have some repeat flowerers, like the centifolia roses of Paestum . . .' I threw back my head, breathing deeply until I settled down. 'I'm thinking about another garden, Helena. A garden beside the Tiber where I once realised I was helplessly in love . . .'

'You're full of snappy talk, Falco.' With only a thin stole, she was shivering. I brought her into my arm so I could wrap my cloak round both of us. She was in a grumpy, defensive mood. 'What are we doing here?'

'You need to talk to me.'

'Oh I do,' she agreed. 'I've been trying all evening, but are you listening?'

'Give me credit. I've come here to listen.'

Defeated by my utterly reasonable attitude, she sighed. 'Thank you.' She forced an arm free and pointed across the water. The river was narrower here than at Moguntiacum, but still so wide that in the darkness we could barely make out the other side. If there were lights, we could not see them. 'Look over there, Marcus. It's almost a different continent. Over there is the antithesis of everything Roman. Nomadic peoples. Nameless gods in wilderness places. No roads. No forts. No towns. No Forum; no public baths; no courts. Nothing organised and no authority to appeal to.'

'And no you,' I said.

I was quite certain she would ask me not to leave. Perhaps she herself had even intended to. Instead, she somehow found a rose-tree and wrenched off a flower for us. With roses it takes some force. She was a girl who had her moments of violence.

We shared the intensity of the flower's perfume. 'I'm here, lady. I'm still listening.'

She was sucking the side of her finger where a thorn had gone in. 'Claudia was right. You defend me. Ever since we met, you have been there – whether I wanted it or not. In those days you even seemed to dislike me, but you were already changing me. I had always been the first-born, the elder sister, the big cousin, the headstrong, bossy, *sensible* one. Everyone always said, "*Helena Justina looks after herself . . .*" '

I thought I could see where she was heading. 'People love you, my darling. Your family, your friends, *my* family – they all worry about you the same as I do.'

'You are the only person I accept it from.'

'Is that what you wanted to say?'

'Sometimes I'm afraid to let you know how much I need you. It seems too much to ask when you have given me so much.'

'Ask whatever you want.' I was still waiting for the big request not to go. I should have known better.

'Just make sure you come back.' Helena spoke without drama. There was no need to reply. For two barleycorns I would have ordered the Emperor to wrap up his mission in vine leaves and run his triumphal chariot over it. But Helena would have hated that.

I told her she was beautiful. I told her I loved her. Being a fair girl and well tutored in etiquette, she made corresponding remarks about me. Then I closed the shutter on the lamp so Colonia Claudia Ara Agrippinensium (Ara Ubiorum) should not have to know that on its neatly dressed quayside a plebeian with all the status of a frowsty water-rat was taking extravagant liberties with the daughter of a senator.

XL

We left the next day. I managed to shed Xanthus, but Justinus, who ought to have known better, smuggled his dreadful dog aboard.

Once again my imperial pass had obtained transport in a vessel of the official fleet. I also discovered that Justinus equipped expeditions in style. He had brought along horses, three leather tents, arms, provisions and a chest of cash. Only the quality of his manpower proved a disappointment, though since I was used to travelling solo on missions like this, I did not complain. One moment of uplift came when Justinus and I went to the dockside: the centurion supervising the loading of our ship was Helvetius.

'What's this?' I grinned. 'You commanding my escort? I thought you had too much sense for a crazy detail like that.'

Not for the first time I caught that fractional hesitation before he quipped back, 'Unluckily for you. It means your escort is two tent parties of my knock-kneed recruits.' It was bad news, but some of them were within earshot so we had to be fairly polite. 'I tried to pick out the best for you.' Helvetius had still brought me a basket of windfalls that were growing heavy mould.

'We've a hundred miles of sailing yet,' I told the centurion. 'And plenty of room on deck. I can help with extra arms practice.' It would get me in shape too. 'We should have them drilled into decent material by the time we disembark at Vetera.'

The same hint of diffidence darkened his face. 'So you're starting from Vetera?'

I thought he suspected me of being just another sightseer. 'There's nothing ghoulish in it. I'm starting where Lupercus left.'

'Wise.'

His laconic reply convinced me I had been prodding at some personal tragedy.

We were sailing out into the great plain of the lower Rhenus. The right bank between here and the River Lupia formed the territory of the Tencteri, a powerful tribe, and one of the few in Europe apart from the Gauls who made considerable use of horses. They had been firm friends of Civilis during the rebellion, eager to cross and harry our supporters – especially Colonia. They had retreated back across the water now. Still, wherever the channel allowed it, our ship clung to our own left bank.

Beyond the Tencteri lived the Bructeri. All I knew about them was their legendary hatred of Rome.

Since we had brought the pedlar Dubnus with us, we sometimes asked him questions about the east bank. His evasive answers only churned up our fears. Dubnus was producing a poor response to the lure of adventure; he seemed to regard himself more as a hostage than our fortunate scout and interpreter. He complained a lot. We were disgruntled too, mainly about him, but I laid down that we were all to coddle him. He had to believe we were sympathetic if we were going to be able to trust him as a guide.

Our days were spent exercising. We passed it off as a leisure activity; it was the easiest way to cope. But we all knew that we were hardening our bodies and preparing our minds for an adventure which could finish us.

Camillus Justinus had now confessed to me that he had his commander's permission to come the whole distance. I made no comment. His legate probably thought the lad had been working too hard; they both probably saw this excursion as a reward for enterprise.

'I wondered how we had managed to acquire the fabulous supply train! So it's down to your honoured presence . . . I take it you never told Helena?'

'No. Do you think she realised?'

'Whether she did or not, you'd better write to her from Vetera.'

'I will. She won't forgive me otherwise.'

'More to the point, Justinus, she won't forgive *me*.'

'Will she think you encouraged me?'

'Probably. And she won't like having both of us at risk.'

'She seemed very concerned about you,' he remarked. 'Visiting the witch in the woods, I mean. Was that based on past experience?'

'Your sister knows any suggestion of me succumbing to Veleda is a lie!' He looked startled by my anger. After a moment, I sighed. 'Well, you know the traditional method of dealing with a fatal beauty among your enemies.'

'That's part of the lecture on strategy I must have missed,' Justinus answered, rather coolly.

195

'Well, you take them to bed and give them a night of pleasure like nothing they have ever known. Next morning, thanks to your fabulous equipment and brilliant technique, they sob and tell you everything.'

'Your niece is right. You make things up, Falco.'

'It's just a myth.'

'Ever done it? In your past life, of course,' he added, in deference to Helena.

'Ha! Most women I know would cry, "Push off, chancer, and take your puny equipment with you!",' I hedged modestly.

'So why is my sister so worried?'

'The myth,' I said, 'is very deep-seated. Think of Cleopatra, Sophonisba – '

'Sophonisba?'

'Daughter of Hasdrubal and wife of the king of Numidia. She was notoriously beautiful.' I sighed again. This time it was an old man's sigh. 'How much education did they waste on you? The Punic Wars, sonny. Ever heard of Scipio?'

'I certainly never heard of the mighty Scipio bedding Carthaginian princesses!'

'Quite right. Scipio was a wise general.' And probably a good Roman prude.

'So?'

'Scipio made sure he never met her. He sent his lieutenant, Masinissa, to the beauty's tent instead.'

'Lucky old Masinissa!'

'Perhaps. Masinissa was so deeply smitten he married her.'

'What about her husband?'

'Mere detail. Masinissa was in love.'

Justinus laughed. 'So was the princess won over to our side?'

'No. Scipio reckoned she lured Masinissa the other way, so he had a few quiet words with him. Masinissa burst into tears, retreated to his tent, and then sent his bride a cup of poison. His message said he would have liked to fulfil the duties of a husband, but since his friends had advised against it here at least was the wherewithal to escape being dragged as a captive through Rome.'

'I assume that luckily for history she quaffed the poison down, and Masinissa redeemed himself . . .'

It was a boy's reply.

Helena had once read me Sophonisba's cutting answer to her bridegroom of the previous day: *I accept your wedding present. Nor is it*

196

unwelcome from a husband who can offer nothing better. However, I should have died with greater satisfaction had I not married so near to my death . . .

Too subtle, I thought, for a tribune. Even one who, according to my horrid niece, had sensitive eyes. He would learn.

Helena Justina highly approved of Sophonisba, needless to say.

We had passed the limit of my previous experience of Germany. That ended at Colonia Agrippinensium, where the great Claudian road ran off westwards through Gaul towards the crossing-point to Britain. The large fortresses of Novaesium and Vetera had until now been only names to me. I had probably read of the minor outposts of Gelduba and Asciburgium, but you can't remember everything. Apart from Britain, these forts marked the ends of the Empire. Our hold in the north had never been tenacious, and Rome had only ever kept control by negotiating special relations with the marsh-dwelling Batavii. Re-establishing our outposts and winning back the Batavian alliance as a buffer against the savage eastern peoples would call for highly efficient diplomacy.

Now that we were past the Ides of October, the weather took a surreptitious shift, as we moved north. Nights were noticeably darker, earlier. Even during the day the golden light which had enhanced the scene at Moguntiacum was reduced to something gloomier. Once again, I felt horrified by the great distance we had to travel.

The scenery, too, was slowly changing. We lost the dramatic crags and dreamy islands. Sometimes there was attractively hilly country, where the Fourteenth's legate could have been taken on his hunting trip – if he *was* hunting. Far above us tremendous flocks of geese and other birds were migrating, adding to our anxious mood with their urgent flight and lonely cries. As the recruits became more excited, their centurion grew more silent. The pedlar scowled. Justinus was smitten by a sense of romantic melancholy. I simply felt depressed.

More and more we began to sense our approaching nearness to the other huge waterways that poured into the delta: the Mosa from Gaul, the Vaculus forming a second arm to the Rhenus, and all the tributaries, each one more powerful than the rivers we were used to in Italy. The sky assumed the lowering greyness I knew belonged to the remote Britannic Ocean – the wildest waters in the world. Sometimes we saw sea birds. The riverine vegetation of oaks, alders and willow became interspersed with sedges and marsh flowers. In those

197

days there was no real military highway along this northern stretch. Habitation along our bank of the river dwindled to infrequent Celtic settlements, many bearing scars from the civil war, and most with sombre Roman watch-towers guarding them. On the other side, nothing was ever visible.

We stopped a night at Novaesium, where the newly rebuilt fort was full of activity. Then we sailed on past the mouth of the Lupia to our right, and finally made landfall on the left bank at Vetera.

Frankly, I did not relish disembarking there myself. And our centurion Helvetius flatly refused to leave the boat.

LXI

The ship's master had struggled to make Vetera before nightfall, not wanting to be caught out at a temporary mooring where the surrounding country must be regarded as unsafe. It was already dark when we landed, however – the worst time to arrive even at an established fort. We could all have stayed on board, but space was cramped and the lads were eager to be within walls, especially in such a famous place.

To organise billets we would have to shift ourselves. Justinus started protesting to the centurion, ready to order him down the gangplank.

'Leave it!' I said curtly.

'In Jupiter's name – '

'Just leave him, Camillus.'

Helvetius was standing to attention on the far side of the boat, staring out across the river with a set face. 'But why does he – '

'I'm sure Helvetius has his reasons.' I had realised what they were.

We marched the recruits off, made ourselves known in a dark reception building, and were allocated quarters. We knew the fort itself lay some distance away from the river, so were startled to find ourselves staying near where the ship had tied up. Our billet was just a wooden hutment, virtually on the quay. The recruits, who had expected the luxuries of a major base, were muttering about the strange set-up, and even Justinus looked mutinous. When we had stowed our kit, I made everyone gather round. The dim light of a taper gave our faces lurid shadowings, and we all spoke in low voices, as if even in this Roman enclave enemy forces might be listening.

'Well, this is a bad start . . . Lads, I know you're wondering why we haven't been allowed to march up and park in the fort. The Batavian rebels must have caused such destruction that they've had to abandon it. The troops here are living in tents and temporary barracks while they select a new site.'

'But why can't we shelter inside the old battlements?'

'You'll see in the morning what the situation is. Just use your imaginations until then. People stay outside the fort because Romans suffered and died there in great numbers. Take your cue from the troops who are stationed here: treat the place with respect.'

'Sir, I thought the legions at Vetera traded with the enemy?' They had no sense of reverence. Tomorrow would cure that.

'No, soldier.' This time Justinus answered. Quick to grasp what I was saying, his voice now was patient and informative. 'The legions at Vetera held out in desperate circumstances. Some of Vocula's relief force did sell their services to the Gallic Empire at one point, but we all have to remember that from here it looked as if the whole world had been torn apart and the Rome to which they had given their oath no longer existed.'

The recruits reacted at first with some scorn. Most of them knew nothing of recent history beyond local episodes like Vitellian soldiers killing a cow in a village three miles down the road. But as Justinus talked to them, they settled down, like listeners absorbed in a Saturnalia ghost story. He was a thorough lecturer: 'Up here, the Fifth and the Fifteenth had the worst of everything. It's true they executed a legate.' He was referring to Vocula. 'But they only surrendered when Civilis had starved them to the point of exhaustion. Then they were massacred. Some were killed as they marched out unarmed. Some fled back to the fort and died there when Civilis burned it in fury. Whatever those men did, they paid for. The Emperor has chosen to sponge the slate clean, so who are we to disagree with him? Listen to Didius Falco. None of us can judge the legions who were here, unless we can be certain what we ourselves would have done.'

The recruits were a rag-tailed lot, but they liked being spoken to sensibly. They were quelled, though still fascinated. 'Sir, why wouldn't Helvetius come ashore?'

Justinus looked to me for help. I breathed slowly. 'You'll have to ask him.'

My guess was that the centurion had been at Vetera before. I had deduced that Helvetius probably belonged to one of the four disgraced German legions that Vespasian had reassigned elsewhere. If I was right, he must be one of the few survivors of the Fifth or the Fifteenth.

In that case, his motives in joining my expedition were ones I would have questioned had I known about them before leaving. I knew now that we were carrying a man whose mental scars could prove dangerous. It was the last thing I needed. But with an escort

200

of only twenty untrained and untested boys, plus Camillus Justinus to look after, it was too late to act. If I shed any of our party, they would not be replaced. And we might need every man.

So I kept the centurion. In the end I was glad of him. He had volunteered to come. And even had he known what was to happen, I believe he would still have chosen to go.

XLII

Next day we unloaded our horses and rode out for the obligatory look at Vetera. The huge double fort lay empty but for the relics that confirmed all the bad reports. Siege engines which Civilis had made his prisoners build. Toppled platforms which the defenders had smashed by hurling down stones. The great Artimedorian grab which someone had managed to dream up for hooking the enemy off the ramparts. Internal faces of the turf walls gouged out from the search for roots or grubs to eat. Intense fire damage. Embedded missiles. Collapsed towers.

The fabric had been assaulted over a long period, then finished with firebrands. Reinvested by Civilis, Petilius Cerialis had battered it down again. The area had been cleared of bodies for a year now, but the dank smell of tragedy still hung everywhere.

We built a small altar. Justinus raised his hands and prayed aloud for the souls who had perished. I presume most of us added a few words for our party, too.

Coming back, chastened, we found Helvetius ashore, although I noticed that he kept his eyes averted from the road inland. He was talking to one of the regularly stationed troops. A dilemma had been offered us: despite the rumours further south, everyone here believed that Civilis was in his own territory, somewhere on The Island.

We talked it over, Justinus, Helvetius and I.

'This could be the old "He's on our patch" syndrome,' I said. 'You know, convincing themselves that a villain is hiding up locally because they want the credit for catching him. I've a friend who is a watch captain in Rome. He reckons that the minute he hears "Your man has been sighted just down the road", he starts searching at the opposite end of town.' Petronius Longus had been on my mind. I was missing the old rascal. Rome, too.

'The problem is,' Justinus argued cautiously, 'if we set off east among the Bructeri without following this up, we won't relish going

202

north again afterwards. You know what will happen if we do manage a meeting with Veleda? We'll come back down the River Lupia so relieved to be alive we'll only want to go home again.'

I wanted to go home already. 'What do you think, Helvetius?'

'I hate The Island, but I agree with the tribune – it's now or never. Now, we can somehow wind it into our itinerary. The detour will be too long later.'

'How did you acquire your local knowledge?' I queried in a bland voice.

'The way you think,' Helvetius said.

The tribune and I avoided one another's gaze. I took the plunge: 'The Fifth?'

'The Fifteenth.' His face stayed expressionless. The Fifth had just about saved their reputations, but the Fifteenth had broken their oaths pretty desperately.

Justinus followed up my question in his quiet, courteous way. 'So what was your story?'

'I'd been wounded. They shipped me out during the hiatus that followed Vocula's relief. I was in the hospital at Novaesium until Novaesium came under attack too. I ended up groaning on a stretcher in a nursing post they had managed to set up on board a barge at Gelduba. I was there throughout the last assault by Civilis on Vetera – and through its aftermath.' The result was obvious, and understandable. The survivor felt guilty that most of his comrades were dead. He even felt half guilty that he had never sworn faith to the Gallic Empire and lost his honour with the rest. 'Am I banned?'

'No,' Camillus Justinus stated. 'You're in the First Adiutrix now.'

'We need you,' I added. 'Especially if you're an expert on the territory.'

'I'm more than that.'

'How come?'

'I've been over in the east.'

That startled me. 'Tell us, centurion.'

'I was stationed in this hole for four years, Falco. Everyone needed a hobby; it was always a desolate post. I never cared for gambling or joining cliques of fancy boys. I did become very interested in the old Varus mystery, though. I read up the story. I used to save my leave and slip across – illegally of course, but everything was quieter then. I was curious about the battle site, fascinated by the idea of finding it.'

So this was what his talk of taking tribunes on hunting trips had meant. Soldiers love to forget their own troubles by reliving other wars. They always want to know what *really* happened to their predecessors. Had it been the enemy's treachery, or just another case of sheer stupidity from the command?

'Did you locate the site?' I asked.

'I was sure I was close. Damn sure.'

I had never liked obsessive types. 'Dubnus knows,' I told him wickedly. Helvetius whistled with annoyance. 'Forget it,' I grinned. 'That's one mystery we can leave to the exalted Germanicus. Let them lie, man. That was our grandfathers' disaster. Vespasian has given us enough to do, and so far I'm not planning to visit the Teutoburgerwald.' He was looking happier anyway, now that we had talked.

I then let myself be persuaded to search The Island. I knew as soon as we set off that the journey would be a waste of time.

I also knew that once we had travelled north, the Teutoburgerwald with its doom-laden reputation would be the sensible route back down to the haunts of the Bructeri.

We were riding. This came as a shock to the recruits. Jupiter knows why they thought we had brought thirty horses. Normally the legions march, but the distances we had to cover were too great for footwork. Besides, our boys were not exactly experienced at marching for days on end. In fact, they were generally such a shambles that most of the troops at Vetera piled out to see us off, wanting to stare at the hand-picked bunch of ninnies I was taking into the wilderness.

The recruits were like any group of adolescent boys: untidy, lazy, complaining and truculent. They spent all day discussing gladiators or their sex lives with an astonishing mixture of lies and ignorance. They were starting to have identities now. Lentullus was our problem baby. Lentullus couldn't do anything. Helvetius had only brought him because he wanted to come so badly, and he had a touching face. Then there was Sextus, who had worse sore feet than the rest of them, which meant they were virtually rotting in his boots. Probus, whom we reckoned would never learn to march with both legs at once. Ascanius, the town boy from Patavium, whose jokes were good but timed with utter tastelessness. The one whose country accent nobody could understand; the one who smelt; the one no one liked; the one with a big nose; the one with big privates; the one who had no personality. My mother would have said not a lad of them was safe to leave in charge of a cooking pot.

Mind you, she said that about me.

Leaving Vetera, we looked like a highly disreputable merchant's caravan emerging from the Nabataean desert after fifteen days of storms. Out of twenty, nineteen recruits had never ridden a horse for more than three miles before; the one left was Lentullus, who had never been on anything four-legged at all. They all seemed to have vaguely wandering eyes, their ears stuck out behind their cheek-guards like steering paddles on a ship, and their swords seemed too big for them. The horses, though Gallic, which should have been a good pedigree, were an even less attractive bunch.

Justinus and I rode first, looking as trim as possible. We were not helped by the tribune's little dog yapping round our horses' hooves. In the middle of the line we were keeping Dubnus on his bow-legged pony, which had a tuneless set of sheepbells stitched to its bridle. We made the pedlar muffle them, but the wadding fell out after the first mile. Helvetius rode last, struggling to keep a tight pack. We could hear him cursing with dreary consistency amidst the *tonk* of the pedlar's bells.

Near the pedlar rode Helvetius's servant, his treasured entitlement as a centurion. He was a mournful dot, who looked after his kit and his horse. While the rest of us kept trying to poach his services, he kept whining to Helvetius that he wanted to apply for an immediate transfer to Moesia (Mocsia is a disgusting post edging the bleakest corner of the Euxine Sea). Justinus, in contrast, had brought no retinue, though his rank rated a large one. He said the dangers of our trip made it unfair. Eccentric lad. Fairness has never featured in the terms of employment for senators' slaves. Still, despite his pampered upbringing, Justinus managed to look after not only himself, but his dog too.

We were all armoured. Even me. I had found a quartermaster who sorted me out a corslet that fitted.

'We have plenty to spare, as a matter of fact!' A bald man with some sort of Gallic accent and a wry sense of humour, he was one of the army's congenital experts. Where his ghostly racks of kit came from was obvious; some of it was still marked with dead men's names. 'Are you sure you want to stand out like this? Why not all go in hunting gear and hope to meld in among the trees?'

I shook my shoulders, testing the familiar weight and the cold burn of the back hinges through my tunic as I hooked the plates together on my chest and tucked in a red neckerchief. It had been a long time. I was wriggling inside the armour like a crab in a lobster shell.

'Disguise is no use. Over there all the men are taller and heavier, with white flesh and huge moustaches you could use to sweep floors. Twenty compact and swarthy brown-eyes with naked chins will be spotted as Romans from miles away. We're in trouble the minute we cross the border. At least a breastplate and groin-protector give a nice feeling of false confidence.'

'What if you run into trouble?'

'I have a plan.'

He made no comment. 'Sword?'

'Always use my own.'

'Javelins?'

'We brought a load downstream with us.' Justinus had arranged that.

'Greaves, then?'

'Forget it. I'm not some flash officer.'

'Bonce pot?' I did let him kit me out with a helmet. 'Take this, too.' He pressed something into my palm. It was a small piece of soapstone engraved with a human eye speared by various mystical emblems. 'Weapons aren't going to be much use to you. Magic's the only other thing I have in store.'

Generous fellow. He had given me his personal amulet.

We spent more days than I cared for paddling in the morass. The Island must have been a dingy place even before the troubles. It was real delta country, all slime and salt flats. There were so many watercourses the land seemed a mere extension of the sea. A bad winter during the Cerialis campaign had brought down even more floods than usual. Untended by the stricken population ever since, the ground was recovering only sluggishly. Tracts that should have been farmed remained sodden. Civilis had also deliberately broken down the Germanicus weir, smashing its mole in order to devastate large areas during his last stand. We thought about Petilius Cerialis and his men, struggling to keep their horses' feet dry on the picket lines, dodging arrows and rainstorms while they splashed away looking for the shallows, constantly taunted by Batavians trying to lure them to destruction in the marshes.

The Batavian capital, Batavodurum, had been razed. Now sternly renamed Noviomagus, it was to be rebuilt and garrisoned. Vespasian had mentioned that to me but it only carried impact now that we were standing among the flattened homes, surveying the painful and desultory attempts of the population to revive their settlement while they lived under awnings with the family pig and chickens. Things must be taking a swing to the better, however, for we met Roman military engineers conducting a survey. They were on detached duty, discussing with local councillors how to bring in material and skills.

During the rebels' last stand, when he retreated to his homeland, Civilis had been besieged at Batavodurum, then driven deep into The Island. He had burned everything he was forced to leave behind. Any farms that escaped were destroyed by our forces – except for those belonging to Civilis himself. That was the mean old strategy of sparing the leader's estate so his suffering supporters grew jealous and angry, while he himself never reached the crucial state of having nothing left to lose. We followed his path inland. The selective scorched-earth policy meant we could see the estate where he should have been. But he had given up on his drenched fields and low dwelling-huts. None of his large family were living there, and there was no trace of him.

Perhaps the strategy had worked. The Batavians were a ruined people – temporarily at least – and their attitude to the prince who ruined them now appeared ambiguous. For the first time I began to doubt whether Civilis was still plotting. I wondered if he had simply fled in fear of the assassin's knife.

We felt no danger while on The Island. The atmosphere was sullen, but the populace had accepted peace and the old alliance. Once again they were a free people within the Roman Empire, exempt from taxes in return for armed manpower – though we all knew Batavian auxiliaries would never again serve in Germany. They let us pass among them without insult. And when we left, they were restrained in showing their relief.

By the Calends of November I was sick of searching, sick of crossing rivers on wobbly pontoons, and sick of half-submerged old roads on lurching wooden duckboards. I announced that we were moving out to seek dry toes and firmer ground.

And so we set off across the territory of the Frisii.

PART FIVE:
SWAMPS AND FORESTS

GERMANIA LIBERA
November, AD 71

'The legionary commander Munius Lupercus had been sent along with other presents to Veleda, an unmarried woman who enjoyed wide influence over the tribe of the Bructeri.'

Tacitus, *Histories*

XLIII

It was hard to believe that Rome had once laid claim almost as far as the River Elbe. Drusus, his brother Tiberius, and his son Germanicus, had slogged away for years, trying to enclose a huge bight of Free Germany. They had used a double-ended pincer movement, invading from Moguntiacum in the south, and across the northern delta flats. Varus and his ineptitude had ended that. Some traces still remained from when Rome had fooled herself that she controlled these wild wetlands. Instead of returning to Batavodurum, we took the Drusus Canal from the mouth of the Rhenus to Lake Flevo, partly because the old canal was a wonder we might have no other chance to see.

We landed again. South of the lake there was little trace of the Roman occupation that had ended sixty years earlier. Lentullus, who was permanently impatient, asked when we would come to the first town. I explained, somewhat roughly, that there were no towns. It started raining. A horse stumbled and pulled a hamstring. We had to unpack and leave it, still within sight of the lake.

'So what do we know about the Frisii, Marcus Didius?' Justinus chaffed, as we surreptitiously made our first camp.

'Let's tell ourselves they are a placid, ranching, cereal-growing people with a yearning for the sea – and hope that their cattle are more dangerous than they are. The Frisii were conquered – no, I'll rephrase that tactfully – they were settled on Roman terms agreed by our esteemed Domitius Corbulo. That's quite recent history.' Corbulo was a real soldiers' general; one who made Petilius Cerialis look like a reject from the Roman fire brigade.

'So where were they in the rebellion?'

'Oh, keen supporters of Civilis, naturally!'

We had not yet reached the forest and were still in flat coastal country. To us it seemed a low, drear, dull land, lacking features as much as it lacked warmth. But perhaps if you were born in a byre there, Batavia and Frisia were a challenge, with their endless fight against floods from rivers, lakes and seas, and their wide stirring vistas of open grey skies.

Much of this region seemed deserted. There were few of the settlements that flourished in Gaul. Even Britain was a populous, companionable place apart from its wildest parts. Germany, however, wanted to be different. All we saw were a few isolated houses, or at best crude huddles of huts and byres.

Here the people matched their reputation and lived a solitary life. If a tribesman could see his neighbour's smoke, he grew twitchy. He would want to ride over there, not for a meal and a game of dice, but to kill his neighbour, enslave his family, and plunder his goods. The presence of Romans just across the great river could only have made matters worse. Now the tribes had the decent excuse of trade to make warlike attacks on each other, seizing prisoners to meet the endless demand for slaves.

'Sir, will they try and capture us, then?'

'They know they can't sell Roman citizens back to Rome as slaves.'

'So what, sir?'

'They'll kill us, probably.'

'Is it true the barbarians are all head-hunters?' jested Ascanius.

'If it is, they'll have no trouble spotting your big noddle anyway.'

I was growing concerned about the pedlar. Dubnus appeared inexplicably restless. I had told him he could trade with the natives, yet he made no attempt to do so. When a man ignores a chance to pursue his living, I always deduce he has hopes of some bounty – and bounties are usually suspect in origin.

On one of my turns to be kind to him, I asked about trade. I knew that the great routes into the interior of northern Europe ran along the River Moenus from Moguntiacum, up the Lupia, and around the Baltic amber coast. The Moenus and Lupia traders, along with others who came up from the Danube, tended to converge in a market among the Bructeri, where we ourselves were heading. 'I've done them all,' the pedlar said. 'All except the sea. I won't sail. I'm a loner. Sometimes I just prefer to wander on my own.' Was that why he hated being in our group?

'Is there a good trade with the tribes, Dubnus? Do they buy or sell?'

'Sell mostly. Converting their plunder.'

'Which is what?'

He was feeling uncooperative. 'Anything they may have snatched from someone else.'

'All right. So what do they snatch?'

'Oxhides and furs. Drinking-horns. Amber. Ironwork.' Dubnus must still be annoyed at being taken into custody and dragged along with us. He grinned evilly. 'In this area they still have a good stock of Roman armour and gold!'

He was trying to rile me. I knew what he was getting at. Twenty thousand men had perished with Varus – along with the field army's complete equipment, the commander's personal treasure, and boxes of soldiers' pay. Every household between the Ems and the Weser must have been living comfortably for decades off pickings from the massacre. Every time they lost a calf, all they had had to do was brave the whitening stacks of bones and gather up a breastplate to use in barter for a new animal.

I asked evenly, 'What do they like to buy? I've heard there's a fairly constant market for good Roman bronze and glass.'

'No tribal chief who takes a pride in his reputation is buried without a silver tray by his head and a full formal Roman drinking set.'

'I expect you can always find buyers for brooches or pins?'

'Trinkets. They like silver. They love coins, though only the old ones with milled edges.' Nero had devalued the currency the year before the Great Fire of Rome. I preferred the old coins too – they felt more substantial. In Rome the State guarantee held just as good for the new adulterated sesterces, but out here the weight of the metal would count.

'Do the German tribes use money?'

'Only when they barter with traders.'

'Coins are more for status and ornament? And is it true they ban imports of wine?'

Dubnus inclined his head. 'Not completely. But this isn't Gaul, where they'd give you their mother in exchange for a drink. Fighting is the serious business.'

'I thought they loved feasting. What do they drink?'

'Mead. Fermented mixes of barley and wayside fruits.'

'Pretty resistible! So, the German tribes tolerate our fancy goods, but Rome hasn't much else to offer them. They hate what we regard as civilised arts: conversation at the bathhouse, harmonious formality – a good binge on the Falernian.'

'They just hate Rome,' said Dubnus.

I gave him a sideways glance. 'You're a Ubian. Your tribe came from over the Rhenus once, so you have Germanic roots. What about you?'

'A man has to earn a living.' He let me hear an undertone of contempt.

But the conversation ended there, because we rode into our first group of Frisians. We drew to a halt like polite visitors. They approached us cautiously.

They were bare-headed – red-headed – blue-eyed, tunicked and cloaked in sombre wool, the way they were supposed to be. We had been telling ourselves that chroniclers exaggerated everything. Maybe it was the Germanic angry temperament they had chosen to misreport.

'Step up, Falco!' Justinus commanded cheerfully. 'Time for this famous plan of yours.'

We all breathed with more care than normal. I hauled Dubnus forwards. 'Please tell these gentlemen we are travelling to pay our respects to Veleda.' He scowled, then said something. I did catch Veleda's name.

The tribune's dog proved our best ally. He rushed up to each Frisian, barking, wagging his rump and trying to lick faces joyfully. They could see that no one who brought such a hopeless hunting hound could have hostile intentions, and that claiming our scalps would be an insult to their manhood. Fortunately, the pup forgot to nip anyone that day.

The Frisians stared at us. Since they were doing nothing more dramatic, we smiled, saluted, and passed on our way. They followed us at first, like curious cattle, then drifted off.

'Veleda seems to do the trick.'

'You mean, they looked as if they'd never heard of her!' Helvetius scoffed.

'Oh I think we can assume they had,' the tribune reproved him in his grave way. 'I believe that explains the pitying looks they all sent after us!'

He rode on, petting the dog, which peered out from a fold of his cloak looking pleased with itself. It was small, smooth, white with black patches, constantly hungry, completely untrainable, and fond of exploring dung. Justinus called him Tigris. It was inappropriate. He was as much like a tiger as my left boot.

Next day we began to encounter stretches of light woodland, and at nightfall we hit the real edge of the forest. From now on we would need all our skills to find paths and keep to the right direction. From here the tree cover continued unbroken across the whole of Europe. Frankly, as a town boy I had always felt the continental arboretum to be excessive. I like foliage – but I like it best when the greenery is leading to a pergola over a stone bench where a freelance wineseller is conveniently hanging about, and I have an appointment to meet my favourite girl under the pergola in about five minutes' time . . .

Camping for the first night on the damp, prickly forest floor, knowing we now had to endure weeks of this, our spirits flagged and tempers rapidly coarsened.

By now the recruits had worked through all the normal stages that afflict soft lads being taken out camping in rough country to harden their characters. We had run the full gamut of moans, theft of personal treasures, spoiling the evening meal, losing equipment, bedwetting and black eyes. Whatever the rough communal living was doing for them, the three of us in charge were exhausted, battered, and welded into a strong defensive team.

One evening, after a particularly sour day and a fight where we had caught them with their daggers out, Helvetius laid about him so angrily that he broke his vine stick. Then Camillus Justinus lined them up for a strong dose of tribunal rhetoric.

'Listen, you bastards!'

'Good approach!' Helvetius muttered subversively to me.

'I'm tired. I'm filthy. I'm sick of marching-biscuit and I'm sick of pissing under oak trees in the rain!' His unorthodox address had startled the group into silence. 'I hate this country just as much as you do. When you behave like this, I hate you too. I'd like to say that the next troublemaker will be sent straight home. Unhappily for all of us we have no convenient wagon going to headquarters, or I'd be first on it myself. Face facts. We all have to make the best of it, or *none* of us will be going home.' He let that sink in. 'Make up your minds. We all have to pull together – '

'Even Lentullus?' cried Probus.

Justinus scowled. 'Except for Lentullus. The rest of us will pull together – and we'll all look after him.'

They laughed. We would spend a quiet night now, and next day everyone would be wonderful.

'He'll do,' Helvetius decided.

'Infinite patience with them,' I agreed.

'Seen it before – they start off thinking he's a worthless snob, and end up dying for him.'

'Camillus won't thank them for that,' I said. 'He'll be martyred if he goes home without a single one of them.'

'Even Lentullus?'

I groaned. 'Especially bloody Lentullus! So, the tribune's all right, is he?'

'He'll probably keep us out of trouble.'

'Thanks! What about me?'

'Mithras, don't make me laugh, Falco. You'll be the one who gets us into it!'

The next morning everyone was wonderful for about half an hour. Then Lentullus in his amiable way piped up, 'Sir, sir, where's Dubnus gone?'

XLIV

I drew a heavy breath. 'What's that, Lentullus?'

'He's not here, sir. And his pony's gone.'

Justinus sprang up, on the alert. 'Anybody know when he left?'
No one did.

I was on my feet too. 'First tent, come with me! Helvetius, you
keep the second tent, pack the kit, then follow us . . .'

Helvetius was running at my heels as I raced for a horse. 'What's
the panic? I know the terrain. I can tell roughly where we are – '

'Use your head! How are we going to converse with Veleda?
Dubnus is our interpreter!'

'We'll get by.'

'It's more than that,' I gasped, bridling up frantically. 'So far we've
been unobtrusive. No unfriendly groups have spotted us. But Dubnus
seemed broody. He was plotting, I'm sure of it. We don't want him
bringing a war party on our heads!'

'Falco, maybe he just wants to get on with his trade.'

'I told him he could do that . . .' Now, however, I was afraid the
pedlar was hoping to make a packet from a new line: selling hostages.
'We can't take the risk that what he's intending to trade with may
be us!'

We tracked him northwards for a long way. It was the wrong direction
for us; perhaps he was using that knowledge in the belief we would
give up, though it only made me stubborn. I hoped he would grow
careless. I hoped he might think we were so single-minded about our
mission that he was free from pursuit altogether.

My party was the slower of our two tracking groups. We were
trying to pick out just one set of hooves among the litter on the forest
floor, whereas Helvetius was following our great swathe. He soon
caught up with us, and we all went on together, first bending east,
then south again.

'What's he up to?'

'Mithras, I don't know.'

'I'm not sure I care.'

Dubnus must have left us early and travelled by night. His start was too great. I decided we would follow until the evening, and then abandon it. We lost the trail by the afternoon.

We were among taller, more thickly growing trees than ever before, in the dense silence of truly ancient woods. A huge horned insect glared at us from the curl of a dead leaf, outraged at this intrusion. There was no other sign of life.

Taking stock, we agreed that the one certainty about our present location was that we had never expected to be in this area. With good luck, no one hostile would expect us here either. Bad luck meant none of our friends would know where to bring a rescue force – but we had ruled that out, anyway. Justinus and I had left behind instructions that if anything went wrong there would be no point in a rescue attempt, so no one was to try.

Our journey from The Island had brought us across most of southern Frisia, but by now we had to be in Bructian territory. Coming this way had been unorthodox, but less exposed. We were a long way from normal trading routes. We were also a long way from both the Roman fieldworks that still survived in the delta area and the old forts that I knew had been planted along the River Lupia. We were approaching the famously hostile Bructeri not from where they were always watching for strangers – along their home river – but by surprise from the north.

During much of our trip we had been about a hundred Roman miles, give or take forty or fifty in this endless hardwood wilderness, above the Lupia's course. That offered some safety, but we had to turn south eventually. The place to change our present easterly direction would be marked by the heights of the Teutoburger ridge. We knew the famous escarpment curved down to the sources of the Lupia. All we had to do was find the northern end, then follow the hills. Helvetius had mentioned an ancient track, but none of us relished taking it. Once there, we would have another forty-mile trip before the heights petered out at the river. By now we had come far enough to be keeping our eyes peeled for the high ground whenever the forest allowed us to scan the countryside.

We began turning south.

Our detour to look for the pedlar had disorientated us slightly. This was easy country in which to lose your way. There were certainly no roads, and forest ways are notoriously aimless. Sometimes the one we took petered out altogether, so that we had to batter through brushwood, perhaps for hours, until we reached a new path. The trees crowded so thickly that though there could have been a much better track only a few strides away, we stood no chance of finding it. Helvetius, who had been near here before for his historical research, reckoned we were still some way from the topmost end of the Teutoburger escarpment, though had we not been in deep forest, the heights might have been visible in the distance. We hacked on through the dismal woods, believing him because we had no choice. Anyway, going south could never be entirely wrong. We would come to the Lupia eventually.

At dusk we stopped. While the tents were pitched, various members of the party vanished on their own for the oak-tree routine. It was cold. The light had sunk but not gone entirely. We were heating mess tins for each tent, but they were nowhere near ready. Helvetius named the night's sentries, whilst his servant groomed his horse. Justinus had a conversation going with Sextus and one of the other lads. They were teaching him some dialect words from the Adriatic coast, since he seemed interested in languages. I was just worried and miserable as usual.

I saw Lentullus creep back after his pee in the woods. He looked furtive, which was nothing unusual. He also looked frightened.

He said nothing to anyone. I decided to ignore it, then found that was impossible. I strolled across to him.

'All right?'

'Yes, sir.'

'Anything to tell me?'

'No, sir.'

'That's a relief.'

'Well, sir . . .' *Oh dear!* 'I think I saw something.'

Lentullus was the type who would spend three days wondering whether he ought to mention that a large army of warriors in wicker chariots with war horns and broadswords was heading our way. He never knew what was important. Lentullus would get us killed rather than say anything to worry the command.

'Something alive?' I asked him.

'No, sir.'

'Someone dead?'

Lentullus paused and would not answer me. All the hairs on my neck and arms rose slowly to attention.

'Come along, Lentullus. Let's you and I take the tribune's puppy for a walk.'

We hacked through the woods for about ten minutes. Lentullus was a shy soul. We had lost him twice already when attending to nature had led him so far from the camp that he couldn't find us afterwards. He stopped to take bearings. I kept quiet rather than confuse him completely. The thought struck me that we could be out here all night while Lentullus searched for his treasure again.

I hate forests. With everywhere completely motionless, it would be easy to become terrified. Among these trees bear, wolves, elk and boar all roamed. The chill air smelt damp, with an evil autumnal unhealthiness. The vegetation was a rank, flowerless kind, with no known herbal use. Fungi like lined faces hung in ancient trees. Undergrowth caught at our clothing and flesh, snagging our tunics and scratching our arms vindictively. My breastplate had become splattered with some sort of insect juice. At this spot we seemed to be the only things breathing apart from eerie watchers from the Celtic spirit world. We could sense a lot of them, both remote and close by.

Twigs snapped, too near for comfort, the way forest twigs do. Even Tigris was subdued. He stayed close to us instead of rushing off to scavenge for woodvoles and bad smells.

'I don't like it here, sir.'

'Show me what you found, then we can go.'

He led me through a few more thickets, over a giant log, past a dead fox which had been torn at by something much larger – something that was probably planning to come back for the rest of it just about now. Tigris growled worryingly. A cloud of midges was mobbing my forehead. 'This is where I was standing. I thought that it looked like a path.' Maybe. Or just a coincidental space among the crowded trees. 'I went along it for a look . . .' He was congenitally curious. And daft. Lentullus would pick up a scorpion to see if it's true they sting.

I still had no idea what he had seen, except that its effect on the recruit chilled me. 'Come on then.'

We took the supposed path. Maybe deer came this way. The air smelt even more hostile, and the light was fading fast. Dew had made our boot-leather swell, and our feet dragged with clumsiness. Leaves crunched under foot louder than I liked. Our progress must have been audible for a couple of miles.

Then the trees stopped.

I was tired. I was cold and uneasy. At first my eyes refused to focus, fighting disbelief. Then I understood why the recruit had been afraid of his discovery.

The silent clearing we had entered lay hung with mist. It was a big clearing, or had been once. Ahead of us lay a strange low sea of brambles. The brambles and brushwood sank slightly nearer to us, then rose many feet away to a regular berm of woodland. The moat-like depression stretched sideways in each direction. The canes dipped, as if the ground beneath their tangled mass had been cut away. And so it had. We knew that, even without venturing forwards – which would have been deadly dangerous. Almost at our feet the ground must fall steeply, deeper than a man's height. Below us, invisible in the brambles, fiendishly sharpened stakes no doubt snarled. At the bottom of the ditch would be a trim channel one spade wide for drainage, then the farther wall would rise diagonally into a bank, before falling back to level ground. There, woodland filled the berm. Comparatively young woodland, not the ancient trees we had been struggling through all day, which must have been standing sturdily in the old times of legend when Hercules visited Germany.

It was a different legend we had found.

Beyond the wood there was a rampart. We could glimpse only the upper part above the vegetation. But there had to be a patrol track, faced with a timber palisade and broken by the shape of familiar square towers. Further on in the gloaming we made out the formidable bulk of a standard fortress gate.

It was silent. No sentries were patrolling and no lights showed. But here, a hundred miles from the Roman provinces, stood a Roman camp.

XLV

'Sir, is anybody there?'

'Dear gods, I hope not!' I was in no mood for exchanging travellers' tales with dead men or their ghosts.

I started to move.

'Are we going in?'

'No. We're going back.' I turned him round.

'Sir, we could camp inside – '

'We'll camp where we are . . .'

Few of us slept much that night. We lay awake, listening for trumpet calls from Hades, then nodded off just before dawn. I woke early and rose while it was still dark, stiff and snuffle-headed. The rest emerged too. After a cold drink and some biscuit to brace us, we packed, brought the horses, and then set off in a close group to make a morning call on our colleagues' camp. At dawn, it managed to look even lonelier.

This was no Vetera. It was a field army's camp, and a large one. Though intended as a temporary construction, it stood in its isolation with an air of permanence. There were no signs of siege warfare. Decay, however, clung tenaciously. Apart from the rich clothing of brushwood on the outworks, some of the towers had lurched and the palisades collapsed. We could see now that further along from us the actual breastwork was broken down.

We battered a path to the gatehouse. One of the great wooden doors lay off its hinges. We edged just inside, no more. A spider the size of a duck's egg watched us entering.

The vegetation was dramatic. Everything within the ramparts was wrecked.

'Sir, was there a fight?'

'No bodies left, if there was.' Helvetius, alone of us, dismounted and wandered forwards to explore. Even he had no intention of going far. He stopped and picked up a small object. 'I don't think the place was abandoned,' he murmured in a puzzled voice.

He began to make his passage further in, and this time we followed him. It would have been a tented camp, so there were large tracts of open ground where the long leather 'butterflies' would have been pitched in rows. But wherever the legions stay for any length of time, the storehouses and the Principia are made from permanent materials. These should have been evident, in their familiar locations, as squares where only a low covering of thin weeds grew, because of their solid floors, yet rotting old timbers and mounds of other wreckage occupied their sites.

'What's your verdict, centurion?' Justinus asked. He was white-faced from the early hour, lack of sleep and anxiety.

'It was an empty camp – but not dismantled normally.'

'They had left for the winter,' I said. I spoke with some confidence. The shrine and strongroom, built of stone, still stood erect. There were of course no standards and no eagles in the shrine. I had seen the gold eagles that once flew here. I had seen them in the Temple of Mars in Rome.

Helvetius looked at me. He too knew what we had found. 'That's right. The buildings were all left here. Bad practice, but they expected to come back, of course.'

He was deeply upset. I turned to the others to explain. 'You all know the rules when you leave a marching camp.' The recruits listened attentively, looking innocent. 'You pack everything reusable in the baggage train. You take, for instance, all the staves from the palisade to use at your next stopping-point. Every soldier carries two of them.'

We all stared back. On the fortified ramparts behind us, stretches of the wooden defences lolled across the patrol track, still partly laced together, like estate fences that had suffered in a huge gale. Other pieces must have rotted; so had the stairs. Time had done this, no other force.

'You burn the rest,' Helvetius said. 'You leave nothing an enemy could use – assuming you think you have an enemy.' He was turning the remains of an old storehouse door. 'This was an empty camp!' he exclaimed, almost protesting at the breach of etiquette. 'It's been trampled pretty thoroughly, by looters, I'd guess. The camp was built by Romans, Romans who stupidly believed the area was so safe they could go out like householders, leaving their door-key under the gatehouse mat . . .' The centurion was burning with a slowly increasing wrath. 'The poor bastards hadn't the slightest inkling of how much danger they were in!'

He strode back to us, clenching his fist around the item he had taken up.

'Who were they, sir?'

'The three legions who were massacred in the forest by Arminius!' Helvetius raged. 'There was a fight – dear gods, there was – but there are no bodies because Germanicus came afterwards and buried them.'

He held up his find. It was a silver coin. It carried the special mint mark which P. Quinctilius Varus had used on his soldiers' pay.

Not many of those ever circulate in Rome.

XLVI

Somewhere in this area had to stand the burial mound. The one whose first turf Germanicus had laid with his own hands – against the rules of sanctity, since he was at the time also holding office as a priest. Here he would have been a soldier first. Standing here, we understood. We too were overwhelmed by our emotional response.

We did not search for the mound. We did not even raise an altar as we had done at Vetera. We honoured them in silence. All of them: the dead, and those who had made it a duty to find them. Gripped by the past, all of us must have wondered whether, if we were killed here in this forest, anybody who cared for us would ever even hear our fate.

We left the camp in the mist by way of its broken Praetorian Gate, on the tough old relics of its exit road. It was easier riding than any other route through the forest, and we wanted to cover distance fast. Our forebears' road did eventually become overgrown. We made the usual complaints about useless engineers, though after sixty years without maintenance some potholing and weeding-over could be excused.

We kept going. Like the army of Varus, we were moving south. Like theirs, that was where our destiny lay in wait. The only difference was: we knew.

It was impossible not to keep churning over the history. Even Justinus had now joined in: 'We know Varus was heading for winter quarters – either the forts they had built on the banks of the Lupia, or possibly right back somewhere along the Rhenus. He must have left that camp wrongly believing he had secured the territory, and all set to return there the next spring.'

'Why couldn't they stay there in winter, sir?'

'Too far from supplies to sit it out. Besides, I expect his troops were nagging for a break somewhere civilised.' The tribune's own troops thought about his solemn remark, then slowly grinned.

'And this is the way they went,' Helvetius said. He was really

225

feeling it. He loved to dramatise; he loved to speculate. 'Everyone believes they had hit the ridge when it happened, but why not here, much further north? All we really know for certain is that Germanicus found them somewhere east of the River Ems.'

'Sir, sir – ' Now they had left the lost camp the recruits felt braver and more excited. 'Will we find the famous battleground?'

'It's my belief,' Helvetius answered heavily, as if he had just worked something out, 'the battlefield is all around us. That would be why Germanicus had such trouble finding it. You don't cut down twenty thousand men – veteran campaigners, after all – in a space like a backyard.'

I agreed. 'We think it was quick, but the engagement may have lasted. No – it *must* have done. Clearly Arminius fell on them and did much damage. But after the first shock, the hardened soldiers would have made a stand.'

'Right, Falco. No choice. We know they did, anyway. Germanicus found whole heaps of bones where they had fought back in groups. He even came on the remains of some who had struggled back to their camp and been slaughtered there.'

'The camp we found?'

'Who knows. After all this time – and Germanicus clearing it as well – you'd have to spend days there to find any clues.'

'So after the initial assault,' I said, 'they faced a drawn-out agony. There were even survivors. Arminius took prisoners: some were slung up on tree branches to propitiate the Celtic gods, but some were held in gruesome pits.' We found none of those, I'm glad to say. 'Some eventually got home to Rome. A few poor sods even came back here with Germanicus.' Every war produces masochists. 'But agreeing a surrender is not the point for the tribes. It was a Celtic fight – to kill and take heads. Any legionaries who tried to make a getaway would have been hunted through the woods. Just like in Britain when the Boudiccan tribes rose.' I heard my voice growing husky with old pain. 'The chase is part of the terrible game. Blood-crazed warriors happily whooping after victims who know they are doomed . . .'

'Arminius may even have prolonged the fun deliberately,' Helvetius informed the rest. 'The upshot would have been bodies all the way from here to – '

'To the next river in any direction, centurion.'

'Tell us, Falco?'

'The warriors stop any remaining fugitives at the water's edge.

Their heads and their armour are dedicated to the gods in the running stream.'

We rode on very quietly. It took us two days, even with fine weather and favourable luck, to reach the Teutoburger hills.

I know that when we rested each evening some of the recruits vanished for long periods into the undergrowth. I know they found various items. They were boys. They cared about their old colleagues, but they found relic-hunting irresistible.

The general mood of our party hardened. Meanwhile, Lentullus would sit with Justinus and me near the fire, taking no part in the secret search for souvenirs. He was withdrawn, as if somehow he thought everything was his fault.

Once I laughed, briefly. 'Here we are, stuck in the middle of nowhere with a whole basket of our own troubles, sounding off like strategists using apples on a tavern table to relive Marathon and Salamis.'

'Shut up about taverns, Falco,' murmured Camillus Justinus sleepily from the depths of his camp-bed. 'Some of us could really use a drink!'

Since I had stayed in his house and tasted his awful table wine, I knew just how desperate His Honour the tribune must be.

Next day we tackled the Teutoburger heights.

We traversed the long escarpment strangely without incident. It seemed too good to be true. It was.

On our descent, all to order, we found the headwater of the River Lupia. At sunset we camped discreetly, making no fires. I noticed that Probus and another recruit went off together and stayed absent for too long. They were no doubt scouring the terrain for antique scabbards and studs again. At first we made no comment, as usual, but we had soon finished distributing rations and still they had failed to appear. That was unheard of. Helvetius stayed in the camp whilst Justinus and I went out to search for our lost lambs. We took a recruit each. He chose one called Orosius. With my luck I got Lentullus. In case I needed more company, Tigris gambolled happily along with us.

As you might expect, it was Tigris, Lentullus and I who stumbled into the sacred grove.

It just seemed like any other clearing when we first went in. It must have been generations old. We marched boldly among the crook-armed trees, thinking the open ground between them had occurred naturally. An angry wind was rousing itself, rustling tirelessly through the dark, dry, November leaves. Tigris, who had bounded on ahead, raced back madly, bringing us a stick to throw. I bent and after the usual noisy struggle I forced him to release it.

'That looks a funny one,' said Lentullus.

Then we saw it was a human fibula.

While the dog barked in frustration, waiting for his game, Lentullus and I gazed slowly round and noticed at last that this place had a special atmosphere. There was a smell of moss and misery. The silence blocked our throats. Panic leapt. It took a few moments to recognise that empty eyes were watching us from every side.

'Stand still, Lentullus. *Stand still!*' I don't know why I said it. No one else was there . . . yet there was *presence* everywhere.

'Sorry, sir,' Lentullus croaked. 'Oh great mother! I've done it again, haven't I?'

I tried to sound cheerful as I whispered back, 'Yes. It seems to be another of your terrifying finds . . .'

Ahead of us leaned a grotesque statue in rotting, rough-hewn wood: some god of water, wood or sky – or perhaps all of them. He loomed up like a huge gnarled oak trunk, beaded with livid orange mould and rooted in decay. He had emerged from a few strokes of a crude adze. His limbs were barely indicated caricatures. He had three primitive faces, with four staring Celtic almond-shaped eyes distributed among them. Atop him the wide antlers of some massive elk draped themselves as if trying to embrace the sky.

Before the god stood a basic turf altar where the priests of the Bructeri came to make their sacrifice. Upon it lay the head of an ox, badly decomposed. Like us, they predicted the future from the entrails of animals. Unlike us, it was their custom to hack to pieces any horses and other captured animals belonging to their vanquished enemies. They also conducted worse kinds of sacrifice. We knew that because all around the grove, nailed up in the ancient trees, were human skulls.

XLVII

Lentullus, who normally knew nothing about anything, knew about this. 'It's death to enter a druids' grove, sir, isn't it?'

'If we wait around, a druid may come along and answer that . . .' I gripped his arm, then slowly backed out the way we had come.

To our right something stood among the trees: a trophy pile. There were innumerable weapons – long, unfamiliar German swords, war axes, round shields with sturdy bosses – among other items whose Roman design we recognised with an unhappy shock.

Lentullus squeaked and tripped over a root. Only that spring I had managed to lay hands on part of Caesar's *Gallic Wars*, going cheap now that Rome had some nasty new wars to occupy its attention. According to Julius, the Suebi worshipped – in those days anyway – in a grove which people could visit for religious purposes, but if they happened to fall down there it was required practice that they should roll out of the grove horizontally. No doubt Caesar quoted other reassuring facts that might have helped us to extract ourselves from this terror, but I had never owned enough money to buy the next scroll in the set.

Here the ground was particularly rich in unpleasant flora, deer droppings, and milky-coloured fungi of the etiolated, squashy kind. I glared at the hostile wood carving and defiantly ruled out Caesar's rite. Rolling like a log to propitiate local deities was not in our recruits' training course, and this one would never have mastered it anyway. I hauled on his arm and pulled the young fool upright. Then we turned round and started to leave conventionally.

We regretted it.

We were now forced to walk past something else we didn't like.

The edifice at the grove exit was square-built, like another and much larger altar. It was set around a massive stake, and made from various narrow-shaped items, irregular or round-ended, and grey in colour. The construction must have been built up over many generations until now it was two strides in each direction and waist-high.

Its components had been laid down in rows extremely neatly, first one way, then crosswise, like twigs in a well-ordered bonfire. But they were not twigs.

It was a giant pile of bones. Bones from human arms and legs. Hundreds of victims must have been dismembered to contribute to this ossuary – first hung in the trees as offerings, then smitten into pieces with casual savagery, like choice cuts from meat carcasses. From what I knew of Celtic rites, most of them had once been young men like us.

Before we could stop him, the tribune's dog went up to sniff this wondrous hoard of bones. We looked away, as a gesture of respect to the dead, while Tigris saluted each corner of the ossuary with his special sign of doggy reverence.

We left the grove very fast.

XLVIII

We started back to camp. That was when the next nightmare began.

Yet again I was out in a wood at dusk with Lentullus. This time it was not the silence that unnerved us. Suddenly we were surrounded by noise – something, or somebody, crashing through the trees in haste. We were already petrified. Then we heard a shout. Foreign voices filled the night. From the start it seemed like pursuit, and from the start we understood that we were their quarry. I forced Lentullus to change direction, hoping to give the rest of our party a chance.

'I'm with you, sir!' he promised.

'That's comforting . . .'

We had lost our path and were blundering over treacherous ground where branches and deceptive clumps of moss lay in wait to throw us headlong with wrenched limbs. I was trying to think as we dashed onwards through the brushwood. I felt fairly sure no one had seen us leave the grove. Perhaps we had not been seen at all. Somebody out there was looking for something, but perhaps they were hunters trying to fill the pot.

We stopped. We crouched amongst bushes while the sweat careered off us and our noses ran.

Not the pot. Whoever they were, they were making a lot of noise for men trying to lure animals into nets. They were thwacking at the bushes in order to flush out fugitives. Harsh laughter alarmed us. Then we heard dogs. Some sort of great horn boomed. Now the boisterous party was coming straight for us.

They were so close we broke cover. They would have found us anyway. Someone glimpsed us. The shouts renewed.

We set off again as best we could, unable even to glance back to see who our pursuers were. I had lost Lentullus. He had stopped to call the tribune's dog. I kept going. They might miss him; they might miss me; we might even escape.

No chance. I was putting distance between us, but sounds broke

231

out that could only mean one thing: they had caught Lentullus. I had no choice. Groaning, I turned back.

They had to be a band of the Bructeri. They were standing round a deep pit, laughing. Lentullus and Tigris had both fallen into it. Perhaps it was an animal trap, or even one of the pits like larders that their hero Arminius had dug for keeping prisoners fresh. The recruit must be unhurt, for I could hear him shouting with a spirit I was proud of, but the warriors were taunting him by shaking their rough wooden lances. He must have been badly shaken by the fall, and I could hear that he was terrified. One of the Bructeri raised his lance. The threat was clear. I started to yell. I was tearing into the dell when someone big, with a very hard shoulder, sprang out from behind a tree and crashed me to the ground.

Lentullus could not see me, but he must have heard my fall. For some reason my presence seemed to hearten him.

'Sir, how are we going to talk to these men without an interpreter?' *That boy was an idiot . . .*

The world stopped spinning. Since my answer might be the only friendly words he ever heard again, I had no heart for rebuking him. 'Speak slowly, and smile a lot, Lentullus . . .'

He may have had problems deciphering it. It was difficult to sound as clear-witted and self-assured as usual when lying face down on the forest floor with my nostrils pressed into the leaf-mould, while a gigantic, bare-chested warrior, who could not possibly have understood my joke, stood with his foot in the small of my back and laughed heartily at me.

XLIX

Dear gods, I hate large, simple-minded jovial types. You can never tell whether they will simply mock you, or mock you with that jolly guffaw, then swipe off your head with an axe . . .

My captor in fact hauled me to a more or less standing position, stripped off my sword and dagger, which he sneered at, but kept, then threw me further into the dell where the others were. They then encouraged Lentullus to scramble out of the pit by poking him with their lances. He brought out the dog, who immediately showed his loyalty by running away.

The happy band stood us side by side and assessed their collection like naturalists collating a set of rare beetles. These lads did not look immensely sophisticated. They probably counted creatures' legs and feelers by picking them off. I started twitching nervously in limbs I didn't even own.

They all towered over us. So did the group who soon turned up whooping triumphantly and bringing our friends from the camp. They had our missing Probus and his treasure-hunting companion. They must have discovered them first.

I anxiously looked them over for damage. Helvetius was sporting a black eye and a terminal case of bad language, and some of the recruits had been knocked about a bit. The centurion's servant appeared to have taken the worst of it, but this was not necessarily a sign of cruelty in the Bructeri; he was such a pathetic character, he was crying out to be beaten up. The lads told me afterwards they had let themselves be taken fairly quietly. After all, our journey's motives were supposed to be peaceable. The warriors had turned up suddenly at the tents. Helvetius had properly followed the rules by trying to converse. It was only when our group had started to be manhandled that he had ordered them to reach for arms. By then it was too late. There had never been much we could hope to achieve by fighting, not in such small numbers and so far from home.

The warriors had then scoured the woods for stragglers. With Lentullus and me they clearly felt they had a complete set.

'Sir, what about – '

'Whoever you're about to mention – *don't!*' Justinus and Orosius were not here. They were our one hope now, though of what I dared not speculate. 'Don't speak of them – don't even think about them, in case the thought shows in your face.'

They might be dead already, as we expected to be soon.

To my intense relief we were not being taken to the grove. At least not yet.

It was now quite dark. They jostled us in a riverward direction, though we never seemed to come to the bank. That was another relief. If they chucked me off a jetty as a morsel for a river-god, I would immediately have to surrender my soul into his webby hands. I couldn't swim my way out of it. I had not much hope for the recruits either; they must have been on the same army water-skills course as me.

We stumbled along, surrounded by tribesmen. They seemed cheerful enough having somebody to jeer at. They offered us no worse harm, though we didn't push our luck by asking who their chieftain was, or when we would be stopping for a snack break.

After what seemed hours we reached a settlement. Rectangular buildings in timber and daub, with steeply pitched roofs which came down almost to the ground. A few pale faces staring at us in the light of smoky torches. A lowing ox.

Our drovers whooped us through a door in an end wall and into a long byre attached at right angles to the largest house or farm. Cattle had lived here very recently; we knew that from the smell. We had tumbled into an area which had a central aisle and stalls separated by posts and hay containers. At the other end there were no stalls, just a bare hearth. We heard a mighty bar closing the door outside. Exploring this squalid guest-suite did not take us long. We just squatted on our haunches and looked round from where we were.

'What happens now, Falco?' We had reached that point of disaster where people have no other option but to turn to me. This was when they were all likely to remind me that the trip to the River Lupia was my idea.

'Have to wait and see.' I sounded moderately confident. 'But I don't think we can expect to be asked which highly articulate defence lawyer we would like to hire from their sophisticated legal pool.'

'How did they know to look for us, sir?'

'My guess is Dubnus alerted them.'

We braced ourselves for a long wait, with not much to hope for at the end of it.

'Maybe a beautiful virgin will bring us a pail of dinner, fall in love with me and lead us to escape,' Ascanius mused. He was the skinniest and most hygienically sordid recruit we had.

'Unwise to expect dinner either, Ascanius.'

Halfway along the building was a shutter. Fascinated blond children opened it and silently peered in at us. Helvetius rapidly tired of that and went to close them out. He said the big warriors were standing about in groups debating in an aimless way. He ducked back inside in case the sight of his grizzled Roman head gave them murderous ideas.

They must have been waiting for someone. He came after an hour or so. The hum of debate increased to a livelier note. They all jabbered on in a way that reminded me of a gathering of my relatives pointlessly arguing whether Great-auntie Atia's birthday was in May or June. Even the man of note must have grown sick of it, for eventually he barged open the door and sauntered in to have a look at us.

He was about fifty. As the russet hair had thinned and faded, he must have increased its length to compensate. Wild skeins of it ravelled behind him. Xanthus would have been horrified. He also had a long moustache, much in need of an enriching pomade, above which were a bulbous red nose and rather watery pale grey eyes. He was a big man in every way: broad shoulders, heavy bones, big head, big hands. He wore brown woollen trousers, a long-sleeved tunic, a green cloak, and a round gold brooch that not only pegged his ensemble together but rose and fell dramatically to show how far his chest expanded every time he breathed. Some of the others may have looked undernourished, but this fellow was fit.

He was followed by his bodyguard. Younger men, any one of whom would have made a handsome model for a Noble Tribesman statuette had they been fattened up and taught to exhibit a mournful Celtic gaze. Left to themselves their gaze was as vacant as village youths anywhere. Most of them did without a tunic to indicate how tough (or poor) they were. They spat a lot on principle, and glared at us whenever they remembered they were there to use objectionable behaviour towards the prisoners. They all had immensely long

German swords, apparently so they had something grand to loll on while their chief was occupied. He looked the type who was always wandering off to pursue other interests, and he had an air of eccentricity that gave him character. Even in Rome that faint impression of madness sometimes works for election candidates.

We were feeling depressed and annoyed with ourselves, so when he made no attempt to communicate we stayed where we were, sitting in two rows on either side of the aisle. We let him wander up and down. None of us spoke. We were hungry and tired, and we let it show, though without appearing demoralised. A man with a proud Roman heritage to bolster him can look truculent even when squatting on two feet of compacted dung. Well, Helvetius managed it, though he had the advantage of being a centurion; it's a snooty rank.

The chief-was a man who walked slowly, with a tread that consolidated ground. He paced back to his starting-point, then turned round to us again. He made a sharp noise through his teeth, as if spitting out a raspberry pip. It seemed to be his evaluation of our group, and was resonantly an expression of contempt. I was surprised that he could find two teeth to do it through, for conspicuous along his gums were large gaps.

'Somebody should tell him to watch that,' Ascanius said derisively. 'It's probably how he lost the rest.'

The chieftain's eyes fell on our joking boy. We all realised he had understood.

I stood up like a spokesperson.

'We come in friendship,' I announced. M. Didius Falco, the ever-hopeful innocent. 'We are travelling to see Veleda, your renowned prophetess.' Veleda's name produced as much effect here as trying to interest a carrion crow in lunching off a lettuce leaf.

'You come in friendship?' The chief's chin rose. He folded his arms. The pose was something of a cliché, but in the circumstances that was his prerogative. 'You are Romans in Free Germany.' His Latin accent was terrible, but good enough for snorting at a frowsty group of renegades. 'You have no choice. We are the Bructeri,' the chief informed us haughtily. '*We do!*'

He did his disgusted tooth noise again, then strode out.

'It's definite then,' Ascanius exclaimed incorrigibly. 'He's cancelling the virgin. No dinner for us tonight, lads!'

He was right, too.

236

L

The beautiful virgin must have been busy next morning, for she sent us her sister instead. Her sister had a figure like a tent-post, a face like the underside of a boulder and a negligible personality. That might not have depressed us, but she was the one who couldn't cook.

'Thank you, my dear,' I saluted her courteously while the others were grimacing. 'We are delighted to make your acquaintance, and that of your gracious porridge pot.' She had brought four bowls between twenty-two of us, and a lukewarm metal cauldron of some glutinous gruel.

She ignored me and stomped out. I pretended I preferred women who are not too obvious.

The breakfast was something everyone ought to experience, so whatever else he had to scoop out of a skillet in his future life he would know it could be worse.

This branch of the Bructeri were slow risers. We were in a sleepy hamlet that would have been an ideal recuperation spot, had the people liked us more. Only towards the end of the morning did we hear activity. 'Attention, men, something's happening . . .'

We looked out of our shutter and saw that runners had been back to raid our camp.

Helvetius and I shoved the others aside while we stood and counted in our baggage and horseflesh. 'I make that six beasts and one tent missing – '

'Plus the cash box, the javelins – '

'Probably some rations, and the tribune's personal kit . . .'

'Oh he'll do!' Helvetius murmured proudly. 'Mithras, he's a *good boy!*'

It looked as if Camillus Justinus would at least be able to report to Rome how the Bructeri had taken us. He had supplies, mounts, and a companion in Orosius The tribesmen were off guard now they had captured us, and would not be watching out. He should get away. It was the best we could hope for. What else could we expect of one gently reared young officer, aided by a rather dim recruit?

Something stupid, normally. (Helvetius said that.)

The arrival of the horses signalled a change for us. Its good face was that we were saying goodbye to our smelly byre. The gloomy aspects were that they were leaving all our baggage behind, that Ascanius had lost his chance to make love to the porridge girl, and that the Bructeri were going on horseback – *our* horses. They were running us alongside them, on foot. They were rapid riders. And wherever they were taking us turned out to be several days away.

'Look on the bright side. At least we're pointing west. They could have been driving us even further into the interior . . . Every mile we trudge is a mile nearer home.'

'How far is it to Rome from here then, Falco?'

'Jupiter, don't ask!'

As soon as the Bructeri grew tired of herding us like geese, with irritating whistles and much active use of sharp thorny sticks, we settled down into a regular formation and showed them how empire-builders march. Even the recruits were now inspired to smarten up. I was worried for the centurion's servant, but it turned out that after twenty years in the army he could not only make his boots cover ground efficiently, but he could complain at the same time.

We even sang. We invented a marching-ditty that started, *Oh I love my little mess tin with my name punched in the rim* . . . and then proceeded to list numerous items of a legionary's kit (there are plenty to choose from) before reaching his girlfriend, after which the form remained constant but we introduced some obscene counterpoint. The recruits loved it. They had never made up their own song before.

'Sir, this is a really good adventure, sir!'

'How true. Swamps, forests, ghosts, glades full of skulls; filthy, frightened and famished; then all ending up as slaves . . .'

'Sir, what I think is, the people we never mention are going to rescue us. What do you think, sir?'

Helvetius gave his opinion in one word. It was anatomical.

I said that assuming the people whom we never mentioned had done what was sensible and scampered for home as fast as they could ride, I was prepared to consider suggestions for us rescuing ourselves. No one had any.

We sang another thirteen verses of the mess-tin song, to pretend to the red-headed Bructeri that they could never make Romans lose heart.

So, with blistered feet and our anxieties as well disguised as possible, we arrived in a large clearing on the riverbank, where more Bructeri were gathering near a suspiciously high tower. At the base of the tower, in some smart little daub houses, lived a group of skinny tribesmen who had managed to equip themselves with debonair quantities of gold bracelets and jewelled cloak-brooches. This seedy lot looked like the horse-thieves who live on the Pontine marshes and earn a living beating out buckled pots. They were as shifty-eyed as I had already heard, yet every man of them possessed a natty torque, a belt with good enamelled trappings, and various silver or bronze scabbards. Unlike everyone else, they wore several layers of clothing and oversized boots. They kept some very pretty hunting dogs as pets, and the latest model of wicker-framed chariot was ostentatiously parked at their compound.

These men were a lanky, long-chinned, unimpressive selection whose power to attract rich offerings must be entirely derivative. When they whined after presents, nobody could argue. Among the Bructeri nobody wanted to. For these, without question, were Veleda's male relatives.

We were all roped together, but allowed to wander about.

We made a beeline for where the prophetess must live. I should have known all along. When did Celtic tribes ever build high towers? Veleda had ensconced herself in an old Roman signal post.

Some adaptations had been made to this now ironic edifice. It still had the platform on top for watching and for making the bonfire, but that had been built up even higher with wattle walls, then provided with a snug timber roof. The near-overthrow of the Empire had definitely been supervised from one of our own buildings. We turned aside in disgust.

The headstreams of the Lupia had long since joined each other. The river here had widened enough to carry shipping. Along the banks were various native craft, including high-sided boats with leather sails, wherries and coracles. Also one much bigger, superior ship, which looked oddly out of place. The recruits were fascinated by this vessel and kept ignoring our guards' shouts to wander back and crane at it. I had forgotten that many of them came from the Adriatic seaboard.

'That's a Liburnian!'

239

Liburnians are light, swift, double-banked galleys derived from Mediterranean pirate ships and much used in the Roman fleet. This one had a decorative portrait of Neptune on the prow and an elaborate cabin at the stern. She was afloat, though half her oars had been robbed and her rigging looked in a fine old tangle. There was no evidence that the priestess kept her trim for floating picnics. She must have lain here deserted for many months.

I said, 'That must be the flagship which Petilius Cerialis had pinched from under his nose.'

'Cor, she's lovely, sir. How could he let that happen?'

'In bed with his fancy bit.'

'Oh sir!'

'Never mind the general's carelessness. Like his splendid Liburnian galley we must have been brought here as presents for the prophetess. So keep quiet; keep together; and keep your eyes peeled for trouble. The lady's last gift of a live Roman was never seen again. And as sure as ambrosia makes heroes belch, the poor beggar's not alive any more.'

I experienced a vague hope, nevertheless, that we would run into the missing legate, Lupercus, and discover he had gone native and was living here with Veleda like a prince. The hope was so vague that it made me feel slightly sick. I knew only too well the more likely alternatives. And I knew they applied to us.

'Is the prophetess up in that tower now, sir?'

'I don't know.'

'Are you going to ask to see her?'

'I doubt if they would allow it. But I want to see what the situation is before I speak.'

'Ooh don't go up in the tower, sir. You might never come out.'

'I'll bear that in mind.'

The Bructian moot appeared to be a prearranged gathering.

It must have been hard work for the caterers. Celtic tribes are famous for turning up to appointments anything up to three days either side of the given date. Here a feast was in progress on rough trestle-tables. It looked fairly permanent. Presumably it was to pass the time until something like a decent quorum deigned to put in an appearance. I wondered who had issued the invitations to this casual assembly. Then I tried not to wonder how the assembly would affect us.

Our group, with its interesting string of prisoners, aroused bursts

240

of excitement. Other chiefs' retainers felt obliged to swagger up and try to outface our chief's successful troupe. They did this by the usual offensive and threatening gestures against us, which we ignored, though plainly our captors could not allow other people to torment us when that privilege was theirs. By now we felt a proprietary interest in the party we were used to, so we cheered them on and managed to get quite a lively fight going. None of them appeared grateful for our encouragement, and eventually they all grew bored and settled down to feasting.

We were fed too, in a small way. The warriors were tucking into plain but hearty fare: loaves, fruit, hot roasted game and I think some fish. For us the cook had gone to some trouble to produce another of their speciality porridges; it was like eating a wound poultice. There was drink (some kind of fermented cranberry juice), but I warned the lads to go easy in case we needed clear heads later. The women were judged a great improvement on our brush with the virgin's sister; the girl who brought round the juice jar was definitely worth flirting with. I ordered them to lay off that too, and was firmly voted least popular man in our group.

Time went by. I leaned on a tree thinking about it. Time seemed to have no real importance. Still, what else can you expect from feckless tribes who have never invented the sundial, let alone imported an Italian water-clock for sternly governing their free hours? Dear gods, these savages seemed to believe life was about doing what you wanted, and enjoying it whenever possible. If ever the ascetic tenets of Greek philosophy filtered through these lazy forests, people were in for a bad shock. And they were so disorganised, it was no wonder the sons and step-grandson of the supremely ordered Augustus had never managed to line up enough of them together to make a decent show of surrendering to Rome. Rome had a systematic way of schooling tribal peoples – but you had to sit them down and explain the benefits first.

Here, the Bructeri made *us* sit about and wait. We took a haughty view of this breach of diplomatic etiquette.

Nothing happened. There was little sense of anybody else waiting for anything to happen. In fact to us the whole occasion made no sense at all. We sat apart, tied together in our miserable skein of rope and bursting with impatience for some formality, even if it turned out to be the formality of our trial.

Ascanius winked at the juice-jar girl. She ignored him, so he tried grabbing the hem of her rough woollen skirt. At that, with the air of a girl who had done it before, she emptied what was left in the jar all over him.

Some things are the same anywhere.

As she spun off with her pretty nose in the air, I smiled at her wearily and she gave what was really quite a nice smile back to me. My standing rose again.

Watching other people feasting is a soulless exercise.

More time passed. Evening approached. Whatever Dubnus had told me about Germanic attitudes to drink, the cranberry wine was obviously one of those country potions that have an insidious effect. My Great-auntie Phoebe made a similar linctus with myrtleberries which regularly caused a Saturnalia riot. They would have liked it here. Soon the hum of conversation rose into pricklier shouts of debate. As happens anywhere, most of the women decided that if there was going to be an argument they would take themselves off to mutter somewhere else. A few hard cases remained – obviously the ones who had been let down in life. They looked even tipsier than the men. The men, who had appeared to be able to sup their rich red jollop without losing sweat, now glistened up angrily. Opinions were being bandied, always a danger sign. Stronger opinions were offered back in slow, slurred voices that were soon emphasised by table-thumps. Then our chief swayed to his feet with drunken grace and burst into impassioned speech. Obviously a vote was being sought.

Well, naturally we would have been pleased that our own man had proved a hot debater; every prisoner likes to feel he has been captured by a worthy foe. The only problem was it became clear from fierce glances cast in our direction that the issue at stake was our fate. We also received a definite hint that the chief with the pip-spitting teeth had decided to enhance his status by offering his prisoners for use in some grove as the next human sacrifice.

It was a long speech; he enjoyed a rant. Gradually the noise changed, as the warriors began to clash their lances on their shields.

I knew what that meant.

The clashing of shields grew louder and faster. Instinctively we all scrambled into a tighter bunch. A lance, thrown with great accuracy, thrummed into the turf right at our feet.

The noise quietened. It reached the nearest to silence that can ever be achieved in a large group of people who are exhausted by eating and arguing. Attention focused gradually.

A woman had ridden into the clearing, bareback and bridleless, on a white horse.

LI

Helvetius grabbed my arm. 'I'm betting that's the prophetess.'

'No takers, man.'

Two of the lanks who carried messages for visitors walked either side of the skittering horse. Had it not borne a rider I would have said the creature was unbroken. It was undersized, with a shaggy coat and a manic eye. Each of the lanks had a hand on its mane for steerage and looked nervous, but there was no doubt who was in control of them, and of the wild horse, too.

Veleda dismounted among her people. Claudia Sacrata had said men would think her beautiful. Claudia was right. There were twenty-two men in our party; we all did.

She was tall, calm and unhesitant. She had the pale colouring that makes men seem weak and pretty but women mysterious. Her swathe of light gold hair fell to her waist. It was in perfect condition. Helena would have said that a woman who spends most of her days in a tower by herself has plenty of time with the comb. She wore a sleeveless purple gown and was sufficiently well developed for its scooped neck and loose armholes to distract the eye. Her eyes were blue. More importantly, they held the confidence of power.

I tried to detect how she had acquired her honoured position. She looked aloof but assured. She looked as if she could not only reach decisions, but make other people see that whatever she decreed was their only course. For us she spelled doom. The prophetess of the Bructeri was too old to be a young woman, yet too young to be called old. For Rome, she was the wrong age altogether. She knew too much to forgive us, and too little to tire of fighting us. I knew at once that we had nothing to offer her.

Helvetius knew too. 'Best of luck, Falco. Let's hope for all our sakes we haven't turned up on her doorstep at a bad time of the month.'

I had five sisters and a girlfriend who all let rip when it suited them; I had learned to dodge. But I was beginning to think that this lady might call *any* day she had to deal with Romans the wrong one. A knot of tension, caused by bad food and too little sleep, was forming in my gut.

She moved among the feasting men as if she were welcoming them. As a hostess she was neither cool nor flushed with grating charm. Her manner was open, yet highly reserved. We saw her take no food (part of her aura – no need for sustenance), but once she raised a cup to the whole company, and then applause and cheerful noise broke out anew. As she went round the tables people spoke up to her as equals, but they listened to her replies very steadily. Only once did we see her laughing, with a warrior who must have brought his adolescent son to an assembly for the first time. Afterwards she spent several minutes talking quietly to the boy, who was so overawed he could hardly answer her.

People handed her gifts. The warrior who had captured me gave her my knife.

Our chief gestured to us. She must have thanked him for the donation. She looked once in our direction, and we felt as if she knew everything about us without being told.

She was moving on.

With both hands I broke the rope which tethered me to the others. I strode up to her – though not so near I earned a lance through my throat. She was taller than me. She wore a handsome torque in twisted gold alloy, less heavy than some but more intricate; it looked Hibernian. Her earrings were Greek – gold crescents with extremely fine granulation; they were exquisite. So was her fine clear skin. For a moment it was like approaching any attractive girl who has been fortunate in the heirloom stakes. Then I met the full impact of her personality. Close to, the first impression was of formidable intelligence, sharply applied. Those blue eyes seemed to have been waiting to confront me. They were utterly still. Never had I been so aware of meeting someone so markedly different.

Most dangerous was her honesty. The circus of tinkers who surrounded her might well be composed of charlatans. But Veleda held herself separate and shone, untouched by their tawdriness.

I turned to the chief. 'Tell your prophetess I have travelled all the way from Rome to speak to her.' I was surprised no one moved for a weapon, but they seemed to take their cue from her. She gave none. The chief did not respond to my request either. 'Tell Veleda,' I insisted, 'I wish to speak with her in Caesar's name!'

She made a small impatient movement, presumably at my

mentioning the hated and feared word of Caesar. The chief said something in their own language. Veleda did not answer him.

Diplomacy is hard enough when people acknowledge you trying. I lost patience. 'Lady, don't look so hostile – it spoils a lovely face!' Once I had set off so irritably without bothering whether she would understand, it would have been feeble to stop. 'I came in peace. As you will see if you inspect them, my escort is extremely young and shy. We pose no threat to the mighty Bructeri.' In fact their experiences – and possibly the example of living with hard nuts like Helvetius and myself – had stiffened the recruits visibly.

Talking did seem to have aroused some contemptuous interest from Veleda, so I quickly continued: 'It's bad enough bringing a peace mission that nobody has asked for. I did hope to experience your legendary German hospitality; I'm disappointed, madam, by our present plight . . .' I gestured to the rest of my party again; they pressed closer together behind me. This time a warrior, probably drunk, misinterpreted and jerked forward aggressively. Veleda showed no reaction, though someone else held him off. I sighed. 'I wish I could say communication doesn't seem to be your tribe's strong point – but it's painfully clear what they intend. If you refuse to listen to my message, I ask you simply, let me return with my companions and tell our Emperor we failed.'

The prophetess still stared at me, without a sign. In a lifetime of hard conversations this was plumbing new depths. I let my voice lighten. 'If you really propose to make us all slaves, I warn you my soldiers are shore-bred fisherlads; they know nothing about cattle and not one of them can plough. As for me, I can manage a little light market gardening, but my mother would soon tell you that I'm useless in the house . . .'

I had done it. '*Silence!*' said Veleda.

I had achieved more than I bargained for: 'Right. I'm a good Roman boy, princess. When women speak to me firmly in Latin, I do what they say.'

We were getting somewhere now. As usual, it was down an alley where I would rather not have gone.

The prophetess smiled bitterly. 'Yes, I speak your tongue. It seemed necessary. When did a Roman ever bother to learn ours?' She had a strong, even, thrilling voice which it could have been a pleasure to listen to. I was no longer surprised. She made everything she did or said seem inevitable. Naturally, when traders came she wanted to exchange the news and ensure they never cheated her. Much the same went for any ambassadors who crept out of the woods.

I did have a smattering of Celtic from Britain, but so many miles lay between these tribes and those, it was a separate dialect and useless here.

I fell back on the normal degrading rites of diplomacy: 'Your civility rebukes us.' It sounded like a comic play translated from a poor original by some hack poet in Tusculum. 'I would be praising the lady Veleda for her beauty, yet I believe she would rather hear me compliment her skill and intellect – '

The lady Veleda spoke in her own language, quietly. What she said was brief, and her people laughed. The expression was probably much ruder, but its import was, *This man makes me feel tired.*

So much for diplomacy.

Veleda tipped her chin up. She knew her striking looks, yet despised using them. 'What,' she enquired deliberately, 'have you come here to say?'

That was straightforward. However, there was no way I could simply answer, *Where's Munius, and will you kindly stop your warriors attacking Rome?*

I tried the frank grin. 'I'm getting the worst of this!'

Some trickster must have grinned at her like that before. 'You are getting what you deserve.' She sounded like another high-handed girl I often quarrelled with.

'Veleda, what Vespasian sent me here to say is vital to all of us. It cannot be bandied about like a cheap exchange of insults in a drunken shouting match. You speak for your nation – '

'No,' she interrupted me.

'You are the venerated priestess of the Bructeri – '

Veleda smiled quietly. Her smile was completely private, with no shared human contact. Its effect was to make her seem untouchable. She said, 'I am an unmarried woman who dwells in the forest with her thoughts. The gods have given me knowledge – '

'Your deeds also will never be forgotten.'

'I have done nothing. I merely provide my opinions if people ask for them.'

'Then your mere opinions have given you great powers of leadership! Deny ambition if you will, but you and Civilis nearly ruled Europe.' And nearly ruined it. 'Lady, your opinions lit the whole world like a lightning storm. Perhaps you were right, but now the world needs rest. The fight is over.'

'The fight will never be over.'

The simple way Veleda spoke alarmed me. Had she been a conventional power-seeker, these boisterous warriors would have sneered at her and Civilis would have seen her as a rival instead of a partner. She might have roused the rabble once or twice with furious oratory, but probably the Bructeri themselves would have seen her off. Even the hero Arminius had been defeated by his own people in the end. A leader who would not seek the trappings of leadership would be beyond comprehension in Rome. Here, her very rejection of ambition increased her strength.

'It's over,' I insisted. 'Rome is herself. To fight now is to run against bedrock. You cannot defeat Rome.'

'We did. We will.'

'That was then, Veleda.'

'Our time will come again.'

However confident I sounded, Veleda too felt secure. She was turning away once more. I refused to be silenced by a woman presenting her back to me. All my adult life women had been treating me like a bathhouse scraping-slave who hadn't earned his tip.

With nothing to lose, I tried making it personal. 'If this is the vaunted Gallic Empire, I'm not impressed, Veleda. Civilis has bunked off, and all I see here is a clearing in the forest with the kind of tawdry sideshow that turns up at every horse fair. Just another girl with a yearning for show business, trying to make a name for herself – and what's more, discovering that success means all her hangdog relations expect her to find them a job in her retinue . . . I'm sorry for you. Yours look even worse than my own.' From their impassive faces the lady's relations were either dumber than I thought, or had not shared her Latin tutor. She herself now faced up to me. Family feeling, I dare say. I carried on more quietly: 'Excuse the jibes. My people may be low, but I'm missing them.' She did not appear to have taken my point that Romans were human too. Still, I had her attention, probably.

'Veleda, your influence rests on your successful prophecy that the Roman legions would be destroyed. An easy feat. Anyone who watched the struggle to be emperor could see the Roman stake in Europe was at risk. With only two straws to draw, you picked the lucky answer. That won't work now. Rome has full control again. Once Rome was revived, Petilius Cerialis marched his men along the western bank of the Rhenus from the Alps to the Britannic Ocean, and Rome's enemies fell back before them all the way. Where is your triumphant Civilis nowadays? In the sea, probably.'

The official version of our own commander's fighting prowess may have pleased his urbane mistress in Colonia but it cannot have impressed a shrewd, scornful woman who could see the Cerialis flagship moored on her personal landing-stage. Yet Veleda knew as well as I did that he may have been disorganised, but even Cerialis had won.

'I hear,' said the prophetess as if she hoped to enjoy my discomfiture, 'our kinsman Civilis has dyed his hair red again.'

Well that was an unexpected bonus. I had not dared hope for news. And it didn't sound as if the rebel was in hiding here.

'He's not with you?'

'Civilis only feels at home on the western bank of the river.'

'Not even on The Island?'

'Nowadays, not even there.'

'Rome will barber Civilis. The question is, resourceful prophetess, will you now have the courage to see that the legions were *not* defeated, and help reconstruct the world which we all so nearly lost?'

I ran out of appeals. The prophetess was still so calm I felt like a man eating grit. 'The decision,' she told me, 'will be made by the Bructeri.'

'Is that why they are here? Veleda, give up your fanatical life of opposing Rome. The Bructeri, and other peoples, will listen to you.'

'My life is irrelevant. The *Bructeri* will never give up opposing Rome!'

Looking around the Bructeri, I was surprised they had ever listened to anyone.

Veleda stayed as aloof as a Greek oracle or a sibyl. Her routine with the tower was just as much of a fake as their terrifying rituals at Delphi or gumae. But Greek and Roman prophets envelop destinies in riddles; Veleda used the open truth. Her best ploy, I thought, was that, like an orator who voices the people's secret thoughts, she drew on deep feelings which already existed. They believed they were making their own choices. We had seen it here: she was hosting this gathering as if she intended to play no part in the coming arguments. Yet I still believed that the prophetess would achieve the result she wanted. It would be the wrong result for Rome. And Veleda's belief in it looked unshakeable.

This time my intervention was over. Veleda's rare public appearance was ending. She began to move and her supporters regrouped to protect her from being detained.

Once again she turned back to me. It was as if she read my thoughts: that if big decisions were about to be made at this gathering, we might have arrived at the right time. She took pleasure in telling me I would have no chance of affecting events: 'You and your companions are a gift to me. I have been asked to endorse a fate which you can probably guess.' For the first time she looked curious about us. 'Are you afraid of death?'

'No.' Only angry.

'I have yet to decide,' she announced cordially.

I managed to fight back one final time: 'Veleda, you demean yourself and your honoured reputation by slaughtering an old soldier, his servant, and a group of innocent boys!'

I had offended everyone. The chief who brought us felled me with a stupendous blow.

Veleda had reached her tower. Her male relations assembled at the foot of it, facing out towards the company. As the slim figure glided away alone into her retreat, the shadow of the great Roman doorway fell across her golden hair. The signal-tower abruptly swallowed her. The effect was sinister.

It roused all the more anxiety if you were lying on the grass with your pride lopped and a pain in your head, facing the thought of a grisly death in a Bructian sacred grove.

LII

Helvetius made a cursory attempt to help me rise. 'Didn't do too well there!'

I shook him off. 'Anyone who thinks his winning words stand a better chance than mine can go and try his luck in the tower!'

The scathing quips dried up.

Two of the lady's relations had been deputed to relocate us in a long stockade made of twiggy hurdles that still looked as if they were growing. This must be where she kept live gifts prior to their ritual butchering. They herded us over there, and penned us in. It was occupied already. The specimen we found huddled in a corner seemed unlikely to propitiate the hoary god whom Lentullus and I had seen in the grove.

'Oh look everyone, we've found Dubnus!'

Our lost pedlar had come in for a heavy battering. He must have been bruised in a rich pattern, then some days later somebody had gone over him with the deliberate aim of filling in any gaps that had shown between the previous contusions. 'What was this for?'

'Being a Ubian.'

'Don't lie! You came selling the Bructeri information about us. They must have used the information, but shown you their contempt!'

He looked as if he expected us to attack him too, but we made a point of explaining that we never hit people whose tribes were officially Romanised. 'Not even two-timing ones, Dubnus.'

'Not even runaway interpreters who skip just when we're needing them.'

'Not even Ubian bastards who sell us into captivity.'

'Not even you, Dubnus.'

He said something in his own tongue, which we did not need an interpreter to understand.

What happened next was a surprise. Hardly had Veleda's shambling adherents roped up the wattle and left us to ponder, than they were there again removing their feeble wisps of lashing and pulling open the exit fence.

'Mithras! The witch has changed her mind. We're all getting nice new cloaks and going to be guests of honour at the feast . . .'

'Save your breath to cool your gruel, centurion. That one won't change her mind.'

The lanks dragged us all out. The sight of Dubnus seemed to remind them that they might enjoy feeling big. He was too mashed already to be worth making him squeal again, so they started giving the odd thump to Helvetius and me. When we shoved them aside angrily, they joined the trend and picked on the centurion's servant instead. This time Helvetius decided he wasn't having it and squared up to defend his man. We braced ourselves for trouble – and trouble duly arrived. Not what we expected, though.

First Veleda popped back out of her stone retreat.

A trumpet sounded. 'Jupiter Best and Greatest – *that's one of ours!*'

It was a short, slow call on a clear but subdued instrument. Its mournful tremor sounded Roman, yet not quite right. It came from the forest somewhere close. It was blown on the twisted bronze horn which sentries use, and the call was recognisably the signal for the second night watch. It was four hours early tonight.

Then Tigris ran into the clearing, went straight across to Veleda, and lay down with his nose between his paws.

I hardly had time to guess that the prophetess must have spied the embassy from her signal-tower when someone else arrived. It was Helena's younger brother. I had long suspected this character of harbouring deep qualities, but it was the first time he had shown us his talent for makeshift spectacle.

He clip-clopped into the clearing with Orosius as an outrider. Neither of them had the trumpet, which subtly implied someone else did (they must have left it propped against a tree). They looked good; one or both of them had spent all afternoon combing plumes and buffing bronze. Helena's brother was tackling the Bructeri as if he had an army of fifteen thousand waiting down the road. There was no road, but Camillus Justinus gave the impression he might have had one built for him. There was no army either; we knew that.

For a man who had spent the last month under canvas in the wilderness, his rig was immaculate. His air of restrained bravado was also pitched perfectly. He had the best of our Gallic horses. He must have raided our supplies for olive oil and burnished the beast so that even its hooves gleamed with their unorthodox marinade. If the horse was well groomed, so was he. Somehow, in the depths of the forest, he and Orosius had managed to shave. They made the rest of us look like the riff-raff with fleas and funny accents who can never get a seat at the races even when the gatekeeper has gone to lunch and left his ten-year-old brother as bouncer.

Justinus wore the entire panoply of his tribunal rank, plus a few details he had invented for himself: a white tunic hemmed in purple; spanking greaves with ornate gilding; a thrusting horsehair plume atop a helmet that had a shine which flashed round the forest every time he moved his head. The breastplate which sat over his heavily fringed leathers looked three times as bright as usual. Looped up around its heroically modelled torso our lad wore his heavy crimson cloak with a debonair swing. In the crook of one arm he was carrying – in an extremely relaxed manner – some sort of ceremonial stave, a novelty he had apparently copied from formal statues of Augustus. His expression had that Emperor's noble calm, and if the noble calm was disguising fright not even his friends could tell.

He rode halfway across the clearing, slowly enough to give the prophetess a good stare at his turnout. He dismounted. Orosius accepted his reins – and his stave – with silent deference. Justinus approached Veleda with a firm spring in his tribunal boots, then swept off his helmet as a sign of respect to her. The Camilli were a tall family, especially in triple-soled military footware; for once she was looking a Roman directly in the eyes. The eyes she would be seeing now were big, brown, modest, and momentously sincere.

Justinus paused. He coloured slightly: nice effect. Removing his gilded pot had allowed the lady to receive the full benefit of his frank admiration and boyish reserve. The sensitive eyes must be working their magic, and he matched the deep stillness of the prophetess with his own steadiness.

Then he said something. He seemed to address Veleda confidentially, yet the pitch of his voice carried everywhere.

We knew the man. We knew the voice. But none of us had the slightest idea what he said to the prophetess.

Camillus Justinus had spoken in her own tongue.

He did it with the lilting fluency I remembered from his Greek. It took Veleda longer than she could have liked before she recovered; then she inclined her head. Justinus spoke to her again; this time she glanced in our direction. He must have asked her a question. She considered her answer, then abruptly replied.

'Thank you,' said Justinus very civilly, in Latin this time, as if paying her the compliment of assuming she would understand him too. 'Then I'll greet my friends first, please . . .' He was not asking her permission; it was a statement of intent. Then he turned back to her with a good-mannered apology: 'My name is Camillus Justinus, by the way.'

His face remained impassive as he walked across to us. We took our cue from him. He shook hands with every one of us, in a measured and grave style. With the eyes of the entire Bructian gathering upon him, Justinus did little more than speak our names, while we muttered as much information as we could.

'Marcus Didius.'

'She claims to be just a woman who dwells in the tower with her thoughts.'

'Helvetius.'

'Somebody should give her something else to think about!' Helvetius could not resist this typical shaft.

'Ascanius.'

'We're all due for a nasty death, sir.'

'Probus.'

'Tribune, what have you said to her?'

'Sextus. We're going to talk things over quietly; let me see what I can do. Lentullus!'

When he had greeted us all, his bright eyes met mine directly. 'Well, you've left me everything to do here! I even had to blow the bloody trumpet for myself.'

He was using the joke to hide some anxiety; behind the glint of amusement his face looked sad. I suddenly stepped up to him, pulling out the amulet I had been given in Vetera; he saw what it was and ducked his head to receive it round his own neck. 'If it's any help, a contact told me Veleda may be yearning for some decent conversation . . . That's for Helena. Watch yourself.'

'Marcus!' he embraced me like a brother, then I took his helmet from him. He walked bravely away from us.

He went back to Veleda. He was a shy man, who had learned to answer challenges alone. Veleda was waiting for him like a woman who thought she was likely to regret something.

I whipped round towards the pedlar, the only one among us whom the tribune had pointedly ignored. 'What did he say to her, Dubnus?'

Dubnus cursed, but answered me. 'He said: "You must be Veleda.

I bring you greetings from my Emperor, and messages of peace . . ." '

'You're holding back! He made an offer – that was obvious.'

Without bothering to question what I had in mind, our reliable Helvetius stomped up behind the pedlar and hoicked his arms back in a wrestling hold that bit persuasively. Dubnus gasped, 'He said: "I see my comrades are your hostages. I offer myself in exchange." '

I had known it. Justinus dashed into danger with the same offhand courage his sister showed when she decided impatiently that someone had to be businesslike. 'So what did Veleda answer him?'

' *"Come into my tower!"* '

What the pedlar said was true. The moment Justinus reached her, Veleda strode back towards her monument. He followed. Then we watched our innocent tribune walk into the tower alone with her.

LIII

I strode to the tower base. The goat-thief guards were standing about looking mystified, but they closed ranks when I appeared. I stood at the door with my head thrown back, staring up at the old Roman stonework with its rows of red brick-tile strengthening. There was nothing I could do. I returned to the troops. The tribune's dog remained behind, sitting at the entrance to the tower and watching intently for his master to reappear.

The recruits were taking bets on his chances, half terrified and half envious: 'She'll eat him!'

I wanted to concentrate on other things. 'Perhaps she'll spit him out . . .'

How was I to tell the tribune's sister about this? She would blame me, I knew.

'Why has he gone in there, sir?'

'You heard him: he's going to talk things over quietly.'

'What things, sir?'

'Nothing much, I expect.'

Fate. World history. His friends' lives. The tribune's death . . .

'Sir – '

'Shut up, Lentullus.'

I went back to the hurdles. I eased myself into a squatting position, trying to keep off the ground. It was the wrong time of year for sitting on grass; tonight would have a heavy dew. It was starting to feel like the wrong time of year for anything.

The others all fell on Orosius, then slowly joined me, settling down to wait for the unknown. Orosius had little to say for himself except that in his opinion the tribune was all right. I tweaked his ear and told him we knew that.

I should have known. He had an appetite for information. Camillus Justinus would not spend three years safeguarding the frontiers of a province without learning how to speak to its people. Now he was on his own with much more than the language.

256

He was so thorough it shook me. With his fresh-faced way of getting to know every soldier he commanded, this unlikely soul had even persuaded some hardbitten *bucinator* to teach him to sound a passable trumpet alarm. A month of woodcraft had depressed him, but left his ingenuity intact. Having come on this adventure in the first place, he would not give up. But he was twenty. He had never been exposed to harm. He stood no chance.

He had never been exposed to *women*, but perhaps we were safe there.

'Are foreign priestesses virgins, sir?'

'I believe it's not obligatory.' Only Rome equated chastity with holiness; and even Rome installed ten vestals at a time, in order to give latitude for mistakes.

'Is the tribune going to – '

'He's going to talk about politics.' Even so, the novel combination of the destiny of nations and the most attractive woman he had ever had to talk to might prove a heady mix.

'The witch might have other ideas!' They were bolder now. 'Maybe the tribune doesn't know what to do – '

'The tribune seems a lad who can improvise.'

But I certainly hoped I never had to tell his sister that I had let some mad-eyed prophetess make a man of her little brother at the top of a signal-tower.

When the torches had waned and the feast died down, I ordered our lads to rest. Later, I left Helvetius on watch, picked my way between the slumbering Bructeri and stole near the tower. One guard with a lance lolled asleep on the entrance steps. I could have grasped his weapon and closed his windpipe with its shaft, but I let him be. Others were inside the tower base, so entering was impossible.

I walked round outside. Moonlight draped the wall with sheaths of startling white. High above shone a faint glimmer from a lamp. I could hear voices. Difficult to tell which language they were using; the level of conversation was too low. It sounded like discussion rather than argument. It sounded more as if they were talking over a concert or the merits of a wall fresco than ascertaining the Empire's horoscope. At one point the tribune said something that amused the prophetess; she answered, then they both laughed.

I could not decide whether to groan or grin. I went back to my men.

Helvetius thumped my shoulder. 'All right?'

'They're talking.'

'That sounds dangerous!'

'More dangerous when they stop, centurion.' Suddenly I confided, 'I want to marry his sister.'

'He told me.'

'I didn't think he knew I was serious.'

'*He's* worried,' said Helvetius, 'that you may not be aware it's what his sister has in mind.'

'Oh, she's a frank woman! I imagined he thought I was just a low-life adventurer who was playing around with her.'

'No, he thinks you're the man for the business.' Helvetius clapped me on the back. 'So this is cosy – now we all know where we are!'

'True. The man I want to be my children's favourite uncle is – '

'Is likely to come back to us with a rather stiff walk and a queer look in his eye! You can't make his choices. He's not a baby.'

'No, he's twenty, and never been kissed . . .' Well, probably. With anyone else I might have wondered whether he had acquired his slick mastery of German from a girl. 'He's never had his throat cut with a sickle in a sacred grove either, centurion!'

'Get some rest, Falco. You know what he's like when he gets an interesting chat going. If the lady feels just as talkative, it's going to be a long night.'

It was the longest night I spent in Germany. When he came back, all the others were asleep. I was watching out for him.

It was dark. The moon had travelled into a deep band of cloud, but our eyes were adjusted. He saw me stand up. We clasped hands, then spoke in whispers, Justinus in a light, excited tone.

'Lot to tell you.' His adrenalin was running at a fierce rate.

'What's going on? Are you on parole?'

'She wants time alone. I have to go back when the moon comes out, and she'll tell me if it's war or peace.' He was exhausted. 'I hope her lunar forecast is reliable . . .'

I surveyed the sky. The heaviness above was an unshed storm; I could see it would pass over. 'She's right – and like all magic, that's observation, not prophecy.'

We crouched down by a tree. He gave me something. 'A knife?'

'Yours. She had her presents on a coffer; I recognised it. I told her it belonged to my brother-in-law.'

'Thanks – which includes the compliment. It's my best knife, but if she's handing out hospitality gifts I can suggest more useful things.'

258

'I think she gave me the knife to show she was detached, and not influenced by presents.'

'Or on the make!'

'Cynic! What should I have asked for?'

I made a silly suggestion, and he laughed. But his task was too oppressive for jokes. 'Marcus, I've nothing to offer. We should have brought presents.'

'We brought the cash box.'

'That's to pay the recruits!' He had a strange simplicity.

'They'd rather be living than dead but paid up.'

'Ah!'

'I'll fetch the money from where you left it. Orosius can show me. Now tell me what you and Veleda talked about.'

'It was quite an experience!' That sounded ominous. 'We talked ourselves all round the forum. I've done what I could for the Emperor's mission. I told her we all ought to accept that the people on the west bank of the Rhenus have *chosen* to be Romanised, and that unless there is a threat to their security, the Emperor has no ambitions for crossing to the east.' Justinus dropped his voice. 'Marcus, I'm not so certain that will always hold.'

'It's policy. Things may change along the Danube, but don't complicate the issue with what may never happen. She's shrewd enough to draw conclusions for herself.'

'I've no training in this. I feel so badly equipped!'

Our one hope was that Veleda might trust him for his transparent integrity.

'Have faith. At least she's listening. Before you did your parade-ground stunt, I spoke to her myself – '

'I heard some of that. Orosius and I were hiding in the trees. We couldn't get close enough to catch everything, but I've tried to follow up what you said about the legions being in power again.'

'She has to be convinced that if the tribes fling themselves against the disciplined might of Rome it can only be suicide.'

'Marcus, she knows that.' He spoke quietly, as if with loyalty to her.

'That's not what she said.'

'She was in front of her people – '

'And arguing with a shyster of course . . .'

'No, I think your words went home. She seems deeply troubled. I fancy she was brooding on the future before we ever came here. That may be why she called the tribal gathering. When I urged her to tell the tribes the truth about what she foresaw for them, I could tell from her face the responsibility alarms her.'

'Use that.'

'I don't have to. Veleda is already suffering.'

'Dear gods, this is just like talking to you about the barmaid at the Medusa!'

I had meant it as a joke, but Justinus dropped his head. 'Something I should have told you. I owe you an apology.'

'What for?' Our rissole lunch at the Medusa seemed a thousand years ago.

'After you left for Colonia there was a rumpus at the tavern. Somebody noticed a funny smell, and it wasn't the dish of the day that time. They found the body of the legate's bedchamber slave buried under a floor. Regina confessed. When they were quarrelling she lost her temper and hit him too hard with an amphora.'

I said it made a change from battered barmaids anyway.

'You knew she was trouble. So Marcus, tell me about this one!'

'Use your initiative – you seem to have plenty. I keep away from prophets; my mother says nice boys don't mess with venerated girls.'

We were still giggling when the moon re-emerged.

'Marcus.'

'Justinus.'

'It's Quintus,' he offered wryly, like a someone making friends rather belatedly after going to bed.

'I'm honoured. I didn't even know your private name.'

'I don't tell many people,' he said quietly. 'Now, what am I doing? *Exchanging gifts, ending the battles –* '

'A snip! And *exercising caution*. Don't end up like Lupercus.'

'Ah! *Asking about Lupercus*.' I myself had been prepared to forget what had happened to Lupercus, in case the recollection gave Veleda bloodthirsty ideas. 'The first thing is to persuade her to release the rest of you . . . I hope you get back.' He could not disguise the crack in his voice.

'I hope we *all* do! Listen, when you climb the tower again, if you find Veleda in her best gown with her hair braided specially, my advice is forget the Empire and do a runner straight back here.'

'Don't be ridiculous!' he answered, in a rare mood of tetchiness.

At least during this absence I found an occupation. I woke Orosius and we crept off through the woods to where he and Justinus had left their tent and supplies. We packed everything and brought it nearer to the tower. Then we led forward the horse with the cash box, and I whistled an alert to the tribune.

The prophetess herself pushed out of the doors through a clump of her relatives; Justinus was not with her. She was extremely pale, and tightly gripping a cloak around herself. We dumped the strong-box on the ground and I opened it to show her the silver. Veleda inspected the money cautiously while I tried to sound as clean-living as Justinus. 'I know: the Bructeri cannot be bought . . . That's not the intention, lady. This is a sign of the Emperor's friendship.'

'Your negotiator made that plain.'

'Where is he?' I asked bluntly.

'Safe.' She was sneering at my anxiety. 'You are Falco? I wish to speak with you.'

She led me just inside the lower portion of the tower. There was a bare octagonal basement, with stairs leading up several storeys round the neatly coursed Roman brick of the inner walls. Each storey was slightly reduced in diameter to provide stability for the tower; only the top was floored, since only the open roof had been built to be used. That, with some modifications for comfort, was where the prophetess lived. She did not invite me to ascend.

Veleda was frowning. I tried to sound sympathetic as I asked, 'Do I deduce that Luna reappeared prematurely?' I was right. Veleda had still not decided what to do. The uncertainty was knotting her like a snaggled fishing net.

'I have two things to say.' She spoke hurriedly, as if she had been pressurised into this. 'I have agreed to your departure. Go tonight. No one will hinder you.'

'Thanks. What's the other thing?'

'The death of Munius Lupercus.'

'So you do know? A woman among the Ubians told me otherwise.'

'I know now,' she said coldly. Obviously they had less in common than Claudia Sacrata had convinced herself. She handed me a small fold of crimson cloth. Inside were two more trifles from her curio cabinet – miniature silver spears of the kind legates receive as good service awards from the Emperor. Lupercus would have been due for his third at the end of his fatal tour in Vetera.

'So he did come here?'

'He was never here.' She spoke with her usual assurance, perhaps relieved to be distanced from the sordid tale. 'Those were brought to me later. I am content that you should return them to the man's mother or his wife.'

I thanked her, and then she told me what had happened. Even Veleda looked subdued when she had finished. I had no sympathy with legates, but it set me back. 'Have you given this information to the tribune Camillus?'

'No.'

I understood why. She had established a friendly pact with Justinus; this could wreck it.

Civilis had sent Munius Lupercus across country with what Veleda chose to call a mixed group from various tribes. I did not press her for more detail; she was right not to provide fuel for recriminations. The legate had been wounded; he had lost his fort and seen his legion slaughtered; he had thought the Empire was disintegrating too. Whether he begged for release or for death, or whether his guards simply lost patience and wanted to be back with Civilis at the fighting, they suddenly accused Lupercus of cowardice. Then they treated him to their version of a coward's fate: he was stripped, bound, half garrotted, thrown in a swamp, and pressed down with hurdles until he drowned.

To do her justice, Veleda looked as though she hated telling it as much as I hated hearing it. 'They had deprived me of my gift, so the truth was slow to emerge.'

I buried my jaw in my hand. 'This truth were better submerged in the swamp with him.'

'If I were his mother or wife,' said Veleda, 'I would wish to know.'

'So would my mother and my future wife, but like you, they are exceptional . . .'

She changed the subject. 'That is all I can tell you. You and your men must depart discreetly; I have no wish to insult the chief who brought you here by exchanging his present too openly.'

'Where's Camillus?' I demanded suspiciously.

'Above. I still wish to talk to him.' Veleda paused, as if she read all my thoughts. 'Naturally,' she said softly, 'your friend will say farewell.'

I was desperate. 'Does it have to be an exchange?'

'That was what was offered,' smiled the prophetess.

At that point Justinus himself came out on to the stairs above us and clattered down to the basement. 'So what happened to Lupercus?'

262

'The legate,' I relied carefully, thinking as I spoke, 'was executed on his way here. Too much time has elapsed for the details to be known.'

Veleda's mouth was pinched, but she went along with it. Then she passed Justinus and left the two of us together. As she climbed the stair her cloak slipped. I could not see what gown she wore, but her rich gold hair was now braided extremely neatly into a plait the thickness of my wrist. Justinus and I avoided each other's eyes.

I made a small snort of annoyance. '*Eheu!* I meant to ask her about horses . . .'

Justinus laughed. 'I asked her for what you wanted.'

She had agreed to my silly suggestion. 'Quintus, you smooth-talking devil! I hope you never come to me trying to wheedle a loan . . . Right, I gather she needs more of your verbal fluency. Don't bite your tongue off chattering! She wants us to leave quickly, but we'll have to wait until first light . . .'

'I must do what I have to here, Marcus.' He looked strained.

'Too many good men have said that, then thrown away promising careers with no public thanks. Don't be a fool – or a dead hero. Tell her the exchange is off. I'm expecting to see you before we leave, tribune. I'll load up, then we'll sit it out and wait for you.' He and I were responsible for the lives of Helvetius and the recruits. We both knew what had to happen.

'Leave at dawn,' Justinus said tersely. He seized the old wooden newel post and swung back up the stairs.

I left him, uncertain whether he intended to come with us. I had a bad feeling that the tribune might not yet know himself.

However, I was damn sure that Veleda knew what *she* was intending for *him.*

Outside, I quietly roused everyone. They huddled round as I whis pered what was happening.

'The witch is letting us steal away, but her colleagues may view it differently, so don't make a sound. Thanks to our fearsome nego-tiator, she's giving us new transport.' I paused. 'So the question is, how many of you horrible seaside beach bums are at home on a Liburnian?'

As I had thought, for once we had no problem. After all, the legio First Adiutrix had been formed from discards of the Misenum fleet. These were the best troops I could have chosen for bringing the general's flagship home.

PART SIX:
GOING HOME (PERHAPS)

GERMANIA LIBERA, BELGICA AND UPPER GERMANY
November, AD 71

'After his first military action against the Romans, Civilis had sworn an oath, like the primitive savage he was, to dye his hair red and let it grow until such time as he had annihilated the legions . . .'

Tacitus, *Histories*

LIV

We managed to board without alerting the Bructeri. At first I refused to take the pedlar, then I relented, in order to make quite certain by keeping him with us that he could not inform on us again. The two mounts Justinus and Orosius had arrived on had been swiftly appropriated by our hosts, but we did tice our remaining four up the gangplank, probably because they could not see where we were leading them.

Fumbling in the dark we struggled in silence to untangle ropes and free wedged oars. Under way with an experienced crew the Liburnian would outstrip anything in these waters, but her condition was uncertain, we lacked manpower, and none of us knew the craft, let alone the river we were about to sail. A group of recruits slipped along the waterfront, putting a spike into boats that might pursue us, but the noise worried Helvetius and we recalled them.

The recruits were in their element. They could all sail and row. Well, all except Lentullus. Lentullus was still our problem boy who couldn't do anything.

The tone of the sky was lightening; I was starting to feel desperate. 'Helvetius, if Camillus doesn't come soon, you take the lads and get out of here.'

'You're not going ashore again?'

'I won't leave him.'

'Forget the heroics. Here he is!'

I admit, I was amazed.

We had eased the ship from her moorings and re-anchored in the channel. Probus was waiting at the quay with a bumboat to row the tribune out to us. We already had the anchor up as we hauled them in.

'Is it war?'

'It's peace.'

It was too dark to see the tribune's face.

267

Justinus walked to the stern of the ship without another word. I looked at his set back, then signalled the others not to bother him. He settled himself in a black corner, leaning against the general's cabin and staring back towards the shore. His little dog lay down at his feet, whimpering as it recognised unhappiness. Seeing the tribune's despondent pose, my own heart sank.

We had plenty to do. We let the ship ride on the current at first, for quietness. As the light increased, the full extent of a year's neglect became obvious. Soon we had half our troops furiously bailing while Helvetius cursed and tried to fix a dried-out bilge pump. It had been a sophisticated apparatus once. So sophisticated, a period out of commission had left its wood and calfskin utterly defunct.

We drifted on, with no sign of pursuit. Ascanius and Sextus had found the sails. The leather had stiffened so much it was almost unmanageable, but we stamped it flat as best we could. The smaller triangular jib went up fairly soon, though the square sail took much longer to organise. Then we found our ship sheering too near the bank. A Liburnian is a big vessel to be manoeuvred by a band of novices, some of whom are also idiots, but I still shook my head when eyes were cast sternwards.

'The tribune could add his weight here!'

'The tribune's done enough.'

'Sir – '

'He wants to feel gloomy. Let him be!'

With all other hands assisting on the danger side, we just shipped the oars in time to avoid crashing them, then held our breath as the galley scraped and bumped along the shallows. Somehow we succeeded in turning her back into the channel. She limped on in the grey light of a cold November morning, while we spent another hour working on the sail. It finally jerked into position to a weary cheer. After that it was a mad rush back to bailing duty, then we took stock.

We had no weapons apart from the javelins, and little food. Only two of us had armour. We had salvaged four horses – who might well end up grilled. We no longer possessed cash for bartering. We had the Bructeri on the north bank, and the Tencteri on the south, both contemptuous of Romans in distress. Landing would be fatal until we came to the River Rhenus, which must be over a week away. The way our ship was listing and dragging foretold a week of hard work.

We were alive and free. That surprise was so pleasant we put half the recruits to rowing while the rest jettisoned lumber to lighten their burden, attended to the sails – and sang.

Helvetius screwed some thrust from the pump.

Then, at last, I let Ascanius take the rudder while I walked astern to investigate what Veleda had done to our boy.

LV

'What ho, Masinissa!' Justinus was too polite to tell me to remove my happy grin. 'I'm glad the amulet worked.'

'Oh it worked!' He said it in an odd voice.

I assumed my sombre uncle attitude: 'You look tired.'

'It's not serious.'

'Good. I was afraid it might be due to a broken heart.'

'How lucky we know that's not true,' he answered, much too quietly.

'She's too old for you, you have nothing in common, and your mother has enough to endure with Helena and me.'

'Of course,' he said. He might have argued the point about me and Helena.

'Well Quintus Camillus, I'm glad you can be philosophical. You're a decent lad and deserve some fun before you settle down to a dull old life as a senator, but we both know what happened back there had all the makings of a significant experience – the kind that has been known to bruise a thoughtful man's morale.'

'The Senate has been ruled out for me.'

'Wrong. You've rewritten that. I believe there are advantages, if you can tolerate the bores and hypocrites. You only have to attend the Curia once a month, and you get front-row seats in theatres.'

'Please don't jolly me along.'

'All right. As a matter of interest, did you escape or did the lady throw you out?'

'I meant my offer of an exchange. I said I had to stay.'

'Ah well. Some women can't stand pompous types who stick by their principles.'

He was silent.

'Do you want to talk about what happened?'

'No,' he said.

We watched the river slipping away behind us. We were travelling slower than I liked for safety, but it was too fast for the tribune. He had been overwhelmed, then wrenched away before he could adjust. Now he felt racked by the scale of his feelings.

'Be prepared,' I advised. 'People other than me will ask you – people in high positions. A junior officer who has talked to the enemy has a duty to explain.' I was turning to go.

Justinus asked suddenly in a wry voice, 'What happened to Masinissa?'

I stopped. 'After he threw away his princess? He lived with honour for many years, devoting himself to kingship and such.'

'Ah, yes of course!' I waited. He was forcing himself to complete the day's official business. 'When I went back upstairs she had already decided. She will tell her people that a free Gallic Empire can never be established. That Rome will not in our lifetime lose the western Rhenus bank. That liberty in their own territory is worth more than pointless war . . . Can she make them listen?' He sounded desperate.

'She never uses compulsion. Leaving people free to choose sometimes pressures them into choosing the harder course.'

'Oh yes!' he said, rather heavily.

'Was she upset?' A fleeting thought assailed me that he might have been consoling her.

He did not answer my question but asked his own: 'What will happen to her?'

'She'll either become a crazy wraith, or she'll marry some thickset red-haired hulk and have nine children in ten years.'

After a silence Justinus said, 'She prophesied to me that if the eastern tribes resume their nomadic life, invading each other's territory, the Bructeri will be wiped out.'

'It's possible.'

For a long time neither of us spoke.

We heard Ascanius calling that he wanted a relief. I had ordered Helvetius to rest so that he could take a later watch; I had to go. 'One thing puzzles me, Quintus. If Veleda had already decided, why did it take her until dawn to throw you out?'

His pause was almost undetectable. 'She was desperate for some decent conversation, as you said. So was I,' he added.

I laughed, then said he had a subtle knack of being rude, and that I could take a hint.

I loped back to supervise Ascanius. When Ascanius demanded for everyone, *'Did he, or didn't he?'*, I confidently answered no.

Justinus never did return to me the quartermaster's amulet. I was rather surprised he kept it. In fact sometimes, especially when he was wearing that painful expression he had brought with him to the boat, I almost thought he looked like a man who had given it away as a love token to some girl.

Fortuna had protected him. He was not in love; he had told me so. Quintus Camillus Justinus, senior tribune of the First Adiutrix, had proved himself one of the Empire's natural diplomats. Diplomacy involves a certain amount of lying – but I could not believe that Helena's brother would hide the truth from me.

LVI

We soon found ourselves short of time for speculation.

The flagship of Petilius Cerialis was as impetuous and unreliable as the general himself. Apart from the sorry effects of neglect, her rudder must have taken a bad knock while the rebels were towing her away. She steered like a wilful camel and sailed with a high old lack of regard for wind or current. All her weight seemed to lean to one side for some reason, a problem which worsened by the day. We had slipped off in a vessel of character – the kind of riotous character my elder brother Festus used to bring home after a night he could not remember in a tavern a long way from home. Taking her down-river felt like riding a horse who wanted to go backwards. She drew water with all the grace of a sodden log.

Most of the trouble derived from our scanty crew. In the right hands she would have been wonderful. But she was meant to have her double banks of oars fully manned, rigging-hands, a master, his deputy and a complement of marines – not to mention the general, who would no doubt have taken his shift on the oars in a tight corner. Twenty-five of us were simply not enough, and that was counting in Dubnus, who proved useless, and the centurion's servant, who made it plain he preferred to be counted out (the plea for a posting to Moesia had cropped up pathetically again). Then, as the days passed and the river grew wider and deeper, our food supplies dwindled. We were weakening when we most needed strength.

The Rhenus junction caught us unawares. The ship had been making water. We had hauled in her sails and many of us were below, frantically trying to stop the leaks. When Probus shouted, no one heard at first. When he threw back his head and roared, we floundered up on deck. There was some cheering before we realised our grave plight. The undertow had strengthened. The flagship, still trailing a wing to starboard, was now dangerously low in the water and nearly uncontrollable. We were in no condition to tackle turbulence.

I shouted to drop anchor, but it failed to hold.

Just as safety seemed to be in sight, it was being snatched from us. The grey skies made everything seem more ominous. A chill north wind brought the smell of the ocean, cruelly reminding us we wanted to turn our backs on it. We were hoping to pass out into the main river; we had always known that without trained oarsmen we would have to turn downstream. We needed to drift across the Rhenus to the Roman bank, then wind gently down to Vetera. Tackling the upriver current would be impossible. For amateurs who were fighting to stabilise an oversized and leaky galley, things would be delicate enough the other way. At least if we managed to join the Rhenus safely we might hail a fleet vessel to tow us – or even take us off, for we would happily have abandoned any kudos which attached to reclaiming the Liburnian in favour of a quick journey home.

Fate had been generous for long enough, and now she turned her glamorous back on us. Impelled by the increased current and weighed down by a flooded bilge, the flagship slowly started to rotate. Even to us it became obvious she had decided to sink. This was desperate. In November, the river was at its lowest, but it still surged formidably and we were not exactly web-footed coots.

Helvetius shouted 'We have to put her in – *before* the Rhenus takes her!'

He was right. We were the wrong side of the river – still on the *wrong* river – but if she sank in midstream we would lose everything, and men would drown. The recruits might have grown up as harbour boys, but only the famous Batavians had ever swum the Rhenus and survived to boast. I said nothing, but at least one member of our party (me) had never learned to swim at all.

Luckily, although the cantankerous galley strongly objected to sailing nicely to safety, it was perfectly willing to run aground on a hostile shore.

We brought her in, which is to say she bumbled of her own accord up the muddiest beach she could find, with a rending crunch that told us she was now ready to rot. Although the ship was beached, her bitter crew had to wade through a spreading morass of turgid water and silt to reach what for human feet counted as land. She had chosen the Tencteri bank. At least, we hoped, they would not know we had slipped away from Veleda's tower in circumstances their Bructian colleagues might have wanted to query.

The junction of these two great rivers was a sombre scene. The air felt cold. The whole area was unwelcoming. With the ground too spongy for farming, the place seemed lonely and deserted. A sudden flock of heavy geese overhead, silent apart from the eerie swishing of their wings, startled us more than it should have done. We were on edge to the point where it could cause mistakes.

We were in sight of the Rhenus, so we despatched a small party to squelch to the riverbank and look for a Roman ship to hail. For once there were none – naturally. Our bored watch party came back, against orders, feebly maintaining that the ground was too marshy to cross, but we were too dispirited to harangue them. Helvetius being a centurion, made a tiresome attempt to revive us with action.

'What now, Falco?'

'I intend to dry my boots, then spend at least three hours sitting on a hummock and blaming other people for what went wrong . . . What does anyone else suggest?'

'Tribune?'

'I'm too hungry to have brilliant ideas.'

We were all hungry. So Helvetius proposed that since we were trapped here, and since the area was teeming with marsh birds and other wildlife, we might as well unpack our unused javelins and seek out prey with some flesh on it. I could remember what he had once said about stupid officers wanting boar-hunts in places they knew were dangerous, but the recruits were morose with starvation, so we let him lead off a forage band. I sent Lentullus out with a bucket looking for crayfish, to keep him out of our way. The rest of us unpacked the galley and loaded the horses, temporarily reprieved from the pot now that we needed them. Then we set off for drier ground where we could camp.

I had wet feet, and the prospect of sharing one eight-man tent with twenty-four other people was already causing misery. The flints in our tinder-box were now so worn nobody could start the fire. Helvetius had the knack – he was competent at everything. We were, therefore, badly in need of him just at the moment when Orosius and the others sloped into camp with a couple of mangled marsh birds but no centurion, admitting that Helvetius seemed to be lost.

It was so out of character I knew straight away that some disaster had occurred.

Justinus stayed on camp duty. I took Orosius, a horse, and our medical casket.

'Where were you last with him?'

'No one was sure. That's why we all came back.'

'Jupiter!' I hated the sound of this.

'What's happened, Falco?'

'I think he must be hurt.' Or worse.

Inevitably the lad could not remember where the party had strayed. While we were searching the marshes we seemed to hear noises as though someone was tracking us. We could have imagined it, for the sounds were intermittent, but we had no time to investigate. We came to a place where side-channels stagnated amongst giant reeds. There, on a ridge of firm turf, alongside a creek, we found our man.

He was alive. But he had not been able to call for help. He had a Roman throwing-spear piercing his throat, and another in his groin.

'Dear gods! Orosius, one of you careless young bastards will be strangled for this . . .'

'Those aren't ours – '

'Don't lie! Look at them – *look*!'

They were Roman javelins. No question about it. They had nine-inch spikes with soft iron necks which had bent on impact. That was by design. Stuck in an enemy's shield, a long wooden shaft dragging on a crooked head impedes movement and is impossible to pull out and throw back. While the victims struggle, we rush them with swords.

The centurion's eyes were pleading – or, more likely, giving me orders. I refused to meet their deep brown, agitated stare.

Somewhere nearby a bird rose, screaming.

'Keep watch, Orosius . . .'

Blood should never make you panic, a surgeon once told me. He could afford to be philosophical; there was money in blood for him. At this moment, if that surgeon had stepped out from a willow tree, I would have made him a millionaire. Helvetius moaned, proudly holding in the noise. Faced with a man who was suffering so horribly, it was hard not to be terrified. I dared not move him. Even if I could get him to camp, there was no advantage; what had to be done might as well be done here. Then we could think about transporting him.

I rolled my cloak into a bumper to support the lower spear; Helvetius, still unaffected by shock, was gripping the other himself. Breaking the wooden shafts would help lessen their weight, but with the iron stuck in those positions I dared not try . . .

Voices. Orosius, glad of the excuse, disappeared to investigate.

I was muttering, partly to reassure Helvetius, but more to calm myself. 'Don't look at me like that, man. All you have to do is lie there acting brave. It's my problem . . .' He kept trying to say something. 'All right. I'm going to do my best – you can give me your list of complaints later.'

I knew I had to work quickly, but it would have been easier if I had felt at all confident. Most of the blood was coming from the neck wound. One barb had failed to penetrate, which could mean the whole thing was extractable. I closed my mind to the thought that the other wound might be bleeding internally. You have to do what you can.

Our medical box was one item Justinus had managed to save from the Bructeri. Its contents were mainly salves and bandages, but I did find a couple of slender bronze hooks which might help me hold back the surrounding skin enough to free the barb. There was even a gadget for extracting missiles, but I had once seen one used: it had to be inserted, twisted under the point, then pulled out very skilfully. It was a skill I lacked. I elected to try without it first.

There was movement or noise in the channel to my left. Not quite a splash, more a skirling of water. It was so slight that I hardly registered it as I bent over Helvetius; I had no time for otters or frogs in the bulrushes.

'Aurochs . . .' Our tough old soldier was halucinating like a fevered child.

'Don't try to talk – '

Then came a flurry in the osiers, a rush, a cry, and a group of men sprang from nowhere. They had their spears up for hurling, but thoughtfully held on to them with a tight grip once they discovered us.

LVII

It was a hunting party, led by some high-class bastard in discreetly well-woven brown wool. He had a Spanish horse, several reverent companions, two bearers bringing extra spears, and a bad case of apoplectic rage. He stared round, spotted me, and it was in perfect Latin that he spat, 'Oh Castor and Pollux – what are *people* doing here?'

I stood up. 'Existing – like yourself!'

My own Latin stopped him dead.

He hurled himself from the horse, dropped its bridle, then strode nearer – but not too near. 'Thought you were Tencteri. We've heard them about.' That was all I needed. 'I've lost my quarry. Something big – '

The haircut he was tearing at was black and cleanly layered to show the handsome shape of his head; the teeth he gnashed were even, orderly, and white. His belt was nielloed with silver; his boots were supple jobs whose tassels were affixed with bronze studs; his signet-ring was an emerald. His rage was the kind you can see any day in the Forum of the Romans after some inattentive donkey-driver has barged aside a man of note coming out of the Basilica Julia.

I was very tired. My body ached. My heart had rarely been more dreary. 'Your quarry's here,' I said quietly. 'Not quite killed yet.'

I stepped aside so the man with the ear-splitting senatorial vowels would have a better view of our centurion, lying wounded at my feet.

'This is Appius Helvetius Rufus, centurion of the legio First Adiutrix. Don't worry about it,' I said courteously. 'Helvetius is a realist. He always knew he stood in less danger from the enemy than from the crass incompetence of senior staff . . .'

'I am a Roman officer,' the leader of the hunting group informed me haughtily, raising his well-groomed eyebrows under his neat black fringe.

'I know who you are.' Something in the caustic way I dared return his stare must have warned him. 'I know a lot about you. Your finances are based on a complicated debt structure; your domestic life is in turmoil. Your wife is restless, and your mistress deserves better. And both of them would *hate* to know you visit a certain party in Colonia . . .'

He looked amazed. 'Are you threatening me?'

'Probably.'

'Who are you?'

'My name is Didius Falco.'

'Means nothing,' he barked.

'It should do. I would have introduced myself six weeks ago, if you had been available. Then you would also have avoided an officeful of unanswered despatches, including Vespasian's critical letter about your legion's future.' He was about to speak. I continued without raising my voice or hurrying: 'He's also questioning *your* future. Your name is Florius Gracilis. Your legion is the Fourteenth Gemina, and we'll just have to pray they have sufficient experience to survive a legate whose attitude to command is casual beyond belief.'

'Listen – '

'No, you listen, sir!' I used the title as an insult. 'I have just found you using army-issue spears for private purposes, on the wrong side of the Rhenus, in company which the Emperor will certainly call unethical – '

One of the legate's companions made a sudden obscene gesture. I recognised the rapidity of the movement as much as his cleft chin and vivid sneer.

I looked the man straight in the eye. 'You're a very long way from Lugdunum!' I said.

LVIII

The Gaul I had last seen arguing with the two German potters squared up angrily. I had been in another world since I had travelled through his province on my way to Upper Germany, but the quarrel at Lugdunum and finding the potters' bodies now came back to me vividly. The big Gaul with the sneer said nothing. Just as well. It would keep. Out here, feeling vulnerable, I was reluctant to tackle him.

I sensed more than saw the faint movement from Helvetius. I knew he was warning me. Suddenly I understood why the centurion was lying on this ridge of turf with two spears in him. I remembered a conversation I had had with him before we left Moguntiacum. He too had seen the Gallic potter arguing with Bruccius and his nephew at Lugdunum; he had even seen the Gaul tailing them later. Maybe the Gaul had seen Helvetius. In court, a centurion's word would be enough to convict a provincial. Finding Helvetius alone out here in the wilderness must have seemed like a gift from the gods to a man who had killed twice already.

I wondered if Florius Gracilis knew just what kind of 'accident' had befallen the wounded man, but from his face when he first saw Helvetius I doubted it. Involving himself in corruption was one thing; murder would be too foolish.

Not knowing the full story, Gracilis opted for bluster. No doubt he believed he had covered his tracks on the tendering fraud and could fudge matters generally once we reached home. 'A tragedy,' he muttered. 'Let me know if I can help . . . Most unfortunate. Accidents will happen. Whole trip has been most inconvenient from day one. I was supposed to be meeting some pedlar who said he could show me the Varus battlefield. Hopeless crook. Took my money to equip himself, then failed to show.' Dubnus.

'If he's a Ubian with a long lip and a strong line in grousing, I hijacked him,' I said. My position strengthened subtly. Dubnus was also a witness to the legate's junketing, and now I had control of

Dubnus . . . I saw Gracilis narrow his eyes; he took the point. To reinforce it I added another: 'The pedlar betrayed us to the Bructeri, and it's safe to say he was planning the same fate for you.'

'Oh I doubt that!' Even after years of watching senators, this man's arrogance took my breath away.

Somehow we had to get home. I was prepared for bargaining. I set my feet more stubbornly and told the legate bluntly, 'If this Gaul is a friend of yours, you should be more careful. There are two dead men in Cavillonum he may be called to account for.' I offered him a get-out. 'The victims were local to your command. The community at Moguntiacum will look to you to deal with it.'

I had judged him correctly. 'Sounds as if I have something to investigate!' The legate distanced himself imperceptibly from the man with the cleft chin. Sharp practice has a lovely habit of working both ways eventually. 'I have no idea what you are doing here,' he challenged me. It was the cool, smooth, patrician voice of a man who expects to get away with everything on the grounds of his cool, smooth, patrician ancestry. 'I myself am engaged on a political reconnaissance.'

That was one way to describe his expenses-paid sweetener. 'Oh really?' Annoyance at the airy way he spoke made my voice rasp. 'Civilis, was it? The Island? Batavodurum? Spend much time in Vetera?'

'I was interested to sniff around the place . . .' A sightseer. Helvetius jerked restlessly.

I too was losing my temper. 'See the damage, smell the disaster, pick a stone out of the rampart to take home as a souvenir? After that a few days off for the *real* chase, and hard luck to any solid Roman veteran who is standing in the way of your loose spears . . . actually, I thought you might have gone across to negotiate with the prophetess.'

'Veleda?' Gracilis seemed genuinely shocked. 'Vespasian wouldn't want anyone to tangle with that witch!'

I chose not to disillusion him. 'And did you find Civilis?'

'No,' he said. Ah well. He was a senator. He would probably win a laurel wreath just for making the attempt.

After our own hardships, I must have lost control. I knew better than to hope Vespasian would demote this unsavoury character unless I came up with some scandal much worse than fiddling a tender award or going on a game-hunt in barbarian territory. His crimes included sex and death and money – but no sex lurid enough to startle Rome into a bout of sanctimony. No bribes costly enough to hire lawyers to exact revenge. And not enough death.

'You're out of bounds, legate.' Out of bounds in every way. But at my feet Helvetius was weakening all the time. 'I have an exhausted and half-starved group of men, and this badly wounded centurion. We have been on an imperial mission which I cannot discuss in public, and we're stuck here without transport, armour or supplies. May I suggest you restore your reputation by assisting us back to base?'

I had misjudged it. The Gaul muttered something. The Four-teenth's legate cynically weighed our helpless predicament against the evidence we held that could blacken his name.

'I'll see you in Hades first!' said Gracilis.

But he had made a mistake too. His was worse than mine.

Several things happened rapidly. Helvetius let out a wretched moan that made me drop to one knee beside him. The Gaul raised his javelin. He was stopped by bright voices. At the other end of the ridge Orosius appeared through some coarse bushes with Lentullus, still carrying his shrimp bucket, and the centurion's servant. I gripped Helvetius by the wrist to warn him to keep still while I dealt with any trouble.

Then he violently convulsed.

He knocked me sideways. He meant to – he was warning me.

As I sprawled on my back, my cry of protest dried in my throat. Three strides from me, snorting at the legate, stood the biggest bull I had ever seen.

LIX

I lurched upright, then clapped my arms against my sides and muttered *"Hup!"* in a pleading tone. The aurochs tossed its head disdainfully.

No byre could hold this bovine. The beast was a brownish colour with black tips to its tail fur. It had a straight back, a massive head, short legs, and shoulders that could demolish civic masonry, hung with a deep collar of heavier foxy-red pelt. Its upswept horns were strong enough and wide enough to lash a maiden to them – some Dirce who had managed to offend people who could dream up frantic punishments. Its breath rasped like a Cyclops in the last stages of pneumonia.

They are untameable. The aurochs belonged centuries before man invented placid domesticity. This one was huge, yet must have been capable of moving with great delicacy – the kind of nifty footwork that also goes with bursts of tremendous speed. Its angry eye told us the spears that were stuck in its coat like briar thorns had already maddened it and now, having tracked the perpetrators with malicious stealth, it was planning to do serious damage to anything that moved. To emphasise this, it emitted a long, strained bellow that spoke loudly of primeval rage and pain. It glared at the legate broodily, as if sizing up where it could hurt him most. Then it stamped.

We all stood very still.

Now, I hate to remember what happened to Florius Gracilis. The worst was, he saw it coming. He gurgled slightly, and broke into a run. Bellowing, the great beast swung after him so fast he stood no chance. He was gored, tossed, trampled, and then stamped to death. Some of those who had been with him tried to throw spears, but once Gracilis was on the ground terror gripped everyone. They fled.

I and my party stayed.

The aurochs must have liked my face; I could tell it had chosen me next.

283

I had to protect Helvetius. I began stepping slowly to my left. It was the only direction open, and pretty soon I had to stop, for I was nearing the edge of the creek. The bank dropped down for a foot or more, and then there was a sinister overhang of long dirty grasses. The last thing I wanted was to end up in an uncertain depth of water, wallowing helplessly while the massive creature charged.

The aurochs breathed ferociously, giving the bloodstained body of the dead legate a final contemptuous toss with one tremendous horn. It waited until I stopped, then it began to move.

The rest was fast, messy and unheroic.

Behind the aurochs my three startled comrades came to life. Orosius began whooping and reached for a dropped javelin. I saw the servant race towards Helvetius. Lentullus bravely hurled his shrimp bucket. It hit the aurochs on the nose. The aurochs flung up its head, but kept coming. It was like being rushed by a rapidly moving house.

The sting of the shrimp bucket didn't stop it – nothing could. But while it blinked, I just had time to jump somewhere. Trapped by the creek, there was only one direction: I flung myself sideways. The beast passed me, so close that I snatched in my arm.

The aurochs turned on nothing. Its head was down. If I had run it would have gored me before my second stride, but something did stop it this time: Lentullus. He had run out and grabbed it by the tail. His face was contorted with effort as by some fluke he held on. The powerful animal swung angrily away from me. With a violent shake to and fro of its shoulders it dislodged the young idiot. The whiplash from its rump flung our boy far into the creek. By then another idiot was doing something stupid. M. Didius Falco, who had once seen a Cretan wall fresco, chose this dank German riverbank as an arena to revive the lost art of bull-dancing. While the aurochs was still bellowing at Lentullus, I skipped straight for it and leapt astride its back.

Its pelt was as coarse as nautical rope and smelt of the wild. A tail clogged with dung lashed my spine. I had only one weapon, in my boot as usual: my knife. Somehow I freed it. My other arm clamped around a horn. There was no time to think: death was reaching for one of us. I gripped with both knees, heaved with all my strength on the mighty horn, hauled up the head, leaned round a flicking ear and savage eye, then started hacking through the aurochs' upstrained throat.

The kill was neither clean nor quick. It took more time, and a great deal more energy, than anyone would ever think having stood in a sparkling white toga to watch the refined priests of Jupiter conduct a taurine sacrifice on Capitol Hill.

LX

'*Mithras!*' I thought the awed cry came from Helvetius, but it must have been his servant.

My left arm was locked so tightly where I had clung on that it was hard to free. The smell of the beast seemed to permeate my own clothes and skin. I sank to the ground, shaking. Orosius rushed up and dragged me clear. Lentullus staggered from the creek, then neatly passed out. 'Must be the shock,' Orosius muttered, turning aside to attend to him. 'Finding something he could actually do . . .'

I felt disgusted – with myself, with the animal whose anger had forced me to this, and with the hot blood all over me. I dropped my forehead on to my hand, then whipped away my palm as I felt more blood on that. I managed to limp across to Helvetius. His servant, whose name was Dama, looked up at me.

'I knew I should have gone to Moesia . . .' he ranted bitterly. Then he burst into tears.

Helvetius was dead.

Hardly had I fought back my own distress when some of the legate's hunting party ventured to reappear. They were led by the Gaul with the sneer, no doubt intent on self-preservation.

It was a brief confrontation. I was still kneeling by Helvetius, gripping his hand. I said to the Gaul, 'I don't want ever to see your face in Free or Roman Germany. You've killed to protect your industry, and you've killed to protect yourself. This is where it stops.'

'Proof?' he jibed, gesturing to the dead centurion.

Suddenly Dama gave voice. He addressed himself to me, as if he could not trust himself to speak to his master's killer. 'Helvetius Rufus was a private man, but he talked to me while I was arming him. He told me what he saw in Gaul.'

'Would you give evidence in court?' He assented.

The Gaul raised a spear. His intention was obvious. But we were no longer unprotected. Both Orosius and Lentullus lifted javelins themselves, ready to throw.

I stood up, covered in blood. I must have looked terrible. 'One word out of place, or a gesture I don't like, and I'll be happy to show you how the aurochs feels now it's dead!'

The men in the hunting party all backed off slowly. I waved them away with an angry gesture. They moved equally slowly out of sight, taking the Gaul from Lugdunum. I do not know what happened to them afterwards, nor do I care. As Celts, they were at far less risk in Germania Libera than we were.

That night we dined on aurochs steaks, but they had a bitter taste. We set a double watch. No one slept much. We broke camp early, then set off in a southerly direction, hoping that somewhere along the riverbank we might find the dead legate's ship.

We were going home. We had two corpses to bring with us, and more than one of us felt broken-hearted. Soon we all were.

Because, as we tramped on mournfully, we came to a wooded area. A little while after we entered it, we found there were other occupants. There were five times as many of them, and they had spotted us. They were a war band of the horse-riding, Rome-hating Tencteri.

LXI

We were surrounded before we had any inkling, but they did not attack immediately. Perhaps they were as surprised as us to find other people in their woods.

We formed up the recruits into a square – quite well, considering they had only learned the manoeuvre theoretically. Helvetius had taught them, however. As a formation the result was passable. But we all knew that we had too small a square.

The real point of a square is to lock shield-rims all around it in a protective wall. We had no shields.

Justinus was too tired and upset for a flamboyant oration, but he told the recruits to do their best. They exchanged frank glances like veterans; they understood the situation we were in.

It was late afternoon. A fine drizzle filled the woods. We were all unwashed, unfed and cold, with mist spiking our hair. I noticed that our boot-leather had set hard and was curled at the edges, with white tracery from mud and salt. The trees had turned colour in the last week or so. Winter was issuing warnings in the frosty air.

I could smell leaf-mould and fear. This was one crisis too many. It felt like a nightmare where you slither through endless ludicrous disasters, *knowing* it's a nightmare and that you must escape soon, yet unable to break free and wake safe in your bed with someone friendly soothing you.

We could not understand why the Tencteri had made no move.

Sometimes we could glimpse them between the trees. They were on horseback. Their presence was palpable on every side. We heard their mounts stamping restlessly and their harnesses chinking. Once a man coughed. If he lived in this rising river fog, it was understandable.

They were just out of spear range. For what seemed ages we stood there, straining for the first movement that would mean the end for us. We heard the shuffle of hooves in the crisp fallen leaves. We heard a shifty breeze rustle overhead.

I thought I heard something else.

Justinus and I were standing back to back. He must have sensed my tension for he looked round. I had my face raised full into the drizzle, struggling to catch sound or sense. I had nothing to tell him, but that odd quiet soul had brought back from Veleda's tower his habit of solitary action. He listened too, without comment. Then he let out a yelp and before we could stop him, he broke from the square.

He raced the ten strides to where we had left our scant baggage. Luckily he was zig-zagging, for a lance hissed out of the trees. It missed. Next minute he crouched, with some shelter from our horses. We could see him rummaging furiously. Soon he stood up. He leaned his elbows on a horse to steady himself while he held something. It was the twisted, wide-mouthed trumpet he had brought in his baggage for a lark.

When he blew, it came out as more of a waver than the notes he had produced among the Bructeri, but it still retained clear traces of the second night watch. It must have been the only call he had learned to play.

A shower of Tencterian arrows and spears tried to silence him. Justinus dropped to the ground with his head covered. But he must have heard, as we all did, another note: clear, high, and professionally sustained. Somewhere, somewhere not far away, a second bronze Roman trumpet had sweetly answered his.

We never saw them leaving. The Tencteri must have silently melted away.

Not long afterwards a vexillation of legionaries from the Fourteenth Gemina marched out of the woods. They were all volunteers. The force had been put together and brought downriver on the initiative of the man who was leading them. Despite my prejudice I have to admit that he was Sextus Juvenalis, the prefect of the camp.

They were looking for their missing legate, but the Fourteenth have always boasted about being thorough, so as well as claiming his body they also rescued us.

LXII

Moguntiacum.

A bridge, a tollbooth, a ridiculous column – and the girl I was longing to see.

The journey had taken sufficient time for us to start readjusting to the real world. However, it might take the world longer to adjust to us savages. Along the river had been civilised towns with baths and Roman food. Civilised contact, too, with men we understood, though for most of the journey we had found ourselves clinging in a tight clique of our own, quarantined by an adventure that seemed too big to discuss.

When we finally landed and returned to the fort we had started from, we took the centurion's ashes to rest in the Principia shrine. As we left the parade-ground, the recruits said goodbye. I would certainly be leaving soon, and their close contact with their senior tribune must also end when Justinus resumed the normal loftiness that was expected from his rank. Our tattered band left us on the Via Principia almost tearfully, but just then a group of passing comrades called out a welcome; we watched a swagger hit them, and they went off visibly boasting. Only Lentullus turned back at the last minute, with a shy wave.

Justinus was having some trouble with his throat. 'I hate to say I'll miss them.'

'Don't worry.' Even I felt subdued. 'You're back in harness, Quintus. There will be plenty of other annoyances . . .'

He swore cheerfully, in one of the several languages he had picked up for chatting to women.

He had the good idea of sending a message to his legate's secretary that there was so much to report he needed a proper appointment – later. This dodge left us free to go off to his house, pretending to stroll lazily as if we had nothing special in mind.

Helena was in the garden. It was too cold for her to be there, but it had ensured her solitude. She was grieving for us. Her brother and

I came out into the portico side by side. Her face seemed to light with excitement almost before she heard our steps; then her only dilemma was which of us to rush to first.

We both held back, to let the other have her. I won in the politeness stakes. I intended to. I meant to let Quintus hug her once, then when he passed on the bundle I would feel free to keep hold of her afterwards. But Helena Justina careered past her brother and fell on me.

He had the grace to smile, before he sadly turned away. 'Stay, friend . . .'

Helena was very quick. As if she had always intended it, she broke from me and threw her arms round him joyfully. 'Falco, you horror, what have you done to my brother?'

'He grew up,' I said. 'An affliction most people manage to avoid, but when it does strike it tends to hurt.'

She was laughing. I had forgotten just how much I loved that laugh. 'How did this accident happen?'

'Don't ask. It must have been so terrible he won't say.'

Helena assumed the stillness that said young Quintus should resign himself because she had in mind that he soon would confess. She held him off for one of her fierce inspections. 'He looks taller!'

Quintus only smiled again, like a man who could keep his own council, and intended to do so.

That was when I realised I might have made a small mistake about the tribune's adventure in Veleda's tower. I had no chance to ask him, because my horrid niece and Little Flaxen Pigtails must have heard of our arrival. They galloped out screaming in a way that passed for greetings, then the tribune's dog made himself at home by biting a servant, and after that a message came that the First's legate was so delighted at our safe return he had cancelled the rest of his schedule and wanted to see Justinus straight away . . .

After he left, I waited for Helena to ask pertinent questions, but although he was her favourite and I knew she loved him dearly, for some reason she only wanted to involve herself with me.

I could have argued, but the girl was evidently set on hauling me off into a dark corner for a bout of something shameless, so rather than disappoint her I went along with it.

I had taken my mission as far as I could – and further than Vespasian had a right to expect, though I knew better than to persuade myself that that unreasonable tyrant would agree. The old miser expected to extract his full money's worth before he let me home; I still had coercing Civilis on my rosta for one thing. But I had done well enough to earn my fee. My curly mop would not be welcome back on the Palatine until the last possible moment now that more than basic expenses would be called for from the Treasury.

For reasons of my own I was in no hurry to shift from here. Decisions were looming painfully, all the worse because I already knew what the answer had to be. Since she refused to make her own decisions, I had to force the right ones on Helena.

I pretended I was staying on at the fort to complete my report on the Fourteenth. I made out that it was difficult. A credible plea. I hate reports. I was perfectly capable of producing it, but lacked the will to start.

I spent a lot of time in the tribune's study chewing the end of a stylus while I watched Helena Justina playing draughts against herself. I wondered how long it would be before she realised I had noticed she was cheating. In the end I felt forced to mention it. She flounced off in a huff, which was annoying because I much preferred dreaming and watching her.

I struggled on. The stylus was a digit shorter now. Bits of soggy wood kept breaking off and splintering my tongue. As I spat them out I registered that my niece and her friend were hanging round the door engaged in secret whispering. There had been efforts at obvious mystery ever since I had arrived back. I was so bored with the report that this time I crept up, jumped out with a roar, and grabbed the pair of them. Then I dragged them into the study and sat them down, one on each knee.

'Now you're captured. You'll sit there until you tell nice Uncle Marcus why you keep peering round the architrave. Are you spying on me?'

At first it seemed like nothing. I was today's suspect. They spent a lot of time playing at being informers. It was not a compliment; it was for the same reasons that Festus and I had always wanted to be rag-pickers: a dirty, disreputable existence, and our mother would have hated us doing it.

'But we're not going to tell you anything we've seen!' Augustinilla boasted.

'Suits me. That saves me having to do anything about it.' She seemed satisfied. It fitted the family view that her sordid Uncle Marcus would sooner lie in bed all day than exert himself turning an honest denarius. I grinned evilly. 'You'd have to be clever to produce anything useful. Most informers spend weeks on a stake-out and still never find out anything . . .'

I could see Pigtails feeling torn. Unlike my niece, she was clever enough to want to have her intelligence recognised – though not enough to hide it and make full use of her advantage. 'Tell him about the boy with the arrows!' she burst out.

Something struck a chord. I was interested now, so I tried looking bored. Augustinilla dealt with that. She shook her head vigorously. I asked Arminia directly where they had seen this boy.

'Augusta Treverorum.'

I was shocked. 'Whatever were you doing there?' My niece opened her mouth and pointed to a reddened hole where a tooth had been. 'Stop fooling. I can see what you had for breakfast wriggling through your gut. Who had you gone to see?'

'Mars Lenus,' she informed me, as if talking to an idiot.

'Mars who?'

'Mars the Healer,' Arminia consented to explain.

This was hard work. I filled in some gaps myself: 'Augustinilla had toothache – I remember that from before I went away.' The ladies looked unimpressed by this subtle reference to the forests full of fog and ferocious animals I had just endured. 'So Helena Justina took you to a shrine – '

'The tooth fell out before we went,' Arminia told me with some disgust. 'Helena made us go there anyway.'

'I wonder why that was.'

'To look around!' they chorused.

'Ah yes. How obvious! Did she see anything worthwhile?' No. Helena would have mentioned it, though she would not trouble me with news of a pointless trip. Not while I had my report to write. She regarded that as serious. 'But you saw this boy?'

'He was shooting at us. He said we were Romans and he was in the Free Gallic Empire, with permission from his father to kill us dead. So then we knew,' Arminia said.

'Tell me, Arminia.'

'Who he was.' That was more than I knew. She whispered nervously, 'The chieftain's son. The one who shoots real prisoners!'

I resisted the urge to grab them closer protectively. These were two tough women; neither needed me. 'I hope you ran away?'

'Of course,' Augustinilla scoffed. 'We knew what to do. He was pathetic. We shook him off, then doubled back and followed him.'

They cackled with delight at the ease with which they had bam-

293

boozled him. No boy was safe with these young hags on his tail. In different ways, they were both destined to be man-eaters.

I let them see me swallow. 'And then?'

'We saw the one-eyed man.'

'The man with the red beard. The beard that's *dyed*,' the little flaxen treasure specified. Just in case I had not realised what completely brilliant sidekicks I had somehow attracted to work with me.

Helena said she would write my report.

'You know nothing about the subject!'

'So what? Most men who write reports know less. How about: "The Fourteenth Gemina Martia Victrix are a sound operative unit, but they need a firmer hand than they received from their recent command structure. The appointment of a new legate with strong supervisory talents will no doubt be a priority. The Fourteenth appear amenable to relocation in Germany on a permanent or semi-permanent basis. This option enables closer control of them; it will also permit full exploitation of their considerable experience with Celtic peoples, which should be particularly appropriate in the delicate political climate that exists in the Rhenus corridor . . ."'

'This is rubbish!' I interrupted.

'Exactly. Just what a secretariat wants to hear.'

I left her to it. She reckoned she could rattle off and stitch together several pages on the same pretentious lines by my return. Her handwriting was neater than mine too.

I would have liked to take Helena with me, but Augusta Treverorum was ninety miles away and I had to ride hard if I wanted to be back at Moguntiacum by the Emperor's birthday and the coming parade.

A man needs a travelling companion, however, so I took someone else instead. Xanthus, who so loved to see the world, was the obvious candidate.

LXIII

Augusta Treverorum, capital of Belgica.

It had been founded by Augustus, who had taken an empty site at a strategic crossroads on the River Mosella and begun with a bridge, like any sensible man. His bridge was a decent affair, with seven pillars of ashlar set on piles. The whole structure was built on a massive scale because the river is changeable there. The town had been planned neatly. There were new vineyards struggling to establish themselves, as well as cereal crops, but the local economy thrived on two staples: ceramics and wool. The sheep supplied official mills that wove cloth for army uniforms, and the redware pots also went under contract to the legions. As a result, I was not surprised to find that the fat cats of Augusta Treverorum had managed to provide them selves with some of the largest and best-appointed villas I had seen since leaving Italy. This was a town that would attract the attentions of anyone who had learned to appreciate Roman life in its most civilised aspects (wealth and show). Someone like a high-ranking, Romanised Batavian, say.

The Temple of Mars Lenus honoured both our own god and his Celtic equivalent, *Tiw*. This was not Mars the warrior, but Mars the healer – a natural corollary, since the god of soldiers needs to mend their wounds also if he wants to bump them back into the battleline as soon as possible. Mars the god of youth (young spear fodder) was also represented.

The temple was the centre of a flourishing shrine for the sick. There was a high quota of slack taverns and sour-smelling rooms for hire, plus booths and bothies where sellers of trinkets and trifles were also grimly trying to get rich quick before their custom literally died. It had the usual depressing hangers-on selling votive models of every anatomical part from sexual organs (both sexes) to feet (left or right) and ears (indeterminate), plus the whole grasping range of apothecaries, quack dentists and doctors, dieticians, fortune-tellers and money-changers. These characters all flocked to the shrine, feeding on hope and despair in equal measure while they raked in their usual sharp percentages. Occasionally I did spot somebody who was actually lame or ill, but they were encouraged to keep out of sight. Pale, sad faces are bad for trade.

Like all these places the turnover in shady entrepreneurs must be fast. People could come and go without much explanation. Few questions would be asked by those who preferred to remain unobtrusive themselves in case an official came round asking questions about licences. A man who wanted to hide could live among this shanty town more or less openly.

I never saw his son, the child with the arrows. It was just as well. I was intending to give him a thrashing, for not shooting straighter at my niece.

I found Julius Civilis looking like a man on his uppers, sitting on a stool at a shack outside town, whittling uneasily. He was keeping an eye out for trouble but he only had one eye to look out with. My informants had been efficient: I knew which dusty track he lived down, and I had a personal description. I circled round in the local fields and silently approached him on his blind side.

'The game's up, Civilis!'

He spun round and saw me standing there. I took my sword out slowly and laid it on the ground between us. It served to establish a truce for us to talk. He must have guessed I still had my knife, and since Civilis had been a cavalry commander I had no doubt he was hung about with daggers for cutting stones out of hooves – or carving notches on imperial agents' ribs. To catch me out he would have to be first into action, and quick with it; he looked too dispirited to try.

He was older than me. Taller and much more solid. Probably even more depressed than I was. He wore leather trousers to just below the knee and a cloak trimmed with strands of raddled fur. He was heavily scarred and moved stiffly, like a man who had fallen from a horse once too often. His missing eye looked as if it had been taken out by something like an artillery bolt, leaving a deep twisted seam. His good eye was sharply intelligent. He had a beard down to his cloak-brooch and long strands of wavy hair; both were red. Not the bold red I had been promising myself, but a sadder, more faded colour that seemed to mirror what was left of the rebel's life. That too was showing grey at the roots.

He let me introduce myself. 'So this is what it feels like meeting a footnote to history!'

'Less of the footnotes!' he growled. I found myself liking him. 'What do you want?'

'Just passing through. I thought I'd look you up. Don't be surprised. A child could find you here. In fact a child did – a mere eight-year-old, and not very bright, though she had help from a much cleverer Ubian. Worried?' I asked gently. 'You know what it means. If a child can find you, so can any smouldering legionary whose mate you killed at Vetera. Or any disgruntled Batavian, come to that.'

Julius Civilis told me what he would like me to do with myself; it was wittily devised and succinctly phrased. 'You say that in much the same terms as the famous Fourteenth Gemina, who also think I stink. Must be the Roman influence. Do you miss all that?'

'No,' he said, but jealously. 'The Fourteenth? Those braggarts!' He himself had commanded an auxiliary detachment in Germany before he had tried for glory; he would have heard about their parent legion from his kinsmen in the eight famous Batavian cohorts who deserted. 'I suppose we have to talk. Do you want the story of my life?'

He had the right background; this interview would be businesslike. I could have been dealing with one of our own. Well, I was really. 'Sorry.' I hoped he could hear that my regret was genuine. I would have given a lot to hear the full story from the rebel's own lips. 'I'm due in Moguntiacum for the Emperor's birthday parade. I've no time to listen to the drivel about twenty years in the Roman camps, then your only reward being Imperial suspicion and the threat of execution . . . Let's get down to it, Civilis. You took the money. You enjoyed the life. You were grateful to be exempt from taxation and gain the benefits of a regular income and a structured career. If things had been different, you would have taken your discharge diploma and retired as a Roman citizen. Right up to the moment when Vespasian became Emperor you could have basked in his friendship and been a great force locally. You threw it away for a dream that became pointless. Now you're stateless and hopeless too.'

'That's pretty bilge! Have you finished?' His single eye regarded me with more good judgement than I liked.

'No, but you have. Events have passed you by, Civilis. I see here an exhausted man. You're saddled with a large family; so am I. Now that your stand against fate is in tatters I can guess how you must be being nagged. You're suffering earache as well as backache and heartache. You're sick of trouble and tired of the campaign – '

'I'd do it again.'

297

'Oh I don't doubt that. In your shoes, so would I. You saw a chance, and made the most of it. But the chance is over. Even Veleda accepts that.'

'Veleda?' He looked suspicious.

I said smoothly, 'Imperial agents have just interviewed the lady in her signal-tower. Incidentally, my own view is we ought to charge her rent for that . . . She concedes the peace, Civilis.'

We both knew the Batavian's independence movement was nothing without support from Free Germany and Gaul. Gaul had long been a lost cause for rebellion: too comfort-loving by half. Now Germany was opting out too.

'So much for freedom!' murmured the red-haired man.

'Freedom to run wild, you mean? Sorry. I sound like every father there ever was berating a child who wants to stay out late in unsuitable company.'

'You can't help that. Rome,' he replied drily, 'is a paternalist society.' It felt strange to be addressed in refined, lightly satirical Latin by a man who looked as if he had spent a month huddled up against a gorse-bush on an open moor.

'Not always,' I confessed. 'My father ran away from home and left the women to get on with it.'

'You should have been a Celt.'

'Then I'd be fighting with you.'

'Thanks,' he said. 'Thanks for that, Falco. So it's parole again?' He was referring to the times other emperors had pardoned him. I hoped he realised this emperor was here to stay. 'What am I required to do?'

'You and your family will live in Augusta Treverorum at a fixed address. Protection will be arranged at first, though I reckon you should soon be assimilated into the local community.' I grinned. 'I don't feel Vespasian will want to offer you a new legionary command!' He was too old to care. 'Apart from that, here comes somebody whom I asked to meet us specially . . .'

A familiar figure had approached, incongruous among the run-down hovels where Civilis had lain up. He had a haircut that shrieked quality, and unacceptable shrimp-pink shoes. Undeterred by his own dramatic turnout, he scrutinised Civilis with visible pity.

'Falco! Your friend has a florid crop of foliage disfiguring his pediment!'

I sighed. 'This character has developed a putrid line of rhetoric since he met me . . . Julius Civilis, prince of Batavia, may I introduce to you Xanthus, one-time barber to emperors – and the best barber on the Palatine at that. He has shaved Nero, Galba, Otho, Vitellius, and probably Titus Caesar, though he never reveals the names of current clients. He has something in common with Celts, I think; he collects celebrity heads. Xanthus,' I announced gently to the rebel chief with the ghastly locks, 'has come to Augusta Treverorum all the way from Rome in order to give you a snappy trim and shave.'

LXIV

I managed to speak to Helena Justina during the parade. I hoped that in a public place politeness would oblige her to restrain her reaction to what I had in mind. Well, it was worth a try. I expected trouble anywhere I broached the tender issue. She would never like what I now had to say, even though I told myself she would have to accept that I was right.

The Fourteenth had made it pretty plain that this, like everything else at Moguntiacum, would be their show. It was the usual tiresome business. Lack of cash and too much cynicism meant there were hardly ever decent spectacles, even in Rome. Here we were in Europe, and seventeen days into November was no time to be holding outdoor festivities. It ought to be a rule that no one can qualify for emperor unless they can claim a midsummer birthday. The only exemption might be for people born on the Aventine thirty years ago in March . . .

As I expected, both the crowd and the glitter were spread far too thinly; the weather was freezing; and the catering was terrible – where you could find any. The formalities took place on the parade-ground, which unlike a decent amphitheatre had no easy exit gates. The few women of Roman extraction who attended were of course subject to strict public conventions. Three of them, along with a couple of guests, had to sit on a dais wrapped in jewelled silks while twelve thousand hairy males stared at them pointedly. Nice work, if they liked it. I knew one lass who was hating it.

The event was due to last all day. I only felt obliged to stay for the presentation of the Hand. Once we had dealt with that, I intended to say my piece to Helena – assuming I could get near her – then slip away.

Both legions were actually taking part, which slowed things to a leaden pace. Patterned marching, even by men in dress uniforms with helmet plumes, has never been my idea of stimulating theatre.

The action drags, and the dialogue is terrible. The promoter here had even failed to provide an orchestra; all we had was military silver and brass. Seeing everything twice over so that both sets of troops could affirm their loyalty to the Emperor increased the tedium to torture. I had been miserable enough in the first place.

It started to rain.

This was what I had been waiting for. The ladies on the dais were shrieking with alarm in case their dresses shrank or their face-paint ran. The group of slaves who were supposed to raise a canopy above them were making a splendid mess of it. I could see Helena losing her temper, as she did when other people became disorganised and it was not her place to interfere. Knowing she would excuse me if I saved the situation, I leapt up on to the dais, grabbed one of the supporting poles, and helped the slaves to lift the canopy.

The women we were protecting were the legate's wife of the Fourteenth, Maenia Priscilla, an older more sensible body who must be the mother hen of the First Adiutrix, Helena Justina, another visitor who was a schoolfriend of the mother hen, and Julia Fortunata. Presumably she had been invited because her status was too high to ignore and her position in the life of the late Gracilis too low to acknowledge. In any event, Maenia Priscilla, clad fetchingly in mourning white, was making the most of her role, while Julia took every opportunity to pet and comfort her. No public statement was to be made about the ex-legate's non-exemplary behaviour, but his women had both been told. As a result neither felt obliged to mourn him too sincerely. I was pleased to see that widowhood, or its equivalent, was bringing out the best in them. Their bravery was wonderful to watch.

It stopped raining. The ladies relaxed. We furled the temporary roof, then I crouched down at Helena's side, ready to spring to attention on awning duty if disaster struck again.

I thought her ladyship shot me a curious look.

Out in the field they were reaching a climax in the elaborate ceremonial. Cohorts of auxiliary cavalry came out to stage a mock battle. The First Adiutrix now came into their own, for the Fourteenth had not yet had their lost Batavians replaced, which at last gave the First an opportunity to sneer as they fielded theirs. These were Spaniards I think. Their small sturdy horses were well matched, and tricked out in full parade regalia with winking discs on their leatherware, gilded eye pieces, and huge roundels on their chests. The riders wore indigo uniforms that contrasted with the brilliant scarlet saddlecloths. They swept round in ceaseless whorls and circles, shaking feathered spears and brandishing round shields with pointed bosses centred on exotic patterns alien to Rome. The air of mystery was compounded by their formal parade helmets, which covered their faces like calmly expressionless theatrical masks. For half an hour this noble equestrian chorus rode the windy parade-ground like haughty gods, then they suddenly swooped out through the great gates to the Via Principia, leaving all the spectators bereft and dismayed.

Warm drinks were supplied on the dais.

Not before time.

I wondered rather pitifully whether I should speak to Helena now. She was enjoying her refreshments, so I chose to let the moment pass.

'There's Julius Mordanticus!' Helena called to me, waving at the local crowd. One of the huddled group of pointed hoods raised an arm back to her. He and his friends were happy. I had been interviewed by the provincial governor about the ceramics franchise fraud, and afterwards I had been able to bring the local potters good news. 'I meant to say,' Helena told me guiltily, 'while you were in Augusta Treverorum he gave us a present of a superb set of dinner bowls. What a pity,' quipped my insensitive sweetheart, 'we have no dining-room to use them in!'

We never would have now. I looked away.

The pause in formalities was lingering as people clutched hot refreshments tightly, trying to warm their hands. Helena continued chattering. 'Is it true when Xanthus shaved the rebel, you brought the trimmings away in a little bag to impress the Emperor?'

'It's true.'

'How did you persuade Xanthus to take part?' Xanthus would do anything for me nowadays; I had given him a *genuine* aurochs' horn. If he had it made into a drinking-cup, he would drown himself, it was so big. I had told him to take great care, because apart from the one I owned myself, there would be no repeats. 'He seems an odd choice to supervise a rebel,' hinted Helena.

'Xanthus is looking to settle down and make his pile in a town where Nero's name will give him massive prestige, but he can rise above his past existence as a slave. Augusta Treverorum fits: refined, but not too snobbish. He'll be shaving the cream of Belgican society on his portico, while poor women queue up at his back door to have

302

their golden tresses sheared to make expensive wigs for society dames in Rome.'

'I don't think I approve of that.'

'They could sell worse things, love. Anyway, I bet our lad with the puce shoelaces will end up a substantial citizen, donating temples and civic columns with the best.'

'And Civilis?'

'Xanthus gave him an ebony rinse to stop him being recognised. He'll be safe from assassins, and secure for us. The barber will be visiting his house to shave him every day. If Civilis absconds, his disappearance will be noted immediately.'

It was the perfect bail. And the unfortunate chief would never get a chance to rabble-rouse, now that he would be battened under hot napkins listening to gossip most of the day.

Helena smiled. I loved her smile. 'Marcus, you're wonderful.' The mockery was fairly delicate.

Out on the parade-ground the provincial governor, his head covered, was preparing to take yet another set of auguries. He was assisted on behalf of the Fourteenth by their senior tribune, Macrinus, who was standing in for the dead legate. I could see Maenia Priscilla getting excited. She stood no chance now. Ambition had superseded all else. Given this chance to show off as a substitute, Macrinus was rapt in pursuit of his public career.

I did not need to peer at a sheep's sickly liver to know the omens were bad for me. 'What's the matter?' asked Helena quietly.

'There is something I have to say to you.'

'Well then, you had better get on with it.'

The standard-bearers were carrying their poles to the central arena. Giant men with bearskins or wolfskins, the animals' heads resting upon their helmets, and the paws crossed on their chests. They walked with their sombre pace to surround the governor, then speared the ground with the stout spikes of their carrying poles. The spikes held – the gods were in favour. So there the standards of the Fourteenth Gemina Martia Victrix stood. The golden eagle with the legion's number. The individual markers for each cohort of foot-soldiers, and the fringed square flags used by the cavalry. The Emperor's portrait taking pride of place. Battle honours from half a century. Their statue of Mars. And now, presented to the legion before the entire assembled company palm outwards as a symbol of either power or friendship, their mighty Hand.

Still kneeling beside Helena, I stared hard at the ceremony. 'I have finished my mission. It's time for me to leave. I've been thinking. Some women can achieve more good for the world than men.' Her finger was tickling the back of my neck; in a moment she would know it was inappropriate and she would stop. I forced myself to speak: 'Helena, for the sake of Rome you ought to marry Titus. When you answer his letter – '

A blaze of trumpets interrupted me.

Brilliant. My life's big gesture shattered by a misplaced musical blast.

The standard-bearer with the Hand received the governor's approval, then began to pace through the entire legion to display Vespasian's gift. He approached the cohorts. At each one their particular signal party went through a short routine of acknowledgement before he set off to the next. Throughout his slow march all the trumpets in the legion brayed.

Helena's hand lay completely still against my neck. To lose her sweet consoling touch would be unbearable. But I was tough. I would do it. I would make myself. If Helena Justina chose the Empire as her duty, I would send her back to Rome alone, while I opted for permanent exile, roaming the wilder edges of the Empire, or even beyond it, like a miserable ghost . . .

Just as I was about to spring from the dais and depart like a hero, Helena bent down to me. Her hair brushed my cheek. Her perfume enveloped me in a cinnamon haze. Her lips moved softly right against my ear: 'You can stop looking so pathetic. *I wrote to him the day you left Colonia.*'

Helena sat back. I crouched where I was. We watched the standard-bearer stamp his way decisively round two more infantry cohorts, then the trumpets stilled.

I looked up. Helena Justina tapped me gently on the nose with her knuckle, the one wearing the silver ring I had once given her. She did not look at me. She was gazing across the parade-ground with an expression of refined interest like any other high-born lady wondering how soon she could go home. Nobody but me could realise how obstinate, and how beautiful, she was.

My girl.

The chief standard-bearer of the XIV Gemina represented their senior tribune with the Emperor's Iron Hand. It was a handsome item, two feet high, and the man in the bearskin must be breathless from the weight. An armourer had regilded the chips in its decoration, but I happened to know that it had a dented thumb where I had bashed it against a bedstead in some crummy travellers' doss-house on my journey across Gaul.

'Are you staying with me, Helena?' I dared to ask meekly.

'No choice,' she said (after pausing to think about it). 'I own a half-share in your samian dinner service, which I don't intend relinquishing. So stop talking nonsense, Marcus, and watch the parade.'